G000298934

DJ Oakley Publications Ltd

Presents

DEATH ON THE GOLF COURSE

One body found, one policeman killed, one bad week

David Oakley

Cover design & map by
Ben King

Illustrations by
Miranda Oakley

First Printing Edition, 2022

ISBN 978-1-7396812-1-0

Picture Credits: Page 38 *"The Nag's Head"*, Page 69 *"The Old Barn"*,
Page 121 *"The Arch Bridge"*, Page 241 *"St Margaret's Church"*
© *Miranda Oakley 2022*

Layout based on a free book template by Used to Tech: usedtotech.com

For Sam

ACKNOWLEDGEMENT

My biggest debt over the 28 years it took me to write this book after many stops and starts and the birth of three children, is to my wife Sam. My advice to anyone who wants to write a novel is to avoid starting it the week before your first child is born. Sam has been a constant support and excellent proof-reader.

I would also like to thank my exceptional daughter Miranda for her illustrations and social media skills and Ben King for his wonderful designs for the book's cover and website. His knowledge of the media, publishing, editing and design and advice has helped make the publication of this book possible.

CONTENTS

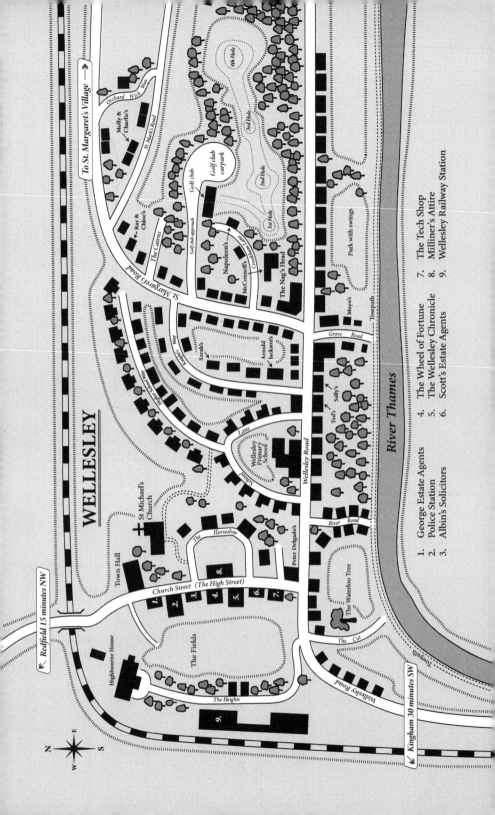

CHAPTER 1

The young man sipping his pint only had two hours left to live. But Peter Delgado was fortunately oblivious to his fate. It had been an emotional day, and he was at last cooling down as he drank from a pint of strong beer after an awful row with his brother. The balance of malt and hops was perfect in this particular ale, just what he needed to compose himself and clear his head. He eyed the small wooden door at the entrance of the pub, where he had taken refuge after the fight with his brother. Now he was calming down, he half hoped Ray would walk in, convinced he could finally make him see sense. Ray was tempestuous and quick to anger, but he was also fair minded. He took another swallow of beer, finishing the last drops of his pint. He needed to talk to his brother one more time to make him change his mind.

Jack McConnell's desk was orderly and business-like. A laptop, a notepad, a pair of matching gold pens and a small desk clock stood at neat angles to each other. McConnell sat straight-backed and alert in a swivel chair behind the desk, his attention on the clock in front of him. The clock said 8.45pm.

At the far end of the pub, John McConnell - Jack's son - lined up a shot on a pool table. He drew his cue back and used all his strength to power the white ball across the baize. With a crack, it bulldozed into the black eight ball, spinning it wildly into the bottom right-hand corner pocket. McConnell flashed a patronising smile at his opponent, a man in a denim jacket, and gathered up his winnings, which amounted to five pound coins stacked on the side of the table. "Time for another drink," he said to no one in particular, and made his way to the bar.

In a small corner by the pool table, Molly took a sip from her glass of white wine. She was depressed and angry in about equal proportions. The bar was too crowded, her white wine was tepid, and her husband was more interested in playing pool than talking to her. Charlie, her husband and the man in the denim jacket, was now at the bar trying to fix a rematch with McConnell.

He had been cool towards her for most of the evening and she was regretting leaving the comfort of her sofa and book at home for the pub. She didn't like The Nag's Head. It was dirty and cramped with small tables and pew like benches that were not designed for comfort. There was also a cloying whiff of old polish, which could not quite mask more insidious smells – stale sick or maybe urine from an intoxicated punter. Charlie only insisted on drinking at the pub because it was a 10-minute walk from their house.

She looked at her phone one more time, but she was now thoroughly bored with her social media feeds. Just as she was about to stand up, Charlie emerged through the bodies at the bar. "I'm going to give McConnell one more game," he said. "And I'm going to leave," she snapped back. She didn't wait for a reply, picking up her bag and slipping through a narrow passage of drinkers as she headed for the door. She brushed past Delgado, who only moments before had taken a similar route to the exit and was standing on the steps outside the pub's entrance. He was looking purposefully across the road. Molly followed his gaze and noticed a thin man wearing a raincoat and fedora hat, smoking a cigarette. The man looked familiar, but she couldn't place him.

It was a quiet, still evening and the fresh, pure air made Molly feel better almost immediately. She glanced again at the thin man, but she still couldn't place him. It was a lovely evening, she thought randomly, with a gibbous moon lighting up the street in a yellowish, almost romantic hue.

She carefully negotiated the weather-beaten path that led from the pub to the pavement, avoiding the muddy and mossy patches.

"Where are you going?" a voice said from behind her. She looked round and met her husband's eyes with a cold stare. "I'm going home," she said and continued walking.

"Molly," Charlie said in a slightly breathless voice. He tried to say more but Molly stopped and interrupted him.

"The only time you notice me is when I'm not there. If you want to play pool fine, but don't expect me just to hang around." She started walking again, but at a quicker pace, turning on to the pavement. Charlie jogged alongside her to keep up.

"I'm sorry. I'll come home with you. I don't like playing pool with McConnell. He really rates himself," he said, breathing heavily.

"Then, why do you? If you ask me, John McConnell is trouble," she said.

"Yes, I know." Charlie said sheepishly. Molly suddenly stopped and peered into her husband's eyes. He looked vulnerable, like a little boy lost. He was a pain, but he seemed genuinely sorry.

"All right, apology accepted." Charlie smiled, relieved that he had been forgiven. He embraced her and she smiled too.

"Come on then. Let's go home," she said. He put his arm around her shoulders, and they carried on walking, but more slowly.

Delgado had discreetly watched the exchanges between them from the pub's steps. He didn't want to be recognised by his boss while he argued with his wife. He continued to watch them as they walked up the road and lowered his scarf, which he had pulled up over his mouth and nose as a makeshift disguise.

The cloak and dagger antics were probably unnecessary. Charlie was too busy trying to placate his wife to spot his junior planning officer. He smiled to himself as they suddenly stopped and embraced. He would have to pass them if he was going to return to his brother's house. He could wait for a while, but it was cold, and he wanted to tackle Ray now. He crossed the road to avoid them and took one last look at the thin man, whose eyes were shielded by the peak of his fedora, before walking quickly in the direction of his brother's home.

In the pub, John McConnell downed his third shot of whisky and prepared the pool table for his next challenger. No one was going to beat him tonight. The whisky had convinced him of that.

———————————◆———————————

The clock said 9.00pm. Jack McConnell's eyes remained fixed on the hands of the clock. He sighed heavily and unwrapped a packet of cigarettes.

———————————◆———————————

It was morning at last and the sun was penetrating through the thin curtains of the bedroom in little forays of golden light. Ray Delgado folded his arm under his girlfriend Chloe's shoulder and stretched his legs until they poked out from under the duvet. He felt oddly relieved. He had confronted Peter. It was over. A smile flickered across his gaunt face, and he fell back to sleep.

CHAPTER 2

◆

John McConnell woke early with a pounding headache. He lay in bed for a while thinking unconnected thoughts about the previous night at The Nag's Head, his father and whether he should get a job before making his way to the bathroom. There, he relieved himself and found two pain killing pills for his headache, which he swallowed with a mouthful of water in one swift gulp. He looked at his crumpled, sleepy face in the bathroom mirror and decided against going back to bed. The pounding hammer in his head would stop him falling back to sleep. A bracing walk in the fresh air would be a better palliative and might spur the tablets to work more quickly.

It was pitch black outside his parents' house and bitterly cold. As he pulled his scarf up over his face, he noticed a vague numbness across the fingers of his hand, which was starting to throb. He must have picked up the injury in his fight with the Buckler brothers, two losers from the other side of town. He had knocked over one of their drinks with his pool cue at the pub and things had escalated.

He also now remembered that the landlord had banned him and the Bucklers from the pub, which was annoying. The Nag's Head was his favourite place to drink. He sucked on a loose tooth at the side of his mouth, another injury from the fight, and wondered why the Bucklers were drinking at The Nag. They didn't usually drink there as they lived on a rundown, former council estate on the west side of the town.

He hadn't seen the Bucklers in The Nag before, now he thought about it. He looked up at the sky, still wondering why the Bucklers had decided to pick his pub for a drink. It was too dark to see much, but it would be light soon, an ideal time for a walk on the golf course, which backed on to his parents' road. It was pretty and peaceful on the golf course in the early morning dawn, he thought to himself, as he unsteadily trudged towards the first tee, which was just by the road.

CHAPTER 3

◆

A smoky mist hovered in the hollows of the golf course in expectation of a beautiful autumn day. The first cracks of light were poking through the clouds and thousands of tiny dew drops clung nervously to the tips of the luscious fairway grass before the sun's rays could evaporate them.

Jack McConnell walked quickly across a speckled purple carpet of heather, which lay before the smooth green expanse of the fairway. A small bird watched him from the high trees that stood to attention along the sides of the first hole, which dog-legged to the flag on the putting green. Jack would be the first of many that day, with their clubs, beating their way over the hills, through the trees and across gaping ditches and tiny streams that made up Wellesley Golf Course.

Jack looked at his watch. Six fifty-eight and his ball was safely on the first green. He would finish his round before breakfast. For Jack, a round of golf under 80 shots was extremely satisfying, but a round under 80 shots in an hour-and-a-half or less lifted his spirits to an even higher level. Playing a good round of golf quickly was an accomplishment that set the tone for the rest of his day. It meant he would be in the office before 9am and before everyone else, which as the boss he considered important. It highlighted his commitment, energy and discipline to the rest of his staff, who all knew he played golf without fail early every Thursday morning.

He bounded on to the green and expeditiously lined up his putt. Eighteen feet from right to left and slightly downhill. He firmly stroked the ball and, with keen eyes, watched it create a narrow curving avenue in the dew. The moisture slowed the ball's momentum and it fell five feet short of the hole. Cursing, he eyed the ball angrily, then stared skyward as if God was responsible for his misjudgement. He continued quietly reproaching himself and squatted down to find the line for his next shot, but something in the corner of his eye disturbed his concentration and he turned sharply to where the grass blended into scrub and trees at the back of the green.

His eyes widened and he stood perfectly still. He swallowed and carefully and tentatively moved towards the scrub. A human arm lay outstretched between a small bush and a large tree. Its owner appeared to be propped up behind the tree. For a second, he was afraid the person might reawaken and leap out at him. He stopped a few feet away from the body and took two deep breaths before edging closer. The sight of a lifeless body - the man was clearly dead - was bad enough. But, lying in such familiar surroundings, made it more macabre and horrific.

CHAPTER 4

◆

Molly popped a tea bag into a mug and poured boiling water over it. She watched the clear, steaming water diffuse into a brownish colour and switched on the television in the corner of the kitchen. It was early and Charlie was asleep. He went to work after her and was naturally a late riser.

The post and a local newspaper arrived with a clatter through the letterbox in the front door. Molly picked up the paper and some of the post from the floor and unwedged the rest from the door.

Upstairs, Charlie was rousing from a restless sleep. He rolled on to his back and groaned for a while, staring blankly at the ceiling. He focused without thinking on the small nodules of the ceiling's Artex design. They were unevenly spread and different sizes. He counted a few and came to a big fat one in the corner. He sighed deeply and rolled back on to his side. Life was unfair. He cast an eye at the bedside clock and thought about being one of life's big fat ones with power, influence and, most importantly, money.

Molly put a tea bag in another mug and filled it with boiling water, while watching the television on the kitchen wall. The local news was on, and a reporter appeared to be standing in Crookham Lane, which was only a few roads away. She moved closer to the television set. It was definitely Crookham Lane. Surprised, she turned up the sound. A man had been found dead on the golf course behind the road earlier that morning. He was in his mid to late twenties, but the police were not naming him. Crookham Lane was just down the hill on the way into town. It was a private road with some of the biggest and most expensive houses in Wellesley, which was itself one of England's most affluent country towns. "Molly," Charlie yelled from the bedroom. "Can you make me a cup of tea, please? Thanks."

"Yes, I'm already making you one," she shouted back. He sounded tired, but for him relatively chirpy. He wasn't a morning person and of late he had been more grumpy than usual. Work was troubling him. She sighed with resignation. At least, the cry for tea was an improvement on morose silence. She took his steaming mug upstairs with the local paper folded under her arm and put the tea on the bedside cabinet, perching herself on the side of the bed.

"They've found a body on the golf course, near here," she said.

"Blimey! Did they say who?" Charlie asked, sitting up and propping himself against two pillows.

"No. They just said a man in his mid to late twenties. I wonder who?"

"Yeah. I wonder." He picked up his mug and took a sip. "Thanks for the tea," he said. "What's in the paper? Can I have a look?"

She showed him the front page, which was dominated by the headline "School land row rages on". It was a long running dispute in Wellesley – two developers wanted to build on the same site where one of the town's primary schools was about to be demolished. Charlie shook his head angrily and took another mouthful of tea.

CHAPTER 5

◆

Chief Inspector Napoleon sipped the bitter tasting coffee his sergeant had placed on his desk and reflected how appropriately it matched his mood. He stared ahead at the blank office wall and tried to remember the days when he had enthusiasm and a passion that drove him without question even through the most tedious aspects of police work. He eyed the papers on his desk. All he could feel now was a jaded disenchantment.

He had risen to chief inspector quickly, but his career had stalled soon after the promotion. He had become involved in a missing child inquiry around that time and his failure to find the boy had affected him deeply. A possible error of judgement when interviewing the boy's father still hung over him. It was now a distant memory, but it had stirred the beginnings of self-doubt in his ability and those of the police force.

Doubt had gnawed at his confidence ever since, making him irritable and leading to dark, volatile moods that were difficult to shake off. He had also grown more aware of the imperfections of the job, which fed his disillusion and chipped away at the tough-minded singleness of purpose that had made him a very good detective.

Today, as on many days of late, he could feel his mental wounds more acutely. Police work was like putting sticking plaster on an haemorrhaging artery – futile and pointless. He smiled wryly at the gloomy thoughts. Melodrama was another fault to add to his list of flaws. He had a lovely wife, four healthy children, and police work was certainly better than going down the mines as his father had done as a colliery electrician.

A knock at the door broke up the internal debate and his sergeant appeared. The sergeant surveyed the familiar scene in his superior's sparsely furnished office. The desk was the usual rock pile of pens, police reports and newspapers, which surrounded his desktop computer. A lamp poked through the clutter at the side of the desk with a photograph of his family standing at a drunken angle against it.

"Yes, sergeant. What can I do for you?" Napoleon said. The sergeant coughed out of habit.

"I thought you should know sir. A body has been found on Wellesley Golf Course near Crookham Lane, where you live. It's a man in his mid to late twenties. There's not much info at the moment, but the scenes of crime team are already down there."

"Thank you," Napoleon said. The sergeant nodded and left. The chief inspector leaned back into his chair and glanced at the clock on the wall. There was plenty of time until his next meeting. He took one more look at the papers on his desk. It was an easy decision. He would make an unofficial trip to Wellesley.

CHAPTER 6

◆

Napoleon unlatched the gate, which was usually open, at the entrance of Crookham Lane and spotted the smallish, shambling figure of Jackson, one of the senior pathologists. He was casually leaning against an ambulance, writing notes on an iPad. Around him, intense where he appeared carefree, a team from forensic buzzed and hummed. The inspector could see a paramedic ask Jackson something, while pointing at what he presumed was the body, which lay covered on a stretcher. The pathologist then spoke to an earnest-looking man from the forensic team circling him and nodded at the paramedic. It was unusual for Jackson to go out on a job, but Napoleon suspected he was here because he lived nearby, like the chief inspector.

He brushed past a couple of newspaper photographers and ducked under a tape cordon, noticing a television crew, which had set up outside one of the houses on the opposite side of the road. A dozen or so people stood with the television team and watched the body being lifted into the ambulance.

Jackson saw Napoleon walk towards him. "Hello inspector. What a nice neighbourhood we live in." His lips curved into the familiar sardonic smile and his eyes crinkled. He gave his bald head a scratch and brushed a leaf off Napoleon's collar. He was remarkably and oddly meticulous with everything but his own appearance.

"You might be interested in this when the scenes of crime boys are finished." His eyebrows arched, inviting a question. Jackson tended to impart specific information only when asked directly, otherwise he would ramble on teasingly.

Napoleon smiled and asked laconically: "Do we know his name?" After years of working with Jackson, the chief inspector knew his cue.

He didn't understand the other man's idiosyncrasies, so he just worked along with them. "Peter Delgado," Jackson said. "Lived locally, according to his driving licence."

"What did he die of?"

"Internal injuries, probably. Looks like his skull was broken, right femur broken, too, smashed pelvis, severe trunk injuries and lacerations to the arms and legs. The type of injuries you would get from being hit by a car."

"I was told at HQ he was found on the golf course, way off the road," Napoleon said.

"Yes. By the first green. If he was killed from the impact of a car, and he almost certainly was, then he was moved there. Forensic might find some interesting fingerprints. I should imagine the body would have been carried through that alleyway." Jackson pointed to a narrow path, tucked between two houses, that led from the road to the golf course.

"It wouldn't take a minute to get from here to the first green."

"But wasn't it possible someone beat him up?" Napoleon asked.

"It's possible, but the injuries are similar to what you would expect from a head-on collision."

"So where would this collision have happened?"

"You'll have to ask this lot what they've found on the road," Jackson said, his eyes following two forensic officers. "But I can't see signs of it in Crookham Lane. On a gravel road, like this, dirt would have kicked up everywhere from the car braking, assuming the driver braked sharply. Even if he didn't, the body would have cartwheeled over the car and skidded along the road, hence the lacerations. There should be some marks on the road. I've only had a general look, inspector, not my area, but Crookham Lane, no. It probably happened on St Margaret's Road. The driver could have turned into Crookham Lane from St Margaret's Road to offload the body. Cars travel at 40, 50, 60 mph on St Margaret's. The car would have been travelling at about 40 to do those kinds of injuries. I wouldn't have thought many would go that fast up Crookham Lane."

"Unless the driver was drunk," Napoleon said.

"Well, you're the detective." The little man brushed the collar of Napoleon's raincoat, this time for no obvious reason.

"When did it happen?" the inspector asked.

"Late last night. I might be able to be more specific later." Jackson was about to say more, but hesitated. A stocky, sandy haired man appeared at Napoleon's side. Chief Inspector Patrick Rankin was the last person Napoleon wanted to see. He quietly sighed. The brusque, officious Rankin would disapprove of his informal visit. Rankin would be in charge of the investigation as the senior officer at Wellesley police station.

"Everything's under control Napoleon," Rankin said. And sod off to you too, Napoleon thought. Deliberately and slowly, he turned back to Jackson and asked about the dead man. Average height, slight build, dark skin. In his mid to late twenties, Jackson said with a grin.

Not for the first time, Rankin's small eyes bored furiously into Napoleon. His thin lips quivered, and the muscles bunched in the bull neck. Napoleon smiled inwardly as the full force of Rankin's anger appeared to edge momentarily close to a violent reprisal.

CHAPTER 7

◆

"He was hit by a car," Jackson said. Napoleon nodded. They were sitting in an office that Jackson used at the headquarters of Valley Police in Kingham, where Napoleon was now based. Kingham was a small country town near Wellesley, similar in size but without the affluence. It had been an ideal site for Valley Police headquarters because it was in the middle of the force's catchment area and the land was plentiful and relatively cheap for development.

Jackson was about to go home, but he was in no hurry despite the late hour. He never was when the conversation turned to corpses. He had a fascination with the causes of death, which you would expect in a pathologist, but Napoleon still found macabre. The inspector was grateful, though, for Jackson's willingness to talk. He wouldn't get the same co-operation from Rankin.

"You're certain?" Napoleon asked, shifting from side to side in an effort to make himself more comfortable on a long leather sofa that was pushed up against an inside wall of the office. "Absolutely. Hit head-on by a small to medium-sized car, I should think, at about 40 mph. Not much chance of survival. Eighty-five per cent of people hit at that speed are killed. I should think his head hit the roof of the car or something hard as he was thrown over it. That would have killed him instantly. And I would say he died around 10 or 11 O'clock in the evening."

"He was definitely hit by a car?"

"Pretty certain. Brain scrambled like eggs. He would have been travelling at 1.4 times the speed of the car, which was say 40 mph, so his head would have hit the roof at, say, 56 mph. It doesn't take much imagination to work out what happens to your brain when that happens. Like I said, scrambled.

The poor sod might have died from other internal injuries, anyway, if his head hadn't taken such a whack."

"Have we any idea where it happened?"

"Shouldn't you ask Rankin? He is heading this case," Jackson said provocatively. He laughed loudly and stretched, his eyes beaming at Napoleon. "I understand from scenes of crime that the accident, or murder," Jackson raised his eyebrows, "appears to have happened on St Margaret's Road, near the Crookham Lane turning, as I originally suspected. There are some marks and blood on St Margaret's Road that forensic are analysing. The man was possibly walking in the road when it happened."

"Hmm," Napoleon said. "Anything else?" Jackson stood up and picked up a red pencil from the desk where he was sitting, opposite the inspector. He stuck it behind his ear and rubbed his hands. "He was tipsy," he said.

"So, he staggers into the road and was hit by a passing car," Napoleon said.

"And the driver decides not to report it because he's afraid, drunk, or irresponsible, young kid maybe," Jackson added. He slid the pencil from his ear and bit into the end of it, leaving small crenulations where his teeth had been.

"Strange that the person should move the body," Napoleon said.

"Panic," Jackson said, taking the pencil out of his mouth. "Someone in a panic would be more likely to drive away in a hurry," Napoleon replied.

Jackson frowned at Napoleon. "I think you should leave this to Rankin, Robert," he said in a facetious, superior tone.

"Yes," Napoleon said. "He was obviously keen to involve me this morning." Jackson produced a lop-sided smile, enjoying the sarcasm, and took another bite of his pencil.

Napoleon had decided to leave the scene after roughly the fifth time Rankin had insisted everything was under control. Napoleon could take a hint and he did have a press liaison meeting to attend. Jackson placed the pockmarked pencil back on the desk and searched around for another to chew. Slipping a long, scar-free red pencil into his mouth he dropped himself back into his chair and gave Napoleon a knowing look.

"You're not going to leave this alone, are you Robert?"

"Well, press liaison's not really my thing."

"Yes, I thought it was funny when they put you in charge of that little show."

"Yes. Gregarious old me. Mr Media as my wife says."

Napoleon grimaced and stood up. He didn't want to talk about himself. It was time to leave.

"Thanks for your help, Arnold," he said.

"No trouble. Just raise my profile with the press. I could do with a bit of adulation." A twisted smile took hold of his face again and he continued chewing his pencil.

CHAPTER 8

◆

"You should leave it to Rankin, Robert. It's his case. He's the chief inspector in charge of Wellesley police station, not you. No wonder you irritate him." Sometimes, Mary Napoleon found her husband extremely exasperating. "He irritates me," Napoleon said grumpily.

"Oh, forget it," Mary said. "You're quite hopeless on the subject of Patrick Rankin." It wasn't worth trying to reason with her husband on certain things and Patrick Rankin was one of them. "I've got better and more interesting things to do, like doing the washing and putting the bins out, rather than arguing with you," she said sarcastically and left Napoleon brooding in the living room.

Mary Napoleon was a down-to-earth, no-nonsense woman, who was no longer prepared to tolerate stupidity in other people, particularly her husband. She was 45, three months younger than Napoleon, but age had had a different effect on her. While his life experiences had made him slightly bitter and disenchanted, bringing out a stubborn, belligerent side to his personality, she had grasped the essential need to compromise to get through mundane day to day situations, both at the office and in the home. This had not diminished her youthful convictions on politics, women's rights, and equality. On these issues, her views had hardened, and she was no longer prepared to give ground, but on trivial and less important matters she understood the benefits of pragmatism, something her husband often failed to grasp.

She had met Napoleon at university and at first had thought he was a big, ignorant oaf. In many respects, he still was with his stupid attitude towards Patrick Rankin and his childish obsession with football, a pointless game played and watched largely by morons. But he possessed two qualities that mattered greatly to her – a strong moral compass, with a natural and instinctive understanding of what was right and wrong, and a good sense of humour. He was also very handsome – dark and tall with shy but expressive hazel eyes.

For Robert Napoleon, the attraction had been more immediate. Mary was blonde and feisty, which was enough to stir his blood. She also had an ability to speak to anyone in any situation, qualities he lacked and admired in her. He had first noticed her at one of the university's many political rallies. He couldn't remember why he was there. He had no interest in politics. But she had caught his eye with a fluent speech on something political. The details of what she said were a blur in his memory bank but her confident delivery in that posh, husky voice had caught his attention. She had a deep voice for a woman. Her address was particularly impressive to him as public speaking was not his strong point, owing to physical shortcomings of shaking hands and a quivering voice. The thoughts might be nimble and eloquent, but the words came out stuttering and jumbled. "Leave it to Rankin," Mary repeated to her husband. She put two cups of tea on the coffee table in the centre of the living room and sat down on the sofa adjacent to where Napoleon was sitting in a big armchair. "You know how they hate your freelance operations."

"What does that mean?" Napoleon was hurt by the remark.

"You know what I mean. The police force does not encourage those individual enterprises of yours. You're supposed to be part of a team and in this case, you're not even supposed to be in the team."

Napoleon said nothing. His wife was right. He might have been a superintendent by now if he had been a team player. Well, what did it matter? He was going to be a chief inspector for the rest of his career, so he might as well enjoy it. His investigations would continue and no one, including Mary, need know.

CHAPTER 9

N apoleon was always interfering in that quiet, arrogant way of his. Rankin banged his fist on the desk. He stood up and then sat back down again in frustration, as much cross with himself as with the other policeman. He knew there was no point in an unproductive trawl over his irritation with Napoleon, but the tedium of the computer checks he was making made it difficult to concentrate. His dimly lit office, one of the bulbs in the light above him had blown that morning, didn't help his black mood – and it was raining. He hated the rain and this time of year when everything was dying. Autumn was his least favourite season. He tried to focus again.

The investigation was proceeding as it should. He hadn't missed anything. A computer search was being made for relatives of the dead man, while other police officers continued combing the woods near where the body was found. None of the residents in Crookham Lane or nearby had seen or heard anything unusual or suspicious the night before.

Forensic had confirmed the young man had been hit by a car, most probably in St Margaret's Road where tyre marks and blood had been found, just before the Crookham Lane turning. The body had then been moved to just behind the green on the first hole of Wellesley Golf Course.

He had decided to come back to the office to go through the police files on driving offences, particularly drink-related, but his mind kept wandering to his old sparring partner.

Since he had moved to the Valley force, he had crossed paths and swords with Napoleon far too frequently for the good of both of them. In his first spell at Wellesley, he had worked under Napoleon, who was the detective chief inspector in charge of the station, as a detective constable. They had worked together for two years, but never became close. Napoleon was aloof and kept his distance from his men. Was it shyness or arrogance that made

Napoleon such a cold fish? His withdrawn nature certainly limited him as a detective, in Rankin's view. If you weren't closely working with your team, then it could restrict your understanding of a case.

He supposed Napoleon had been cold to him because he was ambitious and possibly a threat to his authority. But it wasn't a crime to want to progress. Just because Napoleon didn't seem to care about promotion, didn't mean everyone had to be like that.

He cast his mind back to one of the unsolved cases while he and Napoleon were at Wellesley. A young boy, Sean Cropper, had gone missing after a local derby at Wellesley football ground. The boy, who would have been 17 now, was surely dead. That was 10 years ago. Napoleon had been newly promoted to chief inspector and Rankin had only just arrived at the station.

An investigation and incident room had been set up and all the high-flyers from Valley headquarters had been shipped in with one of the force's top detectives, a superintendent by the name of Jim Hunter, put in charge. Napoleon, for all his pretence of not caring about promotion, had wanted to make a name for himself, Rankin guessed, and had worked tirelessly. But he had kept Rankin on the sidelines. Only towards the end of the case, had he included Rankin in the interviews and more important aspects of the investigation.

What had not occurred to Rankin was that Napoleon had assigned him to the more laborious, less glamorous parts of the case because he was organised, thorough and had an exceptional eye for detail. Napoleon needed someone disciplined enough to check every minor fact, however trivial.

But, despite the grudging respect, Napoleon had struggled with Rankin personally, probably because they were both naturally introverted and needed a more open, less self-conscious person to bring them out of themselves. Finding the extrovert in Napoleon was the key to knowing him, Mary had once said. The same could be said of Rankin, although he was an assiduous networker, when it came to mixing with his superiors.

The Cropper case had hardened the resentment between the two of them, Napoleon finding his detective constable's fastidiousness increasingly annoying. The always neatly folded handkerchief in the breast pocket of his suit and the pathologically ordered desk made him suspicious of the other man. He also suspected Rankin of wanting promotion simply to satisfy a blown-up ego.

After Sean Cropper's disappearance, any tolerance Napoleon might once have had for ambitious types, as he had pigeon-holed Rankin, had dissolved. Rankin seemed to view the investigation as a platform for promoting his career as well as gaining justice for an innocent child, who was probably murdered. Mixing ambition with duty in this way was unacceptable as far as Napoleon was concerned. Jim Hunter, the superintendent in charge of the investigation, was of a similar mould to Rankin and Napoleon didn't like him either.

The Cropper case not only diminished Napoleon's tolerance towards other people's flaws, but also redefined his goals. He had risen through the ranks swiftly, not perhaps with the blinkered determination that would inevitably lead to Rankin's promotions, but all the same with an eye to his own prestige.

His own prestige was no longer as important. Perverts had likely murdered a lovely little boy and a good friend's grandson. He wanted to catch those disgusting people for them. Promotion and the respect that came with a more important title mattered less to him than it once had.

The investigation had a profound, although different, effect on Rankin. He was 10 years younger than Napoleon and had no family or children, just a carefree and satisfying relationship with a long-standing girlfriend. He wanted more control and influence in bringing people to justice, like those involved in the little boy's death, and that meant promotion. He was not openly critical, like Napoleon, of Superintendent Hunter's arguably realistic opinion that the men responsible for Sean Cropper's disappearance would not be found when the early inquiries came to nothing.

He was also more philosophical about the darker side of the human psyche, but he was in his own and perhaps more constructive way determined to do something about it. Sniping at the man in charge was plainly counter-productive. In the 10 years since the boy went missing, Rankin felt he had been proved right. He was in charge at Wellesley now and a chief inspector, like his former governor, whose once blossoming career had died on a plateau of his own choosing.

Rankin tried to concentrate on the file on the computer screen he was supposed to be reading but remained distracted. Napoleon's crash landing didn't particularly please him, even if there was no warmth between them. "He won't interfere," he said to himself, more in hope than conviction.

His desk phone started ringing, yet another distraction. He stared at it, then picked up the receiver, still thinking about Napoleon. It was his detective sergeant. "Sir, Peter Delgado. He has a brother, Ray. He lives in Wellesley."

"Thanks, sergeant," he said.

"We'd better inform him of the bad news."

CHAPTER 10

◆

Ray Delgado had identified his older brother. Rankin and his detective sergeant had then interviewed the young man and his girlfriend at their home. The young man had been surprisingly composed and almost unmoved by his brother's death, Rankin thought, but shock had different ways of affecting people. The police officers had taken a short statement and left the young man and his girlfriend to grieve. She also seemed calm and unaffected by the tragedy.

There had been a row over dinner at the younger brother's house on the Wednesday, the day of Peter Delgado's death. The older brother had stormed out and the younger brother had then tried to find him in his car and ended up in the university library in Redfield, a big minster town a short drive from Wellesley, where he was studying. The younger brother had read some newspapers and tried to find a book for an essay he was writing, but he had not spoken to anyone while he was at the library, returning to his house late that night. His girlfriend had stayed at home alone, which meant neither of them had an alibi.

Pathology had confirmed the man was knocked down and killed by a fast-moving car late on the Wednesday evening at about 10.30pm. Rankin's sergeant had checked the young man's car, which showed no signs of being in a collision, while forensic had been dispatched for a more thorough inspection of the vehicle. Peter Delgado's injuries suggested the car was travelling at 40mph. At that speed, the body would have left its mark on the car.

Rankin had decided he would interview the young couple again more thoroughly later. On the one hand, the row, and the fact the younger brother was out in his car with no alibi put him high up on the list of suspects, but his vehicle was clean, which seemed to rule him out. For now, he would continue sifting through the reports on driving offences in and around Wellesley in the past year.

The body was found about 200 yards from Crookham Lane, but the collision was unlikely to have taken place there. It was a narrow, private road that was made up of gravel and loose stones. There was also a sharp bend only three or four houses into the road with great potholes emerging randomly when least expected. Even the most skilled and reckless driver would have struggled to hit 40 mph in Crookham Lane. If a driver had ploughed into someone at that speed, one of the residents in the lane would also surely have heard it, even late at night.

Delgado's body had therefore been moved and a long way from where the collision happened, almost certainly on St Margaret's Road, which was odd and risky. It would have surely been much easier simply to drive away. It was a puzzle.

Rankin's mind wandered back again to the Sean Cropper investigation. He always associated the word puzzle with the Cropper case. He could still see the boy's face - large eyes, big red cheeks - from the photographs they had given to the press. He had been convinced the father was involved in his son's disappearance. Frank Cropper had been pulled into the police station for questioning three times.

On the final occasion, he was kept in a cell overnight and repeatedly asked about his whereabouts on the afternoon his son was last seen. He had claimed he was at the local football match with Sean and had lost him in the crowd, yet he didn't know the fans had been kept in their seats for 30 minutes after the game because of police fears of a crush. They had then only been allowed to leave in stages.

Cropper had claimed he was too drunk to remember much of the aftermath of what had been a small piece of history for Wellesley Football Club. They had beaten local rivals Millborough in the FA Vase, the cup competition for lower league football teams, to reach the final for the first time.

The landlord of The Rising Sun, just yards from the ground, verified Cropper's drunk claim. He had been in the pub drinking on the morning of the game. But he would have remembered being stuck in the ground, had he been at the game, and no-one could recall him or his son being there. They were both well known, and with a few drinks inside him, Cropper was very loud. Someone would have remembered seeing him and Sean, but they hadn't and their whereabouts remained a mystery.

Napoleon and Rankin had been close to cracking Cropper, but just as they were on the verge of opening him up, he had committed suicide by hanging himself in his police cell. It had blown the investigation, as Cropper was the only serious suspect. With his death, the events surrounding that victorious and tragic afternoon were marked down as yet another unsolved conundrum on the police files.

Napoleon had not been as convinced as Rankin and Superintendent Hunter that Cropper knew anything, but gradually he had come round to their way of thinking.

Napoleon had a soft spot for Cropper from the start because of his love of football and Wellesley in particular. Rankin felt it was a chink in the chief inspector's armour. Napoleon took his son to see Wellesley play whenever he could, as did Cropper. A fellow Wellesley fan could not have been involved in the murder of his own son, was the way Napoleon had seen it. Well, he was wrong and so was failing to come down harder in the interviews of Cropper. Napoleon had eventually realised that.

Cropper wasn't a bright man and he always needed money. He had admitted he used his son in soft-porn videos to make a bit on the side for racing and beer. That confession had opened Napoleon's eyes. The chief inspector had visibly shuddered when Cropper had confessed to the video nasties. He had torn into Cropper with such force, the man had been reduced to tears, begging him to believe he had not killed his son or allowed anyone else to. He had stopped allowing Sean to be used in any videos months ago, he said. He pleaded with Napoleon to back off, but the chief inspector wouldn't. Napoleon had eventually stopped the interview in the early hours of the morning. "We'll let him stew in his own disgusting juice and then we'll wrap this case up," he told Rankin. But later that morning Cropper had been found hanging in his cell. He had used his shirt for a rope and noose and the bars of his cell window for a makeshift gallows. The timing of his death had been a blessing for those involved in Sean's disappearance and a disaster for Napoleon, Rankin, and the police.

Rankin, for all his contempt of Cropper, didn't believe he had murdered his son, but he either knew who the murderer was or knew something connected to the videos, which would have led to the person or persons responsible for abducting his son.

Cropper's death was down to one of those quirks of fate. The custody sergeant had been told to check Cropper every 15 minutes. Cell inspections were usually every 30 minutes, but Napoleon and Rankin were worried about Cropper's mental state. Napoleon had stopped the interview with Cropper as he had started hysterically sobbing. He knew that this was the time when confessions could easily be made, but he didn't want to contrive one. Rankin had wanted to carry on with the interview, but he was overruled.

The two policemen had left the station together at three in the morning, Napoleon telling the custody sergeant to keep a constant watch on Cropper.

There were two people, including Cropper in the cells that night. The other inmate was a youngster, no more than 16, who had been detained for being drunk and disorderly. The custody sergeant had tried to contact his parents during the night but had failed to reach them.

At just after three, the boy's father had burst into the station in a state of panic over his son's whereabouts. When the custody sergeant explained he was in a cell, the father had lost his temper and thrown a punch at the policeman. It took another officer on duty to restrain the man, but the commotion had been ideal cover for Cropper to quietly take his own life.

Rankin had blamed Napoleon for not finishing the interview in the early hours and had made his views known to Superintendent Hunter when questioned the next day. Hunter had gone ballistic, and Napoleon's career had not properly recovered since, which Rankin felt partly responsible for. He wished he had kept his thoughts to himself. He wasn't a vindictive man but, as he now saw, Hunter was.

In truth, however, Napoleon's career had stalled because he had since that day gradually lost his appetite for the job. More hours were spent with his family, and he had given in to Mary's pleas for a fourth child. He had found happiness outside his career. His family life was now more fulfilling than at any time in his life. The job simply paid the mortgage, and that was fine as far as Napoleon was concerned.

Rankin continued pulling up police reports on his computer screen, ambivalent thoughts about the Cropper case still disturbing his concentration. John McConnell. He read the name again on the computer file. There was something familiar about that name. The report on McConnell's drink-driving case was dated June. McConnell had been nearly four times over the limit and had been banned for driving for a year. He noticed the address: Crookham Lane, Wellesley.

Of course, Rankin slapped his hand on top of the desk. John McConnell was the son of the property developer Jack McConnell, who had found the body on the golf course. Jack McConnell had also been responsible for knocking out the custody sergeant on the night Cropper killed himself. It was his son who had been locked up for disturbing the peace. How very interesting, Rankin thought. He had questioned the father, who he knew vaguely, at the scene. The son, who according to the police records lived with his parents in Crookham Lane, would definitely be worth talking to as well.

CHAPTER 11

◆

Rankin rapped the heavy door knocker and waited. The house was a large mock Tudor, with protruding wooden beams and ivy sprawling decoratively up and around the windows. A long time ago Rankin had yearned for such a house with its five, maybe six bedrooms, beautifully manicured front lawn and a back garden that stretched out of his myopic focus towards the blur of Wellesley Golf Course.

He had also once longed for children and a loving wife, but that was a forgotten dream. He couldn't say whether his solitary life had been a choice, or something imposed from above. It certainly wasn't a conscious decision. It was just that work had become more important and time consuming. It was his obsession with policing that had driven Clare, his only long-term partner, away. They had lived together for two years, but in the last months they had shared little, except for the house, and breaking up became the inevitable and natural course.

"Yes?" a tall, slender woman answered the door. She was probably in her fifties, but still very attractive with long flowing auburn hair and an air of haughtiness that sometimes comes with wealth.

"Does John McConnell live here?" Rankin asked.

"Yes. Who are you? The police, I suppose."

"Why do you suppose that, madam?" Rankin said.

"He's always in some kind of trouble. Pornographic videos, fenced bicycles, you know the kind of thing."

"Pornographic videos?" Rankin repeated.

"Well. Are you the police? Before I give anything else away about my son's extra-curricular, if you can call them that, activities."

"Yes madam. Chief Inspector Rankin." Rankin showed her his identification and asked if he could step into the house. He wanted to make some progress, which he was unlikely to do in

32

the doorway. It was now Friday, and he still hadn't tracked down the McConnell boy, as there was no one at the house when he called the day before.

"My son's not here. He's probably at The Nag's Head. It's just down the road."

"Already?" It was only 9.30 in the morning.

"My son wouldn't want to shatter his carefully crafted drop-out image inspector. He likes drink, he likes women, he likes cars, and he likes gambling. He doesn't like work, golf, his father, or me. Oh, and he doesn't like policemen."

She went to shut the door, but Rankin put his hand up to prevent her. "I would like to talk to you about your son," he said.

For a start, he wanted to know more about the pornographic videos and fenced bicycles. It was a flippant remark, but even so it was an unusual one for a mother to blithely blurt out to a stranger, a stranger who happened to be a detective chief inspector. He also wanted to find out more about the son from the mother. McConnell had been in a lot of trouble in the past and lived only yards away from where the body had been found by his father. His father had been at the golf course bar until late on Wednesday night, the evening of the man's death, and dropped home by car by a friend, which had been corroborated by the friend, ruling him out as a suspect. But the coincidences looked decidedly suspicious. He didn't expect much co-operation from McConnell junior when he finally caught up with him. His mother might prove more informative.

Rankin made himself comfortable on a wooden fiddle-back chair and admired the ornate, spacious kitchen, with its marble work surface, pine table and chairs and intricate silk mural draped across a far wall. Spices were neatly arranged in a rack next to the main window, which looked out on to a long and impressively cared for back lawn. By the rack, six sturdy mugs dangled from a cup tree. Above them were two pine wall cupboards. Mrs McConnell, who insisted on being called Jo or Joanne, took out a tea pot from one of the cupboards and filled a kettle with water. She sat down next to Rankin while the kettle boiled.

They drank tea from two of the mugs on the cup tree, Rankin's had the name John imprinted on it, Mrs McConnell's the star sign Gemini with twins embracing below to signify its meaning.

"Your husband discovered a body on the golf course yesterday," Rankin said, taking out his notebook and writing the date at the top of the page.

"Did he now? The old rogue. Whatever could he have been up to? He always plays golf on a Thursday morning, but I thought it was a respectable game."

"You didn't know that he'd found a body?" Rankin could not contain his surprise. "Your husband didn't tell you he found a dead body on the golf course?"

"No," she said, shrugging her shoulders and raising her eyebrows. "We don't talk much and I was out all day yesterday until very late and we didn't see each other. When I woke up this morning, he had gone. So, no he didn't tell me he'd found a body. I must taunt him about it when he gets home. Old rogue."

Rankin gave her a pitying look. Someone had died. It was not a joke or funny. "The person was killed late on Wednesday evening," he said tersely, not bothering to disguise his distaste at her flippancy.

"Oh dear. What's going on in Wellesley. I thought our town was safe and respectable, like golf."

Rankin gave her another pitying look, but she did not seem to notice or care. She took a sip of tea and continued: "My husband seems like the obvious suspect then, as he was the person who discovered the body." She gave Rankin a lopsided smile and raised her eyebrows again.

"Does your son have a car?" Rankin said.

"No. He was banned - and he is very law abiding, as you probably know. Anyway, what has that got to do with anything?" she said.

"It's not particularly relevant," Rankin lied, and wondered if she ever dropped the sarcasm. Her patronising smile suggested not. She also seemed oddly unconcerned about his questions, just angry and bitter. But that seemed to be directed at life in general, rather than his inquiries.

"Do you know where your son was on Wednesday night?" he asked.

"No, I don't. I was out very late on Wednesday night, like I was last night. But he was tucked up nice and snugly in bed when I got home at about two in the morning. Does that clear him of any of the crimes?"

"No. Not quite," Rankin said, taking down some notes.

"Maybe I got home earlier, then," Mrs McConnell said, watching Rankin as he wrote.

"Maybe you did." Rankin played along with the little game. "So where were you on Wednesday night?"

"Oh, so I'm a bloody suspect now. Well, I was at a friend's house all day and night and I walked, sorry staggered, home. So it wasn't me, who done it, inspector. And like John, I don't play golf so that clears me of anything to do with the body on the golf course."

"Do you have a car?"

She took another sip of tea, then said in a hard, abrupt tone: "No. They stop you drinking. My husband drives a Jaguar, but I don't need a car as I have nowhere to drive it, even if I was sober long enough to do so." She smiled lopsidedly again, but this time her expression had a mean edge.

Rankin had taken a look at the McConnell Jaguar when the body had been found. Silver and pristine, it had clearly not hit anything or been involved in a hit-and-run accident.

"Was your husband at home when you got in?" he said.

"Yes, of course. Unlike me, he has to work. He needs his sleep."

Rankin nodded. Jack McConnell had told him he had arrived home around midnight on the Wednesday evening, which had also been corroborated by the friend who had given him a lift back to the house.

"What does your son do, Mrs McConnell?"

"Jo." She corrected him.

"What does your son do, Jo?"

"Well, as I told you, drink, gamble and womanise."

"And fence stolen goods. Not a phrase I would expect from a respectable person like yourself."

"I was being frivolous, inspector, or can I call you…"

"Inspector will do fine," Rankin said.

"And I'm not respectable. I'm a drunk, like my son. Drunks tend to be familiar with terms like fence. We pick them up in the gutter with the other drunks and policemen."
Rankin ignored the dig at his profession.
"Does your son have a job?"

"I don't think so," she replied.

"You don't know."

"No, I don't, inspector." She emphasised the word inspector to show her irritation at his surprise.

"Right," Rankin said. "Does your son usually sleep here? I know it's his registered address, but does he have a girlfriend or friends where he might stay the night instead?"

"What kind of question is that? Of course, he doesn't usually sleep here. He's a young man, free spirit. You know the type. Wherever I lay my hat, I shag. That sort of thing. He sleeps all over the place. Do you have any grown-up daughters? If you have, then he's probably slept with them. Quite a boy is our John. And I don't know whether he has a regular shag."

Rankin smiled thinly. He was sure he didn't look old enough to have a daughter of consenting age, but he supposed that was half the point of the remark. She could not, it seemed, say anything without extending her claws.

She stood up, opened one of the wall cupboards and took out a bottle of gin and a glass tumbler. The chief inspector watched her pour a generous measure of gin and fill the rest of the glass with tonic water and ice from the fridge.

She leant against the kitchen sink and took a large swig from her glass, letting the contents wash around her mouth. An exploratory tongue licked her lips and front teeth. She did not intend to waste a drop. She gave Rankin a defiant stare and took another swig, more or less finishing the drink.

"Look, inspector, I don't know what John does during the day or where he stays at night, sometimes it's here, sometimes it's not. And I don't know what he gets up to and if I did, I wouldn't tell a bloody copper, would I?" The drink appeared to have gone straight to her head, making her more aggressive.

She poured more gin with just a splash of tonic into her glass. This time Rankin was the one to raise his eyebrows. He wondered if she had been drinking gin before he had arrived, with the tea a stopgap between the alcohol.

"You mentioned pornographic videos. What did you mean by it?"

"Nothing. It was just a flip remark. Look I'm bored with all this." She drained her second glass of gin and leant further back against the sink.

"I think you should go now." She stared directly at Rankin with glassy eyes that were struggling to focus properly. "Yes, just bloody go, bloody boring copper, drinking your bloody boring tea."

Rankin stood up and put his notebook in his pocket. "You said John would be in The Nag's Head."

"Yes. That's what I said." She turned away from Rankin and poured a third drink.

"I'll see myself out," he said and left her staring vacantly out of the window.

CHAPTER 12

◆

"Is there a John McConnell here?" Rankin asked the barman.

"Who wants to know?"

"The police." He flashed his identification.

"Round the corner. By the pool table," the barman said, without looking up from the pint glass he was polishing.

"Thank you." Rankin nodded and made his way to where a big man was sitting, reading his phone and drinking a pint of beer. He was in his mid to late twenties and looked a little unkempt. He had a good two days of stubble on his chin.

"Are you John McConnell?"

"Who wants to know?" McConnell said.

Rankin smiled thinly at the carbon copy response to the barman's – they were a wary lot in The Nag's Head - and stuck to his cue. "The police," he said and produced his identification again. "I'm Chief Inspector Rankin. I'm in charge at Wellesley police station."

McConnell nodded in a knowing way and took a sip from his pint. Rankin sat down opposite him and reached for his notebook. "Do you drive?" he asked.

"Why do you want to know?" Rankin sighed and noticed the paint was peeling on the walls. The Nag's Head was much shabbier than he remembered, but then he hadn't been in the pub for months. "I could make this difficult. I could ask you to come down to the station. On the other hand, you could answer some simple questions and then I'll leave you to your beer."

McConnell took a large mouthful of the golden liquid in his pint glass and drummed his fingers on the table. "Okay, no I don't drive. I don't have a car. I was banned a few months ago. You should have the ban on your records."

"You haven't driven recently, then?" Rankin asked.

"That would be breaking the law, wouldn't it? Is this going anywhere?" McConnell had obviously inherited a sarcastic streak from his mother.

Rankin smiled thinly again. "Your father found a body on the golf course yesterday morning."

"Oh, so the old man found the body. Yeah, that would figure, the old git always plays golf early on a Thursday morning."

Old git, old rogue, Rankin was beginning to feel sorry for Jack McConnell. The bachelor life clearly wasn't so bad. The chief inspector rubbed his chin and looked directly at McConnell. At least he was sober, unlike his mother when he left her.

"You knew about the body being found, but you didn't realise your father was the one who came across it?" Communication was not a strong point in the McConnell household.

McConnell took another swig of beer and eyed Rankin morosely. "I saw the news and heard the gossip about a body being found, but I don't speak to my father. Okay? And what has a dead body on the golf course got to do with whether I can drive or not?"

McConnell put his phone down on the table and sat back in his chair. He certainly wasn't going to mention his little trek on the golf course the previous morning. Maybe someone saw him.

"What's the matter?" Rankin asked.

"Nothing," McConnell said aggressively. "I just don't know where this is going."

Rankin paused and noticed a tall, angular man wearing a raincoat and fedora hovering at the next table. He looked like he was about to sit down, but on seeing Rankin turned back towards the bar, where he sat down on a stool with his back to the inspector and McConnell.

"Do you always have that effect on people, inspector?" McConnell said, grinning. Rankin ignored him.

"Where were you on Wednesday night?" he said coolly.

"I was here."

"What time and for how long?"

"I don't know. Why do you want to know?" McConnell said.

"Just answer the question."

"I suppose I got here about 6.30 and was here until about 11.30. I wasn't keeping track of the time," McConnell said as he theatrically pushed one of his fingers into a nostril, presumably to pick something gruesome inside.

"Can people verify that?" Rankin said, unsure whether the nose picking was intended to be deliberately obnoxious.

"Ask the landlord and any number of regulars. The Buckler brothers would certainly remember me being here as we had a little disagreement," McConnell said, taking his finger out of his nose and wiping it on a beer mat.

Rankin tried not to show disgust on his face but failed. "Over what?" he said.

"I knocked over one of their drinks. I thought it was funny. They didn't. We went outside to have our little argument. I came back in the pub for a few more drinks before I left, which I guess was about 11.30. It was definitely after closing time when I left because I remember Barney, the landlord, telling me I was banned. Someone had told him about my little interaction with the Bucklers outside and he disapproved." He smirked. "But it looks like the ban has been lifted, or Barney forgot to tell the bar staff about it. Stupid sod. Anyway, now I'm here enjoying my beer, or I was until you came along with these pointless questions." This time McConnell's smile was more of a sneer than a smirk, cruel and mirthless.

Rankin ignored the barbs. McConnell seemed to enjoy confrontation. He hadn't needed to tell Rankin about his ban from the pub, and his boast that he had evaded it was said in a provocative, challenging way as if he wanted the policeman to try and enforce it. But McConnell defying a ban from The Nag's Head over what sounded like a minor squabble with the Bucklers was of no interest to Rankin. He smiled thinly at McConnell for a third time. Thin, wry smiles were becoming his trademark, a default position to fend off sarcastic and aggressive comments.

"How did you get home?" Rankin asked. McConnell began fiddling with the beer mat he had wiped his finger on.

"I walked. My parents' house, where I live, is up the road." Rankin nodded. He had just walked from the McConnell home. It was a five-minute walk at a quick pace.

"Did you walk home on your own?"

"Yeah," McConnell said and started picking his nose again. This time he made his nostrils flare as he tried to pick something deep inside it. He grinned at the inspector as he did so.

Rankin produced yet another thin smile, looked at his watch and shut his notebook. "Thank you for your co-operation. It's been a lovely chat." He could match the McConnell sarcasm when he wanted to. "That's all I need to know." He would check with witnesses in the pub to confirm McConnell's story, but it rang true. He didn't have a car and his parents' house was such a short distance from the pub, it made sense to walk, which ruled him out as a suspect in the hit-and-run. Father and son appeared to be in the clear.

It was windy outside. Rankin let the breeze wash over him and admired the pretty, red brick homes, with their elegant window boxes and neat little gardens, on the other side of the road. He shivered. It was cold, despite the bright morning sun.

"What was all that about?" McConnell said to the barman.

"Someone found dead near your house. Seems pretty obvious you did it, I suppose," the barman said, as he wiped one of the beer taps with a cloth.

"Thanks for the vote of confidence," McConnell said. "Pour me another pint, will you?" The barman reached for a glass on the shelf behind him. "On second thoughts, forget it," McConnell said and headed for the door. He had several jobs to do in town and they wouldn't get done with two pints swilling inside him this early.

On the pavement, he saw Rankin was half-way across the road. The policeman was going thin on top. McConnell hadn't noticed before. He felt his own scalp, but his thatch was thick and plentiful. Reassured, as baldness was one of his great fears, he considered Rankin for a moment and then moved to the middle of the road, virtually on the policeman's shoulder. The chief inspector was waiting for a car, which was approaching slowly to his left, to go by. McConnell didn't fancy another tedious exchange with the inspector so he suddenly sprinted to the other side of the road before the car could pass.

As he leapt on to the pavement, he heard a sickening thud behind. Turning sharply, he saw Rankin thrown several feet into the air. The policeman hit the ground and rolled two or three times before crashing into a lamp post. The car on McConnell's side of the road, which Rankin had been waiting for, came to a juddering halt and the startled driver jumped out. The car, which had hit the chief inspector from the other direction, was already speeding into the distance. McConnell, without thinking, dashed to where Rankin lay unconscious in the road.

The barman of The Nag's Head had emerged from the pub to see what was going on. McConnell yelled at him to telephone for an ambulance. The barman was only a few yards away, but the desire to shout was overpowering. Rankin was motionless and bleeding heavily. McConnell tried to keep himself calm. His mind flashed back six months to when he had hauled a man out of the Thames. He had saved the man's life by staying calm and giving him mouth-to-mouth resuscitation.

He felt for Rankin's pulse. He couldn't find anything. He leant his head against the chief inspector's chest and put his hand over his mouth. Rankin had stopped breathing. His chest was still and lifeless. McConnell eased the policeman's head back and held his nose tightly. He took a deep breath and blew hard into Rankin's mouth. Nothing. He took another deep breath and blew into Rankin's mouth a second time. Still nothing. McConnell had never felt so helpless or so frightened. The resuscitation had worked quickly with the young man who fell in the river. McConnell continued breathing into Rankin's chest. He was close to giving up when the ambulance arrived. It had arrived quickly, although it seemed like a lifetime.

Blood from the policeman's head covered his hands and part of his coat. It was thick and warm. Before he could think further, a paramedic team swarmed around him.

"Are you all right?" a ginger haired man asked.

"Yes. It's not my blood. It's his." It was probably a stupid thing to say, but the ginger haired man simply nodded.

"A car hit him. It was going fast," McConnell said.

The ginger haired man nodded again. "Why don't you move on to the pavement? We can take over now," he said.

"Sure," McConnell said.

A matronly woman from one of the nearby houses was asking the driver of the car that had stopped if he wanted a cup of tea. The man nodded. "Did you see what happened?" McConnell asked him.

"I didn't see the car actually hit him," he said. McConnell noticed the man was trembling. "I had my eyes on the other side of the road. I was looking for a parking space. I saw the car, though. It was a small red one, but I didn't see the driver."

"What make was the car?" McConnell asked.

"I don't know. I don't know about cars, and I didn't get a good enough look."

"Do you want a cup of tea young man?" the matronly woman asked. "I'm making a pot."

"No thanks," McConnell said.

At that moment, a police car pulled up. McConnell watched the policemen get out. He took a pace or two back, away from the car, and discreetly slipped away. He couldn't face more questioning from the boys in blue.

CHAPTER 13

◆

The glistening autumn morning moved softly into the Napoleons' bedroom, spreading light and colour as it swept away the mysteries of the dark. Mary stirred, the light reawakening her senses and prompting her out of a deep sleep.

She drowsily checked her alarm clock before gently edging out of bed to avoid disturbing her still sleeping husband. She cast a glance at Napoleon, who was gently snoring, something she found at times annoying, at others endearing, depending on its volume and her mood. The snoring wasn't that loud, and he looked sweet, inspiring affection rather than irritation for now. She smiled and went downstairs to make breakfast for herself and the children.

Napoleon was a long way off, deep in dreams of children's parties, with ice-cream treats for tea and plastic, gimmicky presents for entertainment. Autumn was a special time in the Napoleon household as the chief inspector and his three oldest children had birthdays at that time of year.

Napoleon's dreams sent him back to distant autumn days before his youngest was born and an endless procession of birthday parties filled the house with noise and excitement. He was in the living room of their old house. Toys and wrapping paper littered the floor and there was a festive atmosphere, which reminded him of Christmas. At that moment, his subconscious journey transformed into a vast medieval banquet hall, where Christmas lunch was being served.

Mary slipped her dressing gown off and returned to bed. She had made breakfast and seen the children off to school, leaving Napoleon to enjoy a lie in. He looked relaxed and contented and was probably sleeping easier because he had the day off. She snuggled close to him, and he turned on his back, breathing deeply but no longer snoring. He was still far away, eating and

44

drinking at a great feasting table, which magically turned into a bed. His fourth and youngest child Matthew was at the bed/table and the other children had now grown into their teens. Oddly, his second son Robert retained the size and appearance of a toddler. Then he fell deeper and deeper until all sense and consciousness was lost.

The sound of gunfire was quite close, but gradually, as Napoleon emerged from his dream, he became aware that the rattling sound was coming from one of the bedroom windows rather than his imaginary battlefield. It had been opened by Mary and was banging against the wind on its latch.

He could now sense one of Mary's arms resting on his stomach. He stretched and yawned, and she turned towards him, kissing his cheek with moist lips. He pulled her to him and slowly stroked her back, returning her kiss, first on the lips, then on her nose and cheeks.

They made love in their gentle, familiar way against a background noise of the gusting wind, which swept around the chimneys on the roof of the house and thumped against the bedroom windows. After their love making, they fell back to sleep.

At first, Napoleon thought he could hear a telephone ringing in the distance. He was standing on a huge jetty, which stretched miles out to sea into a soothing mass of aquamarine blue. Slowly, he became more aware of the sharp trilling sound. Then, Mary's soft words nudged him out of his slumber.

"Can you get it, darling?" she said. He disentangled himself from her body and reached for the urgent noise at the side of the bed.

"Hello," he said sleepily.

"Napoleon, is that you? You sound odd." The coarse south London tones of Chief Superintendent Jim Hunter, the head of Valley CID, were immediately recognisable.

"Yes sir, it's Napoleon. I'm fine." He couldn't remember the chief superintendent calling him at home before. Still in that half state between dreams and reality, he guessed he was still asleep.

"Patrick Rankin has been killed by a hit-and-run driver in Wellesley."

"Killed." Napoleon repeated incredulously. He sat up, the sleepy cobwebs blown away in an instant.

"Yes, killed," the chief superintendent said tersely. "There's no sign of the driver. All we know is that the person was driving a small, red car. It's the second hit-and-run fatality in Wellesley in two days. It happened half-an-hour ago on the Wellesley Road, outside The Nag's Head. I understand you live near there?"

"Yes sir, in Crookham Lane, near the golf course, where the young man was found yesterday morning."

"Right. Get down to the scene. Then report back to me at headquarters. As of now, you're back in charge at Wellesley police station, replacing Rankin. I will head the investigation into both deaths, and I want you running the day-to-day operation, reporting directly to me. Right."

"Yes sir," Napoleon said. He put the telephone back in its cradle. The news was hard to digest. Emotions of shock and bewilderment mixed uneasily, yet Hunter had given him the one thing he wanted, to run his old station again. It was probably the only job that could revive his appetite for policing, to be a proper hands-on detective on his old patch. But he didn't want it like this, not at the price of another policeman's life.

"What's happened?" Mary said alarmed. She was now sitting up too, alert, and fully awake.

"Patrick Rankin has been killed by a hit-and-run driver. That was Chief Superintendent Hunter."

"Oh my God. That's awful. It can't be true." She shook her head, upset but also relieved that the terrible news was nothing to do with the children. They were all safe. "When and where did it happen?" she asked.

"Half-an-hour ago, outside The Nag's Head."

Mary's eyebrows arched in surprise. "What, down the road? My God. Do they know who the driver was who hit him?"

"No. The driver's vanished. All they know is that it was a small, red car," Napoleon said. He turned to Mary and hugged her. He noticed there were tears in her eyes. She liked Rankin. "I've got to get down to the scene. Hunter's put me back in charge at Wellesley to replace Rankin."

Mary nodded and wiped her eyes with her hand. "You've got that determined face on, like the old you." She smiled at her husband. "You'll get to the bottom of this, if anyone can. But I still can't believe it, two people dead in two days. What's going on?" She sniffed and reached for a tissue at the side of the bed.

CHAPTER 14

◆

Patrick Rankin lay on a metal tray in the mortuary at Redfield General Hospital. Napoleon stood over him. His eyes wandered the room, taking in the grim and impersonal surroundings. There were several white refrigeration units where the bodies were kept and three large silver tables in the middle of the room. The storage tray that Rankin was lying on had been put on the table nearest the door. Napoleon grimaced. He could never get used to these cold, soulless places, which brought home the depressing and final nature of death. His gloomy spirits weren't helped by a pervading smell of hospital disinfectant that made him feel slightly nauseous. Instinctively, he touched one of Rankin's cheeks. It was cold and hard, symbolic of their relationship. A tinge of guilt welled inside him. Should he have tried harder to tolerate and understand his dead colleague?

Jackson hovered behind him, reading his thoughts. "Don't trouble yourself." The pathologist put a hand on Napoleon's shoulder. "He was a good man, but so are you. We can't all get on."

"No. You're right." Napoleon nodded. He wasn't sure if he was a good man, but he appreciated the consoling words.

Jackson gave the chief inspector an assessing glance. He saw no need for further reassurance and moved swiftly on to business. "The car was going about 30 mph at the time of impact. His upper right leg was broken, but the car didn't kill him, a lamp post did. He was thrown straight into it. Smashed his skull. Death was instant."

Napoleon nodded again. He touched Rankin one last time on his cheek, it was his awkward way of saying goodbye, and left before the disinfectant and death in the room could upset his equilibrium any further.

It was cold in the car. Napoleon switched the heating on to full blast and started the engine. He looked at his watch. He was cutting it fine for the press conference on Rankin's death, which Hunter had insisted on holding, but it couldn't be helped. Redfield, 15 minutes north west of Wellesley by car, was a good 45-minute ride to Valley headquarters in Kingham. The road to Kingham, which was on the other side of Wellesley in the heart of the country, was a winding tour of some of the prettier parts of England's diminishing rural South East, where houses were springing up at an ever faster rate. It wasn't a route built for speed or convenient commuting.

Napoleon shifted the gear stick into first and drove out of the hospital car park, thinking of Rankin. Thirty minutes into the journey, death still preoccupied his thoughts, how it often exposed loose ends. The things you would have said and tied up in an ideal world. He should have told Rankin how highly he thought of him as a policeman, but would he have done so? Rankin was always so pompous and such a stickler for the rules, a believer in perspiration and hard work rather than inspiration and creative thought. But sometimes gut instinct, that indefinable hunch, produced results.

Napoleon slammed on the car's brakes as a muddy, banking countryside verge loomed up at him. He hadn't realised how fast he was travelling. Self-analysis didn't make for a good driving companion. He reduced his speed to one more suited to the twisting road that cut through the fields and farms between Wellesley and Kingham.

On his left, he could just glimpse the entrance of The Plough, Rankin's favourite pub. He had once had a pleasant drink there with Rankin. Clare, Rankin's old girlfriend, had been there too. The Plough served an excellent pint of ale, something the two policemen had agreed upon and enjoyed together. If only Rankin hadn't been so pedantic in the way he followed the rulebook. If only he, Napoleon, had told Rankin how much he admired his dogged organisational abilities. You needed those skills, the perspiration, as well as the instinctive, lateral qualities that accounted for inspiration, to get results.

A long queue of cars clogged the approach to Kingham roundabout. On impulse, Napoleon detoured down a left-hand side street into a small estate of houses. He took another left, two rights and one more left up a particularly narrow road clearly marked no entry. Another left and right put him back on the main road, the roundabout satisfactorily bypassed. His local knowledge, he had once investigated a mindless domestic murder in one of the estate's tiny, terraced houses, had saved invaluable minutes. Rankin would never have driven up a road with a no entry sign, but sometimes lateral thinking meant breaking the rules. A wry smile broke across the inspector's face. Lateral thinking? He silently mocked himself for such grandiose and pretentious thoughts. It was just a small detour, but all the same his quick thinking and change of route meant he would arrive at headquarters with time to spare before the press conference.

CHAPTER 15

◆

M olly sat at her desk in the radio station newsroom, digesting a profile of Jack McConnell on the website of one of the local newspapers. She had just read a similar profile on a man called Derek Keele. The station's newsroom was usually alive and buzzing by late morning, but for once Molly found herself sitting alone, with just the low hum of her computer disturbing the peace. She leaned back in her chair, taking a short mental break from her reading, and enjoying the rare tranquil moment.

She had worked as a reporter and presenter at Radio Valley, which was based in Redfield, for almost three years, and was making notes for a programme on a planning dispute between McConnell and Keele. The two men, who had extensive business interests in the area, were vying for a contract to knock down a primary school in Wellesley to make way for their own particular developments after the council had decided to close it because of falling pupil rolls.

She had nearly finished reading McConnell's profile and had come to the conclusion that the two men were remarkably similar, despite their intense dislike of each other. She had met both of them at various functions over the years and had found them unusually domineering and extremely sure of themselves. They had the overbearing confidence of wealthy men used to success and getting their own way.

Molly had also sought opinions on the men from a number of councillors who had dealt with them on contracts or knew them personally. One had summed them up with a perceptiveness that had prompted Molly to make a verbatim note of his words – ruthlessly ambitious but sheathed in a natural charm that inspired fierce loyalty and unquestioning devotion from friends and subordinates. The councillor had added drily that their friends and subordinates tended to agree with their views and opinions.

They were not men to encourage dissent or outspoken individuality. He personally tolerated their egotism and at times blatant selfishness because they got things done and were pleasant enough to deal with.

Molly agreed with him as far as McConnell was concerned. He had always been charming to her, although now that she thought about it, he had done the talking and she the listening. He clearly liked to hold court and be the one who told the stories, which admittedly had been interesting and funny. She was not so sure about Keele. His friendliness had bordered on the creepy. The other striking thing about both men was their height, which each used to dominate a conversation.

McConnell wanted to build a leisure centre and Keele a supermarket. The council had decided to close the school as falling pupil numbers had made it difficult to justify keeping it open. But opposition against the closure among local people, many of whom were themselves former pupils, had taken the council by surprise.

The strength of feeling had even inspired the school's most famous alumnus, Henry Llewellyn, one of Britain's leading actors, to form an action group to fight the proposals. Llewellyn, who lived in a converted farmhouse on the outskirts of Wellesley, had called the group SOS - Save Our School. It was a corny slogan, but it had been effective in gaining support among residents in the town. As well as a fine actor, Llewellyn was a clever self-publicist, using his celebrity to gain maximum airtime on the local television and radio stations and coverage in the Wellesley and county newspapers.

He had urged the local people to remember that a community was not built on money-making supermarkets or leisure centres but on the institutions, however small, that gave a place its character. The school was part of the fabric of Wellesley and had been for more than 160 years, he said. To demolish it was to demolish a piece of history.

Molly found Llewellyn's argument unconvincing and overly sentimental. He had conveniently overlooked the fact that the school was very ordinary and unremarkable, and most critically had ignored the obvious problem of falling pupil numbers. In recent years, it had increasingly struggled to compete with bigger, more modern schools nearby, which offered better facilities and results. The school may have been built in the Victorian times, but it had no particular historical significance. There was nothing special or outstanding about the architecture and half the school had been renovated in the most unimaginative way in the 1970s. But Llewellyn had used emotion and melodrama to appeal to the fears of many residents about development in the area, two new housing estates were being built to the east of Wellesley. It was significant that much of his support came from the older people in the community who resented large swathes of the countryside being turned into concrete, even if it was necessary to tackle a growing and alarming housing shortage.

What the council had hoped was going to be a routine planning matter, perhaps naively, had turned into a bad-tempered feud between McConnell and Keele and a publicity extravaganza for Llewellyn.

In Llewellyn's case, Molly was convinced he was driven by the publicity the campaign could generate for himself and his next project. He was to play Hamlet on the stage at Stratford, which was mentioned in almost every story about the school. This had clearly helped ticket sales. The production was now sold out all the way to Christmas and beyond.

Llewellyn would probably have drawn the crowds without the help of the press, but he wasn't a man to leave chance to fate, scrupulously and meticulously preparing for each new acting role. This, together with his ability to bring humour, charm, and an emotional intensity to the parts he played, had made him, in the opinion of some critics, one of Britain's most accomplished actors. He had won plaudits for a number of inspirational performances on television and in the theatre, his most powerful tending to be Shakespearian. He had played Richard III and Hamlet to acclaim. His big breakthrough as an actor had been his first portrayal of Hamlet five years previously, which Molly had seen with Charlie on one of their first dates together.

Since then, she had interviewed Llewellyn twice for the radio station and, consequently, did not need to read up on him as she had with McConnell and Keele. She also remembered him from her schooldays, although, now 32, he was five years older than her. They had both attended Wellesley Primary School and then the large comprehensive on the outskirts of the town.

Even then, he had appeared destined for stardom, showcasing his talent in the regular school plays and amateur dramatic productions at the local theatre. He was undeniably charming. Indeed, charismatic possibly better described him, with his film star looks and deep, sexy voice.

Like McConnell and Keele, he also seemed to be driven by a powerful ego, with an underlying vanity and conceit that often accompanied high self-esteem. He knew he was handsome, talented and a star - and that came across, albeit in a subtle rather than obvious way. Her husband Charlie was just as handsome and, in many ways, just as clever, but he was totally unaware of it. Strangely, Charlie and Llewellyn looked similar, both thin, dark and of average height, which often made her think of her husband whenever she thought about Llewellyn as she was now. But Charlie was a different kind of man, modest and kind with few pretensions or ego to complicate his character.

Despite his moodiness and their rows of late, it was this down-to-earth straight forwardness that made her love him and want to be with him. Charlie, who had been involved in the decision to close the school as the chief planning officer on the local council, had based his views on facts, not ego or because it could gain him publicity or profits. Yet, it was the egos of Llewellyn, McConnell and Keele that were likely to decide the fate of the school, turning what had been a simple decision to close a poorly performing institution into a local soap opera.

In Molly's view, McConnell or Keele, who were both to an extent, men of vision, could use the site to improve the town. A supermarket definitely appealed to her. She had never been keen on exercise despite being thin and a talented long-distance runner as a child.

The thought of the supermarket reminded her that she was hungry and hadn't eaten breakfast. She was also starting to feel slightly panicky as she still wasn't fully prepared for a meeting of the council in the next few days, which was likely to decide the fate of the school. She wanted to broadcast a news programme on why saving the school had struck such a resonant chord with the locals, and the meeting was the ideal moment to present the story, but she needed to get on top of all the facts first.

She was about to type a few more details on McConnell into her computer file, when the station's news editor Jim burst through the swing doors that led to the studio where the news reports and programmes were broadcast. He sat down with a thump in the chair opposite and gave Molly a cursory, pained glance.

"Can you do the police calls?" he said in an agitated voice. The intonation left no doubt it was a command rather than a question. The late morning news had clearly not gone to plan. The police calls were a routine ring round of the local police stations for news on road accidents and crimes in the area. She reached for the telephone, but it started ringing loudly before she could lift the receiver. Jim stared at it irritably. It was a uniformed policeman she knew well at Wellesley station.

She listened for a moment. "Chief Inspector Rankin? Oh my..." Her mouth dropped. "Yes, I know him. Have you got the driver who hit him?" she asked.

"No details yet. Okay," she said. "When did it happen and where?"

"Look, thanks. I really appreciate the tip." Molly put the telephone down. "Jim, a policeman has been killed by a hit-and-run driver in Wellesley. It was a plainclothes chief inspector. I've had a few dealings with him in the past. He was in charge at Wellesley. They haven't got much information yet. My policemen friend didn't know who was responsible for causing the death or whether anyone at the scene knows who the driver was."

Jim considered Molly briefly, then sprang to his feet, dropping the newspaper he had just picked up on to his desk. His disgruntled expression had transformed. There was now excitement and a newsman's sparkle in his eye.

"Write down what you have," he said urgently. "Get on to the Valley Police press office. Ask them to confirm the story and get any details you can."

"It's only just happened, so they probably won't have much," Molly said. "He was hit just outside that horrible pub I was telling you about, the one Charlie always makes me go to because it's near where we live."

Jim nodded manically. "Okay, but we need an official confirmation from Valley police, then we can put out a news flash. Once we've done that, you can get down to Wellesley to get more details."

Molly nodded. But she couldn't feel or share Jim's excitement at the prospect of a big story, or not one that involved an innocent policeman's death.

CHAPTER 16

◆

Napoleon surveyed his old office with a strange ambivalence. The same dusty yellowing map of the county hung above the same oak panelled desk, and there was a familiar musty smell suggestive of the past. It made him feel oddly detached, as if he was in a dream. He had been in Wellesley police station many times since his transfer to Valley headquarters in Kingham, but not in the chief inspector's office. He sighed. The room brought back memories of the Sean Cropper case. His time at the station had been stained by the abduction of the boy. The failure to track down those responsible still rankled.

He would never forgive himself for ending the interview with Frank Cropper on the night he killed himself. It was his big mistake. Rankin was right. They should have pressed on with the questioning. Frank's death had destroyed any chance of solving the case, and sometimes in his dreams he could feel dark forces laughing at his incompetence, teasing, and sneering in the shadows. Napoleon shivered and sat down in his old chair. He cast a weary eye around the office again. It was only a room. He would soon get used to being back, and this is what he wanted. With the exception of the Cropper tragedy, his time in charge at Wellesley had been the most enjoyable and fulfilling of his career.

He stood up and walked to the window. The rush hour was nearly over, but the high street was still busy. He stared unseeingly at the cars and people making their way home. His thoughts wandered to the Cropper case again. It had deeply affected him because it had happened in his home town and involved a family he knew well. He should have taken himself off the case because of that, but he had desperately wanted to find Sean's killers and had kept his links with the Cropper family to himself.

He had first met Ted Cropper, Sean's grandfather, one Saturday afternoon at a Wellesley football match. He and Robert, his second eldest who he took to most games, were queuing for hot dogs at half-time. Ted and Sean were queuing behind them, and the boys started talking. Ted and Napoleon began to chat too and the four of them watched the second half of the game together.

Napoleon liked Ted. He had an amusingly cynical attitude to football and was one of the most pessimistic fans he had ever come across. They usually sat together at home games because Sean and Robert got on so well. They were both seven years old and equally passionate about football.

The chief inspector had discovered little about Ted on those afternoons, except that he lived in Wellesley, repaired washing machines, loved football and lived for his grandson. But what else did you need to know about someone to like them? Sometimes probing too deeply ruined a friendship. There was only one person Napoleon liked and loved right to the very core and that was Mary, and he was happy for it to stay that way.

On some Saturdays, Frank, who was Ted's son, would join them. He rarely spoke to Napoleon, probably because he was a policeman, although the inspector was all too familiar with the likes of Frank. He was a small-time criminal, forever looking for easy money to pay for his beer and gambling. He was predictably unreliable and probably an alcoholic. He preferred lager to tea at half-time and would usually find his way to the pub immediately after the game. On the afternoon Wellesley played Millborough in the cup, Napoleon and Robert had been invited to sit in the director's box, while Ted had been too ill with pleurisy to go to the game. It had been left to Frank to take Sean to the match, and the last time they were seen was outside The Rising Sun pub just before the game had started.

Napoleon looked at his watch and let the past fade into the background. Time to deal with the present and introduce himself as the new officer in charge of the station. A bemused duty sergeant had watched Napoleon head straight for his old office with just a fleeting glance of acknowledgment. He had done it instinctively. It was an unconscious attempt to settle himself, to find his place in a bizarre and unpredictable situation he could not fully comprehend.

He was still coming to terms with the dreamlike events of the day. If at that moment Rankin had walked into the office, he would have been relieved, not surprised. A shrug of the shoulders would have been the end of it, and he would have quietly slipped back to his office at headquarters, the burden lifted and the reassurance of a known routine ahead.

But that wasn't going to happen. He clasped his hands tightly and gazed again out of the office window. Earlier he had felt guilty for being excited at taking charge of Wellesley. But now he felt apprehensive and a little scared. Reality was crowding in. A fellow officer was dead, and it was up to him to find out who was responsible and why. He had to get a grip of himself, the events, and the strange and suspicious circumstances of the two deaths.

After one long indrawing of his breath, he rang the duty sergeant's extension and told him to gather everyone in the main office. He had had dealings or spoken to most of the men and women at the station. Only the American was unfamiliar. Detective Sergeant Joe Mayo had been at Wellesley for nearly a year. Napoleon knew of him because of his nationality, although he had been told he held a British passport through his English mother and had lived in the country for years, ever since his student days.

He took another long breath to steady himself and slowly made his way to the main office. Mayo had positioned himself on one of the chairs at the back of the room. The chief inspector smiled to himself. Weren't Americans supposed to be pushy, front-seat types? But then Mayo was half English. He looked around the room, taking in the faces. Everyone seemed to be there, so he fixed his eyes on an empty chair and introduced himself in the trademark monotone he invariably used when speaking to a group.

What he had to say was not new. The officers would have been briefed on the changes earlier. But it was important for him to address them, to draw an imaginary line in the sand, to begin building his new team around him. He wanted to develop a sense of camaraderie between himself and his officers. Without that comradeship and feeling the officer in charge was in touch and fighting your corner, policing could become a lonely and soul-destroying business.

The day-to-day running of the station was to stay the same, but with Napoleon replacing Rankin. Chief Superintendent Hunter would head the investigation into both hit-and-run deaths and regular press conferences would be held at Kingham.

Napoleon paid a small tribute to Rankin and asked if there were any questions. There was none so he concluded by saying he would be happy to see everyone individually as long as it was in the pub, and they were buying. The parting quip, although not particularly original, provoked genuine laughter and the smiling faces made Napoleon feel a little more relaxed and assured in a new role, which had plunged him into uncharted and potentially treacherous waters.

CHAPTER 17

◆

Molly turned on her kindle and searched for a copy of Hamlet in the library store. She clicked on to the first one in a long list of copies and editions and downloaded it. She had organised an interview with Henry Llewellyn through his agent and felt she should at least try re-reading the play he was about to star in, particularly as he was reputedly an expert on Shakespeare.

She had read the play when she was at school and then again when she had watched Llewellyn play Hamlet for the first time five years ago. But she had always struggled with the Early Modern English of Shakespeare. Its rhyming couplets, iambic pentameters and unfamiliar idioms were mostly an alien language to her, however hard she tried to understand and appreciate them.

She settled in a chair by the French windows in her dining room and randomly clicked through the pages on her kindle, reading a few lines here and there. She knew the play was a revenge tragedy about Hamlet's indecision over whether to avenge the murder of his father. But she would need some sort of literature guide or study notes with background explanations and summaries of the text to help her better understand the plot and characters.

When she had seen the play for the first time with Charlie, she had been more interested in watching Llewellyn and soaking up the atmosphere of the theatre than following the twists and turns of the plot, which she had lost interest in by the second or third act. She searched for a literature guide on her kindle and downloaded it while thinking about the policeman's death and the body on the golf course. The deaths seemed unreal and out of place in a small town like Wellesley, but at the same time they had deeply unsettled her. The deaths were probably unconnected, random events, but there was a part of Molly that worried there was a psychopath on the loose, a mad person who had dumped a body on the golf course and then with a dangerous recklessness mowed down an innocent policeman in broad daylight.

She thought of Llewellyn again and how she had interviewed him once before for the radio station. It was a couple of years after she had seen him play Hamlet in London. She remembered that she had been having difficulties with Charlie at the time, difficulties that she was again experiencing. She had nearly ended her relationship with Charlie back then and sometimes she regretted her decision not to leave him. But, looking back, she could see why she had stayed with him. They got on very well. And, for all his faults and moodiness, he was interesting and funny. He made her laugh a lot. Not for the first time, she wondered if she had fallen in love with the sense of humour rather than the man.

She smiled to herself at the thought and tried to start reading again. But her mind wandered back to Charlie. Her biggest problem with her husband was never quite knowing which Charlie would turn up, the fun and carefree one, who was witty, funny, and laughed all the time, or the moody and difficult one who felt the world was against him.

She continued flicking through Hamlet on her kindle and came across arguably the most famous line in English literature. "To be, or not to be, that is the question…" She smiled to herself again, pleased that she had a vague understanding of this part of the play. It was pathetic really, feeling so clever for understanding one line in Shakespeare's most well-known soliloquy. She had read that the soliloquies in Hamlet were more colloquial and closer to the ordinary speech of the day and not so influenced by Latin than some of his other works, which probably helped her grasp its meaning.

She read on: "Whether 'tis nobler in the mind to suffer the slings and arrows of outrageous fortune or take arms against a sea of troubles, and by opposing them? – To die, - to sleep…"

She lost concentration on what she was reading again and looked out into her back garden. This time her thoughts drifted back to Llewellyn. She was excited at the prospect of another interview with him. The first one had certainly been an education. It had been that interview that had really opened her eyes to his talent as an actor. He had been so bubbly and together in person, yet utterly convincing as the painfully reflective and indecisive Hamlet. He fully deserved the rave reviews, which had first marked him down as a star of the stage. Bizarrely, it was her husband, who over thought everything and then struggled to make a decision who more closely resembled Hamlet in character than Llewellyn. If Charlie could have learned the lines of Hamlet, it was possible he could have played himself and won as many plaudits as the actor.

Charlie had a quiet confidence, but he was excessively analytical and obsessed by detail, which could make him appear hesitant. Everything, from important matters at work to what breakfast cereal to buy at the supermarket, had to be carefully considered. This intellectual fastidiousness made him an exceptional chief planning officer at the district council. He could digest a complex planning proposal and spot problems others would miss with his unusual eye for detail. But mistakes, even minor ones, weighed heavily on him and could push him into a depression for weeks.

His fear of failure, or more simply making the wrong choice, could result in fruitless soul-searching over what to do, leading to the worst kind of indecision and then to dark, despairing moods. If only he could be more like Llewellyn, or at least how Llewellyn appeared to be - confident and almost recklessly decisive.

This brazen lack of fear over making choices and even failure itself had come across strongly when Molly had first interviewed Llewellyn. He had blithely told her that everyone had to come to terms with failure. It was important to respect and fear failure as that was what drove a person to succeed. But when you failed, it was best to admit it, even embrace it. Then, you should move on. No one should be ashamed to fail. It happened to all of us. And when you succeeded, people would forget your failures. "Triumph and disaster were imposters," he had said, referring to the lines in "If –", the Rudyard Kipling poem. She leaned back into her chair and without thinking reached for her mobile phone, which was lying on the dining room table beside her. She clicked it on, tapped the internet icon with her forefinger and did a search for the Kipling poem.

She found it quickly and read down to the relevant part. "If you can meet with Triumph and Disaster. And treat those two imposters just the same."

She remembered her father telling her when she was little that those "triumph and disaster" lines were inscribed above the entrance to Wimbledon's Centre Court to remind the players of the fine distinction between winning and losing, confidence and delusion, success and failure. She smiled at the memory, which had just come back to her like some forgotten old friend. She had loved that Kipling poem and the triumph and disaster section in particular. They rang so true.

She ran her eye over Shakespeare's famous soliloquy again on her kindle. "To be, or not to be." In those words lay the core difference between Charlie and Llewellyn. Charlie struggled with his fate, suffering "the thousand natural shocks" as Shakespeare put it. He was unsure whether he should leave things as they were, "To be", or take action and suffer the consequences "not to be".

Molly looked up the line in her literature guide. It seemed to contradict what she thought it meant. "To be" meant to live the notes said, while "not to be" meant to die. But then to live was to take action and to die, or kill yourself, was just to give up, or was it the other way round. The Romans had believed suicide was honourable, but in Shakespeare's day such a death would not have been honourable, particularly among Catholics. Llewellyn appeared to have no emotional dilemmas. He acted with barely a glance over his shoulder. He was by instinct a decisive man of action – "to be". Charlie was the opposite – "not to be". Was that right? Was this what Shakespeare's troubled and indecisive Hamlet was driving at? Molly puzzled over this for a while and again unconsciously looked out into her back garden.

She turned back to her kindle and was about to read on, but the opening and slamming of the front door disturbed her. She could hear Charlie sigh and drop his case with a thump on to the coffee table in the front room. There was another sigh and the rattling of keys as they also found their way on to the coffee table. She could hear him crash into something, which was probably the sofa. He was in a mood again. He had been irritable and depressed of late. She assumed the planning row over the school was responsible, although he refused to say. He had not expected and could not understand the fierce opposition to knocking it down. He peered round the door into the dining room, where Molly was sitting, smiled wearily and asked the obvious.

"Just reading," she said.

He moved closer, eyeing her book on the kindle. "Hamlet. Very high brow," he said with a hint of condescension.

"I was looking at some of my notes on Wellesley Primary School. It made me think of Henry Llewellyn and Hamlet. You remember, I told you I have an interview with Llewellyn."

"Yes, I remember, but why do you have to get involved with the Wellesley Primary School story?" he said coldly.

"There is a big meeting on the school next week," she protested. "It's my job to report on these things."

"Yes, but there are other reporters at the radio station. I don't see why you have to cover the meeting."

"Why shouldn't I?"

"It might compromise my position."

"No, it won't."

As chief planning officer and one of the main advocates of demolishing the school, Charlie considered it embarrassing having his wife report on the row. But there was no reason why he should have foreseen the protests against knocking it down. Other schools had been closed with little fanfare. Unfortunately, Charlie, like the rest of the council, had not reckoned on the public relations genius of Llewellyn or even considered that he might have an interest in the school.

"Frankly, this argument is silly," Molly said in a sudden burst of anger. "You know a policeman was hit and killed by a car today, and we're squabbling about a stupid school."

"Yes, I heard your report on the radio. Sorry. You knew him, didn't you?"

Molly calmed down, pacified by his apology, and turned off her kindle. "Yes. He was nice."

"Are you upset about Peter Delgado?" she said, changing tack slightly. The police had not named Peter Delgado as the person found dead on the golf course in the press, but Charlie had been told as he was his boss. Molly had also been told by a police contact on condition she did not name him in any of her reports.

Charlie sat down. Heaviness seemed to come over him. "No. Well, yes. He was a nice bloke, but I didn't know him that well." "I know the school thing has got to you, but I just wondered whether the death of Peter had upset you. You have been difficult over the past couple of days."

"I've been difficult for weeks."

"Well, at least you're aware of it. Is it just the school row weighing on you?" Molly asked.

"The school protests make me cross, but it's not a big, big deal. I don't really know why I'm fed up. It's probably a lot of little things building up and having one of your planning officers killed doesn't help. Look, I'm sorry. I shouldn't take it out on you."

"Don't worry," she said, pleased that Charlie was starting to open up and trying to explain his grumpiness.

They smiled at each other, registering the truce. "Let's go for a meal," Charlie said. "I'll pay. We could go for a curry at that really nice Tandoori place. I really fancy a curry and you need a break after your day dealing with that policeman's death."

"Yes. That would be lovely." Molly smiled again and felt the tension ease in her neck and across her back. It had been a long day.

Charlie's spirits, aided by a tall, cool glass of beer, rose noticeably in the restaurant. Beer often cured his black moods, even if it was only temporarily. She knew Charlie had chosen a curry partly because he really liked the draught Indian lager on tap. He had little interest in food and always chose the same dish.

She was in the middle of deciding which dish to choose when she noticed three waiters make a dash for the entrance. The door was opened by the smallest and nimblest of the three. He immediately bowed and the others followed suit as the guests came in.

Henry Llewellyn gave the waiters an effervescent smile and stepped to one side to let his woman companion through, guiding her with a protective arm, which lightly cradled her waist.

He was of ordinary physical dimensions, of medium height with a slight build, but in the flesh, he was extraordinarily handsome with perfectly symmetrical facial features, a clear complexion, and large dark eyes. Molly stared at him, almost transfixed. She had been thinking about him for most of the day and now here he was.

Molly glanced at Charlie, who was sitting with his back to the entrance. He was engrossed in the menu and did not notice her raised eyebrows towards the door.

Llewellyn casually walked to his table, but she could tell he knew the restaurant's eyes were on him. It struck her again how similar he was to Charlie in looks, or at least in the rough dimensions in terms of height, build and colouring.

No wonder she found Llewellyn irresistible, which she now finally admitted to herself. He was a deluxe model of her husband without the moods. Tonight their clothes were similar too. In the gloomy, candlelit restaurant they could have been mistaken for each other. It was a pity the likeness ended so abruptly with appearance and clothes sense. The disloyal thoughts towards her husband made her feel guilty, but Llewellyn looked so relaxed and happy.

Molly's gaze switched to Charlie who was fumbling with the menu while draining his beer glass. Charlie could be nervous in a group or with people he did not know. It was endearing in a vulnerable way, and it encouraged others to take charge. Llewellyn was, in contrast, clearly the type who instinctively took control.

Charlie eventually looked up from his menu and noticed his wife's eyes trained over his shoulder. He turned and stared at Llewellyn. "I see the entertainment has arrived," he said drily. She laughed, refreshed by his lightened mood. He was an unpredictable person and could have easily slipped into a sulk at the sight of his planning adversary.

"So, what are you having?" Molly asked.

Charlie gave her a twisted grin. "For a change, I will have exactly what I always have. It avoids making a difficult decision."

Molly laughed loudly, prompting the people on the next table to look their way. "We seem to be the entertainment now," she said. Charlie smiled and nodded at the four turned heads. They smiled back and then returned to their conversation.

CHAPTER 18

N apoleon flicked through the pages of Rankin's notebook, which had been found in his jacket pocket. The writing was neat and precise, like the man, with the times the notes were taken down clearly marked in the margin. His last interview had been with John McConnell in The Nag's Head and prior to that Joanne McConnell at her home. The notes didn't reveal much. He guessed Rankin had decided to question John McConnell because of his less than impressive driving record. He remembered his string of motoring offences from his previous time at Wellesley. Delgado's body had also been discovered a short walk from his home, coincidentally or not, by his father. He placed the notebook on his new desk, the last and only time it was likely to remain tidy, a legacy of his meticulous predecessor, and pulled out his own notebook.

There was a knock at the door and Detective Sergeant Mayo appeared. Napoleon smiled to himself, noticing the sergeant's colourful tie, much louder than he considered sensible for a policeman, and his expensive suit and shoes. He was shorter than he had at first imagined and also quite thin.

"Sit down sergeant," the chief inspector said.

Mayo made himself comfortable in one of the chair's opposite Napoleon's desk and straightened his tie, conscious of the inspector's eyes on his admittedly flamboyant appendage.

"I'll get straight to the point," Napoleon said, his eyes stuck on Mayo's tie. It really was a gaudy sight.

"A dead body is found on the golf course and then two days later a policeman is killed in a hit-and-run. Not the usual run-of-the-mill week. Thoughts?"

Although Mayo was not expecting a preamble about his background or interests as a conversational opener after being summoned, his new boss was known as a man of few words who shunned small talk, he still found such a direct approach disconcerting, particularly the staccato delivery. "How are you?" would have been nice, considering this was their first one-on-one meeting since the chief inspector had been appointed head of the station. Some consoling words on Rankin would have been appreciated too. Rankin was a great cop and detective, who was fair and principled with first rate organisational skills. His death was nothing short of tragic.

"Well, it is very strange," Mayo said slowly. He arched his eyebrows, the right one rising higher than the left as he spoke, an involuntary action that was often prompted by nerves. "Two violent deaths in two days. It's not something you would expect in Wellesley, and both men hit by cars. But there's no evidence to suggest they were anything other than accidents, although it is odd that Delgado was moved. But then people do odd things when they're drunk or in a panic and the driver might have been both."

"You interviewed Delgado's younger brother Ray with Chief Inspector Rankin. I see he had a row with his brother on the night of his brother's death and has no alibi?" Napoleon said.

The sergeant did the eyebrow routine again, the right one rising even higher this time. "Yes sir. They had a row over dinner and Peter Delgado left. Ray Delgado then tried to find him in his car and ended up driving to Redfield University. He arrived home very late, but I checked the car, and it hadn't been in a collision. Forensic are also doing checks. His girlfriend, a Chloe Smith, was at home all evening on her own, also with no alibi." Mayo straightened his tie for a second time, probably because Napoleon's eyes remained trained on it. It was also another thing he tended to do when he was nervous or ill at ease. "Chief Inspector Rankin was surprised he took the news so calmly," Mayo added. "His girlfriend was also composed, but I felt it was the shock. I didn't consider their reactions that unusual. People react in different ways."

"What about yesterday when Rankin was killed? Do we know where they were then?" Napoleon asked.

"I spoke to Ray Delgado's girlfriend yesterday to arrange a visit as I suspected you would want to see them both. She told me then that she was at home at the time Rankin was killed and he was…" Mayo hesitated, "out of the country. He flew out to Spain early yesterday morning to see his parents."

"You allowed Ray Delgado to leave the country?"

"I'm sorry sir," Mayo said sheepishly. "We didn't realise he intended to go abroad, but it seems fairly regular. His parents are Spanish, and his girlfriend said the family wanted to grieve together and make arrangements for the funeral. His girlfriend told me he'd be back in a couple of days."

"Okay," Napoleon said, clearly annoyed.

"There is nothing to suggest the deaths of Peter Delgado and Rankin are connected," Mayo said, now sounding defensive. "Ray Delgado and his girlfriend met Chief Inspector Rankin for the first time two days ago when we told them about the brother being found on the golf course. They are very unlikely to be involved or connected to the chief inspector's death. Ray Delgado's Spanish visit won't disrupt our investigations."

"I hope not," Napoleon said, frowning. "And you're sure about the car not being in a collision?"

"Yes sir. Certainly not one with a grown man at 40mph. The car was an old Mini – a complete rust bucket, with dents all over it. But they were all small and, as far as I could tell, they looked like they were from old scrapes and bangs. I will follow up with forensic to get their report on the car."

"Good," Napoleon said.

The chief inspector sat back in his chair and began flicking through the pages of his notebook. "Jack McConnell, the property developer, found the body of Mr Delgado," he said, looking at his notes in the book. "I read his statement. Anything to add?"

"Not really. As he said, he plays golf very early every Thursday morning. It was bloody awful finding a dead man next to his favourite green, his words. Beyond that, there isn't much to add."

"And what of his son John McConnell?" Napoleon said. "I see Chief Inspector Rankin visited him at The Nag's Head just before he died."

"Yes sir. The chief inspector discovered he'd been banned for driving over the limit. He also has a number of speeding convictions. McConnell's been in and out of trouble most of his life, as you probably know sir. He's the type who might ignore a ban, leave a pub half cut and run someone over. The body was found close to his parents' home, his registered address, so the chief inspector felt it was worth having a word with him."

"Yes. McConnell is certainly stupid and reckless enough to knock someone down. I think we should speak to him again and also to his father. And we'll continue withholding from the press the fact Peter Delgado was hit by a car. Have you told the brother and his girlfriend how he was killed? That it was a car that hit him."

"No. Not yet sir. We weren't exactly sure how he was killed when we spoke to them, which we explained to them at the time. We told them that Peter's death was from head injuries. They presumed he had been attacked and we left it at that."

"Anything else I should know?" Napoleon said brusquely, still glancing at his notebook.

"Not a great deal. None of the residents in Crookham Lane saw or heard anything the night Delgado was killed and nothing of consequence was found near his body. The scenes of crime team think the body was carried through an alleyway that leads on to the course from Crookham Lane, which only a golfer or somebody local would know existed. Someone like John McConnell. As for the driver who hit the chief inspector, we only have a vague description of the car, small and red and probably a hatchback. John McConnell might be able to provide a better description. He was there when Rankin was hit by the car, but he disappeared from the scene when uniform arrived."

Napoleon nodded. "Yes. I saw the police report on the collision. That John McConnell tried to revive Rankin. As Ray Delgado is out of the country, let's visit The Nag's Head. John McConnell might be there. If not, we'll try the McConnell residence. Who knows? The whole family might be at home as it's a Saturday. They all have alibis, according to Rankin's notes, but I need to question them all again."

◆

Joanne McConnell placed a tray of drinks on an ornamental mahogany coffee table, the tasteful hub of her sitting room. The table looked expensive and handmade, like the rest of the furniture in the room.

"Would you like milk or sugar with your coffee?" she asked. Mayo, who had disappeared into a large armchair strewn with cushions, had three sugars and plenty of milk, Napoleon a splash of milk.

"You said your husband was at the golf club, but the person we really need to speak to is your son," Napoleon said, stirring the milk into his coffee and eyeing a large landscape painting hanging above Mrs McConnell, opposite the sofa where he was sitting. She was seated in what looked like an antique chair by the door leading to the hallway and kitchen.

"What a popular boy, our John is," she said. "Only yesterday, there was another policeman here looking for him."

"Yes," Napoleon said. "You do realise that same policeman was killed yesterday by a speeding car and your son was at the scene. In fact, it was your son who tried to resuscitate him before the ambulance arrived."

"Oh my God!" Her supercilious expression transformed into one of worry.

"Your son is fine," Napoleon reassured her. "He wasn't hurt. We just need to know where he is. We need to talk to him. He obviously hasn't spoken to you about the incident."

"No. I've not seen him," she said unsteadily. "John wasn't the driver, surely. He's been banned you know."

"No, John wasn't the driver," Napoleon said. "He was simply at the scene. He might have seen something. It happened outside The Nag's Head."

"Well, that's probably where he is now. Have you tried The Nag's Head?" she said.

"Yes," Napoleon replied. "The barman said he hadn't seen him since the incident. He suggested we try here."

"Here? Now that's a novel thought." Her composure was returning and with it the slightly offensive sarcasm. "He's not here that often, only to sleep occasionally."

"Does he have another address?"

"He might have. He has many women friends, so he might be shacked up with one of them, but it's not something he would discuss with me." She smiled thinly and took a sip of her coffee.

"Does he have a mobile telephone number that we could reach him on, or does he work in Wellesley? Maybe we could find him there."

"Oh, he doesn't work, inspector," she said, the sarcasm now turned to full blast. "How silly of you to think that someone like John would do something so conventional. And no, I don't have his mobile number. He likes his independence."

"You don't have your son's mobile number?" Napoleon said, surprised.

"No. I don't," she said firmly. She took another sip of her coffee. "Tell me about the accident, or incident, as you put it. You said it happened outside The Nag's Head. Was John in the pub?"

"Another person at the scene saw John crossing the Wellesley Road directly outside the pub, just in front of the policeman when he was killed. John had reached the other side of the road when a car appeared from nowhere and hit the policeman. He died instantly. Your son was quick to react."

"I see," she said, suddenly looking distracted as if another thought had entered her mind. "Would you like some biscuits?"

Mayo looked at Napoleon, but he couldn't tell what he was thinking, that inscrutable poker face. "Why not?" Mayo said, pre-empting a response from the inspector, who had now gone silent and also looked preoccupied.

"You do speak then," Mrs McConnell said to Mayo, who had been quietly taking notes while Napoleon led the questioning.

"When required," the sergeant said, matching her sarcastic tone.

Mrs McConnell gave Mayo a wry smile and stood up.

"I'll get the chocolate biscuits as you're both clearly very important." Napoleon, whose attention had momentarily switched to the landscape painting opposite him, diverted his gaze back to Mrs McConnell. He went to say something, but she was already half-way through the sitting room door before he could open his mouth. He frowned at Mayo as she disappeared. He wanted to get on with the interview, not eat chocolate biscuits.

The inspector stood up, still frowning, and stretched. He then edged round the coffee table to take a closer look at the painting. There was something about it that had suddenly drawn him to it. The scene looked familiar. That was it. He had definitely seen it before. It was either local or he had seen a painting like it somewhere else. It was of a large barn, surrounded by fields. Peering more closely, he noticed the signature of the artist, H G Shilling, flamboyantly inscribed in one corner.

"Oh shit." Mrs McConnell could be heard from the kitchen. She came into the sitting room, looking flushed and tense.

"Can we do anything?" Napoleon asked.

"No. It's the blasted washing machine. It's flooded the kitchen. I'll have to get that smelly man in."

"Smelly!" Mayo said.

"I shouldn't be rude, but the man who repairs my washing machine when it breaks down does give off a pong."

"Not Ted Cropper?" Napoleon asked.

"Why yes," Mrs McConnell said. "Do you know him? Of course you do. You must know everybody in this town."

"Not everybody, but I know Ted. I hadn't noticed that he smelled," Napoleon said, offended for his friend's sake.

"Well, only a bit. It's probably because he's always lugging around those old washing machines and dryers. Sorry. I shouldn't be rude. He's a very nice man. Always willing to do jobs and repairs for me around the house. I've been using him for years. I'll quickly phone him if you don't mind waiting," she said.

After a minute or so, she came back, still looking flustered. "He's not answering his phone, so I've left a message on his voicemail. Do you mind if I clear the water up? It won't take long." She didn't want them to go. She was enjoying the company and the older one was quite dishy.

"There's not much more we want to ask, Mrs McConnell," Napoleon said. He toyed with asking her about the painting but thought better of it. It was nothing to do with the deaths and he wanted to press on.

"Jo," she corrected him.

Napoleon nodded. "Was your son in any trouble?" he asked quickly before she could disappear into the kitchen again.

"He's always in trouble, inspector." She sighed and sat down, appearing to forget about her flooded kitchen. "But in answer to your question, I don't know," she said seriously.
"John wasn't always so aimless. He failed to get into the parachute regiment years ago and he didn't seem to know what to do after that."

"Are you sure you don't know of any trouble he might be in?" Mayo said.

"You're American," she said, ignoring the question. "You've been here for a long time, haven't you? The accent has faded, but you're definitely American. I didn't notice at first."

"Yes," Mayo said patiently

"You'll have to take me for a little holiday over there." She grinned foolishly. "Sorry," she said, apologising for the feeble joke. "I really don't know if John is in any trouble."

"Okay," Napoleon said. "When will your husband be home?"

"I don't know that either. But he'll be at the golf club now. He lunches there today as it's a Saturday. He always does on a Saturday. He's a creature of habit. You should try there."

The two policemen scrunched their way up the gravel driveway, lost in their own thoughts. Despite Mrs McConnell's plea for them to stay longer while she cleared up the kitchen, Napoleon insisted they leave. He wanted to get on with the investigation. He was also finding her sarcastic manner and random questions about Mayo's heritage annoying.

"I couldn't make her out, except that she had the eye for you," Mayo said, breaking up the silence.

"What do you mean?" the chief inspector said testily.

"She fancied you."

"Nonsense," Napoleon said.

"You should feel flattered sir. She's very attractive, despite the sarcasm and smell of booze. She'd definitely had a drink or two before we arrived."

"Yes, I noticed the smell of booze too, but then it is Saturday. There's no law against having a drink, even if it is a bit early," Napoleon said.

They got into their car with Napoleon squeezing into the driver seat. He had borrowed his wife's brand-new convertible Mini Cooper, which he loved despite its awkward dimensions for someone of his height. It had clearly been designed for a person much shorter than his 6ft 2in. But that aside, the little car handled the road expertly and its computerised music system was terrific, much better than the tinny radio in his old banger. He started the car and switched the music system on, syncing it to his mobile phone. After a quick scroll of the playlist on his mobile, he found what he was looking for, the first movement of Beethoven's third symphony. He needed inspiration and he wasn't going to get it from Mayo.

The sergeant gave Napoleon a puzzled look. It wasn't the right moment for classical music, not that it ever was in his opinion. He was more of a Radiohead fan. He shrugged and tried to talk above the symphony, which was now booming out of the stereo. "You live in this road, don't you sir?" he said.

Napoleon nodded. "Yes. Further up and round the corner," he replied mechanically.

"It's a pretty road, and the McConnells have a lovely house. Yet, Mrs McConnell seemed resentful and bitter," Mayo added. "Sad too. Despite the great house and expensive furniture, she seemed very sad. I wonder why?"

"Yes, aren't we all sad," Napoleon said. He wasn't really listening. He was lost in Beethoven's "Heroic" masterpiece, far, far away from the mundane problems of Joanne McConnell. He needed to think and Beethoven's Eroica symphony - the one dedicated to his namesake Napoleon Bonaparte - would help him focus and clear the clutter in his mind. The two deaths had left too many loose ends, too many things that didn't add up, a frustratingly incomplete picture. He was sure they weren't random accidents. He turned the music up louder to shut out Mayo's wittering and pulled away from the curb. He would need the genius of Beethoven to help him fit this particular jigsaw together.

CHAPTER 19

◆

Molly peered into the stream to see if she could see any fish. Sometimes you could see one or two between the reeds and stones. The water was shallow and calm, unlike downstream where the little tributary widened and met the Thames. She often stood there, by the small, red brick bridge outside the offices of the radio station, to gather her thoughts. It was quiet and peaceful and when it was sunny, like today, the water shimmered and glittered, projecting an array of iridescent colours.

She had driven to the radio station to pick up her notebook and some files, which she had left behind in her haste the day before. It was Saturday and her day off, but Charlie had decided to meet someone at the golf club, and she had little else to do. He had been in a surprisingly good mood. It was probably the curry the night before that had lifted his spirits. It had been a fun evening and now he was full of talk about taking charge of his own destiny. He had refused to elaborate further when she had asked what he meant, which she found slightly worrying. At least, she knew where she stood with the old, moody Charlie. She took one last glimpse into the gleaming water, still no fish, and turned towards the offices.

The newsroom was deserted as she had expected. She noticed her desk was covered with Jim's detritus and junk, which she had also expected. He had the habit of sitting at her desk when his became so untidy it was impossible to work on. It never occurred to him to clear his own as it was far easier to move to hers or someone else's. She threw away two half chewed pens, a newspaper and the leftovers of a hamburger takeaway and put his notebook back on his desk. Her notebook was half hidden by a newspaper cuttings file that he had been using. She sat down at her desk and picked up the file, which said police general on the front, and absent-mindedly began sifting through it. One cutting caught her eye. It was a report about John McConnell receiving a bravery award at Valley Police headquarters. He had saved a man from drowning in the Thames. She sat up with a start and read the name of the man he had saved for a second time. It was Peter Delgado. She remembered now. She had covered the story in one of her reports for the radio station.

CHAPTER 20

◆

Napoleon found Jack McConnell in the golf club bar, reading a broadsheet newspaper. He had left Mayo in the car. Despite his sergeant's moans, he felt McConnell would prove more accommodating one on one.

"Can I buy you a drink Jack?" he said, approaching McConnell's table, which was in a quiet corner at the far end of the bar.

"Inspector Napoleon," McConnell exclaimed loudly. "I haven't seen you for ages. Another orange juice would be nice. Thank you."

Napoleon returned with the orange juice and a pint of local bitter for himself, which McConnell eyed enviously. "I'd love one of those, but I'm on a fitness regime," he said, sweeping a big hand through his thick grey hair, the one obvious concession to his 55 years.

"You look pretty fit to me," Napoleon said.

"Yes, but only because of orange juice and regular exercise. Too many of those," he said, pointing at the pint, "and I'd look like Humphrey over there."

Humphrey, who was also drinking a pint of bitter a few tables away, was a very fat man. He lived up to and rather enjoyed his reputation as a heavy drinker and relentless smoker, usually of large and expensive cigars. Although he was a member of the golf club, he rarely played. For him, the action was always at the 19th hole.

Napoleon smiled and looked over at Humphrey. He had a pint in one hand and a monster cigar in the other and was talking animatedly to another very fat man. Napoleon watched Humphrey light his cigar. The golf club bar was one of the few places where smoking was still allowed. It occurred to the inspector that he should speak to the barfly of Wellesley. He would have been in the golf club bar on the night Peter Delgado was killed, as he was most evenings, and may have seen something significant.

"So, what can I do for you inspector?" McConnell said, sweeping another big hand through his crowning glory. "I suppose you want to talk to me about the man I found on the golf course, and now I hear a policeman has been killed too," McConnell added, answering his own question.

"Yes, unpleasant business," Napoleon said. "Where exactly did you find the body?"

"These details are in a statement I made to one of your colleagues after I found the body. Not that I mind repeating them, but this should already be recorded."

"Yes. The policeman who took the statement was the same one who was killed," Napoleon said matter-of-factly.

"Oh," McConnell said, his eyebrows rising as he registered the shocking turn of events. "I can't believe it. I find a body and now this policeman is dead." He looked at Napoleon gloomily. "Well, there's not much to say really. I found the body at the back of the first green. I was about to make a putt when I noticed something in the bushes. I turned and there was a human arm, poking out from behind a tree. I took a closer look and there was a man, propped up against the tree, clearly dead. He looked quite a mess, like he had been in a fight, so I called an ambulance and the police on my mobile and waited for them to arrive. That's it."

"Did you see anyone else on the course? Other golfers, someone walking a dog, anybody?"

"No. I didn't see another soul. I was the first to tee off. I always am on a Thursday morning. I play as soon as dawn breaks every Thursday. It's my routine. I like a routine. It's good for golf and good for business."

"What about the green keeper or any of the boys who cut the fairways?"

"No. There wasn't anyone else around. Just me and the birds." McConnell laughed loudly. "You know, I did my best round for a long time, hit a 78. I haven't broken 80 for seven months."

"Not eight months," Napoleon said, smiling.

"No. I keep a record of every round I play," McConnell said seriously. "Seven months and five days. You would have thought a dead body would have wrecked my concentration, but it had the reverse effect. I was determined just to think about my game, prove I had strong nerves."

"I'm surprised they let you continue playing?" Napoleon said.

"After the first hole, which was cordoned off, the course takes you out into the countryside, so I don't think it was a problem," McConnell replied.

"You didn't feel sick or ill after seeing the body?"

"A little I suppose, but after all the messing around with the police, I felt irritated more than ill. That policeman who questioned me, the one who died, he was very pedantic. He kept going over things. I found the body. That's it. There wasn't a great deal to say. Anyway, after all that, I needed a round of golf to unwind. And it was the best thing I did. I haven't hit the ball that well for a long time. It happens like that sometimes. You just hit your stride." McConnell smiled at the memory. "I'm sorry inspector. You probably think I'm callous, finding a body and still enjoying my golf, but I didn't know the boy and golf is important to me. Apart from my business, it's what I enjoy. It keeps me alive and happy."

Napoleon nodded and jotted down some of McConnell's remarks in his notebook. He understood. A hobby could be all consuming, particularly one like golf. "Do you realise your son was at the scene yesterday when the policeman was killed?" he said. "Your son tried to revive him."

McConnell took a swig of his orange juice and Napoleon noticed his jaw muscle twitch. "No, I didn't realise."

"You didn't see the local news bulletins, appealing for your son to contact the police?"

"No," McConnell said abruptly. His mood had suddenly darkened, the happy memory of the golf round clouded by the mention of his son. "I've been very busy. Someone told me the police were looking for John, but I don't take notice of such things anymore. He's been in so much trouble."

"Do you know where he is or might be?" Napoleon asked, unconsciously twirling his gold fountain pen around his fingers.

"I would be the last person to know. We don't get on, mainly because he does things like go missing when a policeman has been killed in front of him. Ask my wife. She might know where he is but go round early before she's hit the gin."

"Yes, we've spoken to your wife. Can you tell me where you were on Wednesday night and Friday morning?"

"I need alibis." McConnell laughed loudly again and thought for a moment. "I did tell the other policemen my movements on Wednesday evening, but I can repeat them. I was in the office until about eight. I was alone. I'm always the last to leave. Then, I went home and sorted out some papers, watched the news and went to the golf club, probably around 9.30. Again, I was alone. My wife was out. I came home about midnight, a friend gave me a lift, and I went to bed. My wife was still out. Friday morning, I was in the office. Any number of people can vouch for that."

Napoleon took more notes. "Who was the friend who gave you a lift?"

"A guy called Lee Thompson, an enthusiastic golfer like me. He works in the city for one of the big banks, nice bloke. Clever with numbers."

"Who else did you see at the golf club on Wednesday evening?" Napoleon said without looking up from his notes.

"I had a game of cards with Humphrey and Lee. I don't recall seeing anyone else in particular, just the usual crowd."

McConnell finished his orange juice and turned round, scanning the bar as if looking for someone. "Look inspector, I've got to make a phone call and sort out some business. Why don't we continue this conversation over a game of golf tomorrow? My playing partner has pulled out at the last minute. You can take his place and find out what I'm really like." He smiled broadly. "A man's true character comes out on the golf course, especially a challenging one like Wellesley."

"I haven't played golf for months," Napoleon said, finishing his drink too.

"Then you need the practise, dear boy. You're a good golfer. I've seen you play. You'll soon get into the swing. The tee off time is 8.30 in the morning and after the round we can have lunch in the restaurant here."

Before Napoleon could object, McConnell rose to his full height and stretched. "Tomorrow morning then," he said, pulling out his mobile telephone from his pocket. "You're not allowed to use these in the bar, so I'll be off. See you on the first tee." He nodded and strode purposefully towards the door.

Napoleon was flattered by Jack's invitation and he enjoyed an occasional game of golf, but he wasn't sure a round with such an experienced player was a good idea. He didn't want to embarrass himself by playing badly. He closed his notebook and noticed Humphrey again, who was still talking to his big friend. Tucking his notebook and pen in his jacket pocket, he stood up with his glass in his hand, slid past a couple of chairs and casually made his way towards the fat man's table.

"Ah, the inspector," Humphrey boomed. "Have a seat. Let me get you another. That one's deader than the dodo."

"Yes, thanks. A half of the guest beer will do," Napoleon said, handing the big man his empty glass.

"Nonsense inspector. A pint it must be," Humphrey boomed and crashed towards the bar, knocking a tray of drinks off another table in slapstick fashion and following it up with a ridiculous, genuflecting apology to his victims, a youngish couple who looked extremely embarrassed. Napoleon shook his head and introduced himself to the other big man at the table, who said his name was Bob. He was also a regular in the bar, but said he wasn't at the club on the Wednesday night.

Humphrey returned quickly, beer stains on his shirt and trousers from the accident and a stupid grin on his face. "They put these tables too close together. Everything is designed for slim people. Then when one of us, how should we put it, large people, knocks something over, we're labelled clumsy half-wits. Half-wits maybe, but not clumsy. It is this incommodious, thin world that we live in that makes life so difficult inspector."

"Yes," Napoleon said, with a bemused, half smile. He hadn't spoken to Humphrey for a long time and had forgotten about his over-the-top manner. "At least some thin people, like the inspector here, have a sense of humour, eh Bob," Humphrey said.

Bob vacantly nodded. "What brings you here then, inspector?"

"Business."

Bob looked sadly into his beer and said he needed to go to the bathroom. Napoleon watched Bob waddle away and turned to Humphrey. "I hope I'm not interrupting anything."

"No, no inspector. Your enquiries are far more important than idle gossip with Bob. Two people hit by a car in the space of two days. Terrible, just terrible."

Napoleon sat up straight and stared at the big man suspiciously. "Why do you say two people hit by a car?"

"Someone told me I think, or did I dream it. Maybe it came to me in a dream."

"Humphrey. This is serious. How do you know the man found on the golf course was hit by a car?"

Humphrey looked confused. "Err, I really don't know inspector. I must have guessed."

"The body was found on the golf course. It's not something you would guess. Who told you? Why do you think the young man was run over? Were you in the car?"

"Me, in the car. I don't drive and I always walk everywhere. It's the only exercise I get. Everyone knows that. Jack told me the boy was in a bloody mess, but God knows why I thought he was run over. I assure you, I am an innocent man." He spread his arms and looked to his right and then his left as if he was appealing to the rest of the people in the bar, who had now become his judge and jury.

"There's no need to get melodramatic, but you must tell me how you came to think the man found on the golf course was hit by a car. If Jack McConnell or someone else told you, you must say. This is very important."

"I take it then that this person was hit by a car, but you haven't actually told anyone," Humphrey said, picking up his cigar from an overflowing ashtray. Napoleon noticed his hand was shaking.

"Just answer the question."

"Yes, sorry," Humphrey said, puffing manically at the cigar, which seemed to have gone out. "No, it definitely wasn't Jack who said anything. I might have overheard someone say he was hit by a car in the golf club bar, but how would they know? As you said he was found on the golf course, and there aren't any cars on the golf course," he said, producing a weak smile. "Sorry, inspector, I just don't know why I thought the person had been hit by a car. I must have misheard someone talking about something else and for some reason got the wrong end of the stick. I've been drinking very heavily these past few days, even for me. Pressure of work, you know. I may appear to spend my life in this bar, but I do work very hard during the week. Running your own business isn't easy."

"All right," Napoleon said, cutting him off. He didn't want to hear about the fat man's business problems. "Tell me your movements on Wednesday night and Friday morning."

"I was here on Wednesday night. I played cards with Jack and a couple of other people, smoked a few cigars, drank a hell of a lot, the usual routine."

"How late were you here till on the Wednesday night?"

"Until the early hours. Two in the morning, maybe later. I can't recall the exact time. I was in that happy blurred state when life is sweet, and troubles are no more."

"And on Friday morning?"

"I was asleep in my bed, alas alone."

"Okay," Napoleon said. "I want a list of the people you saw at the golf club bar on Wednesday night and an estimated time you think they left. And I want you to make another list of people you have spoken to over the last few days since Wednesday night in the bar here or anywhere for that matter."

"What now?" Humphrey said with a note of gloom in his voice.

Napoleon handed the big man a spare pen and ripped a page from his notebook. "Yes, now. It won't take long if you concentrate. It doesn't matter if you forget a few names. If you remember more names after I've gone, make a note of them and pass them on to me later."

Napoleon sipped his pint and let his eyes roam the room, while Humphrey busily scribbled some names on the sheet of paper the inspector had given him. There were some faces the inspector recognised in the bar, but most of the golf club set were unfamiliar to him.

"Refill?" Bob said, as he returned to the table.

Humphrey nodded while writing and Napoleon shook his head. Bob waddled away again. He may have been similar to Humphrey in appearance, but his personality lacked the colour of the other man. Where Humphrey was sunny and loquacious, Bob was dour with apparently little to say.

Humphrey finally handed the inspector his lists. His handwriting was spidery and only just coherent. "That's all I can remember."

"I see Ted Cropper was here on Wednesday night. according to your list," Napoleon said.

"Yes. I had a bit of a row with him. He's such a prissy sod."

"What was the row over?"

"I can't remember, but he was being his usual righteous self."

"Okay," the inspector said. "I take it you were drinking here on Thursday and Friday night."

The big man nodded.

"And no doubt you're here most nights, if I need to talk to you again."

"Absolutely no doubt," Humphrey said. "There are many uncertainties in life, inspector, but there's one thing you can always rely on, and that is me being here."

"Yes," Napoleon said. "Who was tending the bar on the Wednesday night?"

"Frank. He's on the list. He's a young lad, thin with no waist. He clearly needs to drink more. He usually serves in the evenings. You could probably catch him tonight."

"Okay," Napoleon said. "And if you remember how you came to believe the man found on the golf course was hit by a car, I want to know immediately. Withholding that kind of information is a serious offence." He gave Humphrey a stern, unforgiving stare and stood up. As he did so, he noticed McConnell returning to his corner table with a youngish man, whose face he couldn't see as he had his back to him but looked familiar. Napoleon exchanged nods with McConnell and headed for the door.

Mayo was leaning against the car smoking when Napoleon returned. "Filthy habit," the inspector said.

"Yes, but it stimulates the mind and helps me think," Mayo replied.

"Put it out and let's talk in the car. It's cold out here."

"Yes sir," the sergeant said in his best army cadet fashion.

"Take a look at these lists," Napoleon said. "The top one is of all the people Humphrey Christopher saw while he was at the golf club bar on Wednesday evening and a rough time when he thinks they left. He was there all night. The other one is of all the people he has spoken to in the last three days. He knew Peter Delgado was hit by a car. He says he can't remember how he came to know. Either someone told him, or he overheard a conversation, probably in the golf club bar. I find that very interesting."

"Yes, very. Do you think he was the driver of the car?"

"No. He doesn't drive, and he was in the golf club bar until two in the morning. I'll talk to the barman to verify that, but it's almost certainly true. He must have overheard something, or someone must have told him Delgado was involved in a hit-and-run. If that is the case, that someone could be the person responsible for knocking down Delgado. We were careful not to release that information."

"I see Jack McConnell's on both lists," Mayo said. "But he was given a lift home from the golf club on the Wednesday night by a guy called Lee Thompson, a banker. I checked him out and his car, which had no signs of being in a collision with anything. Not a mark on it."

"Yes. Jack told me this Thompson person gave him a lift, and Humphrey insists it wasn't McConnell who told him. But who knows?" Napoleon scratched his head and looked pensive.

"Should we pull Humphrey in and question him further? This is a very good lead," Mayo asked.

"No. I don't think he can genuinely remember how he came to know that Delgado was hit by a car and I'm not sure he ever will. He's usually half cut by 7 O'clock at night."

Mayo sucked his teeth and went to say something, but Napoleon's mobile interrupted him. The chief inspector reached for the phone in his inside jacket pocket. "Yes," he said. "Okay." He nodded. "I see, thank you." He disconnected and put his phone back in his pocket.

"That was forensic. They've confirmed the traces of blood and skin that were found on St Margaret's Road, near the Crookham Lane turning, were Peter Delgado's."

CHAPTER 21

◆

C harlie turned right at the golf club entrance and walked up St Margaret's hill towards his home. He was in a good mood. He had enjoyed his curry with Molly the previous night and his conversation with Jack McConnell in the golf club bar had been a real eye-opener.

McConnell had phoned him the previous day and invited him to the golf club for what he called a discreet chat about his plan to build a leisure centre on the site of Wellesley Primary School. The telephone call had strangely transformed Charlie's mood. He could not quite figure out why the old lethargy had left him, but it was probably because his day had suddenly become more interesting. A meeting with McConnell might lead to something financially advantageous. The fact it could also land him in trouble made it perversely liberating, even if a little frightening.

"Is this a joke?" he had said on the telephone when he had found his voice.

"No. It's business," McConnell had replied.

"Well, it is hardly discreet to meet at the golf club," Charlie had responded. McConnell had then laughed loudly down the telephone line and declared it was better to confront a dangerous situation than avoid it. It was surely the other way round, Charlie had replied. McConnell had laughed even more loudly at that. "Forget discretion then, dear boy. Let's just have a chat."

"Okay," Charlie had said. He wanted to hear what McConnell had to say. It wasn't illegal to meet the man and he needed some excitement in his bloody boring life. He was a member of the golf club and occasionally came across McConnell there, anyway. Maybe McConnell was right. Maybe it was time to confront danger and take a risk. Why not?

Charlie increased his pace as he approached the steepest part of St Margaret's Road, taking rapid, small steps to propel himself up the hill as quickly as possible. He felt energised. His thoughts drifted to Wellesley and Molly. It was a pretty town, but he felt he had somehow missed out because he had not moved to London like most of his university friends. But he loved Molly and Molly liked Wellesley. She was the cornerstone of his life. What held it up. Without her, he would have probably crumbled into drink and depression, certainly drink. Depression had only recently started to dog him, like some early mid-life crisis as he wondered where his career was going. Maybe it was time he and Molly tried for children, but he wasn't sure. She wasn't sure either. He often wondered whether her reluctance to commit to children was because she felt he wouldn't make a good father. He sighed and slowed his pace a bit.

He could now see St Mark's Road, where he and Molly lived, in the distance. It would make a good home for children. They had lived there for five years since he joined the council, and he was happy there. It was just the job and the councillors that he worked for that had brought on his despondency. They were mostly well meaning, but a lot of them had little understanding of business with misguided and misplaced ideals, which had led to indecision over the school. It had been tiresome watching them dither. A leisure centre or Derek Keele's plan for a supermarket would each bring benefits to the town. Both bids were equally well thought out and workable and a decision could have been made quickly. But Llewellyn's intervention to save the school had played to the emotions of some of the councillors, who had lost sight of the facts. The school was underperforming, needed costly refurbishment, and critically, no longer attracted pupils. It should be closed, but sentimentality and nostalgia had replaced reason and logic, which was too often the case with politicians, even on a local council.

And now, Llewellyn had upped the ante. He had proposed another option, to turn the school into a museum. This would quite likely attract even more support, which was probably why McConnell had decided to initiate the meeting. It was his last gamble to save his bid.

Charlie's thoughts drifted again, to his meeting with McConnell at the golf club. He had his answers prepared should anyone challenge him over the meeting. They had agreed to say they had just bumped into each other at the bar, something that was bound to happen at times.

Although Charlie spent most of his evenings at The Nag's Head, he liked to drink at the golf club on occasions. It was a pleasant change from The Nag. Its panoramic views of the first tee and fairway, and smell of polished wood were certainly an uplifting contrast to the peeling wooden walls and whiff of cat's pee at the dilapidated pub. But The Nag offered nine different ales, which were all good quality, to the two standard ales on tap at the golf club. A great view and clean tables versus a quality beer and a game of pool. Charlie thought of Molly again. He knew which one she favoured.

He had been uneasy at first with McConnell and the situation as they sat together exposed to all eyes in the golf club bar. But it wasn't long before McConnell's charm and bonhomie had made him relax and forget his nerves. There was a confidence and certainty about McConnell that was reassuring and infectious too, particularly after a couple of pints.

He stopped for a moment and took a breather, trying to assess what he thought of McConnell. For all his jokes and affability on the surface, he was a difficult character to read. He sensed hidden depths that were probably quite sinister. He was clearly breathtakingly reckless. His sly and cryptic comment that he would "make it worthwhile" should Charlie support the leisure centre proposal had turned the conversation from a bit of a lark to something serious. There were dangers in dealing with McConnell that could lead to grave and disastrous consequences.

He had laughed nervously at the "make it worthwhile" remark. "So, you want to bribe me?" he had said. McConnell had then given him one of his feline smiles. Charlie had said he could do with £10,000 to pay off his credit cards and take his wife on holiday. McConnell had nodded and smiled even more broadly. The cat had got his cream. They had shook hands, which Charlie assumed meant the deal was complete, although he had no idea how he would receive the money, and didn't ask. He considered the golf club too public to discuss the details of the deal. McConnell presumably felt the same as he changed the subject to golf and the weather, which he happily opined on for the rest of the conversation.

He pondered his situation again. It was his turn to smile. But, unlike McConnell's in the bar, his was a thin, nervous one. He was such a naive amateur. And why had he suddenly become so reckless? It wasn't just the boredom and frustration of his job. It was something else. He was tired of always trying to do the right thing. He watched a car pass on its way up the hill to St Margaret's, the village where Llewellyn lived, and then continued walking at a quick pace. There was no way anyone could find out should he and McConnell go through with their deal.

He could discreetly start stressing the advantages of the leisure centre to some of the key councillors, who McConnell may well have bribed too. It was about time he used his position as chief planning officer at the council to his own advantage. In fact, maybe he should have come out in favour of either McConnell or Keele's bid before. Again, he had been naive. He should have pushed hard for one or the other rather than staying neutral, then a decision might have been made. He had tried to remain above the fray, but now he was prepared to get his hands dirty to break the stalemate. Putting aside the possible financial gain, it was time he backed one of the bids.

He turned into St Mark's Road and scanned the small, terraced houses that lined it. His old anger at being trapped in a dead-end job had dissipated. Instead, he was feeling an odd combination of elation and fear at the thought of carrying out something deeply unethical – and risky. It felt like he was taking his revenge on some inner force that had coerced him to lead a moral life, which had turned out hollow and unfulfilling.

He stopped in front of his house and thought again about having some extra money. The windowsills needed painting and the door could do with being replaced. The thin smile returned. McConnell probably wouldn't pay him £10,000, but it would be interesting to see how this little game played out. If you find yourself stuck in a rut, do something reckless. Maybe he would regret it, but for now he felt exhilarated and excited, even if a little scared.

CHAPTER 22

N apoleon sat in his favourite chair with a black cup of coffee and peered through the patio doors of his dining room into the darkness. A pitch-black blanket covered his back garden. The only thing he could see was his own reflection on the glass doors from the dining room lights.

It was 6.30 in the morning and his sleep had been fitful. He had woken at 6 O'clock feeling more tired than rested. The thought of playing golf, a game he had not quite mastered, with Jack McConnell, was playing tricks with his body, tightening his shoulder muscles and turning his stomach three parts liquid. At least two butterflies were fluttering around in his tummy. He had not felt this kind of nervous tension for a long while. He knew it was stupid to feel so worked up over an innocuous game of golf, but he didn't want to play badly and embarrass himself in front of a man he admired, although quietly and discreetly as Mary disliked him. Personal pride had a lot to answer for.

He took a last sip of the black stuff, despising himself for being so vain, and made his way to the kitchen to make another cup. Caffeine was unlikely to help his anxiety, but he always drank two cups of black coffee in the morning and habits were hard to change. He switched on the kettle and knocked a newspaper lying beside it on the kitchen bar on the floor. He reached down, his back creaking in the process, for the paper and laid it back on the bar by the kettle.

Henry Llewellyn stared out from the upturned page. The newspaper had profiled Llewellyn, examining his obsession with saving Wellesley Primary School from closure. Llewellyn was pictured standing about 100 yards in front of the school under a headline in black italics "To be, or not to be", linking the actor's acclaimed portrayal of Hamlet with the school's precariously balanced fate. There was also a small picture of the head of planning at the council, who was said to back the closure of the school, beside the photograph of Llewellyn. The council official looked familiar – the inspector had seen him around town many times - and was, strangely, similar in appearance to Llewellyn.

Napoleon read halfway through the piece before the writer's analysis of Llewellyn, the driven man, began to irritate him. The piece had a contemptuous and sneering tone, with a number of assertions about Llewellyn that were not backed up with any facts or evidence. How did the writer know whether Llewellyn was driven to succeed as an actor by slights real or imagined in his childhood and adult life? Did Llewellyn have to be driven because of some flaw in his personality? Maybe he just wanted the simple satisfaction of doing something well, which also brought respect, personal contentment and in his case wealth - three important things that went a long way to creating happiness.

The kettle gurgled and steamed, shutting itself off as the water boiled. Napoleon poured himself another coffee and dropped the newspaper back on the kitchen bar before returning to his chair in front of the patio doors. He walked at a slow, middle aged pace because of stiffness in his back, another ailment to add to the list, and sat down tentatively, hoping his spine would loosen after a hot shower.

Immediately, he noticed the bird song. The morning orchestra was at full tilt. He recognised the distinctive whistle of a blackbird and the cooing of the wood pigeons, as a blue glow began to shed light in patches across the lawn. Gradually, he could make out the green of the grass. White pockets were also appearing in the black, grey sky. He took a sip of his coffee, which was stronger than the first but better for it and thought about his golf. He would play a conservative game, use a short and compact swing and aim for the open spaces. No glorious drives over the trees to cut corners to bring down his score, which he was capable of on a good day.

The light was really taking hold now, growing stronger by the minute. Napoleon could see the whole of his back garden - and the golf course beyond was nearly visible. Jack McConnell had found the body just after 7am, which meant he would have driven off the first tee roughly 10 minutes earlier. Napoleon cast his eye at his watch. It was 6.45 and light enough to hit a golf ball.

McConnell's story added up. He had expected it would, but like any good policeman he never took a fact for granted.

McConnell was waiting on the first tee. There were several other golfers ready to play too, which did nothing to ease Napoleon's nerves. "Ah, Napoleon," McConnell said. "What a lovely morning. Do you fancy a flutter? Let's say a pound a hole. Nothing too ambitious."

"Sure." Napoleon nodded.

"What's your handicap?"

"About 20."

"Mine's 10, so I'll give you 10 shots." McConnell smiled broadly. "We're next to go," he added briskly.

Two elderly men had just played off. Both of their shots had landed comfortably beyond the rough. Napoleon could see their balls, lying neatly in the middle of the fairway. If only McConnell would slice his ball into the woods or, preferably, duff his shot completely. That would take the pressure off.

He had not played in two months and a mistimed drive, where the ball dribbled a few yards into the rough, was far more embarrassing if everyone else hit good shots.

McConnell teed up his ball and took a practise swing in the rough area. The old men were ambling up the fairway, taking a long time to reach their balls. Eventually, they played their second shots. McConnell watched them with screwed up, impatient eyes.

There were six other golfers waiting to play, four seemed to be together. Napoleon recognised Ted Cropper among them. He nodded his way, but Ted didn't notice.

There was a crack, followed by the hissing sound of a golf ball in flight. Napoleon turned to see McConnell's ball arching towards the middle of the fairway, then land and skid on the dewy grass about 250 yards away. So much for the duff shot.

Napoleon teed his ball up high to allow maximum scope for head movement or misjudgement. He steadied himself, thought of Mary, then inexplicably of Llewellyn, and blazed his shot 30 yards past McConnell's. He quickly scooped up his bag, feeling relief and pride in about equal proportions. He glanced at Ted again, but he was fishing a ball out of his bag and didn't meet his eye.

McConnell's second shot landed safely on the green, a further 200 yards away. He used a wood to make the distance. It surprised Napoleon that, for a big man, he was not a longer hitter. McConnell, he guessed, was about 6ft 3in, an inch or so taller than himself and much broader.

Napoleon took a six iron, his favourite club, out of his bag and lined up his ball. He steadied himself and tried to keep his swing compact and controlled but, committing his old crime of lifting his head, he clipped the top of the ball. It curved low in the air and clattered into the woods beyond the green. McConnell laughed from behind. "You'll have to play your shot again. That area's out of bounds until the police tell us otherwise. That blue and white tape has cordoned off the wooded area at the back of the green. It's where I found the body."

"Yes, I know." Napoleon dropped another ball and this time played more conservatively, taking a shorter back swing, and running the ball just shy of the green.

He trudged towards the woods to find his other ball, gently lowering himself under the police tape, which had been erected just behind the green. The ball had landed deep in the heather and was probably impossible to play. "So, Jack, where did you find the body?" he asked, reaching down to pick up his ball. McConnell, who had followed Napoleon into the wood, stepped back closer to the edge of the green and walked about five paces to the inspector's left.

"Here." He pointed to the spot. "I only saw the body because the arm was openly in view, fully stretched out and wedged in that bush by the tree. You couldn't see the body from the green. It was propped up behind the tree, but the arm was alarmingly visible."

"You would definitely have seen the arm. It was that clearly in view?" Napoleon asked.

"Yes. Anyone who stepped on to the green would have seen it. I didn't at first because I was so focused on the ball and it's still quite gloomy that early in the morning, but as I was about to make my second putt, I noticed it. It's not something you would miss, even for the most blinkered golfer."

"Someone clearly put the body there?" Napoleon questioned again.

"Well, it didn't fall out of the tree." McConnell grinned mischievously. "Maybe there was a fight in the wood and this lad came off worse and the other person just ran off."

"Hmm." McConnell either didn't know a car killed the man or he was a very good liar, Napoleon thought.

"But you said the arm was wedged in the bush. Do you mean that someone wedged it there on purpose, in open view, in the expectation it would be seen by anyone who stepped on to the green, or did it wedge there by chance?"

McConnell shrugged. "I hadn't really given it a thought. It was wedged very neatly between two branches. At a guess I would have said someone did it deliberately. Maybe it was to stop the body falling over." He shrugged again and turned round to look back down the fairway. "You'd better go and play your ball, or we'll start holding everyone up." The four-ball behind them were now just about in range of the green.

Napoleon went back to where his second ball had landed and chipped on to the green. He managed to hole his first putt but still scored a double bogey six with the penalty shot. McConnell two putted for a par four and won the hole. He smiled with tremendous satisfaction as he sank his ball. Winning meant a lot to him, Napoleon noted vaguely, still preoccupied with the dead man's arm.

Did someone deliberately place the arm in the open, so it could be seen from the green? Why not just dump the body in the wood? The body would have been carried through the alleyway that led on to the course from Crookham Lane. It would have been far easier to dump it in one of the gardens that backed on to the course. Did someone want the body to be seen? But why not put the body on the green, clearly in the open? Then, instead of McConnell, the green keeper might have seen it, or possibly the club secretary, who often opened his office early in the morning. The office had a good view of the first green, overlooking the fairway. Napoleon sighed, perplexed.

The sun's rays gently poked through the small gaps in the tall, fulsome fir and pine trees that surrounded the ninth tee. McConnell was five holes up and suggested they have a drink at the halfway house refreshment tent. It was a cool, bright autumn day and Napoleon was at last feeling relaxed. His back and shoulders had loosened up and the butterflies had flown.

He had won one hole, halved two and lost six. He had not humiliated himself and McConnell seemed impressed with parts of his game, despite its inconsistency. They both drank orange juice and watched the four-ball behind play through from a small table at the front of the tent. Ted Cropper was among the four-ball. His tee shot veered to the right and crashed into a bunker.

"Terrible golfer, Cropper," McConnell said. He paused and glanced at Napoleon to gauge his reaction. The policeman's face showed no emotion. McConnell continued talking but in a softer, more sympathetic tone. "It was awful about his son and grandson. I was at the police station the night Frank Cropper killed himself."

Napoleon looked up. "Yes. I remember. That right hook of yours is legendary."

McConnell smiled sheepishly. "I wasn't proud about hitting that policeman. It was bloody stupid. I don't know what got into me, but I was very tired, it was three in the morning, and I was worried sick. I was incensed that no one at the station had phoned me to say where John was, but of course it was his fault. He had given them the wrong number, probably on purpose. You know, I was very grateful to that policeman I knocked out for not pressing charges. It could have been very embarrassing."

Napoleon sat back in his chair and watched Ted make his way to the bunker. "I wouldn't worry about the policeman. He just had a black eye. Frank Cropper died. If the sergeant on duty hadn't been knocked out cold, he might have stopped Cropper from taking his own life."

Napoleon saw McConnell grimace from the corner of his eye. "I'm sorry Jack," he said, grimacing himself. "I didn't mean to be tactless. It wasn't your fault Frank Cropper died. He was a hopeless case. You mustn't blame yourself."

McConnell looked into his drink and Napoleon noticed his jaw muscle twitch. It was an interesting, involuntary movement. The chief inspector had noticed it before only yesterday when he had mentioned McConnell's son. Then McConnell seemed angry, now he just looked uncomfortable, understandably bothered by what had happened on the night Frank Cropper died.

McConnell frowned. "Talking of hopeless cases, I'm afraid my son is one and so is my wife. I know I have faults, but at least I get on with things. My wife just drinks to avoid reality, and John - well, he just blames everyone else, usually me, for his troubles. He's typical of a lot of lads these days. They think life owes them something and when they don't get what they want, they get angry."

Napoleon watched Ted hack his ball out of the bunker. He mistimed his shot and sent the ball a long way over the green into the rough beyond. "Your wife said John took failing to get into the parachute regiment very badly," he said.

"Yes, he did, but you can't use one failure as an excuse to ruin the rest of your life. And there's no excuse for pointless crime, which I know John got involved in, probably still is involved in."

"So, it's all right, if there's a point to it," Napoleon said wryly.

"If you can get away with it, dear boy, then why not?" McConnell laughed. "I shouldn't say that to a policeman, should I? No, what I mean is the mindless vandalism these kids or youths are into these days. Take my place. It's been burgled three times and the first time, a few years back, the thieves didn't even take anything, except a small silver cross and chain my son had given my wife as a birthday present. It wasn't worth much, but my wife loved it because John had made the effort to buy her something. But from my perspective, it makes no sense. People take the risk of breaking into a house, yet they don't bother taking anything of value. What's the point of breaking in, trashing the place, and then not stealing anything, except a small silver cross? They probably didn't take the cross and chain either. My wife swears they did, but she could have easily mislaid it while in one of her drunken stupors."

"Maybe the thieves were disturbed before they could take anything," Napoleon said.

"They managed to find the time to trash the place. No, I don't think so. It was just misguided, angry kids doing it for kicks. Pointless. I suppose I should be thankful they didn't steal anything. But it still made my blood boil, all that mess."

Napoleon sipped the last of his orange juice. "Have you spoken to Humphrey much this week?"

McConnell leaned his head to one side and swept his hand through his hair. "No, come to think of it, I haven't. I played cards with him on Wednesday night, but we haven't really spoken since. Why do you ask?"

"No reason," Napoleon said.

McConnell's jaw twitched again. "We should get going," he said, watching the last player in the four-ball hole his putt.

Napoleon drove off the long 15th hole with the sun in his eyes, but it didn't bother him. This was his favourite part of the course, where nature and man had blended the physical elements into an uplifting, magnificent setting. If Napoleon could have chosen an idyllic landscape, the 15th hole of Wellesley Golf Course was it, with its lush fairway and immaculate green. The fairway descended majestically into the heart of the course before banking up towards the green.

This was perfectly offset by a thick, purple mass of heather that stretched around and in front of the hole like an unruly haircut. The trees were also more varied here and appeared taller than anywhere else on the course.

Napoleon took a deep contented breath and watched his ball fly straight and long towards the middle of the fairway. His second shot was not quite so accurate. Using his favoured six iron, he tried to run the ball safely on to the green. Except for the mistimed chip on the first hole, his six iron had reliably delivered all day, but this time a squirrel busily digging under a tree disturbed his concentration and his shot spun wildly into the trees.

"Keep your head down," McConnell bellowed.

"It was the squirrel's fault," Napoleon said lamely.

"A squirrel!" McConnell was incredulous. "You take too much notice of everything around you. You need tunnel vision to play this game. I haven't noticed any squirrels."

"It's not as much fun, if you don't notice the squirrels." The offending creature had subsequently darted up the nearest tree, out of sight.

"Winning is fun and I'm winning," McConnell said.

"I don't mind losing on a nice day like this," Napoleon said, putting his club back in his bag.

McConnell walked towards Napoleon. He had already found the centre of the green with a perfectly timed chip, the shot Napoleon had tried to reproduce. "Ah, you may not mind losing but I love winning, so who's better off? Me, I think."

The two men separated as they reached the green, McConnell stopping by the flag near where his ball lay while Napoleon tramped through the thick rough at the back of the hole. He found his ball wrapped in a particularly sturdy looking piece of heather.

He took out his wedge and drove it hard into the weed, which obligingly coughed up the ball, although stubbornly still managing to take most of the power out of the shot. The ball cleared the rough but fell a long way short of the green.

"Who's smiling now?" McConnell said. "Looks like I'm going to win this hole too. I tell you what," he shouted over to Napoleon who was wiping the remains of the weed off the end of his wedge. "Let's make the last three holes double or quits. I can't say fairer than that as I'm eight holes up already."

"You're being greedy," Napoleon said. "It'll be your undoing, but if you want to gamble away your money. That's fine by me."

"Greed is a great motivator. All great men are greedy."

Napoleon nodded, but didn't agree.

"Reckless bet, that last one on the 15th hole," the chief inspector said, swallowing a large mouthful of beer. They were now in the golf club bar and Napoleon had won two of the last three holes.

"Yes, but I was the moral victor," McConnell said, eyeing Napoleon provocatively. "I won the round easily and I should have won that last hole. You were lucky with your final putt, but not to worry. That last bet made the game much more interesting at the end. It was worth the financial loss. We were hardly playing for big bucks."

"But I won," Napoleon said, deliberately trying to wind up his intensely competitive opponent.

"That you did, dear boy, but there's always a next time," McConnell said calmly, refusing to take the bait. "How about a game of cards with me and Humphrey?" McConnell turned round and searched the bar. "He should be here by now."

Napoleon shook his head. "No thanks. I'm expected home for lunch."

McConnell turned back to face the inspector. "Pity. I was sure cards would be your game, with your poker face."

Napoleon smiled. People often commented on his impassive expression. It was, he assumed, the natural default setting of his face. "My poker face comes in useful in police work. It keeps people guessing," Napoleon said. He took another large swallow of beer. "But I'm not much of a gambler. I don't like the uncertainty."

McConnell looked disappointed. "You should live a little. A risk now and then makes everything so much more exciting."

"I'll stick with caution and common sense, thanks," Napoleon said.

McConnell laughed loudly. "Spoken like a true policeman."

Napoleon sensed a patronising tone in McConnell's voice, but smiled all the same. Does taking a risk mean breaking the law, he wondered? McConnell was clearly the type who might bend it.

CHAPTER 23

◆

Henry Llewellyn sat on the floor of his spacious living room, propped against an immense full-grain leather sofa surrounded by four plump cushions, while Molly shifted nervously opposite him on a Victorian chaise longue. The interior of the actor's house, which had been converted from an old farmhouse, was a mixture of styles and periods, reflecting Llewellyn's varied tastes. He had an eclectic mind, Molly guessed, and was the type who probably went through phases, flitting from one interest to the next. Saving the school was the latest fad and the reason she was there to interview him.

The living room was best described as modern in a rustic country barn style. Old wooden beams criss-crossed the high ceilings and large fenestrated windows, which allowed the maximum amount of light to flood in, gave the room an airy feel. The ash wood floor and embedded spotlights in the ceiling were the room's nod to the modern, while at the far end there was a large Victorian fireplace, with a painting of an old barn surrounded by fields hanging above it. A tall, thin antique lamp stood beside the fireplace, which to Molly's eye looked Georgian. An art deco coffee table, between Molly and Llewellyn, added to the diverse mix. The other striking thing about the room was that it lacked a television. One of the country's leading actors, who appeared on television regularly, did not seem to own a wide-screen or even a small portable for that matter.

It was the first time Molly had been inside the actor's home and she was not sure what to make of it. She kept searching for the television, maybe it was hidden in a wall unit or somewhere else, but the room's one bookcase, painted white and in a French classical design, appeared to be just that – with a legion of books cramming its shelves. Apart from the one painting of the barn, there were no other prints on the cream-coloured walls either, which also accentuated the room's size. It was not a home for someone with agoraphobia.

"I don't like to feel hemmed in," Llewellyn said, following her wandering eye and reading her thoughts. "I like to pace around when I think and memorise my lines. This is the perfect room for that. It allows you to breathe and clear your mind. That's why there are no paintings or prints except for the barn. I don't want any distractions."

"I see," Molly said tentatively, turning her attention to Llewellyn. She looked closely at his face, the same face that appeared on magazine covers and was rarely out of the newspapers. It was hard to remain cool in such company. Her nerves were not helped by having to raise her voice when she spoke. The chaise longue and the leather sofa were set back a fair distance from the coffee table in between them.

"I'll have to come closer to allow the microphone to pick you up better," she said loudly.

"Fine," Llewellyn said, smiling.

She gingerly lowered herself on to the hard floor and placed her microphone and recording device on the coffee table next to the cup of coffee Llewellyn had made for her when she arrived. She was still too far away from Llewellyn, so she moved around the coffee table and put the microphone and recording device in front of Llewellyn on the floor.

"You had better take a couple of these," Llewellyn said, handing her two cushions to sit on. "Sorry, I like sitting on the floor and spreading out. I feel more relaxed sitting on the floor."

"Sure," Molly said. "That's no problem. The more relaxed you feel, the better." She was feeling more at ease herself, now she was within comfortable talking range. She noticed he was much better looking at close quarters. The clear complexion and fine, facial bone structure were lost from a distance.

He also looked alarmingly like Charlie, although his eyes and hair were lighter and his nose thinner. Like her husband, he also had small delicate hands and bony feet, which were crossed sockless in front of him. His jeans were rolled up to his knees revealing two thin, hairy shins.

She was beginning to feel oddly intimate with him, sitting so close. It was probably because he reminded her of Charlie.

"Well, should we get started?" Llewellyn said. He smiled and Charlie smiled too.

"Sorry, I'll get settled in a minute. I'm not used to interviewing someone on the floor of a farmhouse."

"It's not a farmhouse anymore," Llewellyn said. He leaned into one of the large cushions. His body language reflected a man completely at ease and comfortable in his own environment.

"Yes, I suppose you're right," Molly said, glancing around the room again. She smiled and coughed a little nervously. "Okay, I'll ask you a few questions on why you've put forward this new proposal to turn the school into a museum, then I'll ask why you, a big star etc, etc, has spent so much time trying to save a small school. This is a recording and not live, so just say what you want, and we can always edit things out to make the replies sharper."

"Great," Llewellyn said. One of his knees poked out of his rolled-up jeans. It was knobbly and a carbon copy of Charlie's.

Molly clicked the microphone on and spoke into it. "Do you think this new proposal to convert Wellesley Primary School into a museum will win over the council?"

She turned the microphone towards Llewellyn.

"I hope so," he said. "The reason I've drawn up this new plan is because it is becoming increasingly clear to me that the council is unlikely to back down over its decision to shut the school because of falling rolls. So here is an alternative idea that will help to enhance the character of the town in a way a supermarket or leisure centre could never hope to."

"Can you elaborate further on what a museum will bring to the town?" she said, swivelling the microphone her way before returning it to Llewellyn.

Llewellyn straightened himself. "Let me explain why I started the Save Our School campaign first. It was for a principle, a principle that stands for our community and our tradition, a principle that does not put money, comfort and convenience before everything else.

"A supermarket or a leisure centre would provide benefits and convenience, but little meaning. The school is a part of the town's past. As I said, I believe the council is determined to close the school. Well, here is a new proposal that has massive support and will bring something to the town way beyond what a supermarket or a leisure centre can. A museum would provide us with insight about our town and our past. It would show us what children in the 19th century experienced. We talk of Wellesley Primary School as a Victorian school, but most of us have little idea of what a Victorian school was like. It might encourage our children to appreciate their own schooling."

"Is turning the school into a museum really going to make much difference to Wellesley?" Molly asked.

"It's just a little idea, but it should be part of a bigger idea to enrich and strengthen the bond between the town and the people who live here. Capitalism has given us the money for more comforts like supermarkets and leisure centres, but it hasn't helped us understand ourselves."

Molly nodded. "But money is important," she said. "The council has to consider finances."

"The museum would be self-financing," Llewellyn said. "I am prepared to put up capital and I have support from a lot of wealthy people who would do likewise. Wellesley is not a town short of wealthy patrons."

Molly clicked off the microphone. "Thanks. That was perfect. I'll just give you a quick breather. I want to make a brief note of your comments. It helps me when I'm compiling my report." She flicked open her notebook and jotted down a few key points. Llewellyn lazily watched her. "You've got nice writing," he said.

"Thanks." She closed the notebook and put it to one side. "Are you ready for another question?"

"Sure," he said.

"Excellent." She took a sip of her coffee and turned the microphone back on. "You're the most successful actor of your generation. You're about to play Hamlet at Stratford, a role you've played before to great acclaim. You've played Richard III at the Barbican, and you've established yourself in Hollywood, so why are you bothered about Wellesley Primary School?"

Llewellyn paused for a moment, gathering his thoughts. "I was brought up in Wellesley and I feel strongly about a school I went to as a child. If you knock it down and turn it into a supermarket or leisure centre, you knock down my past, you take a little piece away from me. I think a lot of people feel like that."

"When I first started this campaign, a long time ago now, most people told me they thought a supermarket or leisure centre was a good idea, but when I began to explain why I felt so strongly, why community and tradition are important, many, many people changed their minds. Now the museum idea is taking off as a serious alternative, should the council insist on closing the school. It has captured the imagination in a way that has even surprised me."

Molly switched off the microphone and stretched. "That's great. It's nice interviewing an actor. They know about soundbites. I won't have to edit much. Have you ever thought about a career in broadcasting?"

"If I'm ever out of work, I'll give the station a call," Llewellyn said, smiling.

Molly smiled back. "Seriously, though." She looked into his eyes. They were hazel with green flecks in the centre near the pupils. "A lot of people say you're abnormally obsessed with saving the school."

"You mean Jack McConnell and Derek Keele, the two developers." Llewellyn pulled out a handkerchief and blew his nose. He even did that in a sexy, debonair way. "Anyway, obsession harnessed in the right way can achieve great things. It's a powerful emotion. It will drive you anywhere you want. You just have to make sure you can control it and use it as a positive force. You mentioned Hamlet. Obsession in his case destroyed him as well as indecision."

He sat forward and said with a curious, quiet intensity: "Have you ever hated someone?"

Molly pulled away from him, mainly because his face was so close to hers. "No, I don't think so." She caught a waft of his aftershave, which was fresh and lemony. She was really quite turned on.

"I have and it has helped me greatly with my acting, especially in roles like Hamlet and Richard III, the other play you mentioned. I hated a boy at school. He bullied me. He was one of those tough types. Fighting to him was second nature and he knew I was scared of him. It helped me to learn never to show fear, even if deep down I did. Whenever I'm nervous about a role, a challenge, I remember that fear and realise nothing can be that bad. And I remember how obsessed I became with that fear. It invaded my thoughts all the time. I think of that boy when I play a character that is obsessed by something."

"You thought of him when you played Hamlet and Richard III?" Molly was now leaning closer to him.

"Yes." Llewellyn scratched a knobbly knee. "Do you want another coffee? I'm sorry for getting so heavy. Let's have a coffee, nothing deep in that."

"Yes. Good idea, but I don't mind deep conversations. It's fascinating."

They stood up and Molly followed Llewellyn into the kitchen, which like the other rooms couldn't make up its mind over style and design, although the end product was a pleasing mishmash. It was, she supposed, Art Deco. There was a small circular glass table with four silver, thin rectangular chairs surrounding it and paintings by Picasso and George Braque dominated the walls. Unlike the living room, it felt cluttered and crowded. It also had that old rustic cottage feel with slightly careworn wooden cupboards on the walls and flowers everywhere. And there was a television in the corner of the room at the far end with a radio standing beneath it.

Molly leaned against the doorway and stared at one of the Picasso prints. It was, she assumed, painted during his Cubism period and, like many of Picasso's paintings, it looked ridiculous to her. Llewellyn noticed her frowning as he ground some coffee beans by a spotless, gleaming sink. "You don't like it. Well, I'm sure it was just a big joke. I think Cubism was the great con of our age. I think the more absurd the paintings, the more satisfaction Picasso had at the expense of his fawning public."

"Why put these on your walls, then?" Molly said, looking around the room.

"I suppose it's because they're wonderfully incomprehensible and the colours are striking. It also gives you a certain perspective. Picasso was a genius, but it doesn't mean all his paintings were masterpieces. In my opinion, Cubism – all of these are from that era – was the great failure of the great artist. Maybe the whole point of it was to see how absurdly he could paint before the cheering stopped, but it never did."

He stopped for a moment, considering his thoughts as he put the ground up coffee into a cafetiere.

"I don't know for sure what was in Picasso's mind," he said finally. "But it certainly makes you think. No actor or performer, as Picasso was in a way, should let themselves be fooled by the public, be fooled by the imbecilic applause. When I'm cheered on stage, I often think of Picasso's big joke. Maybe calling Cubism a big joke is unfair – and I'm not sure whether the joke was on the public or Picasso. Who was fooling who? The paintings are fascinating and magisterial in their way. But there is something unreal about them, something fake. As art, they have failed for me because they don't offer a vision of reality. That is the key goal for me as an actor and an artist." He stopped and looked intensely at one of the paintings as if he was trying to bore a hole through it with the power of his stare.

"I hang these paintings on my walls because it comforts me that even failure can look like success if you have the chutzpah and confidence to pull it off. For me, it is ridiculous, almost laughable, that Cubism was such a success, and that was down to public opinion, which is why I try not to judge my work by public opinion alone. It is a very crude measurement." Llewellyn laid out a tray and reached into a cupboard for some clean coffee cups.

"What do you measure it by then?" Molly asked, smiling to herself at the intense turn of the conversation. Llewellyn couldn't help himself, even when making coffee.

"There's only one person who can judge personal achievement, and that's you, the individual. No one else really matters because art, performance, is subjective. If you believe you've succeeded, and I mean really believe, then no one can ever be more successful than that." Llewellyn smiled. "Shall we go through?" he said, lifting up the tray, which now had a cafetiere, milk jug and two cups neatly arranged on it.

They sat back down among the cushions and Molly admired the painting of the barn, which was definitely local, for a second time, while Llewellyn poured the coffee.

"Why do you really do it, try to save the school, I mean?" Molly said.

"Haven't I answered that?"

"Well, not really. The museum idea sounds great, but the council will probably reject it. I appreciate your point about doing something for a principle, but ultimately if it's likely to end in failure, is it really worth it?"

Llewellyn scratched his chest. He was wearing an open-necked tee-shirt and Molly noticed how hairy it was, just like Charlie's.

"You may be right," he said. "I've known from the start that saving the school was perhaps a vain hope, but you don't always do things because you think you can succeed, sometimes you do them because you think you're right. And maybe, now, the challenge has become an obsession as a lot of people have already told you." Llewellyn smiled cheekily.

"Maybe I want to show Jack McConnell and Derek Keele they can't have it all their own way."

He took a sip of coffee, then gently replaced it on its saucer. "Let's go back to Hamlet and Richard III," he said in a quieter more serious tone.

Molly cast another glance at his chest. He was perhaps a bit hairier than Charlie.

Llewellyn took another sip of coffee. "Well, they were both obsessed. Let's assume I am as well over the school for the neatness of the point, which is that obsession can be a driving force to achieve great things, if channelled in the right way.

"Hamlet is obsessed by his desire for revenge over his father's death but lacks the decisiveness to carry through his actions because he is thwarted by moral conscience. Richard III is obsessed with his ambition, but he is not obstructed by this moral conscience. He is, like Hamlet, supremely intelligent but he is decisive and channels his obsession skilfully.

"Hamlet is driven by grief after the murder of his father by Claudius, who then marries his mother and becomes king. But his problem is that he chronically dithers over how to deal with this grief, whether he should take revenge or not, hence – 'To be or not to be'.

"And it is this which delivers the tragedy, because in the end his indecision brings about the worst of all worlds, his death, his mother's death, his one-time lover Ophelia's death, and the death of her brother Laertes. Okay, so Claudius is killed too, and Fortinbras becomes king with Hamlet's blessing, purging the sickness of Denmark, but what a price? There you have the essence of revenge tragedy."

Llewellyn used his hands artfully to make his points, chopping the air for emphasis, then moving them in circular patterns to help bring his words to life. It was as if he was performing some medieval spell. Molly was captivated. So this was charisma.

"But what has this got to do with the school or Jack McConnell?" she said, still puzzled, despite the irresistible intensity of his argument.

"Well, I know I'm drawing this out, but it's important. McConnell and Keele have spread it around that I'm obsessed with the school. They say that my desire to save it is irrational, unhealthy. The implication is that I might even be a little crazy, simply opposing them because of some misplaced principle. In fact, the inference is that I'm just some mad actor, out of touch with the real world.

"Well, Hamlet was considered mad, perhaps he was a little, but in my case, we're not talking about his kind of obsession. We're talking about an obsession that is no different from say McConnell's arguably obsessive desire to build a leisure centre. He's always wanted to build one in the town, it will probably make him a lot of money, and he's also motivated by a desire to get one over on Keele. I'm sure that would give him more satisfaction than anything else."

Llewellyn stopped for a moment and let his busy hands rest on his knees. "Sorry I'm rambling."

"No, no. Go on. It's fascinating, even if I don't quite follow."

He smiled and leaned back into the cushion propped behind him. "Okay, my obsession and McConnell's are more like Richard III's. Richard is powerful and effective when he has the challenge to motivate him. He is obsessed by the desire to be king and have power.

"His ambition is an intellectual one, rather than a vain one. He plots for the throne to make up for his deformity, his humped back, to show people he is not just a freakish hunchback. But once he gets to the throne his power wanes.

"He has no challenge. We only get a glimpse of his remarkable powers again, just before his demise, when faced with another challenge, the Battle of Bosworth."

Molly grinned. "So, you and Jack McConnell have humped backs?"

"Maybe we do, but invisible ones. What I mean is, I need a challenge. McConnell, I'm sure, is the same. My motivation is an intellectual one like Richard's. It is a possible flaw in my character, but without a challenge I lose my way. People need a purpose in life and for me acting doesn't always fulfil that need. After all, when you boil it down, it's simply prancing about on a stage or behind a camera pretending to be someone else.

"Richard was driven by his deformity and Hamlet by his desire for revenge. In this instance, I'm driven by a principle while McConnell and Keele are driven by a desire to make money, their egos and their obsession with trying to outwit each other. To really enjoy life, most people, I think, need some purpose, some aim. The museum, saving the school, is that aim, at least for the moment, for me.

"It's totally different to acting and it's very refreshing, partly because of that. But it's also very refreshing to fight for something, however insignificant, that means a lot to you and is the right thing to do in principle and for yourself and the small place where you live."

He leaned forward and picked up his coffee cup. "I hope you understand now why I'm doing this, for a little school probably beyond saving."

Molly smiled and took her first sip of coffee. It was cold, but it didn't matter. She understood completely.

CHAPTER 24

◆

Napoleon straightened his tie, a habit he'd picked up from Sergeant Mayo, and knocked on Chief Superintendent Jim Hunter's door. There was what sounded like a growl from inside, the usual signal to enter the lion's den.

Hunter's office was neat and regimented. It was also lacking in something - warmth and personality, Napoleon supposed. There were no photographs of family or friends on the walls and no personal mementoes or souvenirs on his desk, which gave clues about a person's character or past, like there were on Napoleon's.

Hunter eyed Napoleon sullenly. "Sit down," he said. "I hate it when you hover, as if you'd rather not be here. I'm not your dentist. I'm not going to drill any holes in your mouth."

"No sir," Napoleon said and lapsed into the chair facing Hunter.

Hunter continued staring at his chief inspector but could see nothing in his blank expression. "The press conferences have gone quite well so far. Mayo's good at that sort of thing," he said, implying Napoleon wasn't. "We can keep the press at bay with good public relations and bland statements for a while, but it's three days since Rankin was killed. We need to start making progress, so what have we got?"

The chief superintendent was direct and aggressive. At least in that he was always consistent. Napoleon smiled to himself and considered the outline of the man in front of him. The dark fiery eyes, cropped black hair and impressive muscular build, only slightly blemished by a small paunch from too many official lunches and malt whiskies, his favourite and probably only vice.

It painted a picture of power. Unfortunately, the personality behind it was domineering and, in Napoleon's opinion, flawed in its eagerness for results instead of justice.

"Bits and pieces, but nothing solid to go on," Napoleon said. He tried to keep the casual tone out of his voice but failed. He knew his occasional diffidence annoyed Hunter.

"Nothing solid to go on," the chief superintendent repeated the words louder and more forcefully. The dark eyes bore into Napoleon. "Rankin was knocked down in broad daylight. I can't believe no one saw the collision. What about the car that hit him, this small red hatchback?"

"No trace sir. We only have one witness who saw the car and that was only as it was speeding away. There are thousands of small red hatchbacks. DVLA is checking out those listed to owners living in the area."

"Right, and we have no other witnesses?"

"No. The barman at The Nag's Head came rushing out of the pub when he heard the collision, but he didn't see anything. There was a driver going the other way, but he was looking for a parking space and didn't notice the car and there was an elderly lady who was walking into town on the other side of the road from The Nag's Head. She was the one who gave us the description of the car. She didn't see the collision but saw the car as it was speeding away. She has poor eyesight, so small, red and she thinks a hatchback, was the best she could do. And then there's John McConnell, who tried to revive Rankin. We're still trying to find him. Our elderly witness thinks the car came close to hitting McConnell."

Hunter nodded morosely. "Right. What about the traces of blood and skin found on St Margaret's Road?"

"Scenes of crime have confirmed they belong to Peter Delgado."

"I presume St Margaret's Road is the one that runs by the golf club and Crookham Lane?"

"Yes sir."

"Well, surely that's something?"

"Yes sir. The fragments were found on the left-hand side of the road as you come down the hill from the golf club, just before the Crookham Lane turning. So, the suspect could have come from the golf club. And there's something else you should know sir." Napoleon straightened his tie again. "A member of the golf club who was drinking in the bar on the night of Delgado's death knew he was knocked over by a car, despite the fact we haven't given out that information yet, which is interesting."

Hunter leaned forward. "It's more than interesting. I thought you said we didn't have anything solid." The chief superintendent eyed Napoleon suspiciously. "Is this man the driver?"

"No." Napoleon shook his head. "He's a notorious drinker, who doesn't drive. He was in the golf club bar all night and walked home, which has been verified. He thinks someone told him Delgado was knocked over by a car, but he can't remember. He might have imagined it, he says. I don't know what to believe. We're checking on the members of the club. They all have to fill in registration forms, which include details of the cars they own. We might find our small red hatchback."

"This man," Hunter said. "He must remember who spoke to him."

"He can't," Napoleon said, a little too defiantly. "He spends most of his evenings completely inebriated. He genuinely can't remember how he knew Delgado was run over. I'm afraid I don't think he'll ever remember, but it does suggest the driver may be a member of the golf club."

"Is he covering up for someone?"

"I don't think so," Napoleon said.

"Blast. Well, you've got to find something."

"I have a list of the people who were at the golf club on the night Delgado died, which we're following up."

Napoleon fished out his notebook from his jacket pocket. He flipped over a couple of the pages theatrically, which he suspected would irritate Hunter. Sometimes, he just couldn't resist annoying his boss. He found the page he was looking for.

"This is strictly conjecture sir," Napoleon said.

Hunter frowned, his dark bushy eyebrows coming together in an almost perfect V-shape.

"Go on," he said, sounding sceptical.

"Well, it is possible whoever put the body on the golf course wanted it to be seen there." Napoleon read from his notes. He found this a useful tactic with Hunter when he was proposing something not backed up with hard evidence. He felt it gave what he said a more authoritative and official air. "I have no idea why, but it would explain why the body was moved after the collision on St Margaret's Road. It would also explain why part of the body, an arm, was left clearly in view from the green. Jack McConnell, who found the body, said the arm was stretched right out and wedged between two branches of a bush. That seemed strange. Why not just dump the body in a ditch or in the woods? The scenes of crime team concurred that the arm had the appearance of being deliberately wedged between the branches."

"Had the appearance. That doesn't mean much. Why would someone do that?"

"Maybe they wanted Jack McConnell to see the body. It's well known among the golf club members that Jack McConnell is always first to tee off early on a Thursday morning. It's his ritual, a routine he told me he has stuck to for years. The body was put in a place where it could only have been noticed as you walked on to the green, in other words McConnell was almost certain to find the body."

Hunter frowned again. "Do you have any thoughts on who might have done this?"

"No sir."

"No. I guessed not. Well, it sounds highly implausible to me Napoleon. Jack McConnell didn't know Peter Delgado, so why would someone want him to find his body? Your theory just doesn't make sense. But if you're right, it means we may be looking at murder instead of manslaughter, so you'd better be certain of your facts. I don't want you getting sidetracked on some wild goose chase. The arm could simply have fallen like that."

Napoleon lifted his eyes from his notebook and focused on Hunter's mouth. Looking into his eyes tended to unnerve him. "There are other lines of enquiry."

Hunter stood up to his full 6ft 3in. He was the same height as Jack McConnell, Napoleon thought randomly, an inch taller than he was. It was the only time he wished he was taller, when he was with Hunter. Mary, who was 5ft 5in, never worried about height. But Napoleon, who was taller than most people, found it slightly disconcerting to look upwards into another person's eyes, particularly those belonging to his stern and unyielding boss.

Hunter turned round to stare out of the office window. "Nothing solid to go on," he said. "Now I can't stop you talking. Go on then Napoleon, tell me the other lines of enquiry."

Napoleon shook his head a fraction to clear his thoughts. "Yes. Sorry sir. Peter Delgado had a heated argument with his younger brother Ray on the night he died. Rankin and Sergeant Mayo interviewed Ray Delgado and his girlfriend, a Chloe Smith. We intend to interview them again."

"Right. Surely you should have done that already?"

"Ray Delgado is in Spain. We will talk to him when he returns."

Hunter turned round to face Napoleon. His neck had gone slightly pink, the colour gradually spreading upwards, a sign of rising anger and sometimes complete loss of temper.

"A suspect in Spain. Fantastic," he said in a loud sarcastic voice.

"He travelled there on the day his brother's body was found. Mayo and Rankin interviewed him and his girlfriend before he went. Mayo said they didn't realise he intended to leave the country. Apparently, most of his family live in Spain and he wanted to grieve with them and make arrangements for the funeral. His girlfriend assured us he would be back tomorrow."

"Ray Delgado was in Spain then, when Rankin was killed," Hunter said irritably.

"Yes sir. Our best hope on that front is to speak with Jack McConnell's son, John."

"Right." Hunter cooled just a little and sat back in his chair. "But you haven't managed to track him down?"

"No sir. Not yet, but he'll turn up. He won't go far. I've made it clear to his father and mother that he must come forward."

"Good, but go easy on Jack McConnell. I don't want his feathers ruffled unnecessarily. There's no point in it."

"He found the body, sir. I may have to question him again. And he seemed very open to talk. In fact, he invited me to play golf. We had a round at Wellesley yesterday."

Napoleon couldn't help himself. He had to mention the golf round. He knew it would make Hunter jealous. Jack McConnell was, in the chief superintendent's eyes, an important person, someone to be seen with.

"Yes, very clever of you, but be careful when you deal with him. Don't clod about and make my job more difficult. I'm afraid it's a fact of life that people like McConnell have contacts, the chief constable for instance, who can make my position, which means your life, less than easy."

There was an awkward pause, Hunter waiting for Napoleon to assent, but the chief inspector remained silent. He planned to clod about as much as he liked.

Hunter stared hard at Napoleon, trying to prise at least a nod from his subordinate, but it was a Mexican standoff he wasn't going to win. "All right, Napoleon," he said, changing the subject. "Has anything turned up from the garages, cars needing bodywork repairs? That sort of thing."

"No sir. Nothing locally, but we've extended our search across the whole region. We've spoken to two owners of small red cars that have had the kind of damage you might expect from a hit and run, but both were run-of-the-mill shunts with witnesses. And there are no reports of any cars stolen fitting the description we're looking for."

Hunter straightened a sheaf of papers in front of him and sighed. He looked tired and tense. "So, you were right all along Napoleon. There was nothing solid to go on. And if Peter Delgado was knocked down by his brother, then we're looking for someone else who ploughed into Rankin?" The bullying energy was starting to ebb. Rankin's death had left a mark. He was not a man who wasted much time on personal emotion, but for Rankin he had made an exception. Napoleon considered it ironic how the soulless Rankin had brought out the human qualities in Hunter.

Napoleon put his notebook back in his pocket. "Both deaths are puzzling, Delgado being moved, and scenes of crime tell me the driver that hit Rankin appears to have failed to brake as there were no skid marks on the road.

"You would expect someone to brake before impact, unless they panicked and hit the accelerator by mistake, or…" Hunter looked up wearily and finished the sentence. "They deliberately ran Rankin over."

Hunter shook his head. His pallid complexion reflected his sinking spirits. He stared grimly at his chief inspector. Napoleon wasn't sure what his superior saw, maybe a reflection of his own downcast mood, but whatever it was, it revived him, and he crackled with energy once again in the old bullying way.

"We must find something, Napoleon. I'm trusting you on this. I know we've had our differences, but I've always rated you as a detective, your results speak for themselves. I don't want these deaths lying on the file, unresolved. Is that understood? Report back to me when you've interviewed Ray Delgado. And I want to be kept abreast of any developments, however minor. Is that clear?"

"Yes sir," Napoleon said.

At the door, Napoleon turned and smiled awkwardly at his old adversary. "I'm sorry about Rankin sir. He was a good policeman."

Napoleon again noticed the strain in Hunter's face through the tired lines around his eyes and the shadows below them. His pale skin, normally a healthy reddish colour, was sickly grey at the edges. Even the ruddy nose had lost its colour.

For a few seconds, Hunter relaxed and became human. "Yes Napoleon, a good policeman." He smiled forlornly before the hard-boiled chief superintendent returned. "Get out Napoleon. There's work to be done." He motioned Napoleon to leave with a dismissive sweep of his arm.

CHAPTER 25

T he river was still and introspective, like Napoleon, who gazed without seeing into the water, his mind clearly elsewhere. Mary squeezed his hand to release him from his thoughts. "Sorry," he said. "Did you say something?"

"No. I was just wondering what you were thinking about. You look very preoccupied," Mary said.

Napoleon looked at his wife blankly for a moment before focusing on her question. "Patrick Rankin," he said with intensity. "Patrick Rankin might have discovered something that led to his death."

"Hmm," Mary nodded. She should have guessed her husband would be wrapped up in his latest case. She watched two swans glide past on the river. It was her turn to be distracted. They were like her husband, serene on the surface but below the water line, where the eye could not see, they were straining and stretching, the inspector with his exhaustive thoughts, the swans energetically paddling to propel themselves upstream.

"There has to be some kind of link between the deaths of Rankin and Peter Delgado. And Jack McConnell is linked to the deaths too," Napoleon added.

"Yes," Mary said, admiring the swans, which had come to a halt in the middle of the river. A couple of mallards joined them, one tipping itself headfirst into the water in search of fish. Mary watched the duck resurface fishless, and turned to Napoleon, who was deep in thought again.

"Come on Rob. Let's get going. You can walk and think at the same time." She pulled the inspector's arm to prompt him, and they headed towards the waterfall and bridge, Wellesley's unofficial boundary with the village next door.

It was not that far upstream, but here the river seemed to come alive as the water crashed and smashed against the bridge and then frothed and foamed as it dropped over the rocky precipice that made up the waterfall.

Not for the first time, Mary considered the contrast between the violently noisy waterfall and the motionless and silent bridge, which straddled the rushing currents below. People always remarked on the waterfall, its splendid power and beauty, and yet the bridge, if you bothered to look, was equally impressive in the quality of its brickwork and the resilience of its structure.

The bridge carried them to the prettier south side of the river, where a number of boats were moored by a quaint, rustic pub, which served average food and warm beer. Here, the river bustled with activity – smartly dressed office workers on lunchbreaks, mothers with their children and teenagers on bikes and skateboards provided a human rhythm to its natural setting. This part of the river was the town's scenic bolt hole, the ideal place to escape from the routine and humdrum of work or school.

"I love our walks by the river," Mary said. "It is so fresh and pure by the water. I feel closer to nature."

"Yeah right," Napoleon said, nodding sarcastically.

"Oh, shut up Robert. You know what I mean."

"Yes. I know what you mean," he lied. He stopped as they passed the pub and absent-mindedly kicked a large stone, which landed in the water with a loud splash. The inspector watched the tiny bubbles and ripples left in the stone's wake as it sank and, without thinking, produced a small model car from his pocket.

"What on earth is that?" Mary said.

"Eh?" Napoleon looked down at the car as if he had only just noticed it. "Oh. It's an old toy of mine, a matchbox car – an

Austin Maxi hatchback. I dug it out of the cupboard at home. The car that hit Rankin was small and red, like this one."

"Rob," she smiled. "Sometimes I forget how eccentric you are."

"Well, it helps me think and frankly I need any inspiration I can get. There has to be a link between the two deaths and there has to be a link between Peter Delgado and Jack McConnell. I just can't think of any other reason why someone would move Delgado's body."

Mary pulled at her husband's arm again to get him to move, but he remained rooted to the ground, his eyes still fixed on the spot where the stone had broken the surface of the water.

"I told Hunter it is possible the person deliberately put the body on the first green because they wanted Jack McConnell to find it. It's the only way moving the body would make sense."

"But doesn't that suggest murder? And whoever moved the body couldn't be sure Jack McConnell would find it?" Mary said, still tugging on Napoleon's arm. This time he took the hint and they continued walking. A King Charles Spaniel bounded past them followed much more slowly by an old Labrador and his even older owner.

"For goodness' sake, Robert," Mary said. She was starting to lose patience with her listless husband. "Even that old man and his pensioner of a dog are walking faster than you. Come on, or we'll never finish this walk."

"But you see, that's just it," Napoleon said, speeding up a little. "Jack was bound to find the body because he's always the first to tee off on a Thursday morning. It's a routine, one that he has stuck to for years and one that every member of the golf club knows and jokes about."

"So, that's why you think there must be a link between Jack and the dead man. Did Jack know the dead man, then?"

"That's the problem with my theory. Jack didn't know Delgado. It was just a body to him, not pleasant to find, but just a body. If it had been somebody he had known, been close to, then it might explain why the body was moved there, to upset him, to hurt him. Jack was also very calm, unusually so for someone who had just found a dead man, according to Rankin's notes."

Napoleon went quiet for a while. Mary remained quiet too, not wanting to disturb him. She could tell he was thinking something through. "I don't believe Jack's coolness is particularly relevant," Napoleon said at last. "It's just in his nature. It's like when he plays golf. He's always calm and in control. He laughs a lot and he's very loud, but he keeps his emotions in check. I think that's why he's such a good golfer. He has the right, nerveless temperament. Jack's just a naturally cool customer."

"I'm sure you're right," Mary said dutifully, realising her husband was talking more to himself than her, which he tended to do, particularly when engrossed in a complicated case.

They caught up with the old Labrador and its ancient owner, the spaniel was sniffing around a large willow tree in the distance, as the path narrowed, and the river became more remote. The crashing, rushing hum of the waterfall, which was now barely audible, was no longer providing the background music. Only occasional bird song broke up the gentle sound of flowing water.

"Maybe it was mistaken identity," Mary said suddenly. "Maybe whoever knocked down Peter Delgado thought he was someone else or maybe they thought Jack did know him."

"That's possible," Napoleon said, nodding earnestly.

"But Rob, that's unlikely. Surely Peter Delgado's brother is your main suspect if you think it was a deliberate act?" Mary said.

"Yes. We need to talk to him urgently. He's not back from Spain until tomorrow, but if he was responsible, why did he move the body, unless he thought it might confuse things. Yet even that doesn't make sense. If the body had been left in the road, then we would have thought it was careless driving. He had nothing to gain by moving it."

Mary shook her head. "It is very odd, but you'll get to the bottom of it. You always do."

Napoleon smiled at her thinly. "Yes, maybe," he said, but his words were drowned out by an old freight train, thumping past on the nearby railway track. He wished he had his wife's confidence.

After about 10 minutes, they came to a sharp bend in the river, which brought them face to face with a fierce south-west wind.

"That's cold," Mary said.

"Cold but invigorating," Napoleon replied. For no obvious reason, it was here that some of his most intuitive thoughts had come to him, or so it seemed. Nothing sprang from the murky recesses of his mind today, but the scenery was doing wonders for a policeman in need of inspiration.

"Quite a view," Napoleon said, digesting the picture postcard setting on the other side of the river. A row of cottages sat halfway up a slope. They were thatched and built of local brick, which helped them blend into the landscape. The scene was enhanced by a bright, powerful sun. Its radiance brought out to the full the variegated autumnal colours of the trees, with their yellow, red, and browning leaves, which framed everything in a feel-good glow.

They carried on walking, wrapped up in their own thoughts, until they reached an arch bridge, where they sat down on a rickety wooden bench. This was the most secluded part of the river, just before its discreet arrival into the neighbouring village, and the Napoleons' favourite spot. Napoleon thought of the arch bridge as his own special place. There was no sign of anyone here. The colourful little boats and elegant swans that gave the river its more sophisticated character nearer the bigger town were gone. Just a few broken branches and a lonesome duck bobbled on its surface. The banks were also overgrown with weeds and stinging nettles. There was no park keeper to mow and manicure them this far away from the town. The river had taken on a wild appearance and the birds seemed to sing more loudly here.

"What do you think of Jack McConnell?" Napoleon said, finally breaking the silence. He knew his wife didn't like McConnell, but he wanted to hear her thoughts again.

"McConnell," Mary screwed up her eyes. "Not much."

"I like him," Napoleon said.

"You would Robert. You're a man. His bravado and chumminess would appeal to you. All boys together while you have a laugh over a pint. He's charming, funny and a bit of lark but he's also untrustworthy, unprincipled and a bully. Look at the way he treats his wife."

"His wife?"

Mary shook her head. "Why do men go around with their heads in the clouds? We've lived in the same road as them for years and you haven't noticed the way Jack treats his wife. And his son, for that matter."

"I've noticed she has a drinking problem," Napoleon said defensively. He stood up to get a better view of a noisy blackbird perched in one of the trees.

It was belting out a tune not too dissimilar to a high-pitched machine gun. It sounded like an alarm call, although Napoleon could see no sign of predators.

"And why do you think she has a drinking problem?" Mary said.

"You can't blame it all on Jack."

"No, you can't, but he's not helped. Jo may be a weak person, but I often wonder how strong you or I would be without the support of the other. If you kept undermining and belittling me like Jack does with Jo, my self-esteem would suffer too. If the main person in your life, who you see every day, makes it clear his opinion of you is extremely low, it would be debilitating."

"How do you know Jack belittles his wife?" Napoleon said, sitting back down on the bench.

"Jo and I have coffee together sometimes. She tells me what he says. She stays with Jack out of duty. I admire that, although I think it's misplaced. Jack takes no interest in her, except to bully her when he's in a bad mood."

Napoleon nodded. "Jack did tell me once that when the romance was over, so was the marriage."

"That's typical of Jack. When the real work starts, he's had enough."

"Work!" Napoleon was amused.

"You have to work at marriage, don't you? It's hard work, especially with children. When the romance is over, that's the real test of the marriage. That's obvious, but people like Jack miss that point or are too selfish to want to understand it. When the romance was over, Jack was off with some other woman."

"How do you know?"

"I don't know for sure, but he's had a lot of affairs. He's having one with his personal assistant."

"Is that true? I didn't know that."

"For a policeman, you don't notice much, Robert."

"Who Jack McConnell is bedding, isn't police business. His wife should leave him, if he's as bad as you say."

"Misplaced duty, as I said."

"But if Jack's had all those affairs and is in the middle of one now, his wife could get a divorce and a good settlement," Napoleon said.

"It's not that easy for someone to walk out, someone brought up to believe strongly in the institution of marriage, someone who has lost all her confidence, who, for that reason, is too frightened to leave her husband. He does at least provide security with his money and house."

"Yes." Napoleon shivered. A large cloud had blotted out the sun and the bright blue sky of only moments ago had turned moody and grey. "Shall we get back, it's getting cold?"

"Okay. It does look like it might rain." Mary brushed away a couple of leaves that had fallen on to her skirt and slowly lifted herself off the bench. Napoleon watched her and then got up too. "He's not helped that son of his, John, either," Mary said as they began the walk back. "Jack is so competitive, he's ruined the boy. You're far more relaxed. You never put pressure on the children and nor did I. Jack wanted John to be the best but never put the effort in to try and help him meet his expectations. John rebelled and his mother turned to drink, a rebellion in itself."

"But, what about Joanne? She's John's mother. She had a part to play too. You can't blame everything on Jack."

"She kept herself together while John was growing up, gave him security and stability. But when a father treats a mother like dirt, maybe a child begins to believe his mother is dirt, and that has undermined Jo's relationship with John."

Mary paused for a moment, then added: "Jack is happy with his golf, his deals and his girlfriends. His life is just fine, but his wife and son – his family – it doesn't matter to him what their lives are like."

"But Jack's not entirely responsible for Jo and John's lives," Napoleon said. "They have choices too."

"But Jack doesn't care, Rob. Whether Jack is all to blame, or whether Jo and John are partly responsible, is irrelevant. Jack doesn't care about anyone except Jack. He doesn't even care about his only son. Jo told me that when John was trying to get

into the parachute regiment, Jack thought it would do him good.
He said if he got himself killed at least it was something
constructive, not like nicking a car and getting killed in a police
chase. It was supposed to be a joke, but Jo said Jack half meant
it. If John died tomorrow, I don't think it would bother Jack too
much. Sometimes I think he's quite evil. At the very least, there's
a coldness and a lack of empathy for other people, despite all his
laughter and bonhomie."

Napoleon sighed, then shrugged, noticing the pretty cottages
as they passed them again. The doors and windowsills on each of
them were painted a bright blue. Perhaps they were colour co-
ordinated inside too. "Jack's not evil and John's death would
bother him," he finally said, turning his attention back to Mary.
"You're getting everything out of perspective because you've
always disliked loud, over-confident men, which Jack typifies."

"I don't have any problem with loud and over-confident men.
I have a problem with sexist and inconsiderate men, particularly
one who has no empathy or compassion or pity," Mary said. "He
has no sense of feeling for other people. Compassion is what sets
us apart from animals and it's missing in Jack. That gives him a
capacity for evil. You must have seen it in your job."

"Yes, I've seen evil as you put it, but if Jack's evil, he
hides it very well."

"And that makes him worse. If he didn't hide his wicked
nature so well and wasn't so calculating and devious, then perhaps
I could accept your view of him as some kind of harmless,
machismo man, who just wanted a fun time with his mates.
But, Robert, he isn't harmless. He is malevolent," Mary said
fiercely. She wasn't going to back down or compromise her
opinion on Jack.

Napoleon smiled wryly and shook his head. He had only asked
Mary her thoughts on McConnell as an afterthought. He hadn't
expected such a full and relentless character assassination.

After another 20 minutes, they were nearly home.

"Can we take a wander to the first green?" Napoleon said. "I
want to show you where the body was found."

"Sure." They turned into Crookham Lane and passed the
McConnells' house. Everything about it looked perfect from the
outside, from the green, manicured lawn to the neat driveway and

immaculate Tudor entrance. Napoleon had always been secretly envious of Jack's wealth, but perhaps not anymore after what Mary had told him. They reached the alleyway that led to the back of the first green. Napoleon ducked under a blue and white police cordon draped across its entrance.

The alleyway was overgrown with rhododendrons and smelt of old wood. "This is where the body would have been carried, which wouldn't have been easy," Napoleon said. "It's very cramped. The green keeper deliberately keeps it this way to discourage people from walking on to the course."

"It's very dark," Mary said as they emerged from the tunnel of rhododendrons into the wood behind the green. "It's quite spooky."

"There's a lot of trees. It's not a place you'd want to hit a golf ball, although I always seem to hit mine here." Napoleon shrugged at his misfortune. "Come on," he said, and they scrunched through the undergrowth, making their way to the edge of the green, where a golfer was about to putt. "We'd better stop here. We don't want to disturb him," Napoleon said, coming to a halt by a large tree. As they waited for the man to finish his shot, the inspector pulled a small plastic bag with a piece of paper inside it out of his pocket. "We found this scrap of paper in the bushes just here," he said quietly.

"And you've kept it," Mary said, taking a closer look.

"It could be significant, and it reminded me of an old teacher of mine."

The piece of paper had a small circle drawn on it with the words 'Round Tuit' written inside.

"How odd," Mary said.

"Yes. Odd, but interesting. I had a teacher when I was at Wellesley Primary School, who used to write notes on the blackboard just like this. It was supposed to remind people to do their homework, 'get round to it'. It never worked. You know what kids are like. We just thought he was mad."

"So, the teacher is the killer or maybe it belonged to the dead man. Did he go to Wellesley Primary School?" Mary asked.

"Good question. Yes, the dead man did go to Wellesley Primary School, but not while the teacher was there. The teacher died in 1995, when the dead man was two years old. So, it wasn't the teacher's either," Napoleon said.

"But you think the killer might have gone to Wellesley Primary School," Mary said. "And they picked up the habit of writing bizarre notes to themselves from the eccentric teacher."

Napoleon smiled lopsidedly. "Yes. The only trouble is a lot of people in the town went to Wellesley Primary School when that teacher was there, if indeed they did copy his habits. He taught at the school for more than 30 years. And it could have easily been dropped by an innocent golfer and have no significance. Jack McConnell had no recollection of the teacher or his funny notes when I mentioned it at the golf club yesterday, and he was at Wellesley Primary School a few years before me. Forensic couldn't find any traces of fingerprints or DNA on it, either, probably degraded because of the weather."

Napoleon shrugged his shoulders and moved towards the green as the golfer had finished his putt and was making his way to the next hole. "Come on, I'll show you exactly where the body was found," he said.

Mary watched her husband stride purposefully towards the green with the energy and excitement of a teenager. He was so wrapped up in this investigation. He was like he was when he first joined the police force, determined, and focused entirely on the job. She was sure he would eventually find the truth. She hoped it would be soon. He might be a terrific detective, but he was hell to live with when he was involved in a difficult case.

CHAPTER 26

◆

Charlie took a large bite out of a thick beef and mayonnaise sandwich. A quiet corner in the canteen of the council offices had narrowly edged out the pub as a lunch option. He needed a clear head to mull Jack McConnell's offer of £10,000 to support his leisure centre plan for Wellesley Primary School.

Euphoria at being handed a badly needed financial pick-me-up had turned into an uneasiness over whether he might get caught. He had also discovered, albeit late in life, that he genuinely had a conscience. Bribery was wrong and he shouldn't accept the money. But £10,000 was a lot for someone on his salary and his finances were a mess with bills and debts he was struggling to pay. This had created the simple dilemma he was now puzzling over: Should he help McConnell or not? Did the prospect of enough money to pay off his credit cards and book a decent holiday make it worth the risk? Could he compromise his conscience and enjoy the windfall? He wiped some mayonnaise, which had oozed from the side of his mouth, off his chin with a napkin and watched an express train hurtle past the council offices at full tilt. No signal failures today.

The canteen was six floors up and this spot by the window was his favourite place for contemplation. It offered a perfect view of the Berkshire and Oxfordshire Downs - green fields and farmland that stretched for miles and was only broken up by the railway track and the occasional road.

Charlie pondered McConnell's bribe once again. It was not a big crime, but it was wrong, and he would have to live with a decision that might haunt him later. He wasn't like McConnell. He didn't have that swaggering confidence and belief that he was untouchable. There could be negative consequences, getting caught the most obvious. McConnell would also have something over him. Was this the slippery slope? Would McConnell want to bribe him again? He might have no choice but to accept the next time. Would he forever have to do McConnell's bidding?

He sighed. He was only 32, but this was surely what they called a mid-life crisis. Another train whizzed by, rushing into the distance. Charlie followed its path enviously. It had no feelings, no heart, but it had a destination. It knew where it was going. He took another bite of his sandwich, but the taste of the beef and bread made little impression. With the amount he drank, this probably was mid-life, cirrhosis, and premature death in his early sixties a high probability. He put the sandwich down, half finished, as a wave of despondency washed over him.

He was always tired and often depressed, yet he couldn't quite pinpoint the reasons why. The Save Our School campaign rankled and so had Peter Delgado, who had signed the petition to stop the school from being demolished, despite his position as a planning officer. But it was just one of a number of things that chipped away at his confidence and self-worth. At moments like this, he felt like a man gradually slipping into a black hole of despair. A lack of money and a lack of prospects to earn more were largely responsible for his low spirits, but more fundamentally there lurked a terrible, dawning realisation that this was it, that he would never go much higher in his career or do anything of significance in his life.

He also sensed that his wife no longer loved him, probably because he drank too much and was moody, unreasonable and sometimes aggressive. Yet he couldn't stop drinking or break out of the moods that hung over him like some malevolent cloud. He simply wasn't the man he wanted to be – a confident, wealthy success story.

His thoughts turned to Peter Delgado's death, which had naturally upset him. It was a tragedy, but he wasn't grieving. Guilt was probably a better description for the way he felt. His last conversation with the man had been unpleasant, an argument over Peter's refusal to withdraw his name from the save the school petition. He had never really got on with Peter. He was righteous and talked about his religion and church all the time, something Charlie, a committed atheist, found deeply annoying. But still, he could have been kinder towards his subordinate, who was a hard and conscientious worker. This, he was only now fully appreciating, as jobs and paperwork mounted in the office that Peter would have quickly and efficiently dealt with had he been alive.

Charlie stood up and stretched the kinks out of his legs and spine from sitting in one position a fraction too long. The canteen was filling up as the height of lunch hour approached and he didn't feel like making small talk with colleagues whose names he could barely remember. That was the problem with eating in the canteen. There were too many people who knew him just well enough to make sitting at another table appear rude, which meant laboured small talk with a person who was in effect one step away from being a total stranger. He also couldn't face another depressing conversation about Peter's death. It was sad, he was so young, his poor family would be devastated. These were the obvious and trite statements he had repeated more times than he cared to remember.

He put his tray and half eaten sandwich on the canteen conveyer belt for dirty plates and unfinished food and decided to go to the pub. He always seemed to end up in the pub, even today when he supposedly wanted a completely clear head to think. The pub by the council offices was a drab little watering hole, but it was near and had a decent selection of lagers and real ales. Even better, no one from the council offices went there. They tended to go to the prettier and more homely pub on the opposite side of the precinct.

He ordered a lager at the bar. He had a hankering for something light and fizzy, in contrast to his mood, and settled into his familiar seat at a table near the entrance. It tasted good and went straight to his head as he had eaten little, a cup of tea for breakfast and only the half-eaten sandwich at lunch. The beer made him feel better and more relaxed almost immediately. The demons were still there, but the drink had temporarily side-lined them. The walk to the pub had also helped him reach his decision over the bribe. The cool breeze and bright sun had cleared his head of doubts. He had finally convinced his conscience that it would do no harm to take the money, which was in the broad scheme of things a relatively small amount.

More importantly, he had reassured himself no one would find out - and that it wasn't stealing. It was McConnell's money, to do with in the way he wished. The man had pots of the stuff, so he might as well have some of it. It would be the last time he did anything like this. McConnell wouldn't be able to force him into more bribes as he needed Charlie's discretion. They were locked into a secret pact, which would be equally damaging to both should it become public.

As for Molly, he would tell her he had withdrawn the money from his portfolio of shares. She didn't know they were close to worthless. She would be pleased at the influx of cash, which she wouldn't question.

He sank a second pint and just about crushed a temptation for a third. He wasn't an alcoholic yet, and there was work to be done back at the office.

There was a note on his telephone when he returned. It had been fixed by an engineer, although he wasn't aware it had been broken. The line occasionally crackled, but it always worked. He shut his office door and punched in McConnell's number. McConnell's secretary answered and put him on hold. Some familiar baroque classic played in the background as he waited on the line. He noticed there was still a crackle in the background. The telephone engineer was either completely useless or he had tinnitus.

"Yes, dear boy. So, I take it, we are in business?"

"Yes. £10,000."

"I think that was the sum you mentioned," McConnell said with a chuckle in his voice.

"We have an agreement then," Charlie said abruptly. He felt McConnell was patronising him. Maybe he should have asked for more money.

"Marvellous, marvellous," McConnell said, now sounding genuinely delighted.

"Yes marvellous, thank you," Charlie said seriously.

He put the telephone down before realising he had no idea how McConnell would pay him. He couldn't exactly write a cheque, and an electronic bank transfer would look decidedly suspicious. He punched in McConnell's number again. This was farcical. He wasn't cut out to be a crook.

The same efficient voice answered and put him on hold. The baroque classic, which he still couldn't place, played in the background, again accompanied by the mildly irritating crackle. He could do with another drink, or maybe a change of personality would be better, one that was smooth, efficient and didn't forget to ask the blindingly obvious.

CHAPTER 27

◆

T he thin man was sitting in his usual spot at a stool by the bar. He looked like a character out of a 1940s American detective movie, or film noir, with his long trench coat and trilby hat. Mayo watched him sip his drink, which looked like whisky and ice, and decided the hat was probably a fedora rather than a trilby. The brim was too wide for a trilby. The man had a mysterious, shifty air about him, his eyes constantly on the move as if he were worried someone might be following him.

The sergeant wondered what brand of whisky he was drinking. He favoured beer and wine himself, although he liked a malt whisky on occasions. His reverie was interrupted by a playful slap on the back. He turned and came face to face with the familiar bulbous nose of Tony Carter, an ageing detective constable, whose pugnacious appearance matched his belligerent and cynical personality.

"What are you looking at?" Carter asked, following Mayo's stare and scanning the bar.

"I'm not looking at anything and I'll have a lager, thanks," the sergeant said defensively. It was a cliché, but as an American he couldn't get used to the English warm ale. "It's that blonde at the bar, isn't it?" Carter said and winked at Mayo. The sergeant sighed and refrained from answering. Carter grinned and made his way to the bar.

The sergeant moved from his seat at the side of the table to the bench with the wall behind it for a better view of the bar and the thin man, who now seemed to be talking to the blonde woman. Two other police officers walked past his table and headed for the bar where Carter was beckoning them.

Mayo smiled to himself. One of the police officers was Sarah Parsons, a detective constable, who he quite fancied. He also got on very well with her. She was someone he would have asked out for dinner, but it was too much of a risk. He didn't want any embarrassment in the office, if it didn't work out. It was much easier to be friends, without any strings or complications. He watched Parsons and the other detective constable, Barry Williams, give their orders to Carter, who then turned and pointed Mayo's way. Parsons smiled and waved at the sergeant and the two police officers came over to the table, leaving Carter to sort out the drinks at the bar.

The pub, The Wheel of Fortune, was now filling up with office workers. It was a popular place for a drink after work; ideally located on Wellesley high street, only two doors from the police station and near a number of shops and offices, which included a legal practice that specialised in criminal law, a couple of estate agents, a small tech company and the offices of the town's weekly newspaper.

Williams sat down opposite Mayo, and Parsons parked herself next to the sergeant on the bench. It was their usual spot when they came to The Wheel.

"What do you think of Napoleon?" Williams asked Mayo after taking a big slug of his beer. The sergeant sighed. He didn't want to get into some gossipy conversation about his boss. He didn't mind confiding in Parsons, but he didn't know Williams well enough to trust him. "He's a bit moody and difficult to read, but he's pleasant enough," he said, feeling that came close enough to the truth without being unkind or risking some exaggerated and false rumour that he disliked the chief inspector, which could then undermine their relationship.

"He's a grumpy git, you mean," Carter said, sitting down next to Williams with a tray of drinks. "He's a good detective, but he's always pissed off and he doesn't communicate with his team."

Mayo gave Carter a sparing smile and sighed again, regretting his relative candour. He hadn't noticed Carter approaching with the tray of drinks and would have given a blander, more neutral reply had he realised the detective was within earshot. Carter wasn't malicious, but he was a master at the art of spinning gossip and didn't care what he said or who he upset as he was nearing retirement and had never been ambitious in the first place.

The other two police officers remained silent, no doubt thinking similar thoughts to Mayo. Parsons finally filled the void.

"I like him. He's always very nice and pleasant to me. I think he's quite charming."

Carter gave her a pained look. "Well, he would be very nice and pleasant to you, wouldn't he?" he said sarcastically.

"Sorry, Tony, why would he be very nice and pleasant to me?" Parsons said sharply.

"Well, you know?"

"No. I don't know."

"Okay. Sorry," Carter said. "I didn't mean to offend. I was giving you a backhanded compliment. You're very good looking. Any normal man would be nice and pleasant to you."

"Tony, that statement is so wrong on so many counts. We don't live in the stone age anymore, even if you're still a dinosaur."

Everyone laughed, including Carter, which seemed to ease the tension. For all his antagonistic instincts, Carter could always laugh at himself, and this time it seemed to defuse the situation. Parsons shook her head and said no more. There was little point.

Mayo eyed Parsons. Carter's remarks were unprofessional, but there might be some truth in them. Parsons was tall, about his own height, with long, thick dark brown hair and a thin, athlete's body that was still curvy and feminine. She also had darkish skin with deep brown eyes and lots of freckles on her face, which added rather than detracted from her looks. She could have been a model. Napoleon had probably warmed to her because she was intelligent, engaging, and funny, but her looks would have helped too. Any heterosexual man would instinctively be friendly and pleasant to her with those looks. It was just a fact of life, but a fact that was better left unsaid.

As for Napoleon, Carter was right, even if he had been indiscreetly blunt in his assessment. The chief inspector was unpredictable, lugubrious and had a habit of keeping important facts to himself. On the other hand, he was highly thought of for his ability as a detective, as Carter had pointed out, and for his generosity when it came to crediting others for successes and breakthroughs on cases, which Carter had neglected to acknowledge.

Mayo took a swallow of his beer and noticed the thin man again. His expression was curiously intense, suddenly deepening

138

into a frown. The sergeant followed his gaze, which stopped at another man with his share of admirers and detractors. Jack McConnell stood at the entrance of the pub with a young woman on his arm.

"Right," Carter said, finishing his pint. "I'm off." He patted Mayo on the shoulder and winked at Parsons, who ignored him and instead offered to buy the next round. Mayo smiled broadly, pleased she was staying and asked for another lager.

Parsons returned quickly with the drinks, a relief to Mayo as Williams was a struggle when it came to conversation and small talk other than police work. Williams was also clearly more interested in a darts match in the far corner of the pub than making idle chat – his eyes constantly drawn to the game, which involved some of the lawyers from the nearby solicitors.

Parsons sat down in Carter's old seat opposite Mayo and next to Williams. "Go on Barry," she said, noticing his distracted glances at the darts game, too. "Go and play darts. That's what you're itching to do." Williams smiled at her and stood up. He then adjusted his coat and nodded before making his way over to the corner where the lawyers were gathered around the darts board.

Parsons relaxed and took a sip of her drink, a gin and tonic with ice and a slice of lime. "I like Barry, but I'm glad he's gone," she said. "I wanted to discuss something with you before I tell Napoleon. I found this today on St Margaret's Road, near where Peter Delgado was hit. That was where I was this afternoon."

She produced a cassette tape in a small plastic bag. "It's an old tape, like the ones popular in the 1980s, of Beethoven's symphonies. Napoleon asked me to go back to the crime scene on the golf course and follow the route through the passageway by the first green to Crookham Lane and St Margaret's Road, where Delgado was killed, and I found this. It was by the side of the road, very close to where he was hit. It must have been dropped today. We would have found it earlier otherwise. What do you think? Could it be relevant? Napoleon said we've got to use our imagination on this investigation, think creatively, because it's so unusual, so that's what I'm trying to do, with your help."

Mayo laughed. "We're police officers, not Enigma code breakers, but I can give it go." He thought for a moment. He was flattered that Parsons was asking for advice, but at the same time annoyed Napoleon had failed to tell him he had sent her to the crime scene. He also thought the chief inspector was clutching at straws.

"I've no idea whether it's relevant, but I doubt it," the sergeant said. "I'm not sure why Napoleon asked you to go back to the golf course and St Margaret's Road. What did he hope to achieve? That part of the road is no longer cordoned off, so anyone could have walked past there and dropped the tape. Maybe it was Napoleon. He likes Beethoven. I had to listen to Beethoven in his car the other day. But who would still be listening to cassette tapes?"

"It has to be someone quite old," Parsons said. "But you're right. I can't see how it can be relevant to our investigations. I'll tell Napoleon about it tomorrow. He thinks we need to expand our thinking to anything that might be linked to what happened. It's such an unusual investigation. We don't know whether the deaths are linked, whether they're murders or manslaughter and there are no witnesses. Forensics haven't come up with anything, either."

They sipped their drinks in unison.

"What do you think of Napoleon?" Parsons said. "Between you and me, entre nous?"

Mayo took another sip of his lager to give himself time to think. "I like working with him. He has a certain charm, as you said, even if he is grumpy and moody. But I also agree with Carter about his lack of communication. Maybe he'll be more forthcoming as he gets to know the team better."

Parsons nodded. "I think he's an instinctive policeman and can't always explain those instincts or communicate them. Like sending me to the golf course and St Margaret's Road. I asked him why he wanted me to go as the forensic teams had been all over the area with a fine-tooth comb.

That's when he said we need to use our imaginations, but what does that mean? All I've found is a tape of Beethoven, which we both think is irrelevant to the investigation."

She cocked her head to one side and then took a sip of her drink. "Do you remember the Sean Cropper case?" she said. "I'm told Napoleon never really came to terms with not finding the boy or his killer, and I think there's still some blame attached to him over the failure to bring anyone to justice. Carter thinks it's why he's remained a chief inspector. A detective with his abilities should have risen higher."

Most people in the pub were now starting to leave. The Wheel of Fortune was typical of a high street pub early in the week, packed between 5.30pm and 7pm as people sought a quick drink after work before dinner. The thin man joined the exodus, edging towards the door and neatly positioning his hat in a fashionable angle as he did so. He placed a cigarette in the corner of his mouth and flicked up the lapels of his raincoat. Humphrey Bogart, as Dashiell Hammett's private investigator Sam Spade, couldn't have done it with more class, Mayo thought.

"What are you looking at?" Parsons asked.

"Oh, I'm sorry. Nothing in particular. I was just thinking about what you said. Interesting."

Parsons stood up. "Look, I'm sorry, Joe." She looked at her watch. "I've got to go. I didn't realise the time. I want to log this tape with forensics and then I've got to get back home."

"No worries," Mayo said, hiding his disappointment. "I should probably leave too."

He stood up and put on his coat, which he had rested over the chair by the side of the table.

They followed the thin man out of the door and stood on the kerb outside.

Mayo looked in both directions to see if the thin man was still around, but he was gone. Like any decent Bogart-style gumshoe, he had disappeared into the shadows.

He said goodbye to Parsons, who smiled and said they should go for a drink more often. "Yes. Definitely," he said. "Definitely."

She cocked her head to one side, like she had earlier, considering him, and smiled again. He smiled back a little sheepishly. He had sounded far too keen to meet for drinks again. He needed to be cooler in future. "Bye then," she said and walked off up the high street towards the police station.

Mayo sighed again, he had been sighing all night for various reasons, not quite knowing why he was feeling such disappointment at watching the departing back of Parsons, or losing sight of the thin man, a stranger who was merely fascinating because of the tilt of his hat. He patted his jacket pockets to make sure his wallet and mobile phone were in their place, and flicked up the lapels of his own raincoat, in his best Bogart imitation. He sighed one final time and walked down the high street in the opposite direction of Parsons in silent contemplation.

CHAPTER 28

"Are you okay? You look tired," Chloe said casually, trying to hide her alarm. Ray's normally healthy, dark complexion had turned a sickly yellow. He looked shattered. It was going to take time to put the pieces back together after Peter's death. Ray put down his suitcases in the hallway and gave her a weak smile.

"I'm fine. A cup of tea would be nice." He walked slowly into the sitting room and fell on to the large sofa. The trip to Madrid had left him emotionally drained. He had a strained relationship with his family and the death of his older brother had complicated it further.

Chloe returned from the kitchen with a cup of tea and a small plate of biscuits. She gently laid them on a table by the sofa and turned on an overhead lamp. A bright, optimistic morning had faded into a gloomy grey afternoon and the room needed more light.

"I'm afraid the police are likely to turn up this afternoon," she said tentatively. Ray had a short fuse in the best of circumstances. Stress, lack of sleep and a tiring three-hour flight were not the best of circumstances.

"I was half expecting it. Don't worry. I'll tell them the truth, like I did last week when they interviewed us before, and that will be that." he said softly. He was too tired to get angry. Chloe relaxed and stroked his lined face. Peter's death had come at a bad time. The couple were expecting their first child, yet they were both still students. It was going to be a struggle. Chloe sighed and gently patted her pregnant stomach. These were supposed to be the happiest moments of their lives, but everything was so difficult.

Ray watched her and put his hand on her stomach too. He stared at the tiny bulge, which would be his future son or daughter and raised his eyes to Chloe's. "It'll never know its uncle.

I can't believe our child will never meet him. I know I didn't get on with him, but it hurts so much, now he's gone. The stupid, arrogant sod."

"Ray, it's not important that you didn't get on. What's important is that you loved him. You were very different. It's not your fault or his that you didn't see eye to eye on many things. But if he could see how much you cared about him, how upset you are now, that would make him happy." Was happy the right word? She was not sure. Peter rarely seemed happy. But at least he would know how much his brother loved him.

"Yes, but why didn't we at least try to understand each other? You don't necessarily have to be similar to get on with someone. Why didn't I try harder? And why was I so horrible to him on that last night? I just wish…" Ray's words trailed off and he let his head fall back on to the top of the sofa in a state of frustrated resignation over what he couldn't change.

Chloe stroked his face again. "Sometimes opposite personalities can complement each other, but with you two the differences just caused friction. I think it was because neither of you wanted to understand the other. You were just too different and too stubborn. Pig-headedness, that's something you shared. But we've got to look forward. I know it's going to be hard, but let's try to think about the baby and be positive."

Ray looked into Chloe's eyes again. He smiled. She was right. They had to be practical and think of the future. The facts were hard, but they had to be faced. He and his brother were opposites and now Peter was dead. Nothing could be altered.

He had to recognise Peter was his father's son - serious, idealistic, and motivated by his religion, something he had struggled to accept while his brother was alive. He hated his father's influence over Peter. Perhaps an accident of birth explained this hold and the brothers' differences. Peter was born in Spain where he had lived for the first four years of his life, while Ray, seven years younger at 21, had arrived after their parents had moved to Wellesley to take up lecturing posts at Redfield University.

Peter saw himself as a Spaniard and a Catholic, like his father, while Ray considered himself English. He was also an atheist, who preferred swapping bad jokes and discussing football to the religious debates Peter enjoyed.

Religion, humour, and this cultural and intellectual divide were difficult to bridge and explained their fractured relationship, which had almost completely broken down since he and Chloe had started living together. Peter disapproved because they weren't married and, more importantly, because it would upset their Spanish father with his strict Catholic beliefs. Their mother would disapprove too, but she was English, having met her husband while studying in Spain, and could relate more easily with her youngest son.

The brothers had barely spoken to each other for close to a year, but when Chloe became pregnant Ray decided it was time to invite Peter to dinner. He would have to tell him of the news. Even if it ended in the usual row, his brother would have to know. He wasn't ashamed that he wasn't married, and his child would be born out of wedlock. Marriage was an old-fashioned institution and meaningless as far as Ray was concerned.

Peter would have to understand that he would live his life his way. Part of him hoped his brother would refuse the invitation, delaying what could be a messy scene, but he didn't, and it was later that night that he died.

Ray told him about the baby as they settled down to eat. Peter wanted to be pleased. He had guessed Chloe might be pregnant as she had put on a little weight and he knew his brother was making an effort, but still he couldn't conceal his disappointment that the child had been conceived out of wedlock and would be born a bastard. His father and the family would struggle to come to terms with such a bombshell.

Ray could not hide his exasperation at what he saw as his brother's hypocrisy. "Remember you were conceived before our parents were married. Most children are these days. It's not a big deal," Ray had said. It was something he had never mentioned until then – and the effect was like pressing a detonator.

Peter's anger had been frightening. "Can't you see? That is why it is such a big issue for our parents and particularly for our father," he had said. "He does not want to see his sons make the same mistakes as he did." Peter had stood up abruptly, pushed his chair aside and left, snatching his coat off a hat stand in the hallway as he went.

Chloe couldn't believe what she was hearing. "Peter was really conceived out of wedlock? But your parents! They're so strict. Why didn't you tell me?"

Ray sighed. "I'm sorry, but some things you keep to yourself. I suppose I didn't tell you out of respect to the family. I shouldn't have blurted it out, but even so. All that guilt, all that suppressed regret. Suppressed because of a stupid religion, made up by a few zealots 2,000 years ago. I don't see why we have to live by my parents' rules. It's not as if Peter's a bastard. He wasn't born out of wedlock, just conceived out of wedlock. I've never understood the fuss. Maybe it's because I was born in protestant England where religion is mostly for cranks and old people."

Chloe poured some mineral water into her glass and then took a sip. "I think I understand your brother a little more now. You must go and find him and make sure he's all right. I've never seen him like that. So utterly furious. He could do something silly. To himself."

"Yes, you're right." Ray stood up. "I'm glad it's done, though. We had to tell him about the baby. He was never going to like it. We can get on with things now and not worry about Peter, or the family. He'll tell them. He tells them everything. They'll have to decide whether to accept it or not. I don't think I really care anymore what they think."

Chloe clutched Ray's hand. "Try to be gentle with Peter. He's very like your father. Remember, they're both good people, principled people. They just find it difficult to compromise over their beliefs."

"They find it difficult to live in the real world, you mean."

"Your world Ray, not theirs. We're not all the same."

"Yes, I know." He smiled and left. It was 8.25pm. Chloe noticed the clock on the wall as she watched Ray pull away in his car. He didn't return until 12.30 in the morning. He couldn't find his brother and had driven to the university library in Redfield. In truth, he hadn't searched that hard for Peter. He had slowly driven to his brother's flat near the town centre, searching the roads. But when he had reached the flat, he couldn't face getting out of his car to see if he was home, instead driving on to the university. For him, the matter was over. There was nothing more to say. Another confrontation would have probably caused more damage. Their differences were irreconcilable.

Chloe had spent the rest of the evening worrying about Peter and wondering what had happened to Ray. Why did Ray always leave his mobile at home?

Six days had gone by and she was worried for different reasons now. She believed Ray hadn't seen Peter and had gone to the library, but would the chief inspector, who had called earlier? There was a knock on the door. With effort Ray sat forward, still looking tired and dazed.

"I'll get it," Chloe said. "It's probably the police."

CHAPTER 29

◆

The young woman who opened the door was no more than 20 years old. Napoleon noticed the convex, outward curve of her stomach on an otherwise thin frame. To his experienced eye, he guessed she was about six months pregnant. She was nervous and looked tired. "Come this way," she said.

She showed the inspector and Mayo through the hallway to the living room, where a morose young man, who was barely older than her, lay sprawled on a sofa. Mayo had told Napoleon that Ray Delgado and his girlfriend Chloe rented the house, an elegant Edwardian semi, with another student lodger, who was due to return soon from a three-month back-packing trip abroad.

"Ray, the police are here," Chloe said.

"Hello Mr Delgado, I'm Chief Inspector Napoleon." The inspector sat down in an armchair opposite Delgado. "I'm leading the investigation into your brother's death. This is Sergeant Mayo. I think you met him last week." Mayo sat down in another armchair, next to Napoleon's. Delgado nodded.

"You're probably aware that the policeman who was previously in charge of the investigation was killed last week. He was the officer you gave your statement to. It means I must ask you some questions that you've already answered." Delgado nodded again. Napoleon glanced briefly at Mayo, who had his notebook open, and then back to Delgado.

"Please don't take these questions personally, Mr Delgado. They have to be asked."

Delgado and the young woman, who had sat down next to her boyfriend on the sofa, both nodded this time.

"Where were you on the night your brother died?"

Delgado reached out and held his girlfriend's hand: "I left the house around 8.30 in the evening. I was trying to find my brother. We had just had a row here over dinner. He'd left in a temper and Chloe suggested I look for him. I took the car and drove around for a bit but couldn't find him, so I drove to the university library in Redfield instead. I am studying there, so is Chloe. It's where we met. Anyway, I suppose I should have driven back home, but I felt like a drive to clear my head."

Napoleon went to ask another question, but Delgado interrupted him. "Look, inspector, I would really like some questions answered myself, like how my brother died. The police told us last week he suffered severe head injuries, but from what, a fight? You told us it was too early to give out any information last week, but you must know something by now?"

Napoleon straightened his tie. "This information has been withheld from the press, so you must be discreet, but it seems your brother sustained his head injuries after being knocked down by a car."

"But he was found on the golf course? How could he have been hit by a car?"

"That's what we are trying to find out."

"Could a car get on to the golf course?"

"We think your brother was knocked down elsewhere and moved."

"But why?"

"We don't know," Napoleon said. "So, you drove to Redfield and went to the university library. How long were you there and what did you do in the library?"

Delgado paused and pushed his hands through his thick, dark hair. "I was there until about midnight. It stays open late on Wednesdays. I tried to find a book I needed for one of my essays, but I couldn't, so I read some sports reports in the newspapers. I was too tense to concentrate on proper study. The sports pages were a good distraction."

"Did you speak to anyone or see anyone who knows you?"

"No. There were a lot of students there, but nobody I knew. I didn't speak to anyone. I found a quiet corner and kept myself to myself. I don't have an alibi, if that's what you're getting at."

"What sports reports did you read?" Napoleon said.

Delgado thought for a moment. "I read a match report on Chelsea. They won. I read a piece on that manager who quit, some rugby. All kinds of things."

"Hmm," Napoleon said. "Chelsea did win, but you could have read the newspapers any time before then. Maybe in the morning over breakfast."

"Except, I didn't," Delgado said indignantly.

"You said you drove around for a bit. How long for and where did you go before you drove to the library?" Napoleon watched Mayo flick over a page in his notebook as he spoke.

"You think I might have run my brother over?"

"Ray," the young woman said. "They don't and you didn't. Don't be silly."

"Well, that's where it seems to be leading. Inspector, I don't know what happened to my brother. I'm tired and confused and everything seems to have gone wrong. Not only have I lost my brother, but not knowing what happened to him on that last night is very difficult to come to terms with. I appreciate you've got your job to do, but this just seems absurd. Your colleague here asked me all these questions last week."

"I'm sorry Mr Delgado, but I have to ask them again."

Delgado looked at his girlfriend and turned back to the inspector. "Okay," he sighed. "I didn't drive around for very long. I went to Peter's flat by the river, near the high street, but there was no sign of him. Then, I drove to the university."

"Did you get out of the car?"

"No, I didn't. I thought about knocking on Peter's door, but I didn't. I drove to the university, instead. As I said, I wanted to clear my head and it's a nice drive to the university."

Napoleon nodded. The police had searched Peter Delgado's flat and interviewed his neighbours, who said they hadn't heard him return home that evening or heard anyone call for him.

"What time did you get to the university?" the inspector said.

"About 9pm."

"And you read the sports pages for three hours?"

"I wasn't reading all the time. I tried to read some books first as I said, then I had a cup of coffee and did some thinking. I also searched around in the history section, but I couldn't find the book I was looking for, so I found some newspapers instead. I took a long time reading them. I was distracted, thinking about the argument with my brother. It made it difficult to focus, even on a basic thing like a football report."

"What was the argument with your brother about?" Napoleon said, straightening his tie again.

"Do we have to go into this?" Delgado said, exasperated.

"Yes. I'm afraid we do."

"This is so intrusive."

"Please answer, sir." Napoleon frowned as if he was finding asking the questions equally difficult.

Delgado looked at his girlfriend and gripped her hand tightly. "Chloe is expecting a baby. I told my brother the news last Wednesday over dinner. It's starting to become obvious that Chloe is pregnant." His eyes rested on her small bump. "I couldn't delay telling my brother for much longer. He told us we should get married now a child is on the way, but we're not and he got very upset and angry. I knew he would, which is why I held off telling him about the child. He was a staunch Catholic, but I'm not and neither is Chloe. We don't see the need to get married."

"I see. Was your relationship strained before this argument?" Napoleon said. He kept his tone disinterested.

Delgado turned and looked at his girlfriend again. "Yes. I'm not religious. He was. He didn't approve of us living together without being married either. He was a very serious person, who felt very passionately about his religion, like our father. I'm not like that. I'd rather have my teeth pulled than discuss God, which is, was, my brother's favourite subject. We were very different, inspector. We had many rows, but our arguments were just family squabbles. I didn't kill my brother."

"Right. So, you left here at 8.30 and arrived home at what time?"

"I suppose it must have been about 12.30 in the morning. It's about a 15 minute drive from the university, but I was driving slowly."

Napoleon turned to the young woman. "And you can confirm this, miss?"

"Yes. I was here. The boys argued. Peter stormed out. I suggested to Ray that he look for him. It was 8.25 in fact when he left. I noticed the clock on the wall," her eyes drifted above Napoleon's head to where a clock was, "as he drove away, and he returned home at about half past midnight."

"Were you expecting him to go to the university?"

She looked at Delgado and he nodded. "No, I wasn't. I was annoyed with him for staying out so late and not taking his mobile. I told him I was cross when he got back, but he was upset, so I didn't make a big thing of it."

"He was upset," Napoleon said. "More than you would have expected after an argument?"

"Look," Delgado sat up sharply. "I was upset after an argument with my brother. That's all."

"Calm down, sir," Mayo intervened. "We are trying to establish some facts and it will be much easier if you stay calm."

"You're trying to say I killed my brother," Delgado said, ignoring Mayo's advice.

"Don't be silly," the young woman said. "Ray, we know you didn't."

"We do, but they don't."

"Okay, sir," Napoleon said. "I think that is enough questions for today. Can you please inform us if you want to leave the country again. We will also inform you of any further developments."

He stood up and Mayo followed, closing his notebook as he did so.

"Delgado's story has remained consistent," Mayo said as they walked back to the car. "He was much calmer when we spoke to him last week. I think his brother's death is finally hitting him. But he doesn't seem like a murderer."

"Some murderers don't," Napoleon said, opening the driver's door. "We need to speak to Peter Delgado's work colleagues, and we need to find John McConnell."

The inspector started the car and turned on Beethoven. Mayo smiled to himself. He was beginning to enjoy the dramatic openings of the symphonies. Napoleon had agreed the Beethoven tape Parsons had found was probably irrelevant to the case, but it had seemed to disconcert him and he was listening to the symphonies at every opportunity. They really were very good, Mayo thought, as the music boomed. He would definitely add some of the composer's stuff to his own playlist.

CHAPTER 30

N apoleon and Mayo stood dripping inside the entrance of the council offices. It was raining heavily and neither of them had an umbrella. Mayo pulled a handkerchief out of his pocket. He wiped his face and then knelt down to clean his mud-spattered shoes, while Napoleon restricted himself to a good shake, spraying raindrops everywhere.

The offices of the district council were situated on a self-contained complex just outside Wellesley on the road to Kingham. It was a modern site with a big car park, a few shops and two pubs. It had all the conveniences but lacked character, just a group of dull buildings, mainly filled with office workers. Any trace of colour in the neat little bushes and greenery that lined the walkways had been blotted out by a black, miserable sky, while the buildings had turned a darker and even more depressing shade of grey by the incessant rain.

Napoleon, feeling as overcast as the weather, stared down at Mayo, who couldn't resist one more wipe of his smart shoes, which were starting to shine again. "You care too much about your appearance," the chief inspector remarked.

"They're new. I don't want them ruined," Mayo protested.

"All your clothes are new. And why do you have to wear that hat?"

"It is raining," Mayo said indignantly. He loved his hat, an expensive fedora he had bought at a shop on Wellesley High Street that very morning because of the rain. "England must be the wettest place on earth. I should have got a job with the Italian Carabinieri."

"They're part of the army, not policemen," Napoleon said.

"They serve as policemen," Mayo corrected him.

They continued bickering over clothes and the weather as they followed a receptionist, who had offered to show them the way to the lifts. The corridors were wide and long and soulless, despite an attempt to brighten them with exotic plants and colourful wall prints. It was a depressing place, Napoleon thought, as Mayo droned on about the importance of appearance and the general inadequacies of the English climate. Wellesley police station was old, cramped and untidy, but it had a big heart. This place was clinically dead.

They eventually reached the lifts and the receptionist told them to take one to the fifth floor. As they waited, the mirrors on the closed elevator doors reflected their images, capturing in a small way their different personalities. Mayo looked straight into the glass, took his hat off, and flicked his wispy hair into place - a slightly vain and carefree young man with a modern outlook on clothes and style. Napoleon stood a couple of paces behind him, fiddling with his notebook and fountain pen. He was past caring about the wave in his hair or the shine in his shoe. He looked preoccupied and troubled.

A lift presently arrived and quickly and efficiently carried them to the fifth floor, where Charlie Dean had an office. An equally expeditious secretary met them as the lift doors opened, took their raincoats and Mayo's hat, and showed them the way to Dean's office.

Dean was leaning back in his chair and staring out of the office window. He shifted his gaze to the policemen as they entered the room, sitting up straight as he did so. Napoleon recognised him immediately. He remembered the newspaper report of Henry Llewellyn, where he had seen a picture of Dean in a piece about the actor and the planned closure of Wellesley Primary School. In the flesh, he was even more similar in appearance to Llewellyn, perhaps not quite as good looking. But they could easily be mistaken for one another. In fact, Napoleon wasn't sure whether he had seen Dean many times around town or Llewellyn, or both. Like most residents of Wellesley, Napoleon knew all about Llewellyn, the famous actor. He knew very little of Charlie Dean.

Dean assessed the policemen for a long moment before offering them a seat. Mayo took one, but Napoleon remained standing. The chief inspector's manner was cool and aloof, as he normally was during an official interview. Mayo, still getting used to the quirks of his new boss, wondered if his decision to play the bad cop was a conscious one.

The sergeant smiled to himself, politely making the introductions and opening the questioning in an easy, friendly manner. He was more comfortable being the good cop. Napoleon disinterestedly turned to look out of the window and began twirling his pen around his fingers, a habit he had picked up from Carter, although his technique was amateurish in comparison. Dean followed the pen acrobatics with an amused eye and answered Mayo's questions economically. He was not close to the dead man. Yes, Delgado had worked on the day of his death. No, he did not appear to be worried about anything. Yes, he was a good worker.

A tall woman came into the office with three cups of coffee, although no one had asked for any, and said it was terrible about poor Peter. She admired Mayo's suit and moaned about the rain, which was lashing hard against the windows. Dean sighed theatrically and drummed his fingers on the desk. The tall woman smiled at him affectionately and left, still moaning about the rain.

They sipped their coffee and Mayo asked Dean if he knew Delgado's brother. Napoleon seemed to take an interest in this question and finally sat down next to the sergeant, following Dean's answer, which was in the negative, closely.

Napoleon took another sip of his coffee, which was pleasantly strong and bitter, and asked his first question. "You said you weren't close to Peter Delgado, but are you aware of any interests he might have had outside work?"

"Not really. You should ask his brother."

"We have. He went to church regularly and he was a good footballer, but I thought you might know something else. Did you ever drink with him at lunchtime or after work, or do you know of anyone here who did?" Napoleon's manner remained cool, although Dean didn't appear to notice.

"He liked a drink, but we never went to the pub together or anything like that. We really weren't close at all and I don't know if anyone else from work saw him socially. Sorry," Dean said equably.

"Hmm." Napoleon scratched his chin and glanced at Mayo, who shrugged his shoulders.

"He had a lot of friends in the area, old school friends I think," Dean said without prompting. "He came from somewhere around here and he was quite a sociable person. Carol, the woman who fetched the coffee, might be able to give you some names. She liked Peter and they chatted a lot."

"Thank you," Napoleon said, with the first hint of warmth in his voice. He sounded genuinely appreciative.

Dean smiled. "No problem," he said and opened up further. "You'll hear this from Carol, so I might as well tell you. He was a member of that save the school group. I wasn't happy about it. He wasn't technically doing anything wrong, but I felt it was unprofessional and it could have led to complications, a potential conflict of interests. If one of the developers found out, they could have made a big thing of it."

"Hmm. Yes, I suspect they could," Napoleon said. "When did you last see Mr Delgado?"

"The Wednesday night, the night before he was found on the golf course. He was in The Nag's Head, the pub on the Wellesley Road. My wife and I were there that night. It's near where we live," Dean said. "I'm sorry, I suppose I should have mentioned that."

"No worries. You have now," Napoleon said. "Did you speak to him?"

"No. I only noticed him when I was leaving. He left at the same time as my wife and I."

"Was he with anyone? Did he look in any way different or troubled?" Napoleon asked.

"He was alone, standing on the step outside the pub when I saw him. And he looked his usual self, although I didn't take a close look."

"What time was that? What time did you leave?"

"I don't know exactly. Just before 9 O'clock at a guess. Yeah, about nine. We definitely left at the same time. I remember him jogging past us on the other side of the road, up the hill towards the golf club away from town. My wife and I live in St Mark's Road, a turning off St Margaret's Road, just after the golf club. We were going home."

"Who else was in the pub?" Mayo asked as Napoleon took a moment to digest the new information.

"Erm, well, let me think. There was John McConnell. You might know him. He's a very big guy, youngish, full of himself. He's lived here for years. I played a game of pool with him."

"Yes, we know him," Mayo said. Napoleon nodded. McConnell had a criminal record and was well known to the police. An eyewitness had also identified him at the scene when Rankin had been knocked down and killed. McConnell had nearly been hit, too.

"I can't recall anyone else; a few familiar faces but I can't put names to them," Dean said. "My wife Molly might have a better recollection of who was there. She's a journalist. She's got a good memory for things like that."

"Ahh, so your wife must be Molly Jensen, who works at the radio station," Napoleon said, immediately making the connection.

"That's right. She uses her maiden name on the radio," Dean said.

Napoleon smiled. "Where did you spend the rest of Wednesday night after you left the pub?" he asked.

"At home and an early night."

"And when were you aware of Mr Delgado's death?"

"The next day. We were told at work and it was on the local news in the morning, although I didn't know the dead man was Peter at that point."

Napoleon nodded. "And where were you on Friday morning?"

"When the policeman was killed?" Dean said. "I was in the office. Carol or any number of people here can verify that, if you consider me a suspect." He replied with a chuckle. He was amused, rather than affronted by the question.

Napoleon nodded again. "Thank you, Mr Dean. I think that's about everything."

The policemen found Carol, Dean's assistant, by a photocopying machine in the corridor. She was gossiping with another woman, who hurried away as the policemen approached. Carol didn't know who Peter mixed with outside work and couldn't add much to what they already knew. Peter was very nice and Dean, or young Charlie as she referred to him, was a lot angrier over his planning officer's support for saving the school than he let on. Dean, she confided, took the campaign against the school's closure personally, which she thought was silly.

"Okay, thank you," Napoleon said. "Let's get going," he said to Mayo. They collected their raincoats and Mayo's hat and made their way to the lifts. The rain was still bucketing down as they reached the glass doors at the council entrance. The policemen stopped, eyeing the rain, which was now slanted by the wind and pounding like hundreds of furious rapiers into the ground.

"What did you think of Dean?" Napoleon asked.

"He was pleasant and helpful. What did you think?" Mayo said.

"I felt he seemed a bit wary at first, as if he had something to hide," Napoleon said. "There was something in the way he looked at us as we walked in. He looked suspicious, slightly uncomfortable. Some people are just like that. Policemen make them feel guilty, but you're right, he was helpful."

Mayo nodded. "We now know that Peter Delgado was heading towards the golf club at about 9 O'clock. His brother lives a little way beyond the golf club on St Margaret's Road, which suggests he was going back there for another confrontation or maybe to try and patch things up. It was a pity his iPhone was damaged in the collision as we might have got a definite location from that. We need to talk to Ray Delgado and his girlfriend again to make sure they didn't miss anything out. It is possible Ray saw his brother again later in the evening but didn't want to say or possibly Peter knocked on the door and confronted his girlfriend. They may have decided to be economical with the truth."

"I don't think so," Napoleon replied, watching the rain. The policemen had not budged from the foyer by the glass entrance doors, hoping the rain would ease before they made their dash to the car. "I think they were telling the truth. Peter Delgado may have gone back to his brother's house, but decided not to call when he saw the car had gone. He could have waited for a bit and then decided to walk home when his brother didn't return.
He lives on the other side of town and would've walked back past the golf club again to get home. He's then knocked down as he wanders into the road just before Crookham Lane."

Mayo frowned. "That's possible sir, but that would mean he must have waited for at least an hour outside his brother's house, or gone somewhere else. He was killed at about 10.30. It would have taken 15 minutes at most to walk back to his brother's from the pub, quicker if he jogged all the way. That means he would have arrived at his brother's at 9.15 at the very latest. You can add on another 10 minutes or so for him to walk back down the road to the spot where he was killed, so there's an hour unaccounted for. And surely he would have knocked on the door of his brother's house if he'd gone back there, just to check if anyone was home, which as it happened there was."

Napoleon nodded. "Sure, but I don't think Delgado or his girlfriend were hiding anything. There's a street bench outside the couple's house. Peter Delgado could have sat there for a while and waited for his brother to return, or he could have gone somewhere else. We just don't know. But you're right, we need to talk to Delgado and his girlfriend again. We also need to make more enquiries along St Margaret's Road and all the turnings off it to find out if anyone else saw Peter Delgado after 9pm when he left The Nag's Head."

The two men slipped into silence, both still looking intently at the downpour outside. The watery rapiers were more like small kitchen knives now.

"The rain's not quite as heavy," Mayo said eventually, putting his hat on at a neat angle, shielding his forehead. Napoleon didn't respond, subconsciously twirling his pen around his long fingers, but dropping it in the process. His concentration was elsewhere. Dean looked similar to Llewellyn, but what of their personalities? Mary said Llewellyn in the flesh bubbled with charisma and charm. The languid Dean was pleasant enough, but no inspirer of emotions.

Mayo picked up the pen. "Thank you, sergeant," Napoleon said. "Chalk and cheese," he added.

"Sorry sir?" Mayo asked.

Napoleon looked at him vacantly. "Nothing," he said. He pushed the door to the entrance open and decided to take his chance with the rain. Mayo, his hat firmly in place, followed reluctantly.

CHAPTER 31

◆

olly closed the sitting room curtains to shut out the grey evening and gently prodded the fading fire with a poker. It crackled with renewed vigour as she did so, its fine energetic flames licking at the grate and giving the room a pleasant yellow hue. She then snuggled herself between two large cushions on the sofa and reached for her kindle, which was lying on the coffee table, and clicked open the copy of Hamlet she was reading.

The text was heavy going and needed constant references to a crib sheet she had printed out on how to interpret the English of Shakespeare, which she had gathered up from the coffee table too. She was just about coming to grips with the passage she was reading, when the urgent ringing of the house telephone broke her concentration.

"To answer or not to answer," she thought tritely, before hauling herself out of the comfortable arms of the sofa cushions. She stretched for the receiver, which Charlie had left on a cabinet by the sofa. He rarely returned it to its stand in the kitchen, but for once he had discarded it in a convenient place, within reach and where she could find it quickly.

The man at the other end of the line spoke in quick bursts. "My name is John McConnell. Do you remember me?" was the first burst.

"Yes, I remember you," Molly said, wondering what on earth he wanted. She hardly knew him. Maybe he wanted to speak to Charlie.

"I'm Jack McConnell's son," came a second burst.

"Yes, I know who you are," Molly replied. "Do you want to speak to my husband?"

"No. You're Molly Jensen, right?" The words raced through the receiver.

"Yes, I am, but what do you want?" she said impatiently.

"You interviewed me when I won that award for saving that bloke from drowning. Remember?"

"Yes, I remember." Have-a-go hero. She recalled the cliché used in the local newspaper to describe him, a tired and unoriginal phrase she had avoided in her own report. "I know who you are. Just tell me why you're phoning."

"I was there when the policeman was knocked down by the car. The car only just missed me."

"I know," she said brusquely. One of her police contacts had told her, off the record, that McConnell was lucky not to have been hurt. But it still didn't explain the reason for the telephone call.

"I should go to the cop shop. They'll want to talk to me."

"Yes. They will, but what has this got to do with me?"

"You can help me. I can't go to the police because someone's after me. I've got to keep a low profile. I want you to tell the police that's why I'm avoiding them and not going to the cop shop."

"Surely you can make it to the police station, or can't you just phone them? I can give you the number if you want."

"I trust you. Please tell the coppers. They'll believe you." The words sprinted through the receiver for the last time and the line went dead.

Molly dragged herself up from the sofa, looking at the telephone as if it were a Martian asking for directions to the town centre. "Cop shop! Someone's after me! What a lot of melodramatic nonsense," she said to herself.

She wandered, still in slight shock from the bizarre conversation, to the kitchen. Please tell the coppers. Who did McConnell think he was? Some small-time gangster? The telephone call was absurd. She stopped at the kitchen sink and fished out her favourite mug, which she had left in the bowl at breakfast. The water was cold and soapy and made her shiver.

She could picture McConnell now; large and overbearing with a smile like a demented child. He had played pool with Charlie in The Nag's Head on the night Peter Delgado had died. She dried the mug with a tea towel and switched on the kettle.

He didn't seem bright enough to be a son of Jack McConnell. He was quite immature, too. She remembered being surprised that he was 27, a bit of a no-hoper really.

On balance, he was the type of idiot who would phone a reporter he hardly knew, ask her to tell the police he wasn't hiding from them but some dark assassin lurking in the Wellesley undergrowth and then just as mysteriously hang up without further explanation. The police were likely to give as much credibility to the cloak and dagger codswallop as she was. She found a tea bag in a tin and dropped it in the mug.

'Please tell the coppers. They'll believe you.' The request, dressed up like some desperate plea, was ridiculous. And coming from someone who still retained a trace of his public school accent, despite mixing with the Wellesley low-life, made it sound even more ludicrous. The kettle boiled. She poured the water into the mug and reached inside the fridge for some milk.

Still, she would have to tell the police about the call with McConnell, even if it was just to cover herself and her conscience should something happen to him. There was also an outside possibility of a connection between him and the policeman's death. She picked out the teabag from the mug with a spoon and poured in a little milk, watching the mixture coalesce into a rich, golden brown. She took a sip. It had that refreshing, tangy flavour peculiar to a good cup of tea. It made her think wistfully of what might have been, a quiet evening by the fire. She drank the tea slowly, perched on a kitchen stool, thinking randomly about McConnell, Hamlet, her marriage, life. She would have to go to the police station to explain the call. It would be much easier than telling the police on the telephone. She drank the last drops of her tea and peered out of the kitchen window. It was raining heavily, but she would have to go now, she wouldn't have time the next day, and it was a relatively short walk to Wellesley police station. She found her big coat and an umbrella and ventured outside into the wet, uninviting night.

---◆---

The duty officer at Wellesley police station had a pleasant face and manner and politely listened as Molly told him about the strange telephone call from John McConnell. After a few moments, he suggested she wait while he fetched a detective.

She sat down in a corner and cast her eyes around the shabby surroundings of the reception area. It was a good few years since she had been in the police station; the last time was while she was working for the Wellesley Chronicle, the town's weekly newspaper. The place hadn't changed much. It was like a time capsule. There were no new curtains or fashionable light fittings. The delinquents who passed through its doors were probably, like the furniture, much the same too.

Five minutes went by before the officer returned. Chief Inspector Napoleon would see her in his office, he said, and led her through the corridors to the back of the station. She recalled now how the place was like a rabbit warren. It was also much bigger than it appeared from the outside, like Doctor Who's Tardis.

She followed the policeman into the chief inspector's office. He introduced her to Napoleon, who she remembered meeting at various police functions and press conferences. He seemed to recognise her too.

"Would you like anything to drink, tea or coffee?" he asked as she sat down opposite him. He didn't look up and instead focused on a gold fountain pen he was holding.

"No, I'm fine."

He paused. "How are you?" he said finally. He still had that reticent manner and the shy eyes that remained fixed on the pen and seemed reluctant to look at her directly.

"Fine. I think we met a couple of times when I was working for the Wellesley Chronicle. I'm now working at the Valley radio station. It's a lot more exciting than working for the town's newspaper."

He nodded. "Yes. I listen to your reports."

He fell silent again and spun his pen around his fingers. "So, tell me about the mysterious phone call from John McConnell?" he said eventually and for the first time looked directly into her eyes.

She frowned and paused for a moment, recalling the strange conversation. "It's very odd. I don't know why he decided to phone me."

I've only met him once at an awards ceremony for bravery. He had saved someone from drowning. I did a report on it. In fact, coincidentally it was Peter Delgado, the man who was found dead on the golf course, who he rescued."

Napoleon sucked his teeth and slowly opened a notebook that lay on his desk. "It's interesting that he should have saved Peter Delgado, probably quite irrelevant, but interesting. When did this happen?"

"Six months ago, in April. The awards ceremony was a month after that." Molly watched the chief inspector write down some notes. "It's strange. I mean McConnell saving Delgado, Delgado is then killed and McConnell is nearly killed too by the car that hit the policeman. It does make you wonder whether there is a connection."

The chief inspector nodded. "Yes, it does. One of the witnesses at the scene said the car only just missed McConnell." His expression changed a fraction as he spoke. He now looked troubled rather than disinterested.

"I presume the witness didn't see who was driving?" Molly asked.

"No. The witness was elderly and short-sighted. She saw McConnell dart out of the way of the car, but she didn't see the collision itself and could only provide a vague description of the vehicle. The car nearly hitting McConnell is off the record by the way. I don't want it reported, or not just yet."

Molly nodded. She had already been told that by her police contact.

Napoleon made some more notes. He wrote slowly and deliberately. "You did the right thing in coming in," he said. "I doubt McConnell has a mystery gangster on his tail. I've come across him before. He lives in a fantasy world of cops and robbers, but then two people have been killed. It is just possible he's right this time to be paranoid."

The chief inspector looked up from his notes and put his pen down. "He had a fight with Mick and Jim Buckler at The Nag's Head on the night of Peter Delgado's death. They had a quarrel over a spilled drink. It was probably just another unrelated event." He lapsed into silence and flipped his pen around his fingers.

"Peter Delgado was in The Nag's Head on the night he died, and I understand you and your husband were there too? My sergeant and I were going to give you a call," he said finally.

"Ahh, yes, we were there on the Wednesday night. I suppose we should have come forward and told you. How did you know we were there?"

"Your husband told us. We interviewed him at the council offices this afternoon. He told us he was married to you and that you were both at the pub that night and saw Delgado."

"Ahh," Molly said again. "Charlie isn't home from work yet. I haven't seen him since this morning." She smiled and noticed Napoleon was now doodling on his pad. It looked like a drawing of a car. "Peter was at the pub. We both recognised him. He works, or worked, for my husband as I'm sure my husband told you. We didn't talk to him, but he left about the same time as us. In fact, he ran by us on the opposite side of the road as we walked home, up St Margaret's Road."

"And you didn't see him again?"

"No. We went home and had an early night."

Napoleon smiled. She had repeated what her husband had said about the evening, Delgado running past them, then home and an early night, without hesitation, not that she or Dean were suspects.

"Do you remember who else was in The Nag's Head that evening?"

"I remember John McConnell being there, he's so big and loud, but I didn't see anybody else I knew. I don't go there very often, so I'm not that familiar with the people who drink there. John McConnell was still there when we left."

Napoleon took more notes, but he wrote more quickly this time. "Did you see Peter Delgado talk to anyone in the pub?"

"No. He was on his own. But I only saw him as I was leaving. I brushed past him on my way out."

"Did you notice anything unusual about him?"

"No, except..." Molly paused. "I suppose he looked preoccupied. That's it, preoccupied and maybe a little angry. He was standing just outside the pub on the path when I saw him. I remember he was staring at a man across the road. He was looking thoughtful," she paused again, "and he was frowning."

"Hmm," Napoleon took a note. She was a lot more observant than her husband, but then she was a journalist. "This man he was staring at. Did you recognise him? Was he anybody familiar?"

"No. Yes... Sorry. I'm being vague. I didn't recognise him, but he did look familiar, but then I've lived in Wellesley all my life, so there are a lot of people who look familiar who I don't really know or can't quite place."

"If I dug out some police photographs, could you take a look? If the man isn't in our files, maybe you could help us draw up a photofit?"

"I'm sorry, inspector, I wouldn't be able to help you with either. He was wearing a fedora hat and an old-fashioned trench coat, and he was tall and thin, but it was too dark and he was too far away for me to see his face. His demeanour looked familiar, but I couldn't add much more than that."

"Okay," Napoleon said. "And you're sure you can't recall anyone else in the pub that night, apart from McConnell and Delgado?"

"I'm sorry. No, I can't. I'm sure John McConnell would be able to give you a list of names."

"Yes. No doubt."

Molly stretched her legs and rolled her neck. "Is The Nag's Head important. I mean, was it the last place Peter Delgado was seen before he died?"

Napoleon frowned and leaned back into his chair, flicking his pen around his fingers again. "This is not for reporting, but yes it was the last place Delgado was seen."

"So, if you can find out who else was there, they might provide you with some answers?"

Napoleon sat up straight. "They might, but I think the golf club is the key to this case, where the body was found. This is also not for reporting and I'm only telling you because I trust you from our dealings in the past and sometimes it's helpful having a reporter in the know. You might find out something useful, which of course I would expect you to inform me of immediately. Peter Delgado wasn't killed on the golf course. He was hit by a car and moved there. If we can work out why, we'll probably find our killer."

"Wow," Molly said. "What an odd thing to do. I assumed he was mugged, although I did wonder when no details were given out about how he died. Now I understand."

"Yes, and it means I have to take John McConnell's paranoia seriously. His close shave with the car may not have been an accident. His father, Jack, found the body by the way. So, we have a neat and tidy chain of events: John McConnell saves Delgado from drowning, Delgado is knocked down and killed, Jack McConnell finds the body and then John McConnell is nearly knocked down and killed too."

"That's intriguing," Molly said.

"Yes, and that's all it is at the moment, but all the same it's possible McConnell is in danger. So, if he phones you again, tell him he must report directly to me here at the police station. He's one of our best hopes of finding some answers and he's no good to anyone dead."

CHAPTER 32

◆

"Someone at the golf club has to be responsible for the deaths of Delgado and Rankin," Napoleon said, watching Mary stack clean plates in one of the kitchen cupboards.

"Maybe," Mary said, reaching into the dishwasher for more plates. "I know you want it to be two murders, which you can then brilliantly solve. But the deaths could just as easily be two unrelated accidents."

"No, I don't think so," Napoleon said seriously, the sarcastic remarks sailing over his head. "The golf club is the key." It was a phrase he had been repeating to himself like some mystical mantra all day. "Two accidental hit and runs by two different drivers in the space of 36 hours in a small country town is too much of a coincidence. The murders must have been committed by one person with one motive, which means we must focus on why Delgado was moved to the golf course. When we can answer that, we'll find the murderer."

"I see," Mary said impatiently. "Do you think you can widen your focus just for one second to help me unload this machine?"

Napoleon nodded, although he wasn't listening. "Humphrey knew Peter Delgado was hit by a car, yet he can't be responsible. He was in the golf club until two in the morning on the night Delgado died, and he can't drive. So, someone either told him a car hit Delgado or he overheard something. Unfortunately, he can't remember because he was drunk."

"Or he's covering up for someone?" Mary said, handing Napoleon a plate from the dishwasher, while she put cutlery into one of the kitchen drawers.

"I don't think so. Humphrey's not that kind of person," the inspector said, taking the plate and easing himself off the kitchen table opposite the dishwasher and cupboards, which he had been leaning against. "He's more badger than fox. He may be loud and overbearing, but at heart he's a simple soul who likes to drink and

168

eat. He's not cunning and conniving. I don't think he could genuinely remember how he knew Delgado's injuries had been caused by a car."

"I'm sure you're right, Robert, although I don't see Humphrey as a badger. They're quiet and keep themselves to themselves. Humphrey's more like an unruly hippo," Mary said. "And are you going to put that plate away, or are you just going to admire it?"

Napoleon looked at the plate distractedly. It was pretty, embossed in green and gold with an Ironstone hallmark. "Mayo and I have questioned everybody we can think of at the club and not one person seems to be aware of how Delgado was killed, but there must be somebody else, apart from Humphrey, who knows," the inspector said, still looking at the plate. "And then there's the red hatchback, the car that hit Rankin. No one at the golf club owns that type of car, although it's possible one of the members borrowed one like it from a wife or a friend," he added.

He put the Ironstone plate in the wall cupboard and Mary handed him another one, which was plain and white with no pattern. The inspector looked at it blankly.

"Cupboard," she said. "That's where it belongs. Like the other one. You can put it in the cupboard, too."

"And then there are the McConnells," the inspector said, the sarcasm again lost on him. "The father found Delgado's body and the son was nearly killed by the car that hit Rankin, so where do they fit in? We really need to find John McConnell. He was the last person to speak to Rankin before he was killed."

Napoleon finally put the plate in the cupboard and turned to Mary, who was reaching into the dishwasher for the last of the cutlery. "I'm going to the golf club bar tonight just to watch, to see how a normal evening unfolds," he said. "It might trigger something. Give me some ideas. Is there someone who would want Jack McConnell to find Peter Delgado dead on the first green? And is there someone who would want to see John McConnell dead? The golf club is definitely the key."

"Yes, I think you said that before Robert," Mary said. "Thank you for putting away the two plates, most kind. Now why don't you go to the golf club bar before I use one of these knives to kill you. I've heard enough of your ramblings for one evening."

Napoleon looked at his wife with a puzzled expression. "You can come if you like," he said, as if that might make up for his lack of attentiveness and failure to help with the chores

"Tempting! But watching a group of men, whose conversation rarely stretches beyond their last putt, consume huge amounts of beer is not my thing. You trot along on your own." Mary smiled facetiously and put away the last of the knives and forks in one of the kitchen drawers with more than a little menace in her eye.

◆

Napoleon ordered an orange juice at the golf club bar and found himself a table near the door. It was 8.30 and the bar was busy, although he could see no sign of Humphrey or Jack McConnell. He sat down and took a few sips of his orange juice. He planned to stay for about two hours to familiarise himself with as many of the patrons as possible. It might open his eyes to something that would lift the case out of its present rut.

At 8.35, the florid countenance of Bob, Humphrey's drinking companion, burst into the bar. He reminded Napoleon of a corpulent sunflower, his thick yellowish blonde hair and beard sticking out in all directions, neatly framing a fat red face. Two steps behind him was the most notorious paunch in Wellesley and a step behind that, its owner Humphrey Christopher.

The fat man saw the inspector and smiled broadly. It was infectious. Napoleon smiled back. The time was now 8.36 and these two were probably here for the night, which could easily turn into early morning. Up to six hours of solid drinking, and it was only Tuesday night. The life some people lead, Napoleon thought, and for a second was intensely jealous.

The corpulent sunflower and the mega-paunch ordered their drinks at the bar and made their way back to Napoleon's table. The urgency had gone from Bob's step now he had a pint of beer in his hand. He was a nervous, hesitant man and it showed in his gait as he wandered uncertainly towards where Napoleon was sitting, clearly unsure whether to join the inspector.

Humphrey, however, made up for his friend's reticence and steamed towards Napoleon's table, looking the very definition of larger than life with a Cheshire cat grin stretched across his face.

"Ahh, Sir Paunch," Napoleon said.

"Ahh, inspector," Humphrey replied, puffing out his already bulging stomach and looking around the bar as if in search of an audience. A young woman on the next table was watching him, which seemed to act as his cue. "The green-eyed monster is an evil and desperate animal," he boomed, smiling at the young woman. "I know your secret wish is to have a paunch like me." He stepped back apace and looked directly at Napoleon. "It shows I am a man of standing and wealth, able to afford the finer things in life." His eyes swept across the room as if he were on the stage at the National Theatre rather than in the golf club bar. "Never let the green-eyed monster control you. Jealousy is a most invidious and debilitating trait," he concluded, nodding at the young women, who was now laughing, and raising his glass in the air.

"And you like a pint," Bob said. It was the first time Napoleon had heard Bob speak. He had a light country accent, like many people who grew up in or near Wellesley. There were broadly two accents in the town – posh or country, or maybe three if you added the neutral one similar to Napoleon's. Humphrey was posh.

"Yes, dear Bob. I like a pint. And what true man does not like a pint?" He waited for a moment as if he was anticipating applause from his audience, his eyes sweeping the room one last time, and sat down slowly and theatrically next to Napoleon, his pint cradled in his fat hand. Bob followed his friend's lead and precariously nestled himself on a small stool at the end of the table, his fatty folds smothering it like some overweight amoeba swallowing its prey. The beer they were both drinking was dark and looked like special, the strongest ale in the house. For the second time, Napoleon reflected on the amount of beer these two might put away in one evening. It would probably fill the lake by the 10th hole.

Humphrey turned to Napoleon, wrapping a big bear like arm around him. "So, my dear inspector, what brings you here tonight?" he said, lifting his pint glass with his free hand and taking a long, deep swallow of the dark beer, draining nearly half of its contents.

"I felt like a drink and good company," Napoleon said, sitting up straight and trying to shake off Humphrey's arm, which was slightly damp from sweat. The inspector was not a tactile man. With the exception of his wife and children, he tended to avoid bodily contact.

"Well, well. The penny has finally dropped after all these years of living in Wellesley. You have found the heart and soul of our sweet town," Humphrey said, retracting his arm from Napoleon's shoulders and wiping a residue of beer left on his mouth with his shirt sleeve.

"Hmm," Napoleon raised his eyes. "Do you mean you or the golf club bar?"

"Why both, dear boy. The bar is the heart, and I am the soul." It was interesting how Humphrey used the phrase dear boy, like Jack McConnell. Even the intonation was the same, with both words dragged out for dramatic effect.

Napoleon smiled but his tone was now serious. "I want you to try and remember why you thought Peter Delgado was knocked over by a car?" Mary had put doubts in his mind over whether Humphrey was covering up for someone.

"Once a policeman, always a policeman, eh Napoleon," Humphrey said, trying to be light-hearted, although from his nervous expression he clearly realised the moment for gentle banter had passed.

"Well?" Napoleon said sternly.

"I really don't know. I'm sorry inspector. I really think I must have imagined it." He took another large gulp of his beer, which seemed to embolden him. "Anyway, even if I did know, I don't know that I would pass on such hot information. I've never seen myself as a super grass or anything like that, certainly not against a fellow boozer. One day the boozers of the world will unite, and those who police us will be sent to the gulags. I will not betray a fellow patron of this fine bar."

172

Napoleon shook his head crossly. "This is serious. Think harder and give me your answer like a normal person."

"Normal, well let me think. What is normal, dear boy? That is a strange and subjective word." Humphrey tried to be facetious again, but Napoleon was having none of it.

"Just think and reply, Humphrey," Napoleon said. "You must remember why you made such an assumption? Do you know of anyone who might drink and drive?"

"No. Only drink."

"There must be someone here who you suspect of driving while over the limit? I know how tempting it is for some people. You must notice such things."

Humphrey took a further gulp from his pint, emptying his glass. Again, it seemed to bring out the dramatic in him. "I can tell you for a fact, inspector, that however many drinks I have had, however late it is, I always have the observation of the best detective. And the next day, however late I have been carousing, the facts are always at my fingertips. However, my dear boy, I don't drink in the car park, which means I have no idea who might drive while intoxicated."

"So, you can't remember the most important fact: why you knew Delgado was hit by a car?" Napoleon said impatiently.

"It is the one fact that has escaped me, alas. The one that got away," Humphrey replied, raising his eyebrows, and spreading his arms in mock apology.

The fat man stopped in mid gesture as Ted Cropper entered the bar. "Ahh, the prissy sod," Humphrey said, spreading his arms even wider as if to embrace a new companion.

"Hello Rob," Ted said, approaching the table and ignoring Humphrey. He was one of the few people, apart from Mary, who called the inspector by his Christian name.

"Would you like a drink, Rob?" he asked before turning to Humphrey. "And I suppose I can buy you one too, although you don't deserve my generosity."

"A pint would be lovely," Humphrey said. "And I am sorry, sorry for everything. But I cannot…"

"Yes," Ted said, interrupting. "I get it. You're sorry. Bob, what are you drinking? I suppose you're both drinking special," he said answering his own question. Bob and Humphrey nodded. "And do you want to stick with orange juice, Rob?"

"Yes. Thanks Ted," Napoleon said.

Ted returned quickly with a tray of drinks, having caught the barman's attention straight away. He handed the drinks round and placed a pint of old bitter on the table in front of the chair where he was about to sit. Old bitter was less potent than special. Napoleon decided he would have one of those next time round. Two glasses of orange juice was enough vitamin C for one evening.

"Were you here last Wednesday, Ted?" Napoleon said, sipping his orange juice.

"Yes, I was. It was a pleasant evening except for Humphrey."

"I've said I'm sorry, although I have no idea why you got so upset if I am truly honest. Live and let live, accept and understand. Do not judge other people unless you truly know them. That is what I say."

"That's not an apology," Ted said. "That's just more of your meaningless and inane drivel."

Napoleon was amused by Ted's directness. It was unlike him.

Ted caught Napoleon's eye, immediately understanding the inspector's thoughts. "I have to be blunt with Humphrey," he said. "It's the only way to get through to him. And let's face it, it's difficult to get a word in edgeways in a conversation with him, so you have to say what you mean and quickly."

"Oh, you wound me. I am wounded. Wounded by the prissy sod." Humphrey said it with a grin and slapped Ted on the back.

"Yes, the prissy sod," Ted smiled thinly.

"What was the row about?" Napoleon asked.

"It wasn't a row. Humphrey just likes to go on and on about how wonderful Jack McConnell is. He knows I'm not a fan of Jack, so he deliberately tries to rile me by constantly praising him," Ted said.

"I didn't know you didn't like Jack," Napoleon said.

"He's not a moral man. He is selfish and unkind, but Humphrey thinks that is acceptable because he is charming. Humphrey seems to think charm means you can be a shit and act irresponsibly," Ted said with an uncompromising hardness that surprised Napoleon. He wasn't an opinionated person by nature, but he left no doubt about his views on Jack.

"You're the second person I've heard question the morals of Jack in the past few days," Napoleon said. "My wife's not too hot on him either."

Humphrey gave Napoleon a long look and took a swig of his beer. "Supermac's not that bad," he said earnestly. "He might have done a few dodgy deals. And he might be a bit of a cad. He doesn't treat his wife very well, lovely lady, gorgeous, if only she were mine. I would even say Jack is a great man in his way, if you look at what he has done for the community. He just has a few flaws. Every genius, every great man, has flaws. Just look at Churchill. Couldn't stop drinking. Just look at Kennedy. Couldn't stop shagging."

Ted shook his head. "Churchill, Kennedy. What a lot of nonsense. Jack may do a lot for the community, but behind that respectable and charming façade, full of bonhomie and good cheer, is a sinister man who you should never trust."

"Trust, sinister," Humphrey said. "Nonsense. Jack is just out for himself, like all of us, if we are truly honest. To say you don't trust someone is the most naïve thing to say in the world. You should never trust anyone, except maybe your wife or your mother. Every human being is selfish in that they put themselves first. And, as for sinister. What does that mean?"

Ted shook his head again. "Someone who is so selfish and so lacking in trust is sinister, in my opinion, maybe even evil."

"Hmm," Napoleon said, appraising Ted, who looked deadly serious. He knew Ted was a thoughtful, intelligent man, but to come to such a malign opinion about Jack seemed odd, although Mary, who was the most sane person he knew, would probably agree with Ted if she were here.

"Did you have a similar conversation to this last Wednesday night?" the inspector asked.

"Yes. Carbon copy, I would say," Bob said in his light country twang.

"You know how I feel about Jack, Humphrey, but you still go on and on about him being a wonderful man," Ted said. "Why don't you just accept that I'm not a fan of Jack and leave it at that?"

"I don't understand why you dislike him so much. It makes no sense and I like winding you up. I like winding people up. It is fun and funny. It is the contrarian in me, and Jack always buys a round of drinks, even if he is only drinking mineral water. That is the true test of a person's character. It is a selfless act, a kind act, an act of a man you can trust," Humphrey said, winking at Napoleon.

"Maybe we should change the subject," Napoleon said. Ted's face had gone a slight tinge of red, almost the same colour as Bob. "Are you going to the Wellesley game on Saturday?" he said to Ted before Humphrey could respond.

"Yes. They should win I think," Ted said mechanically. His colour had gone back to normal, but he now looked sad and preoccupied.

Napoleon wondered if it was a mistake to switch the topic to football. He knew Ted still dwelt on the disappearance of his grandson Sean at one of the Wellesley games, but it was too late to change tack, so he ploughed on.

"My lad Rob and I will be there for sure. We'll meet up with you if you want," the inspector said.

"Great," Ted said. He smiled and seemed to emerge from whatever distant thoughts were troubling him.

"Maybe I will get a match ticket," Humphrey said. "I haven't been for a long time and I like the football club's hot dogs. Someone also told me the bar in the ground now has special on tap. A hot dog, washed down by a couple of pints of special. Glorious."

Napoleon smiled. He remembered the last time he had seen Humphrey at the football. He had stood at the club bar drinking for the entire game. The inspector doubted the fat man had watched one kick of the match.

More familiar faces filled the bar. Frank, the regular barman arrived for the late shift and came over to the table to collect the empties. He smiled and politely chatted to Humphrey. The crowd was much the same the previous Wednesday night, he said in answer to a question from Napoleon.

Other people came and went. Not one looked like a mystery killer.

At 10 O'clock Jack McConnell appeared at the door of the bar. Ted saw him first and immediately stood up to leave.

"Where are you going?" Napoleon said. "You haven't finished your drink." The inspector then noticed Jack and said no more.

"I was going anyway," Ted said. "So, now seems a good time. See you at the football, Rob." He nodded to Napoleon and then to Humphrey and Bob and walked past Jack at the doorway without acknowledging him.

Humphrey watched Ted go and beckoned Jack to come over to the table. "Ted's silly. Jack's not perfect, but you've got to live and let live, eh?"

The fat man's usual default expression, a supercilious smile, had been displaced by a grave frown, which lined and creased his forehead. Discussions about Jack seemed to bring out the earnest in him.

Napoleon wondered what Jack had said or done to upset Ted, who was by nature a tolerant, easy-going man. He put up with Humphrey, which would have been beyond Napoleon had he been a regular drinker at the golf club.

"Napoleon, Humphrey, Bob. Dear boys," Jack said, smiling broadly. "Another round of drinks?" Everyone nodded and Jack went to the bar.

"See what I mean," Humphrey said. "Jack always buys a round. He's a good man." His supercilious smile was back in place. Everything was back to normal in the world of the fat man.

Humphrey turned to Bob and whispered something in his ear, the corpulent sunflower laughed and went an even deeper shade of red.

Napoleon pondered the fat man for a moment. He was like a huge sponge, soaking up information as well as beer, even if the key fact over how he knew Delgado was hit by a car was lost in a fog of alcohol somewhere deep in his memory bank. Gossip and drink were Humphrey's currencies. And when it came to the golf club, he knew everything and everyone. If the club was the key to the investigation, then it was only a matter of time before Sir Paunch said something significant to open up the case.

CHAPTER 33

◆

John McConnell sat down opposite Napoleon. The inspector looked stern and inscrutable – his standard poker face in police interviews. Mayo, next to him, appeared more friendly, but his expression was also blank and unreadable.

"How are you, John?" the inspector said.

"Not great," McConnell replied. "Someone is trying to kill me."

Mayo struggled to suppress a laugh. "Really? Who?" he asked, raising his right eyebrow in a figurative question mark.

"I mean it," McConnell said indignantly. "The car that hit the policeman was obviously meant for me."

"Really?" Mayo said again. As a policeman, he had heard some bizarre statements – the most memorable from a drunken husband who claimed he had attacked his wife because she was a Russian spy. But, as far as he was concerned, this was up there with the best in the world of fantasy. "So, why do you think that, John?" he said, his scepticism obvious from his sarcastic tone. He noticed Napoleon, who had been grumpy all morning after a boozy evening at the golf club, was now smiling. McConnell's preposterous assertion had worked some kind of palliative magic on the inspector, where four headache pills and two glasses of orange juice had failed.

"I dunno. I just know," McConnell said.

"You dunno. You just know." Napoleon was now laughing. "John, as much as I could do with something to move this case forward, I am going to need more than that." The inspector sat back in his chair and crossed his arms, a curious smile playing on his lips. Mayo's right eyebrow remained in the question mark position, a fraction above the left.

179

"Well, maybe they're not trying to kill me, but someone is after me. That's why I'm here. Why I came to the police station. I knew you would give me a hard time and think I'm nuts. I shouldn't have come."

"All right, John. Calm down. Just tell us, who's after you, and why you think they want to hurt you or kill you?" Napoleon said flatly.

"I dunno," McConnell said again. This time in a less confident, sulky tone. There was silence as the two policemen looked at each other and then back at McConnell.

"The car that ran over the policeman. It was meant for me," McConnell said finally.

"Okay, John," Napoleon said. There was an exasperated edge to his voice. Although he hadn't entirely written McConnell off as a clueless fantasist, his patience was now wearing thin. "Let's start at the beginning. Tell us what happened before the policeman was hit by the car and why you think the driver was trying to run you down."

"All right, but I know someone is after me. I just do."

"The beginning, John," Napoleon said firmly.

McConnell sighed heavily and then recalled the interview with Rankin in The Nag's Head, the awful thud of the car when it knocked the inspector down and how he had tried to revive him by the roadside. The car was a small, red hatchback. He didn't know the registration and couldn't see the driver.

When McConnell had finished, Napoleon nodded and gave Mayo a resigned glance. The sergeant could see the disappointment in the inspector's expression. McConnell had added nothing worthwhile to what the police already knew. Mayo smiled thinly, registering his own disappointment. This interview was going nowhere.

"Okay, John," Napoleon said again, turning back to McConnell. "And now I want an answer. Who is trying to hurt you or kill you, and why? What have you done, or what are you involved in, to make you think someone wants to murder you? I don't want any fantastic tales or nonsense. Just the truth. Now."

McConnell let out another heavy sigh. "I dunno for sure. But I've been selling drugs and porn videos and I think I might be undercutting someone. I think someone wants me out of the way."

McConnell told the policemen about the fight with the Bucklers at The Nag's Head the evening before Delgado was found on the golf course. The brothers had warned him against selling drugs and porn videos and then attacked him. They hadn't used a weapon or threatened to kill him, but their intentions were very clear – to scare him. He had easily fended them off and gone back to the bar for another hour before walking home a little after closing time. He hadn't seen Peter Delgado at the pub that night. He didn't know him, he said, although he had pulled Delgado out of the river about six months ago. Delgado had fallen in while jogging near the bank. He had run into an overhanging branch, knocking himself out and tumbling in close to the waterfall and bridge, one of the most dangerous stretches of the river because of the strong currents. McConnell had been walking a friend's dog nearby and jumped in when Delgado failed to surface, dragging him back to the verge.

Napoleon gave McConnell a reassuring smile. "That was a brave thing you did." The young man was an idiot but he was a courageous one. "If you hadn't jumped in, Delgado might have died."

"And now he has," McConnell said quietly, reflecting the irony.

"Yes, and we need to find out why," Napoleon said. "Let's go back to the Bucklers. You can't seriously think they want to kill you? Maybe scare you, as you said, but not cause you serious harm. They're not the most charming people in Wellesley, but neither of them has killed anyone or hurt anyone seriously to my knowledge. They didn't threaten to kill you, and they weren't carrying any weapons, which suggests they weren't intending to hurt you badly. So why all the melodrama?"

"All right," McConnell said testily. "Maybe they don't want to kill me. But they're out to get me. They said I would get hurt if I didn't stop selling the drugs and the porn. That's the truth, and they meant it," he added, raising his voice in frustration at the inspector's scepticism.

"Okay. Calm down," Napoleon said slowly as if he was talking to a child. "Could it have been one of the Bucklers who was driving the car?"

"I really couldn't tell who was driving," McConnell said less heatedly. "The car was too far away by the time I'd realised what had happened. It was going very fast. It could have been anyone driving. But it's not just the fight with the Bucklers that's made me paranoid. It was only afterwards, when I kept replaying the car knocking over the policeman in my mind, that I realised the driver didn't brake. I know about cars, inspector, and there was no screech of the brakes or sound of locked tyres on the tarmac. The driver was aiming for me, and it was only because I suddenly sprinted across the road that they hit the policeman."

"Our scenes of crime team made a similar observation about the driver's failure to brake," Napoleon said. "There were no tyre marks on the road, which would have resulted if the car had braked sharply. But maybe the driver didn't see the policeman, or you until it was too late. Maybe they were talking on their mobile and weren't concentrating on the road. The fact the driver didn't brake doesn't prove anything."

Napoleon paused for a moment. "Let's turn to the drugs and videos," he said, eyeing McConnell closely. "What drugs do you sell and in what quantities? And what type of porn are we talking about – extreme or the confessions of a window cleaner kind?"

There was a firm edge to the inspector's voice. He remembered Sean Cropper had been used in porn videos and there had been rumours at the time of a ring of paedophiles, who may have been responsible for his death.

McConnell rubbed his chin and fell silent while he thought through his answer. He might as well tell the policemen the whole truth, now he had admitted selling drugs. "It's mostly cannabis and hash," he said. "Sometimes I sell a little coke, but it's all in small quantities - and the videos are harmless. They're more like Carry On films than anything erotic. I thought it would be fun to throw them in with some of the deals. A lot of the punters loved it, getting high and watching porn. I found I could mark up a drug deal quite considerably by throwing in a couple of videos."

"People still use VCRs to watch videos?" Mayo said. "Surely technology has moved on."

"VCRs are making a bit of a comeback, like vinyl records. I sell the VCRs too with the videos if the punter hasn't got one. They're cheap and pretty good quality, even if the technology is old," McConnell said. "A lot of people have loads of videos stored away, old films, family weddings, and they still want to watch them. And the VCRs are good value for the price. It's not a bad market."

"I see, very interesting," Napoleon said in a monotone that suggested he had absolutely no interest in the market for VCRs and old technology. In fact, he wasn't even sure there was one, except in McConnell's imagination. "I want you to bring in any drugs and any videos you have in your possession to the police station. And you are to stop selling drugs or videos. No more dealing. Is that clear?"

"Yes. But what about the fact someone is trying to kill me?"

Mayo snorted, suppressing another laugh, while Napoleon rapped his hands against the table in frustration. His patience had now run out. "John. No one is trying to kill you," he said firmly.

"All right. Trying to hurt me."

"If you stop selling the drugs and videos, then the problem will go away. It's that simple, surely," Mayo said with a crooked smile. It was difficult to take McConnell seriously.

"You're right," McConnell conceded. "But there's something else, and I know it sounds far-fetched, but I've got to tell you. Someone is out to get me and it's not just the Bucklers. Someone's following me. There's this bloke in a mac who wears a hat. I don't know if he's connected with the Bucklers, but he's always there. Everywhere I turn, I see him. I know it sounds ridiculous. But I'm being followed and it's freaking me out."

Mayo laughed really hard this time. It was a laugh he had been trying to contain like some mad genie in a bottle since the start of the interview, and he couldn't suppress it any longer. Napoleon gave the sergeant a bewildered look and McConnell a dismissive one. As far as the inspector was concerned, McConnell might as well have been talking in some incomprehensible foreign language for all the sense he was making.

"There's a bloke in a mac who wears a hat?" Mayo repeated, still laughing. "I don't suppose the hat is a fedora?"

"Yes. That's him," McConnell said earnestly. "You see. I'm not making this up. It's not funny."

"I have seen a man who wears a fedora and a trench coat around town," Mayo said. "But that's all. He was in The Wheel of Fortune pub on the high street the other day. You really think this man is following you and wants to kill you?"

"Well, I don't know if he wants to kill me," McConnell said. "But he's always around, whenever I'm in The Nag's Head or going to the shops. He's everywhere, and then I get this warning from the Bucklers and the policeman is killed by a speeding car. It's got to be related."

Mayo rolled his eyes and said bluntly: "John, why has this got to be related? This man may just happen to live near you. Lots of people go to The Nag's Head or go to the shops. Has he ever approached you, talked to you or threatened you?"

"No," McConnell said belligerently. "But he's always there."

"All right," Napoleon said. He had had enough of McConnell and his wayward, fantastical theories. "We'll talk to the Bucklers. In the meantime, bring all the drugs and pornographic videos you have in your possession to the police station immediately and then keep your head down, and keep out of trouble."

Mayo stood up and escorted McConnell to the police station's reception where he told the duty sergeant to find someone to escort the young man back to his home to get the drugs and pornographic videos. Back in the interview room, he found Napoleon twirling his gold fountain pen around his fingers. He looked pensive and irritated in about equal measure.

"Shouldn't we have cautioned or charged him for distributing drugs?" Mayo said. "And what about the fight? We could have charged him over that too."

"We can deal with all that later," Napoleon said. "McConnell is stupid and paranoid, which isn't probably helped by his own drug taking. If he's dealing in drugs, he's almost certainly using them. But let's forget McConnell for the moment. Our priority is to talk to the Bucklers. Did they really threaten McConnell over selling drugs and if so, what are they selling and who are they working for? And is there really a market for pornographic videos in Wellesley? McConnell's probably just found a few in his cupboard and sold them for loose change.

"We also need to talk to this man in the mac and the hat." Napoleon smiled lopsidedly as he said it. "Now the young fool has got me talking like him. But still, we need to rule this man out as a part of the investigation, and we need to see what the Bucklers have to say before we totally write off McConnell as a crazy fantasist. He just may be on to something."

CHAPTER 34

◆

He was big and handsome, but there was a self-regarding arrogance about him. He also knew he was good looking and made no effort to hide his conceit, an unattractive and contemptible trait. Sarah Parsons watched John McConnell turn the key in the front door of his parents' house as she made the character assassination. She was probably being uncharitable, but she could have done without having to escort the young man back to his home to collect his pornographic videos and drugs. Her heavy workload had not put her in the mood for macho wisecracks and glib small talk. She was about to follow him into the house, but he suddenly stopped with the door ajar as if he feared he might find something unpleasant inside.

"This way," he said after a moment's hesitation and pushed the door wider. His overconfident demeanour had been replaced by an odd edginess. After another short pause, he finally led the bemused Parsons through the hallway and up the stairs to his bedroom where he kept his drugs and videos. He handed her a large cardboard box, packed with videos and several small see-through plastic bags. Some contained what looked like cannabis, while others held a white powder, which Parsons presumed was cocaine. "That's it," he said.

"Okay," she said and carried the box down the stairs.

"Who's that?" a voice said from the living room.

"It's all right mum," McConnell said. "I'm just picking some stuff up with a friend." He smiled awkwardly at Parsons, who shrugged her shoulders and carried on walking towards the door. "You don't need to come back to the police station with me, John," she said. "But make sure you're available for further interviews or questions. Don't go missing."

McConnell nodded. "Sure," he said.

He watched Parsons walk down the driveway and then shut the front door, a good-looking woman who had made it obvious she had no interest in his banter. In fact, she seemed distinctly unimpressed. Maybe, he was trying too hard. He should probably relax and be himself, but sexy women always brought out the show-off in him. He frowned and turned back down the hallway in search of his mother. The living room door needed a hard shove before it would open. A book had lodged itself beneath it. "Fell off," slurred his mother, who was slumped in her favourite chair opposite the door.

He picked up the book and put it back in its place on the bookshelf by the door. His mother was drinking her favourite poison, gin and tonic, with plenty of ice. Judging by her half-closed eyes and unsteady speech, she was already drunk. Thankfully, the policewoman hadn't seen her. That would have been embarrassing.

He frowned again and sat down on a chair next to her. "You need a coffee, mum," he said. His mother looked at him through half-closed, drink-clouded eyes. "What? What are you saying?"

"I'm just saying that you need a coffee."

She smiled. Her son hadn't spoken to her for a while. It was good to hear his voice. "Shure," she said.

The coffee tasted surprisingly good. The room looked better, things looked better. Jo blinked once, then again. John was smiling at her. That was nice.

"You look like you're enjoying that?" her son said.

"Yes, which is surprising." She laughed throatily. It was like an old crone's cackle, she thought, but it made John smile again. The coffee was also sobering her up, which was no bad thing.

"Mum, I'm going to try and sort myself out. The woman who was with me was a policewoman. The box I gave her was full of pornographic videos and drugs. I'm not going to sell drugs or porn videos anymore, and I've got a job at The Nag's Head as a barman."

"I thought you were banned from that pub?"

"No, not really. When the landlord bans me, he doesn't really mean it. One of the barmen is leaving and he's persuaded the landlord to give me his job. It's not the greatest job in the world, but it'll be the first proper one, apart from my paper round when

I was a kid, that I've ever had. It's about time I grew up and got a real job."

His mother didn't say anything. She just took another sip of her coffee.

"Did your father have anything to do with those pornographic videos?" she said finally.

"No. Of course not. Why do you ask that?" John said.

"Well, don't forget he owned that bloody video shop on the high street back in the day, when they were popular. But he closed it, thank God, when was it, a good 10 years ago now? Nobody watches videos anymore."

"Some people do," John said. "People who like porn do."

"Really?" Jo said. Surely, people who liked porn surfed the internet. Sometimes she wondered about her son's grip on reality.

"Were the Bucklers involved in this video thing?" she asked. They had helped Jack run the video shop, which she always suspected meant it was a front for something more sinister.

"How did you know the Bucklers were involved? They warned me against selling the videos. They have their own business selling them and I guess I was undercutting them. We ended up in a fight over it at The Nag's Head."

"The Bucklers have a business selling pornographic videos? I very much doubt it."

"That's what they said," John replied. "Look, sorry, I've got to rush. I've got to see the landlord at The Nag about a few things. I'll be back later. You will be okay, won't you, mum? No more gin."

"I'll be okay as long as you promise to stay out of trouble."

"I promise," John said. He lowered his large frame and kissed his mother on the cheek. It was something he hadn't done for a long while. Jo smiled. He wasn't such a bad son.

She watched her son disappear down the road from the ledge of the living room window, where she had perched herself with her coffee. Cradling her cup and taking small, deliberate sips, she reflected for a long moment on what John had said about the videos. A mist was clearing. She had heard Jack talking to one of the Bucklers on the telephone in his study the other week about sorting someone out. Was he referring to his own son? He had said something about pornography. She remembered now.

Maybe the Bucklers really had given John a warning over selling videos. If that was the case, was Jack responsible for giving them the orders to do so? But why would he do that? She stood up, deep in thought, and wandered over to the living room table, where she bent down and straightened a magazine out of habit, barely conscious of her action. Raising herself up, the landscape painting of the old barn on the wall opposite, which dominated the living room, caught her eye. It had been painted by a young Henry Llewellyn before he had found fame with his acting and was now worth a lot of money. There was something about the painting that always stirred her subconscious. It brought back happy memories of her walks with Jack when they were young. It was a painting of their favourite spot in the Wellesley countryside. After they had married, Jack had bought the barn, which was part of an old farm, and surrounding land, where he had built starter homes. It was his first major step on the road to making a fortune. She took a final sip from her depleted cup, her eyes still on the painting and thoughts in the past, then made her way to the kitchen for more coffee. Another cup might give her memory an extra nudge. She needed the mist to clear a little further to help her see a more complete picture and figure out what her husband was up to.

CHAPTER 35

The wind blew fiercely across the East Stand of Wellesley Football Club. Napoleon savoured the cold bite on his face. He loved the bitterly fresh evenings of the midweek football games in the early part of the season when there was still hope the team might win something. In his heart, he knew they wouldn't, but that didn't seem to matter as he was a true aficionado of the minor league game. It wasn't just about the football either, but the accoutrements that came with it - the half-time hotdogs, the paint-stripper tea, the noisy and excitable fans, the charge-filled atmosphere they created when the result was in the balance and the generally broken-down grounds, which at some venues like Wellesley, had their own unique and cosy appeal. Napoleon enjoyed the matches and occasions, even in defeat.

Robert, his second eldest and namesake, rubbed his hands together to keep warm and moaned at a wayward pass from the Wellesley left back. Robert, now 17, had been watching Wellesley since he was six years old. Like his father, he enjoyed the minor league game for its exciting unpredictability, even if it was at the expense of the quality of the football in the higher divisions, and he loved Wellesley because it was truly his team, the town where he had been born. His loyalty to Wellesley was something he could never transfer to another club, even a glamorous Premiership side, as it was part of his heritage and DNA.

Daniel, Napoleon's oldest son, who was 19, and Matthew, his youngest at nine, had little interest in football. Amy, the chief inspector's 14-year-old daughter, was no follower of the game either. One football fan out of four children wasn't bad, Napoleon supposed, although sometimes he begrudged his wife's influence on them. She variously described the game as boring, mindless, or pointless and that was on a good day.

Robert shook his head at another inadequate attempt to play pass and run football from Wellesley's midfield quartet. "Sometimes dad, I really wish you had brought me up as a Manchester City fan, even a team in one of the higher leagues would have been better than this lot." Wellesley were in the sixth highest division in the English football league system, which meant a large number of their players were semi-professional or amateur. The chasm in ability between the professionals of the English Premier League, the top division, and the mix of electricians, plumbers and even one policeman in the Wellesley side was immense.

"Yes, but when Wellesley win, you appreciate it more," Napoleon said. "It's also a short walk from our house. Anyway, this is real football. You never quite know what is going to happen or who is going to win. What's the fun in watching a team like Manchester City win every week? That would be boring. You don't want to support a club just because they win."

"Fat chance of that," Robert said. "But yeah. I guess you're right, and I can't change now. I love this team, even though they're playing rubbish football."

The referee blew the whistle for half-time before Napoleon could say anymore. Robert stood up from his seat and turned swiftly towards the stand's exit and the hot dog van. The chief inspector followed. He bought a hot dog for Robert and a cup of tea for himself, a ritual they followed at most games. The tea was so strong, it tended to rasp the hairs off your tongue, but Napoleon had acquired a taste for it over the years.

Robert was now complaining about his older brother which, together with Wellesley's less-than-skilful footballers, was his other main grievance of the evening. "He really is tight with his money, dad," he said through a mouthful of sausage, onion and tomato ketchup. "He's got loads of money and he buys me a packet of golf balls for my birthday. I bought him an expensive present for his."

Napoleon smiled. "It's not fair, but what he does with his money is his business. Just because you spend a lot on him, doesn't mean he has to spend the same amount on you, as unfair as it may seem. And next birthday, spend a little less on him."

The brothers' birthdays were only a few days apart and it often caused friction. When they were young, the arguments were about the number and size of the presents. In fact, now Napoleon thought about it, the arguments hadn't changed much over the years.

The chief inspector put a consoling arm around his son. "Jack McConnell was only telling me the other day that his son bought his wife a silver cross for her birthday a few years ago. It wasn't very expensive, but it meant a lot to his mum because his son had made the effort to get her something he knew she would like. Jack said she was very upset when it was stolen in a burglary."

"So, what are you saying? Golf balls are cheap, but Dan thought they would mean a lot to me? I suppose he knew they would be useful, and they were good quality," Robert said grudgingly.

"That's the way to look at it," Napoleon said. "Dan may not have used much imagination or paid out a king's ransom, but you do play a lot of golf. Let's give him the benefit of the doubt."

"Yeah," Robert said. "He's still a stingy git, though."

They both laughed, but as Robert finished his hot dog, he suddenly went quiet.

"What's the matter?" Napoleon said.

"Nothing. The silver cross. Sean had one. I remember. He was always fiddling with it, especially at the football. When he wanted something, he would rub a coin against it and make a wish to try and make it come true. I remember him doing it to bring Wellesley luck on the football field."

"Oh, really?" Napoleon said, surprised by his son's vivid recollection of the past when he and Robert used to meet up with Ted Cropper and his grandson at the Wellesley games. The two boys had been good friends.

"Sean was my first best friend. That's a special thing," Robert said. "I wonder what he would be like now. Would we still be friends, watching Wellesley games together? I wish he was still here."

"So do I," Napoleon said. Sean Cropper's disappearance had affected Robert deeply. Robert was seven and innocent when Sean had mysteriously vanished. Sean's disappearance had stolen that innocence and brought nightmares and insecurity. Napoleon sometimes wondered if it was responsible for Robert's reticent, almost withdrawn, nature. He was a bookish child, who enjoyed the comfort of his bedroom and his home to a degree Napoleon felt was unnatural for a boy of his age. His older brother was the total opposite. Even the youngest, Matthew, was more adventurous and confident than Robert.

Napoleon's reverie was broken by the hooter that signalled the second half was about to start. "I suppose we should go back to our seats," he said.

Robert nodded.

"Are you sure Sean had a silver cross?" Napoleon asked.

"Yes, of course I am," Robert said.

"Interesting," the chief inspector said.

"Yes," Robert replied.

Napoleon smiled at his son, lost in thought again. Sean Cropper had a silver cross and John McConnell had bought his mother a silver cross. In his experience, a coincidence often had an explanation.

"Come on dad, we'll miss the start of the second half if you don't hurry up."

"Yes," the chief inspector said, coming back to earth and noticing that most of the fans were now returning to their seats. He finished his tea and threw the polystyrene cup into a nearby bin. "Thanks Robert," he said absent-mindedly and followed his son back into the stand.

CHAPTER 36

◆

Napoleon sat down unsteadily on a rickety chair at a table in Ted Cropper's back garden. The chair's back legs dug into the earth and tipped him slightly backwards. He sat forward and righted himself, but the chair still felt unstable. The table was large and round and covered with an assortment of trays. Most were filled with bulbs or plants and some with earth. Ted looked up from where he was busily digging in the flower beds by the table and gave the inspector a half-hearted smile.

"I was just passing, so I thought I would drop in," Napoleon said.

It wasn't strictly a social call. He had some questions for Ted related to the deaths of Rankin and Delgado, but it was close to the truth. The inspector was a regular visitor and often found Ted in his garden, watering, planting or just pottering and mending his tools.

Napoleon had become close to Ted over the years and, now more than ever, his friend needed support as his wife had died from cancer earlier in the year, plunging him into a melancholy the inspector feared might turn into serious depression. The dark moods were something Ted had struggled with off and on since Sean's disappearance and his son Frank's suicide in the Wellesley police cells 10 years previously.

The feelings of wretchedness, or the black dog as Ted referred to them, were a result of the tragedies he and his family had suffered. His daughter-in-law and Frank's wife had died in a car accident in Spain shortly after losing her husband and son, and Ted's only surviving family member was an older sister, who had been diagnosed with the early stages of dementia.

"It's good to see you," Ted said, picking himself up from where he was planting. His gloomy expression indicated it was anything but good. He looked tired and strained, with deep lines on his face. He was 65, but he looked much older.

"Now's a good time to plant bulbs, before the winter frosts. The roots can get a hold in the ground before the soil freezes," he said, in explanation of why he was gardening on a bitterly cold, blustery autumn day, with rain clouds threatening to burst at any moment. Napoleon nodded, although he knew the real reason was more complicated. The garden was Ted's solace. The only place where he could find at least some happiness after the series of tragedies.

"But I warn you Rob, I might not be good company," Ted added. "I've not been sleeping well. You know how tough it's been for me this year."

"I can come back another time," Napoleon said, shifting forward again as his chair's back legs dug more deeply into the earth.

"No. It's fine. You're here now," Ted said, sitting down on a chair opposite Napoleon, which looked a lot steadier with legs that didn't plunge into the ground.

Napoleon tentatively eased backwards in his seat and reached inside one of his jacket pockets, pulling out a gold cross and chain. A thread of the woollen gloves he was wearing caught against one of the tiny links. He shook the chain free and placed it on the table, grimacing as he did so. He rarely wore gloves, but it was very cold and his circulation wasn't as good as it used to be. He had found the cross and chain in Mary's jewellery box. It was his cue to ask Ted whether Sean had owned a silver cross. He was sure his son was right about the cross, but he just needed to check.

"What's that?" Ted asked.

"I promised my wife I would fix her cross and chain," Napoleon said.

"It looks fine to me," Ted said.

"Yes, I've just got it back from the repair shop. One of the links was broken," Napoleon said. He felt a little disconcerted by how easily the lie rolled off his tongue, but he carried on anyway. "Didn't Sean have a cross like this?" he said casually.

"Yes, but it was silver, not gold like that one," Ted said. "He loved it. I bought it for him." Ted stood up abruptly and picked up one of the trays of bulbs on the table. "These are tulips. I'm going to plant them here," he said, pointing to the flower bed behind his chair.

"Right," Napoleon said. He stood up too, and moved his chair further round the table, nearer Ted, where the ground looked more solid. "I'm not much of a gardener, but I do like tulips."

"I suppose you don't have the time for gardening," Ted said, picking up another tray of bulbs. "These are daffodils. I'm going to plant them here too. Tulips and daffodils in a sea of yellow, my wife's favourite colour." Ted smiled broadly, looking genuinely happy.

"Joanne McConnell used to have a silver cross," Napoleon said, tentatively sitting back in his chair.

"Really? I wouldn't know. Why are you so interested in jewellery all of a sudden?" Ted said as he knelt on the ground and made a hole in the earth with his trowel.

"I'm sorry. I was just drifting. It's nothing," Napoleon said, carefully putting the cross and chain back in his jacket pocket, making sure it didn't snag on his gloves. He wasn't sure why he had mentioned Joanne McConnell's silver cross. Ted had a good memory and noticed things like necklaces and rings, some people did, but even he was unlikely to recall an item of jewellery worn by a woman he occasionally did odd jobs for that was stolen in a burglary years ago.

"Joanne McConnell doesn't strike me as the religious type who would wear a cross," Ted said as he carefully placed one of the bulbs in the ground, and patted earth around and on top of it. "She certainly blasphemes a lot. You should have heard her last Saturday when I went round to fix her washing machine. In fact, you probably did. She told me you and your sergeant had been there when the machine flooded the kitchen."

"Yes. That's right. We've been questioning a lot of people about the deaths of the policeman and the man found on the golf course."

Ted nodded and stood up. "I've heard about you and your questions," he said, sitting back down at the table. "The golf club secretary was grumbling to me the other day about you bothering all the members for alibis on the Wednesday night when the man found on the course was killed."

"How do you know he died on Wednesday night?" Napoleon asked, suddenly alert. "We haven't given out details on the exact time of his death."

"I'm a suspect now, am I? I don't know. Yes, I do know. Humphrey told me. But I do have an alibi. I was at the golf club on Wednesday night, which you know."

"Hmm. Humphrey again." Napoleon went quiet for a moment. "You only have an alibi for part of Wednesday night. You left the golf club at about 10pm to go home, according to my sergeant's notes. But don't worry Ted. You're not a prime suspect."

The inspector leaned back in his chair, testing the ground, which seemed more solid nearer Ted's side of the table, closer to the flower beds, and reached inside his jacket pocket. He pulled out a plastic bag containing the scrap of paper with the words 'Round Tuit' written inside a sketchily drawn circle, technically it was more of an oval, which had been found near the dead man on the first tee of the golf course.

"Do you remember a teacher who used to write odd little phrases on the blackboard when you were at Wellesley Primary School?" he said, showing Ted the piece of paper.

Ted was 20 years older than Napoleon, but both had been at the school during the teacher's time. The teacher had first joined the school in the early 1960s when Ted was a child and remained there until retiring in 1995. He died of a heart attack at the relatively young age of 58 shortly afterwards. The inspector had double checked the dates of the teacher's tenure at the school and found an obituary in the cuttings' files of the Wellesley Chronicle. The town's weekly newspaper still had files of old stories going back to the 1970s in its library, thanks to the old editor who insisted on maintaining the paper records despite the advance of the internet.

"The teacher's name was John Carter," Napoleon said. "He was a short man, quite austere and old fashioned who wore his university gown all the time. I remember being quite frightened of him. I've never forgotten the funny phrases and sayings he used to write on the blackboard to remind us to do our homework. Round Tuit – get round to it – was one of them. You must remember him?"

Ted looked blank. "No. I don't. It was too long ago. But why do you ask? Is the piece of paper evidence?"

"Maybe," Napoleon said. "But you're sure you can't remember him? You have a very good memory Ted, for everything. Football statistics, for example, and you observe things that others miss."

Ted laughed, then looked extremely serious and shook his head. "I'm sorry, Rob. I have no recall of the teacher or his phrases. What other strange things are you going to ask me? You're full of surprises today."

"There is one more." Napoleon smiled, warming to the absurdities of the conversation. "Do you like classical music and have you got an old cassette tape player?" he said. It was a reference to the tape of Beethoven found by Parsons on St Margaret's Road where Delgado was knocked down.

"Well, that's the strangest question of the lot. The answer is no and no, but I can tell you who likes classical music and who has one of those old tape machines, and that's Jack McConnell. He likes Beethoven and Wagner, like you do, if I recall. There's a cassette player in the McConnells' cellar, which belongs to Jack. I saw it last Saturday when I went down there to check whether the room had flooded like the kitchen. There were lots of old tapes, too, of classical music in a rack. But why on earth do you ask? Are all these questions related to the deaths?"

Napoleon smiled enigmatically, ignoring Ted's question. "That's interesting about Jack."

"Yes. Interesting." Ted laughed and picked up another tray of bulbs. "Come on Rob. Why do you ask? What is all this about?"

"Nothing."

"It's about nothing. This conversation is about nothing," Ted laughed again. "Whatever you say. I'm perplexed, but at least you've cheered me up with all these funny questions."

"Good," the inspector said, standing up and loosening his shoulders. "I wanted to make sure you were all right as you weren't at the football last night."

"No. I didn't feel like watching football. Sometimes I don't. Too many memories. But I'll come next time if you tell me why you're asking all these funny questions. Do crosses, Round Tuits and classical music have anything to do with the death of that young man and the policeman?"

"Probably not," Napoleon said, raising his eyebrows. "But remember, you can always talk to me. I'll give you a call and we can go for a drink or maybe play some golf." He pulled out his fountain pen and notebook from his jacket pockets. "Can you give me your mobile number? I can't find it in my phone for some reason." He handed Ted his notebook and pen. "Write the number in my notebook."

"Sure," Ted said, putting the tray of bulbs he was holding back on the table and pulling off his gardening gloves. He reached inside his trouser pocket for his phone to check the number. "You're so old school, Rob. Always pen and paper with you. You could key the numbers into your phone instead. It would easier."

"Old school," the inspector repeated. "But it's difficult to type when you're wearing a pair of woollen gloves." He raised his woollen-clad hands in a gesture of mock surrender and smiled crookedly.

Ted laughed and shook his head, writing down the number as he did so. He handed the pen and notebook back to the inspector, who was now stretching his shoulders. Sitting in a rickety garden chair was not helping his posture.

"And a drink would be good," Ted said. He smiled, but in a sad, distant way, picking up another tray of bulbs. "Winter pansies. My wife loved winter pansies. She loved flowers."

"Yes. I remember," Napoleon said.

Napoleon left Ted to his gardening and sat in his car for a while, his thoughts on Jack McConnell. He likes Beethoven, has a cassette player, a rack of classical tapes, and then one of the composer's music is found at the crime scene. But Parsons found the tape after the scenes of crime team had searched the area. The SOCO team would have found it otherwise. And even if it was Jack's tape, it wouldn't necessarily mean anything. But there were a lot of things connecting the McConnells to the investigation into the two deaths. Jack had found Delgado's body, his son had saved Delgado from drowning and then nearly been a victim of the red hatchback that hit Rankin. Jack had also been taught by the Round Tuit teacher at Wellesley Primary School, but the piece of paper wasn't his. He couldn't remember the teacher, or his phrases or sayings. His schooldays were a blur, he had said. Then, there were the silver cross and chains belonging to Sean Cropper and the one given to Joanne McConnell as a birthday present by her son, although they had no connection to the deaths of Delgado and Rankin. But it was still another coincidence in a growing list involving the McConnell family.

He held the Round Tuit piece of paper in his left hand and his notebook open on the page where Ted had written his telephone number in his right. He hadn't meant to make Ted write the number down, but suddenly in the cold, overcast garden, with his woollen gloves making his fingers too fat to type on his phone, it had seemed like a good idea to get a copy of Ted's handwriting for a comparison with the Round Tuit note. Now, he was suspecting his friend. That was ridiculous. To his relief, the writing didn't look similar. The inspector sighed and started the car as raindrops began to splatter on to the windscreen. Loose ends and coincidences, but no hard facts or evidence. He was sure there was something he could not quite see that linked everything. Like Ted, he was going to have a few sleepless nights, until he found some answers.

CHAPTER 37

◆

Napoleon decided on a lunchtime walk to recharge his batteries. A brisk walk was his daily constitutional. As well as physically stimulating, he found it mentally relaxing, like an emotional bath. Today he opted for a stroll to The Nag's Head. It was 20 minutes from the police station at a decent pace, longer than his usual walks, but the overcast day had turned pleasantly sunny, influencing his decision to go further afield.

The canopy of leaves along the tree-lined Wellesley Road had turned into an autumnal kaleidoscope of auburns, yellows and browns, with the occasional evergreen conifer breaking up the pattern. One tall and spindly tree, it looked like a sweet chestnut to Napoleon's untrained eye, reminded the inspector of Mick Buckler, the most unpleasant and vicious of the two brothers. Its stringy branches could have passed for Buckler's wiry, muscular arms, while the weather-beaten trunk had the look of his battle-hardened torso.

Napoleon had told Mayo and Parsons to pull the brothers in for questioning. They were the only people at The Nag's Head on the night Delgado was last seen alive who had yet to be interviewed, disappearing after their fight with McConnell outside the pub that evening. But now, Napoleon wanted answers. Not just on what they had seen that night, but why they had threatened McConnell over selling drugs and pornographic videos. The inspector guessed McConnell was undercutting them by selling cheaper drugs, but he was puzzled why they cared about the videos. The boxful that Parsons had brought back from McConnell's house were in poor condition on a primitive technology that rendered them close to worthless. They were also of the soft, amateurish variety the inspector considered more comical than sinister.

"So, what's your poison, chief inspector?" Napoleon had arrived at The Nag's Head to find John McConnell serving behind the bar. He had smiled to himself, thinking the young man looked the part with a tea towel slung over his arm for wiping glasses and a big grin on his face. Maybe this was his vocation.

"I'll have an orange juice," the inspector said. He had lost his taste for a pint. There was no winter ale on tap, his favourite, and he wanted a clear head for the afternoon. Even one pint was probably unwise. If Mayo and Parsons managed to find the Bucklers, he would need to be alert for the questioning.

He sat down on a stool at the bar and eyed the still grinning McConnell. The young man would probably make a good barman, if he could keep his hands out of the till.

"There you go inspector, a lovely glass of cold orange juice," McConnell said.

"Thank you," Napoleon said. He tapped the payment machine with his bank card and reached inside his jacket for his gold fountain pen and notebook. The small notebook was in its usual place in the left-hand pocket, but there was no pen. Annoyingly, he must have left it on his desk. He wasn't a superstitious man by nature, but the pen always seemed to bring him luck, and he wanted to make some notes.

He sighed. "Do you have a pen, John?" he said. McConnell rummaged around under the bar and came up with an old blue biro that had been chewed at the end. It would do, Napoleon supposed. He considered McConnell for a moment, then asked a question that had suddenly pushed its way to the front of his mind. "Do you remember a silver cross you gave your mother for a birthday present?" The question had been prompted by the misplaced pen. Sean Cropper's silver cross had been a lucky charm, although maybe not so lucky given the young child's fate.

McConnell's features creased into a picture of bafflement. He rolled his head from side to side and stared at Napoleon in astonishment as if the inspector had suddenly grown an extra head. "Now, that is an unexpected question." McConnell then smiled broadly. "But yes, I do." He paused and frowned. "But why do you ask? Don't tell me you've found it. It was stolen from my parents' house years ago."

"Where did you buy it?"

"I didn't. I won it in a game of cards with Mick Buckler. He had no money left so he put the cross in the pot. But, come on inspector, why are you asking? Have you found it? This is intriguing."

Napoleon ignored McConnell's question. "When did you win it off Buckler? Be precise."

"I can't be precise. A long time ago. Five years ago, maybe more. I can't remember."

"Try."

"It must be five years ago, I guess. No, probably seven or eight. It was just after I came back from travelling. I won it off Buckler shortly after I got home. I can't be more specific than that. Sorry."

Napoleon nodded and took down some notes with the chewed biro. It moved raggedly across the page unlike his fountain pen, which glided across the paper as if they were made for each other.

McConnell gave the inspector another baffled look. "Come on inspector, what is all this about?"

"It was definitely stolen?" Napoleon said, again ignoring McConnell's question and shaking the biro to try to make the ink flow more freely.

"Yes. It was. It was taken from our kitchen by burglars. My mum was very upset about it. She really liked it for some reason. I suppose it was because it was one of the first birthday presents I ever gave her. She used to leave it hanging from a hook in the kitchen. I remember her telling me. The kitchen wasn't touched by whoever broke in. The rest of the house was trashed, but not the kitchen. Yet they stole the cross. Bizarre."

"The kitchen wasn't trashed but the rest of the house was," Napoleon repeated. "That is odd." The inspector drained his orange juice. "You've been very helpful," he said. He took down some more notes, but the pen ran out of ink before he could finish writing.

"Are you going to tell me why you want to know all this?" McConnell said plaintively.

"I will one day, if it leads anywhere," Napoleon said cryptically.

The inspector stood up and handed the chewed, spent pen back to McConnell. It was time to get back to the office. "But I doubt it will," the inspector added and made for the door. He needed another walk to stimulate his thoughts.

CHAPTER 38

◆

Mick Buckler, the meanest of the Buckler brothers, sat on a chair in one of the interview rooms at Wellesley police station. His folded arms rested on the table in front of him and an aggressive sneer distorted his face. His white tee shirt was taut, straining over a well-developed physique, and the muscles on display in his neck and forearms were bunched in a gesture of defiance. Mayo cast a discursive eye over the muscular outline, the product of hours in the gym, and sat down opposite him.

It was fortunate such a borderline psychopath didn't have a well-developed mind to match the body, the sergeant thought. He let his eyes settle on the little terrier's flexed arms. Would the reckless Buckler try the fisticuffs routine in a police station? The sergeant moved his chair back a little, out of arm swinging range, as Parsons entered. It was better to be cautious when dealing with Buckler.

The detective constable took the chair next to the sergeant and opposite Buckler, who she looked at with obvious disapproval. It had been a difficult morning. They had found Buckler in a pub in St Margaret's, the small village just outside Wellesley where Henry Llewellyn lived. Buckler had been putting up a shed for one of the residents and was taking a break in the pub.

Up until that point, Mayo had considered it an unusually pleasant day. The sun had come out and Parsons had been making him laugh over stories about her four-year-old niece, who she had been looking after over the weekend. Maybe, it was Parsons who had made him complacent. She certainly lifted his spirits with her funny stories, but it was no excuse for not listening to Napoleon.

The inspector had instructed him to bring Buckler back to the station. "Just say it is a routine inquiry and bring him back here,"

Napoleon had said. But surely it would be easier to question him on the spot, where we find him, Mayo had replied. "There aren't any charges against him." Napoleon smiled crookedly. "Just get him in the police car and bring him back. Don't tell him what it's about. Just get him back here."

Now, he all too clearly understood the prescience of the advice. On showing Buckler his police warrant card, the man had become unnecessarily aggressive. The sergeant had then mentioned McConnell and the fight. It had been like pouring petrol on a fire, prompting a stream of expletives from Buckler about policemen and their likeness to a certain farmyard animal. The reaction had been so fierce, it had left the sergeant with little choice but to handcuff him. The man was like a walking detonator, any tiny sound or injudicious word setting him off in a torrent of foul language and threats.

Mayo was just pondering whether to tell Napoleon about what had happened when the inspector pushed open the door. "Ahh," he said. "We've found Mr Buckler." The inspector looked triumphant, although Mayo thought his pleasure was premature. Buckler was unlikely to say anything helpful.

"This is overkill, isn't it? Three coppers to interview me over what, some alleged fight me and Jim had with John McConnell? You've got to be joking. I would call my lawyer, if I could be bothered."

Napoleon remained standing and nodded at Mayo, who clicked on the machine to record the interview. "Just tell us about the fight," the sergeant said.

"No comment," Buckler said, sneering.

"We understand you threatened John McConnell over the selling of drugs and pornographic videos," Mayo said.

"No comment."

"And that John then beat you up," Parsons interjected. She smiled provocatively.

"That's not true. We beat him up," Buckler responded, eyeing Parsons up and down lecherously.

"So, you did have a fight?" Parsons said.

"We pushed and shoved each other. That's all. It was nothing."

"And you threatened him over selling drugs and videos?" Mayo asked again.

"No comment."

"Okay Mick," Napoleon said. He was now leaning forward with his left hand resting on the table next to Mayo, while twirling his gold fountain pen around the fingers of his right. His face was very close to Buckler's, which the sergeant thought unwise. "Do you know Peter Delgado, the man who was found dead on the golf course? He was at The Nag's Head that night you had your disagreement with McConnell."

"Oh, I see. So, you're gonna try and stitch me up for that, are you?"

Napoleon looked into Buckler's eyes, his face still threateningly close to the angry terrier. "Mick, just tell us whether you know Delgado and whether you noticed him at the pub that night? Did you talk to him or see anyone talk to him?" the inspector said.

"I didn't know the dead man. And I didn't see him at the pub. Me and my brother were just in the pub for a drink, then McConnell spilt my pint and we had words. That's all."

"Where is your brother?" Napoleon said, pulling his face away from Buckler's and standing up straight.

"I don't know. Around. We've been in Redfield for the past week doing odd jobs for Jack McConnell."

"Odd jobs for Jack McConnell?" Napoleon repeated.

"Yeah. He has some offices there and we were doing some painting in one of them. That's all. We finished the other day, and I haven't seen Jim since."

"Do you remember a silver cross that you lost to John McConnell in a game of cards?" Napoleon said, again leaning close to Buckler's face to gauge his reaction.

Parsons turned to look at Napoleon, a puzzled expression toying with her features. The inspector was an unpredictable man, but that was a question out of the deep, dark blue. Mayo also glanced at the inspector, raising his right eyebrow as he did so, looking just as baffled.

"What are you talking about? I haven't played cards with McConnell in years and I don't have a silver cross."

"You lost a silver cross to McConnell in a card game a few years ago," Napoleon said, looking deeply into Buckler's eyes.

"You're off your head inspector. I don't know anything about a silver cross. Can I go now? This is bullshit."

Buckler pulled away from Napoleon's face, looking furious. Mayo feared the detonator was about to go off again. The question had clearly unsettled him, like the warrant card. Buckler stood up. "I'm leaving," he said, and told the inspector to do something that was biologically impossible.

"Sit down, Mick," Napoleon said calmly. Buckler looked at the inspector, then at Mayo and Parsons, snorted and finally did as Napoleon suggested. "I haven't done anything. This is bloody police harassment," Buckler said sulkily.

"Cool it," Napoleon said. "We aren't accusing you of anything." He motioned to Mayo to turn off the machine recording the interview. "My office," he said to the two officers. To Buckler, he added: "We won't be long. Don't do anything stupid."

"What was all that about a cross?" Parsons asked.

"I'm not sure. I had a hunch. But after that reaction, maybe it's more than a hunch," Napoleon said. He sighed. "This case might have just got a lot more complicated."

"What do you mean?" Parsons asked. She was utterly confused.

"McConnell won a silver cross in a card game with Buckler seven or eight years ago. A little boy, Sean Cropper, who went missing a year or two before that also had a silver cross."

"You can't mean that it's the same cross?" Parsons said.

"It could be," Napoleon said.

"Have you found this cross, sir?" Mayo asked.

"No. As I said, it's just a hunch, but that was an extreme reaction to an innocuous question," the inspector said.

"But if you haven't found the cross, then it's just speculation," Mayo said. "And it's not connected with the deaths of Delgado and Rankin. It's a blind alley, sir."

"There were rumours of a porn ring years ago. And there is this cross. The cross and the deaths might be related," Napoleon said.

"Sorry sir. You're not making sense," Parsons said. "How can the cross and the deaths be related?"

"I don't know. But there's an undertone. We can't see it or hear it, but there's something that connects the deaths of Delgado and Rankin, and it has something to do with the McConnells. There are too many strange coincidences involving the McConnells."

Parsons looked at Mayo and then at the inspector. "Sir, you'll have to explain."

Napoleon met Parsons' eyes, his expression troubled. "Jack McConnell found Delgado's body, John McConnell saved Delgado from drowning, then John McConnell is at the scene when Rankin is killed. Buckler is in the pay of Jack McConnell and he and his brother have a fight with John McConnell on the night Delgado is killed."

The inspector shifted his gaze from Parsons to Mayo, both looking equally bewildered by this new and beguiling line of thinking. "Okay," Napoleon said, seeing the scepticism written across the faces of his two colleagues. "The cross probably isn't connected. But we need to use our imagination, or we'll get nowhere."

The inspector suddenly stood up from his chair and left the room. He had left his gold fountain pen on the table by Buckler. The villain would take it, if he didn't retrieve it.

Mayo smiled forlornly at Parsons and shook his head as the inspector closed the door behind him. "I think this has been a wasted day. Napoleon is clutching at straws, and he knows it," the sergeant said. "Life is full of coincidences, but they don't mean anything."

"You're right," Parsons said. "The inspector's trying to make a connection that isn't there. Buckler's heated reaction at the mention of the cross isn't that odd. The man's a psycho."

She sighed deeply and flicked back her long dark hair in a way that Mayo found incredibly alluring. She was a very attractive woman. "We should go for a drink. I think we all need one," Parsons said, glancing at the sergeant and cocking her head to one side as she did so.

Mayo smiled again, but this time more broadly and with pleasure. At least one of his colleagues was sane. It was the best suggestion of the day.

CHAPTER 39

◆

The three police officers found their usual table just behind the door at The Wheel of Fortune. "Now we've let his brother go, we need to find Jim Buckler," Napoleon said loudly to make himself heard above a background cacophony of boozy laughter and disembodied conversations. Thursday nights at The Wheel were usually a boisterous affair with the weekend approaching, and the pub was already filling up with drinkers, despite the early hour.

"He's not a psycho like his brother, but he's not likely to be much more helpful," Mayo said, taking his malt whisky and ice from a tray, which Napoleon had placed on the table.

"But he might," the inspector said, before downing a large mouthful of beer.

Parsons took a sip of her gin and tonic. "Sir, shouldn't we be looking more closely at the brother of Delgado? If Delgado's death was premeditated, then Ray Delgado has to be high on our list of suspects. I know his car has no marks on it to suggest it was in an accident, but he doesn't have an alibi for the evening his brother died and we don't know for sure what he did that night. There was no record of him on the university CCTV. It doesn't cover the entire library, but you would have thought he would have been caught on camera at some point during the evening, given he was there for three or four hours. The university security told me yesterday they had dug out the footage of the car park. They couldn't find it last week because it was on a different hard drive. We should go back to the university and check the CCTV again, particularly now we have coverage of the car park."

"Yes. Good idea, constable," Napoleon said, nodding. "Take a trip to the university and go over the CCTV one more time. And talk to the brother and girlfriend to see if their story remains consistent."

211

Napoleon stood up. "I need to go to the bathroom."

Parsons watched the inspector disappear through a crowd of people on his way to the toilets. "He's happy for me to go to the university and talk to Delgado again, but he has no interest in following that line of enquiry himself. He really believes there's some link that connects the McConnells to the deaths, doesn't he?" she said.

Mayo rubbed his chin and drained his whisky in one large mouthful. "He was convinced the golf club was the key to the deaths," he said. "Now, he's convinced the McConnells hold the key, even believing this stolen silver cross is somehow significant. He obsessively pursues one line, then suddenly loses interest, and focuses on another. I'm not sure if he's a genius or a crackpot. But he's wrong about the cross. It's a red herring. As for Ray Delgado, I can see why he doesn't think he's responsible. His story about driving to the university sounds right, his car was clean, and it's not likely he used another vehicle to run his brother over."

Mayo looked into his glass, which was full of ice but deplete of whisky. "Do you want another drink?" he said.

"No, I'm fine," Parsons said.

The sergeant squeezed past two tall men, deep in conversation, to get to the front of the bar, where to his surprise he found Joanne McConnell. "Hello," he said. "Would you like a drink?"

"Oh, that would be marvellous. I've been looking for you and the inspector. The duty sergeant at the police station said you'd be here. I have something important to tell you."

Mrs McConnell sat down between Parsons and Napoleon and opposite Mayo. "Isn't that odd? I've lived in this town all my life and not once have I crossed the threshold into this quaint little pub." She smiled, amused by her comment. The three police officers politely smiled back. "Sorry, you don't want to hear bland observations about my life, which is of no interest to anyone. You want to hear what I've got to say that is so important. Well, I'm convinced my husband ordered the Bucklers to threaten my son last week." Napoleon raised his eyebrows. "Why would he do that?"

"I'm not sure, but I think it has something to do with videos, blue ones. I heard Jack on the telephone, saying he wanted the boy sorted out and warned over the videos."

Mrs McConnell hesitated, then went on: "My husband's quite a paradox, you know. Meticulous and careful about his business. Yet, in other ways, reckless. I've heard him talk about blue videos on the telephone before, most probably to one of the Bucklers."

Her eyes settled on Parsons in sudden recognition. "You were at my house yesterday. I remember now," she said, nodding to herself. "My apologies. I wasn't that welcoming. Too much gin and not enough tonic." She lifted her glass of tonic water and chinked it against Parson's gin filled tumbler.

Parsons smiled. "No problem."

Mrs McConnell smiled back. "It was after you'd gone that John told me about the pornographic videos and the fight he had with the Bucklers at The Nag's Head. John said he wasn't going to sell them anymore or break the law. Well, it makes sense now, doesn't it? Jack on the telephone, wanting someone sorted out over pornographic videos. Then, the Bucklers turn up at The Nag's Head, threatening John and warning him not to sell the nasty things."

"This is all very interesting," Mayo said. "But your husband can easily deny it, and then it's your word against his."

"The sergeant's right," Napoleon said. "There were rumours about Jack and pornographic videos a few years ago. But they were baseless rumours. And I find it hard to believe a father would order someone to threaten his own son."

"You don't know Jack," Mrs McConnell said.

"No. I don't," Napoleon said. The inspector sucked his teeth and took a deep breath. "Mrs McConnell," he said slowly, changing the subject. "Can you remember a silver cross your son gave you as a birthday present some years ago?"

Mayo smiled wryly at Parsons, who discreetly rolled her eyes.

Mrs McConnell went quiet for a moment before collecting her thoughts. "Yes. I do. It was very precious to me, but it was stolen. Have you found it, after all this time? It was stolen at least five or six years ago."

"No. We haven't found it. Was it marked in any distinctive way, a scratch maybe?"

"Is that important?" Mrs McConnell said. "What is all this about?"

"I don't know if the silver cross has any relevance to anything, but I would be interested to know if it was scratched," Napoleon replied. It was a question he should have asked John McConnell. If it was Sean's, it might have had a mark where he rubbed coins against it for luck.

"I can't remember." She shrugged her shoulders. "But if you find it, I would like it back."

"Of course," Napoleon said.

Mrs McConnell considered the inspector's troubled expression. "The cross," she said. "It wasn't worth much. Is it significant to anything?"

No, thought Mayo. He could see why Rankin used to get frustrated with Napoleon. The cross was an irrelevant distraction.

"I don't know," Napoleon replied.

"I don't understand. If you haven't found it, how do you know about it and why are you asking these questions?" Mrs McConnell persisted.

"Forget it. It means nothing," Napoleon said firmly.

Yes, let's forget it, Mayo thought. Parsons rolled her eyes at the sergeant again. She clearly thought the subject of the cross was best forgotten, too.

CHAPTER 40

◆

It was Ray Delgado. She was sure. He was getting into a red hatchback with a smallish, dark-haired woman of about his own age. Parsons hadn't been able to find Delgado in the library on the university CCTV, but now the college security had provided film of the car park, there he was. Time stamp on the recording: 9:03 on the Wednesday evening that his older brother had been hit and killed by a car. Her heart did a little leap and she phoned Mayo. The sergeant would be pleased. This was a significant development.

CHAPTER 41

◆

"**R**ay Delgado got into a red hatchback with a smallish, dark haired woman at 9pm on the night his brother was killed," Napoleon said in the flat monotone he tended to use when talking to Chief Superintendent Jim Hunter. "The car that hit Rankin was a red hatchback. A big coincidence." The inspector scratched his chin as he waited for a reaction.

Hunter raised his eyes from the papers he was reading. "Was this recorded on the university CCTV?"

"Yes," Napoleon said. Hunter was looking calmer and more relaxed than usual. But that was about to change.

"And you've brought Delgado in for questioning?"

"He's on a flight to Spain, sir." Napoleon waited for the explosion.

"Spain." Hunter stood up from behind his desk. "How did you let that happen?" There was no explosion, but the tone was menacing.

Napoleon shuffled awkwardly in his chair. "He promised to remain in Wellesley after his first trip to Spain. We didn't consider him a flight risk."

Hunter frowned. "What now? Have you contacted the Spanish police?"

"Yes sir. We've spoken to them. They're going to collect him when he gets off the plane in Madrid, which should be around lunchtime."

"And the young woman, who got into the car with him. His girlfriend?"

"No, sir. She is a Miss Sally Jones. She was identified by Delgado's girlfriend. We pulled the girlfriend in for questioning this morning. She says her boyfriend's trip to Spain was innocent and because of a last-minute change in the funeral arrangements. The older brother is now being buried in Spain, instead of Wellesley. The girlfriend says her boyfriend is flying back to

216

England tomorrow, and she insists there's nothing suspicious about this Miss Jones getting into the car with him. They're doing the same degree, Economics and English, and often study together. They're good friends."

Hunter nodded morosely and sat back down in his chair.

"And, sir... The young woman was the driver. The CCTV shows she got into the driver's seat. Delgado got into the passenger's side. Mayo and Parsons are at Redfield University now, trying to find her. She should be in lectures this morning."

"Good," Hunter said. "That's something positive. Is there anything else I need to know?" He began reading the papers on his desk again.

"I intend to speak to Jack McConnell. I have some more questions to ask him on various matters."

Hunter looked up and gave Napoleon a long, hard stare. "What various matters?"

"Just loose ends, sir." Napoleon saw no point in telling Hunter about Joanne McConnell's claim her husband had ordered the Buckler brothers to threaten their son. It would only make Hunter angry. A respectable businessman ordering a couple of thugs to threaten his son didn't add up and Hunter was a man who liked things to add up. "He found the body," Napoleon said instead.

"I know he found the body, Napoleon. But don't blunder around upsetting Jack McConnell, an important member of the community, when the obvious answers are staring you in the face. I don't want you going off on one of your wild goose chases."

"No sir," the inspector said. He returned the chief superintendent's stare with a poker face. The two men blinked at each other before Hunter looked away and stood up again.

"You can go, Napoleon," Hunter said, turning to look out of the office window. "But, I mean it. Don't upset McConnell, and no wild goose chases."

It was cold. Mayo rubbed his hands as he waited for Parsons to finish talking to Napoleon on her mobile. They had just arrived at Redfield University and were getting out of the car when the chief inspector called. "I don't believe it," Parsons said, as the pair of them started walking towards the university reception area and the vice-chancellor's office. "He still thinks this case hinges around Jack McConnell, when we have evidence that Delgado was lying to us and got into a car with this young woman on the night his brother was killed."

Mayo smiled. He couldn't help himself.

"What are you smiling for? It's ridiculous," Parsons said, snappily.

"No reason," Mayo lied. He was smiling because he found Parsons very attractive when she was cross. He wasn't sure why. It was probably the set of her face, the pout of her mouth and the expressive eyes, full of angst and determination. "I wouldn't worry about Napoleon," he said. "Once we pick up this young woman, we can find out what happened. Who knows? We might get a confession, then even Napoleon will have to give up on his mad theories."

Napoleon grimaced as he disconnected from the call. He could sense Parsons' exasperation with him. The CCTV of Ray Delgado and the young woman driving away from the university could be a breakthrough, yet he still felt McConnell was involved in the deaths, even if not directly. But maybe he should have kept that to himself and maybe he should have been more positive about Parsons' CCTV find earlier in the day. He sighed heavily as he waited for several passing vehicles at the exit of the car park. The road alongside Valley Police headquarters was a busy dual carriageway and it was often difficult to find a space in the traffic. Finally, one opened up. He put his foot down on the accelerator and nipped in between a blue sports car and a white delivery van, pointing the blunt nose of his wife's Mini Cooper towards Jack McConnell's house and Wellesley.

"Come in, dear boy," McConnell said with a broad smile, his large frame filling the front door. He ushered the chief inspector into the hallway, wrapping an expansive arm around his shoulders.

"I've opened a favourite bottle of wine. The enjoyment of good wine is even greater when there is someone to share it with," McConnell boomed, tightening his arm around the inspector's shoulders. "I thought we would have a light lunch of cheese, cold meats and some bread and biscuits to go with the wine."

He took Napoleon's raincoat and hung it on a peg by the front door. "And we're eating in the cellar. My wife doesn't like me messing up her kitchen or dining room. She's not here and won't be back until a lot later, but I prefer the cellar anyway. It's my den."

Napoleon nodded. He knew Joanne McConnell would be out. She would be at a friend's house, she had said, in his telephone call with her that morning. He had called her to tell her about his lunch with McConnell and his intention of bringing up the threats against her son. Make sure you tell my husband who heard him on the phone ordering the Bucklers to threaten John, she had replied. She sounded defiant, like she wanted a fight with her husband, although she was happy for the inspector to wade in first.

McConnell finally lifted his arm off Napoleon's shoulders and slapped him hard on the back.

"Sounds good," Napoleon said in a breathless voice, the playful slap slightly winding him. McConnell looked Napoleon up and down and punched him on the shoulder, but this time gently, to the relief of the inspector. "To the wine, dear boy," he said and led the way to the cellar. Napoleon followed, still slightly breathless, half in awe, half annoyed at McConnell's physicality. He was like a force of nature, mesmerizing and powerful. It reminded Napoleon of the river on a harsh winter day, the wind whipping across the water, disrupting everything in its path. Like the wind, nothing could break McConnell's stride or change his course. He was remorseless. It was the key to his success in business and the cause of his broken marriage, where his single-minded drive had sacrificed compromise and empathy.

"I will show you something to tantalize the taste buds and lift the spirits," McConnell said as they descended the stairs into the cellar. He smiled broadly again, like a schoolboy about to show a friend his favourite toy.

The cellar was large, with at least a half a dozen corridors leading off into darkness from the main room. The corridors were packed with wine bottles, some lying horizontally, and others stacked at angles on wooden wine racks. In the centre of the room, stood a gleaming mahogany table, furnished with a bottle of red wine, two crystal glasses and a large platter, overflowing with various cheeses, meats, different kinds of bread and a selection of biscuits. Napkins were neatly folded by the side of two plates. Napoleon sat on the nearest of two stools by the mahogany table and peered down one of the dark aisles. It stretched at least 20 feet.

McConnell placed himself on the other stool and followed the chief inspector's gaze. "It's a big cellar. The same size as the ground floor of the house," he said. "I kept expanding my collection of wine and the cellar grew with it."

"An ideal place to hide a body," Napoleon said. "Or some pornographic videos." He focused sharply on McConnell's face. The broad smile gave nothing away.

"I wouldn't hide a body here, dear boy. It might ruin the wine. Now pornographic videos, that's a thought, although they're not illegal as far as I know, so no need to conceal them down here."

"Hard-core pornographic ones are," the inspector said.

McConnell laughed. "So, that's what you're here about. Blue movies."

"Why do you say that?"

"No reason, really. Just a feeble joke. There used to be a racket in porn videos in this area. But you're about 10 years too late to do anything about it. No-one watches videos anymore."

McConnell poured the wine into the crystal glasses. They looked expensive, like the wine.

As McConnell was pouring, Napoleon noticed a large tape cassette player with a built-in radio and protruding aerial on a small table behind him. It was half hidden in one of the aisles, but it looked like an old ghetto blaster from the 1980s before compact discs and then DVDs made them obsolete. McConnell looked round to see what had caught the inspector's eye. "It's my old tape machine from my university days," McConnell said. "I keep it for nostalgic reasons."

"Does it still work?" Napoleon said. He had owned a similar machine when he was young, which had long been consigned to the scrap heap.

"Yes, but the sound is a bit tinny, and a lot of my tapes have corroded with age."

"Hmm," the inspector said. Ted Cropper had said McConnell had a tape machine in his cellar and liked classical music. There was a cassette rack beside the machine filled with tapes, similar to the one of Beethoven found by Parsons on St Margaret's Road, near where Delgado was hit. "You're a fan of classical music, aren't you? Beethoven in particular?"

"Yes. I am. Did I tell you that?"

"Erm. Yes. I think you did," Napoleon said. It wasn't exactly a lie. Ted Cropper had told him, but McConnell might have done as well at some point. "Have you any Beethoven tapes?"

"Quite probably. I'll dig one out for you in a minute. Drink some wine first," McConnell said impatiently. He was keen to start the wine tasting.

Napoleon nodded. "Okay," he said, swilling the wine around his glass and taking a small sip. It was dark, almost brown in colour and full bodied.

"How is it?" McConnell asked eagerly before tasting the wine himself. "Plenty of flavour, full and rich," he said, answering his own question. "But refined and rounded, like it's encased in velvet," he added with an intensity of someone unable to conceal their excitement over an anticipated pleasure.

Napoleon nodded again.

"It's a Chateau Leoville, a full-bodied claret," McConnell said. "It's second cru, but it tastes like a premier cru if you keep it long enough. I opened it today because I've had it in my cellar for exactly 10 years, and it seemed like a good time to try it."

"So, when do you open the Margaux?" Napoleon said. It was the only top range, premier cru wine he could think of.

"For very special occasions," McConnell said. "This is very nearly a very special occasion." McConnell laughed loudly at his joke. He was one of those people who found himself hilarious.

The chief inspector smiled back, taking another sip of wine, rolling the liquid around his mouth to get a true sense of its flavour. It was, as McConnell said, full, refined and rounded. The red wine he usually drank was pleasant enough in a tangy, fruity way, but this had a much deeper and more distinctive flavour, lingering on the taste buds and leaving a lasting mark.

McConnell smiled broadly yet again. "I see you're a fan." He finally took a large sip from his glass, sluicing the wine around his teeth and tongue in a similar way to Napoleon. He looked deep in thought, like he was in a heavenly trance, allowing the wine to soak and marinate his mouth.

The chief inspector put his wine glass down and watched McConnell savouring his first taste of the precious liquid. He waited for his host to swallow and finish his special moment before asking to look at his tape collection.

"Of course," McConnell said. "But the sound system isn't great. If you want to listen to Beethoven or something else, I can get my smart speakers from upstairs. I have an Alexa."

"No. That's okay," the inspector said. "A tape of Beethoven was found on St Margaret's Road by one of our officers the other day," he added.

McConnell shrugged his shoulders and looked blank.

Napoleon stood up and walked over to where the tapes were, bending down and casting his eye over the rows of small rectangular boxes. They were mostly of old 1970s and 1980s rock and punk bands, reflecting McConnell's taste in music in his university days. There were some tapes of classical music, but none of Beethoven.

"I can't see any Beethoven tapes in your collection. Maybe the Beethoven tape we found was yours?"

"I doubt it," McConnell said. "No one has touched those tapes for years."

Napoleon stood up straight and walked back to the mahogany table. Even if the tape found in St Margaret's Road was McConnell's, what did it prove? It was dropped there at least a day after Delgado was killed, otherwise it would have been found in the initial sweep of the road by SOCO, rather than Parsons a week later. It was another frustrating loose end.

"Are you sure you don't want me to get the Alexa from upstairs?" McConnell said. "It would be no trouble, if you want to listen to some music. Beethoven's third and fifth symphonies are my favourites."

"No. Don't worry," Napoleon said. Those symphonies were his favourites too. He and McConnell had similar tastes and outlooks, they were both single-minded and driven. It was why the inspector couldn't help liking the man, despite his selfishness and neglect of his wife.

The inspector sat back down on his stool. "Why did you ask the Bucklers to threaten your son?" he said.

McConnell frowned, looking bemused. "Why would I want the Bucklers to threaten John?" he replied warily, his cheek twitching as he clenched his chin. Napoleon had noticed McConnell subconsciously clench his chin before, when challenged with something awkward.

"You tell me?" Napoleon said. "Apparently, it was over the selling of pornographic videos."

"Ahh. Back to the videos," McConnell said in a guarded way, eyeing the inspector up and down suspiciously. "I used to own a video shop as you probably know. But I have no interest in them now. As for my son, he may need some sense beaten into him, but I wouldn't ask someone to threaten or attack him. I am his father. And frankly, I can't see the Bucklers winning a fight with John. Fighting is the one thing John's good at." McConnell smiled broadly again. "Try some cheese," he said, his good humour returning as his thoughts turned back to the lunch and wine.

"Thanks. I will," Napoleon said. He took a generous slice of Stilton with his knife and put it on his plate.

"Your wife thinks you ordered the Bucklers to threaten your son. She thinks it's to do with the videos. She thinks your son was causing you problems by selling his own pornographic videos."

McConnell laughed loudly again. "The pornographic video business is finished. Not that I was ever involved in it in the first place. As I said inspector, no one watches videos anymore. John would be stupid to try and make money from selling videos in this day and age. Why would anyone buy them? My wife is talking nonsense." McConnell spread some Brie over a water biscuit and took a large bite.

Napoleon nodded, frowning as he did so, and broke open a white roll, spreading his Stilton in the middle and adding some mango chutney and a gherkin. He was a big fan of gherkins. "Your wife overheard some of your telephone calls. She was quite clear about what you said to one of the Bucklers. That it was an instruction to threaten John." The inspector took a sip of wine and then a mouthful of his roll.

"My wife's drunk a lot of the time. I wouldn't put any value on what she says, if I was you inspector."

"Hmm. But your wife was stone cold sober when she made the allegation. Why would she make such an allegation, if it wasn't true?" Napoleon said.

McConnell sighed and looked at the inspector as if he was dealing with a child. "Napoleon. What is the point of all this? Why are you here? My wife's allegation, as you put it, is nonsense. She is an embittered drunk. It is my word against hers. You're wasting your time with this."

It was Napoleon's turn to sigh. McConnell was right.

"Your wife made a complaint against you and we have to question you. So here I am questioning you."

"And now you have the answer to your question. It's nonsense," McConnell said. "Why don't we talk about something else and enjoy our lunch. How's the golf?"

Napoleon nodded again, but his expression was a wry smile rather than a frown this time. "I haven't played since our last game."

"In that case, you can listen to me telling you about my golf. I enjoy nothing better than talking about my game and now I have a captive audience with a glass of wine in their hand and some of the finest Stilton, soaked in port by me personally."

Napoleon nodded yet again. He believed Joanne McConnell had told the truth, but her word alone was not enough to prove it. And, as McConnell said, it didn't make sense. Why would he want his son threatened? He had no interest in the video racket, which probably didn't exist anymore, except in the mind of his son, who appeared to live in a fantasy world half the time. Hunter and Parsons were right.

The police needed to focus on Ray Delgado and the young woman who drove him out of the university car park on the night his brother was killed. Jack McConnell, the threats and videos, the Beethoven tape, were probably just distractions. McConnell, though, was a pleasant diversion, with the wine and smorgasbord of cheese and hams.

"Okay Jack. Tell me about your golf," he said. It wouldn't hurt to forget police work for an hour or two and enjoy the lunch.

CHAPTER 42

◆

"But Ray, it wasn't our fault."

"I know, but I can't tell the police that I was with you on the Wednesday night after the row with Peter. It would upset Chloe too much."

Ray looked across the table into Sally's eyes. The sun was breaking through the clouds on the Champs-Elysees and was now shining in his face. He shielded his forehead with a hand and sipped his expresso. A feeling of pleasure welled inside him; the switching of flights to Paris, instead of travelling to Madrid to see his parents, was the right decision. Seeing Sally had convinced him of that. She looked very lovely, and his heart had done its usual somersault when he had first seen her in the cafe.

She had found a corner table, perfectly located with a view of the Arc de Triomphe and away from the kitchen. It was a typically Parisian café with its wicker chairs and rich odours of pastry and strong coffee. Even its expense on the Champs-Elysees, which emptied the wallet, stirred fond and sentimental memories from their previous visits.

He had been desperate to see Sally for several days, but it was only at Heathrow that his need had become urgent, and Paris was ideal - on neutral ground, away from his parents and Chloe. It also delayed the confrontation with his parents after his father's decision to bury Peter in Spain instead of Wellesley, which had infuriated him. It would be a struggle to control his temper when he met his father, but he hoped Sally might give him the perspective he needed to soften his anger.

"I didn't think it would matter, if I didn't tell the police about you and our drive," Ray said. "But now I'm not so sure. The police say Peter was hit and killed by a car. If someone saw us in your car, we could get in trouble. They might think I was trying to cover up."

"You are," Sally said. "And following me to Paris was stupid. You should contact the police and tell them you're coming home as soon as possible and tell them the truth. If the police want to talk to me, then I will get a flight home too. This was supposed to be a relaxing weekend away with my parents, then suddenly you turn up. I can't relax now."

"I'm sorry, Sally. I'm not contacting the police. I'm going to fly on to Madrid to see my parents. I haven't told them I'm here and they'll be wondering what's going on. I should have landed in Madrid this morning. And I need to phone Chloe. She's left me loads of messages. I told her I would call her once I landed in Spain."

"Ray. You need to get a grip," Sally said, motioning to the waiter that she wanted service. It took a couple of waves before she caught his attention. "You need to call Chloe, your parents and the police and go back home. We need to resolve this. I thought you had told the police the truth about what happened on the night your brother died. We can go back to my parents' apartment and make the calls from there."

Before Ray could respond, he wanted to talk about his parents and his unreasonable father, the waiter arrived. "L'addition, s'il vous plait," Sally said in a perfect French accent. She was bilingual, having been brought up in Paris where her parents still lived for most of the year.

Ray looked at her uncertainly. "We need to sort this mess out Ray," Sally said firmly. Ray nodded. Everything was a mess. His brother's death, his feelings for Sally. His relationship with his father. Everything. But maybe it could be sorted out, with time. And, if he was honest, he was enjoying the drama and break from the routine of study and the tension at home with Chloe.

❖

"I've never been inside Wellesley police station before," Henry Llewellyn said. "I was arrested when I broke into Wellesley Primary School as part of our protests at its closure, but the police took me to Kingham and locked me up there."

"Yes. That sometimes happens. You were a high-profile case, so they probably decided to take you to Valley headquarters," Napoleon replied, levelling his eyes at the thin, young face. "You look different in your photographs."

"People often say that. I'm a very ordinary person. They can do amazing things with lights and make-up in photographs."

"Yes, I suppose they can," Napoleon said, although the chief inspector meant exactly the opposite. Llewellyn was in no sense of the word ordinary looking. Despite his unkempt, almost careworn, appearance - facial stubble, ripped tee-shirt and tatty jeans - he was much better looking in the flesh. The photographs didn't do him justice. The long-lashed hazel eyes were large and clear and his nose and facial bone structure were perfectly crafted. This was complemented with a flawless olive complexion and a shock of thick dark brown hair.

"What can I do for you?" Napoleon said, picking up his gold fountain pen that was lying on his desk and flicking it around his fingers, a manoeuvre that now came as naturally as combing his hair.

Llewellyn opened his knapsack. "I have some information you might be interested in. I say might be, because it would not, I understand, be admissible in court. All the same, it may be very useful to you."

Napoleon nodded, taking in again Llewellyn's handsome outline. He was short, or he was in the eyes of the 6ft 2in chief inspector, and his dress sense was frankly bizarre, flip-flops and thin jacket over the even thinner ripped tee-shirt were a strange choice for the cold month of October.

"I have a recording of a telephone call between Charlie Dean, the chief planning officer of the district council, and Jack McConnell. I think you will find this conversation between them very interesting."

Llewellyn took out a recording machine from the knapsack, placed it on Napoleon's desk and turned it on.

Napoleon immediately recognised McConnell's voice. He sounded relaxed and pleased with himself. The other man sounded nervous and was barely audible, although Napoleon also recognised the voice. It was Charlie Dean.

The chief inspector twirled his pen around his fingers as the recording finished. "So, what does it all mean?" Napoleon said, a crooked smile flickering across his face. Llewellyn was an intriguing fish, and innovative. He must have somehow installed a transmitter in the telephone of Dean or McConnell.

"I think it's fairly obvious. A figure of £10,000 is mentioned. Dean says we have an agreement. Then he calls McConnell again to check how he will be paid. It must be a bribe for Dean, the head of planning at the local council, to back McConnell's scheme to turn Wellesley's primary school into a leisure centre."

"It's too vague and unclear," Napoleon said. "They don't mention specifics and how did you get this recording?"

"No comment." Llewellyn grinned. He had paid a friend who worked for a telecoms company to go to the council offices and fix Dean's phone while he was on a lunchbreak. It was surprisingly easy to put a listening bug in a telephone.

"You tapped the phone of either Charlie Dean or Jack McConnell, which is illegal. I could charge you."

"You could. The publicity would be interesting. It might not hurt my cause to save the school from demolition."

Napoleon smiled briefly again, thinly this time. "Yes. I'm sure it would make the national news. You had better leave the recording here. I'll be in touch. Thank you Mr Llewellyn. And don't bug any more phones, or I'll arrest you."

Llewellyn smiled broadly and left, flip-flops and tatty jeans jauntily disappearing through the door. Napoleon flipped his pen around his fingers again and swivelled his chair around to face the old yellowing map of the county that hung behind his desk. He would have to change it. It dated back to the days before the Valley police area was created. Some of the villages on the map no longer existed as the urban sprawl of Redfield had swallowed them up and the road network was so out of date, it was of little practical use. It did, however, have a nostalgic charm.

He eyed the map for a long while, thinking about illicit recordings and pornographic videos. McConnell was clearly a little too comfortable outside the law, but Llewellyn's recording was not solid enough for a case against McConnell or Dean. As for pornographic videos and McConnell's threats against his son via the Bucklers, that led nowhere either. He needed to find out how Mayo and Parsons had fared at the university. They should have called in by now. Sally Jones should have been easy to find.

CHAPTER 43

◆

Parsons watched Mayo return with the drinks. He was a decent bloke, not bad looking, not a dick like her previous boyfriend, but this was a relationship that would remain strictly business. She had made the mistake of dating another police officer when she had first joined CID and she wasn't about to repeat it.

"Thanks," she said as Mayo put a glass of what looked like white wine in front of her. "But I didn't want an alcoholic drink. Sorry, I should have said."

"It's not. It's elderflower wine and it's alcohol free. The landlord recommended it. I've got a glass too, although I could do with something stronger, after this morning."

Parsons nodded, sipping her drink and smiling to herself.

"Police work can be such a hassle," Mayo said with sudden intensity. "Maybe I should just run a pub like this one. The Wheel would be a nice place to work, in a nice town, surrounded by liquor. What more could a person want?"

"You'd get bored after 10 minutes," Parsons said, taking another sip from her glass. "Good choice on the drink, by the way. I love elderflower." Mayo had a knack of knowing what she liked. Even in the short while they had been working more closely together on the deaths of Delgado and Rankin, she had noticed his sensitivity. It was small things like letting her drive, she hated being a passenger, not talking over her like some of her other male colleagues or making half-witted sexist comments. He was naturally considerate, a quality she had come to appreciate as she had grown older, and definitely not a dick.

"No problem over the drink," Mayo said. "But I don't think I'd get bored, running a pub. At least there wouldn't be all the hassle of police work. Take today. It could have been so straightforward, pulling this Sally Jones in for questioning and maybe getting to the bottom of this case. Then we find out she's gone to Paris for the weekend."

"She could be running away from something," Parsons said, noticing Mayo's straight white teeth. He clearly had a marvellous dentist.

Mayo nodded. "She could be. She could be meeting up with Ray Delgado. They could be running off together."

"He's in Madrid. The Spanish police may have picked him up by now. Then we might get some answers," Parsons said, picking up a menu on the table. "While we're here, we should get some lunch. Napoleon's probably still at Jack McConnell's. We might as well get something to eat."

"Sure," Mayo said distractedly, his attention diverted to the bar. "That's Jim Buckler. The very man we've been trying to track down for the past week. I didn't see him when I was getting the drinks. He must have been in the bathroom."

Parsons turned to face the bar. "And it looks like he's been drinking all morning." Buckler was sitting on a bar stool with a pint in his hand and his head drooping as if it was becoming too heavy to hold up.

Buckler looked up from his drink and caught sight of Mayo. "It's the Yank," he slurred. He stood up unsteadily and weaved his way towards the police officers' table. He looked Parsons up and down, nodded at her as if in approval, and sat down clumsily in the chair next to her, directly opposite Mayo.

"Do you wanna know summing, summing about my brother and Jack McConnell? Summing bad," he said, slurring. He was very drunk.

Mayo glanced at Parsons, his right eyebrow raised. "Why not?"

Buckler looked vacantly into Mayo's eyes, not really registering what the sergeant had said. "I've found summing out, summing about my brother and Jack McConnell, but no-one must know who told you."

Before Mayo or Parsons could respond, he lurched back to his feet. "Meet in the cemetery, 7.30 tonight, by my little brother's grave and I'll tell yer."

"Err," Mayo said.

"Yep. Tell yer," Buckler said and staggered off. He was a small, lithe man, but his speed of movement was still surprising, particularly for someone so drunk. He was through the pub's entrance and on to the street in an instant. Mayo and Parsons looked at each other, bewildered, then quickly followed him.

Parsons was first on to the street, with Mayo just behind. They glanced across the road and to their left and right. There was no one on the other side of the road, but their view was obscured by a group of teenagers to their left and two young women pushing prams, a small baby in each, to their right. "I'll go this way," Mayo said, hurriedly pointing at the approaching teenagers. "You go the other," he added quickly, an instruction Parsons had anticipated. She was already weaving past the young women. "He can't have gone far," she shouted back at the sergeant as she broke into a run.

Napoleon was pushing a small, model car across his desk as Mayo and Parsons entered his office. "Ah," he said, stretching and then placing the red car, a miniature replica of a 1970 Austin Maxi, back in the top drawer of the desk. "It's a model of Britain's first five-door hatchback. I found it in my old toy cupboard. Just in case you were wondering."

The inspector digested the blank expressions. "Look, I don't know why I dug it out. It's a red hatchback, sort of like the one that hit Rankin. It helps me think. Anyway, you two took your time."

"Sorry, sir. We did," Parsons said. She then explained that Sally Jones was in Paris with her parents and not responding to her mobile.

"Do we have a number for her parents, if that's where she's staying?" Napoleon asked.

"We're looking into that," Parsons said. "We've also sent her messages on social media, asking her to contact us immediately. We'll contact the French police, if she doesn't get back to us soon. "But what about Ray Delgado, boss?" she asked. "Did the Spanish police apprehend him at the airport in Madrid as you requested?"

"No. He wasn't on the flight his girlfriend said he'd be on, and he hasn't turned up at his parents' home," Napoleon said. "They live just outside Madrid. And like Ms Jones, he's not responding to his mobile, or to text messages from his girlfriend. She's very upset and worried. She can't understand why he wasn't on the plane. It's possible he's still in the UK. We've got police searching for him at Heathrow and checking passenger lists to see if he took a flight elsewhere. His girlfriend has promised to contact us as soon as he gets in touch with her."

The inspector suddenly sighed and fished out a newspaper cutting from one of the lower drawers in his desk. He carefully placed it in front of him and smoothed down the corners. It featured a profile of Henry Llewellyn with a picture of the actor standing in front of Wellesley Primary School. Mayo and Parsons exchanged glances, bemused. The inspector looked up, smiled crookedly, and then told them about Llewellyn's visit and the recording of McConnell's conversation with Charlie Dean.

"Should we pull Jack McConnell in for questioning?" Mayo asked after Napoleon had finished. "He's clearly illegally trying to fix this property deal. We should question him. And what about Llewellyn? What he did was illegal."

"Llewellyn won't bug any more telephones. We're not taking any action against him. There's no point. As for Jack McConnell, we'll leave him alone for the time being," Napoleon said, putting the newspaper cutting of Llewellyn back in his drawer and thinking of Hunter's warning about wild goose chases and not upsetting McConnell. For once, he agreed with the chief superintendent. Bringing in McConnell would achieve nothing. He would just deny any wrongdoing, and that would be the end of it.

"You think it would be a waste of time?" Mayo said.

Napoleon nodded.

The three officers sat silently for a moment, deep in their various thoughts.

"We saw Jim Buckler in The Wheel, while we were having lunch," Parsons said finally. "He said he knew something bad about his brother Mick and Jack McConnell. He was very drunk, but it might be significant. He staggered off before we could properly question him. We followed him, but he disappeared once he was out on the street." She paused and added with a playful smile. "He wants to see Joe in the cemetery tonight."

Napoleon laughed. "Really?"

"Yes. Just Joe," Parsons said, beaming at the sergeant.

"Don't you want to come with me?" Mayo said, looking hurt.

Parsons shook her head in mock apology.

"Why the cemetery?" Napoleon asked.

"He wants to meet by his brother's grave," Mayo said gloomily. "I never knew there was a third brother."

Napoleon scratched his nose, which Parsons noticed was beaky like Mayo's. He was lean like the sergeant too, but a lot taller. The inspector's teeth weren't quite as white and straight, though. She followed the inspector's gaze out of the office window, while thinking about Mayo's pristine smile.

"The youngest brother died in a car accident about 10 years ago," Napoleon said, scanning the overcast sky. "I doubt Jim will remember to turn up, but you'd better go. You go too, Sarah. Probably best if there's two of you."

"Okay. If I must," Parsons said.

Mayo gave her one of his Colgate smiles. "It'll be fun."

"I doubt it, but if I must hold your hand in the scary graveyard, then I'll go," she said, teasingly. She didn't really mind a trip to the graveyard. She had no other plans for the evening.

"In the meantime, I'm going to see Henry Llewellyn. I want another word with him," Napoleon said.

"Why?" Parsons asked.

"Always with the difficult questions," the inspector said. "I don't really know. I just feel there's something he might know that would help us."

"Can I go with you sir?" Parsons said. "Apparently, he's converted a barn in St Margaret's into some artsy house. I'd love to see inside."

"All right." Napoleon nodded. "You get the graveyard shift on your own, Joe." The inspector grinned, looking out of the window again. The heavens had now opened. "Remember to take your Wellingtons," he said with a snigger. Mayo shook his head and again produced the Colgate smile, but there was a wry, dejected twist to it.

The sergeant had a lovely smile, Parsons thought, even his sad, unconvincing one.

CHAPTER 44

◆

Sometimes perfection can grate. That was it, Parsons thought. Henry Llewellyn was too perfect with his chiselled features and designer jeans and tee-shirt that were torn in just the right places for that affected shabby look. Mayo, despite his beaky nose and receding hairline, was far more attractive. Napoleon had the edge on Llewellyn too, as far as she was concerned, even though he was older and a bit of a grump with his permanently tired and put-upon expression.

"Make yourselves comfortable," Llewellyn said, bringing Parsons back to earth. He smiled broadly. His teeth were perfect, too. Maybe he had the same dentist as Mayo. "There's coffee brewing in the kitchen," Llewellyn added, sitting down on an ornate rug in the middle of his sitting room and propping himself against a big leather sofa. "I'll get the coffee in a minute." Napoleon nodded and seated himself on a Victorian chaise longue opposite Llewellyn. Parsons followed the inspector, although she was tempted to sit on the floor, too, just for the hell of it.

She wasn't sure whether she liked the house. She felt Llewellyn had gone too far with the modern touches. Spotlights embedded in the ceiling's wooden beams looked odd to her, and the sitting room in particular seemed somehow disjointed, the mainly art deco furniture ill at ease with the otherwise rustic feel of the house. Her eye wandered to the fireplace at the far end of the room. Above it was an oil painting of an old barn and men in a field. Next to the canvas was a small print of a black man reclining against a bookshelf. He looked familiar. She was sure he was a writer or something to do with the American civil rights movement.

"Ralph Ellison," Llewellyn said, noticing the direction of her glance. "The print is of Ralph Ellison, the African-American writer who wrote the Invisible Man about a black man living in a racist society. He is seen not for what he is but through the prism of the colour of his skin. It is a great novel. Men like Ellison inspire me. What they achieved, despite the prejudices ranged against them, is a great motivator."

"Yes. That's very interesting," Napoleon said, although the subject clearly bored him. "We came by on the off-chance for a quick chat. I have a few follow-up questions."

"You were lucky. I was about to leave for Stratford. I'm in a production that starts rehearsals next week. Hamlet. You may have heard of it. I need every motivation I can get to really pump myself up for the performance. It's why I dug out the print of Ellison and put it on the wall. Great men inspire me. And he was a great writer."

"Yes. You said. My wife is a fan of Ralph Ellison and American literature," Napoleon said.

"And you're not," Llewellyn responded.

"No. I like murder mystery crime novels."

Parsons laughed, but Llewellyn looked more puzzled than amused, not sure whether the inspector was making fun of him.

"Do you want some coffee, inspector?" Llewellyn said, changing the subject.

"I'm fine," Napoleon said.

"And I'm fine, too," Parsons added sarcastically. She felt invisible at times when interviewing people with a senior male police officer like Napoleon. People tended to address the male officer and not properly see or respect her because she was a younger woman.

"I'm sorry, constable," Llewellyn said quickly, putting his hands up in a gesture of apology. "I didn't mean to direct my question only to the inspector." He shook his head and smiled sheepishly at the irony of his failure to include her. "Women suffer prejudice too."

He smiled again, still looking uncomfortable. "So how can I help you? Both of you?"

"I'm not sure," Napoleon said. "I guess, I would like to go over why you thought Jack McConnell would try and bribe Charlie Dean."

Llewellyn looked intensely at the inspector. "A hunch, or maybe an educated guess. A friend of mine told me that

McConnell had lunch with Dean at the golf club last week. It struck me that when the area's chief planning officer and a man who needs his support to build a leisure centre get together, then they're probably stitching something up. I mean, why else would they be meeting? They're not friends and I'm told Dean rarely goes to the golf club. I'm not sure he's even a member."

"Yes. You have a point," Napoleon said. "But why would Jack McConnell meet Dean in such a public place if he was stitching something up? Bit of a risk, isn't it?" The inspector frowned to himself as he said it. McConnell liked to take a risk. He had said as much in the bar of the golf club after their game at the weekend.

"Over confidence, perhaps. Or complacency. Who knows? But I thought it would be interesting to listen in on Dean. It wasn't going to do any harm," Llewellyn said.

"Except we could have charged you," Napoleon said.

"It would have been good publicity inspector, for my cause to save the school, if I'd been charged, as I think I pointed out in your office."

Parsons pulled out a notebook from her pocket. "Can I ask why you're so wrapped up in this school project? I heard on the radio that you want to turn the school into a museum."

"So many people have asked me that, so many times, and I give them all the same answer. It's because this town is my home. It was my first school and it's a part of me. To see it knocked down would take a little piece away from me. And the past should be preserved to improve the future. If we turn the school into a museum to show how a Victorian school was run, it will remind people of the past and show how we have progressed and changed as a society. Developers have also destroyed too much in this part of the world. I remember when that housing estate just south of here was a huge wood with rabbits, squirrels, foxes, and woodland birds that are now almost extinct. I played there as a child, built camps there, found conkers there, rode my bike there - and now it's gone. Children of the future won't be able to enjoy and appreciate nature as I did as a child, which I think is terribly sad."

"People have got to live somewhere," Parsons said.

"Exactly," Napoleon added, reaching for his gold fountain pen in his inside jacket pocket.

"Yes, and developers like Jack McConnell have got to make money," Llewellyn said.

Napoleon twirled his gold fountain pen around his fingers and eyed the large painting of the barn on the wall above the fireplace. "The painting. It's familiar," he said. He stood up and walked over to it for a closer inspection.

"Yes. It would be. It's of one of the old barns down the road. It's owned by Jack McConnell. I sat in the churchyard opposite when I painted it," Llewellyn said.

"It's very good," the inspector said, noticing the whirling signature of H. G. Shilling in the corner of the painting and remembering there was a similar landscape hanging in Jack McConnell's sitting room. He recalled now how McConnell's painting had caught his attention in the same way. Even to his amateur eye, he could see the skill and attention to detail in the brush strokes. Llewellyn was a talented painter. "H. G. Shilling is you? Jack McConnell has a painting of this same barn, also by you."

"Yes." Llewellyn nodded. "My name is Henry Griffiths Shilling Llewellyn. I dispensed with Llewellyn because I didn't want people buying my stuff because of my acting. Griffiths was my mother's maiden name and Shilling was her mother's maiden name."

"The men," the chief inspector said. Unlike McConnell's painting, there were three men standing near the barn. "My word," Napoleon said. "One of those men is Jack McConnell, the tall one, or at least it looks very like him."

"Yes, very good inspector. Jack and the Buckler brothers." Llewellyn and Parsons had joined the inspector and were peering closely at the painting too.

"Why did you paint Jack McConnell and the Bucklers into the picture?" Napoleon said.

"Hmm. Now, why did I?" Llewellyn screwed up his face in thought. "I did two paintings to capture and contrast the different seasons. The one I gave to Jack McConnell was painted during the summer, 11 years ago, while this one was painted in the following spring. I painted McConnell and the Bucklers into the spring picture because they were around a lot, using the barn to store things. Jack saw me painting around that time and said he would like it when I'd finished. I gave him summer, the one without him and his henchmen. I didn't think he would appreciate being in the picture. He paid me a lot of money, which I gave to charity."

"And you think you did the spring painting about 10 years ago?" Napoleon asked.

"Yes. It would have been 10 years ago. I have a good memory for dates. But I can check for certain. I've got photographs of the barn, which I took at the time to help me do the paintings. The photographs will have the dates when they were taken on the back. Is the year important? Is this leading somewhere?"

Napoleon stepped back from the painting to allow Parsons a closer look. "I don't know if it means anything. Police work is about checking things, gathering loose ends and hoping some might fit together. It's probably totally irrelevant to anything. Do you remember what Jack McConnell and the Bucklers were storing in the barn?"

"It was a long time ago. My memory is hazy. But I do remember them shifting lots of boxes. I've no idea what was in them, but at a guess, I would say books or something like that. They were small boxes and they carried them fairly easily. It wasn't heavy equipment or anything like that. I remember thinking an old barn was a strange place to store books."

Llewellyn sat back down on the ornate rug, crossing his legs, while his two visitors returned to the Victorian chaise longue opposite.

"Can you check the date you did the paintings now?" Napoleon said.

Llewellyn looked at his watch. "Sure, but you might have to wait a while. The prints of the barn will be in my desk or bureau in my storage room upstairs, but I'm not exactly sure where. I might have to wade through a lot of clutter to find them."

Llewellyn stood up. "I suggest you both make some coffee while I dig around for them." He emphasised the word both, gave Parsons a knowing smile, and pointed them in the direction of the kitchen, coffee machine and cups. "I take my coffee black, no sugar," he said.

CHAPTER 45

M ayo parked his car by a crossroads, about a mile outside Wellesley in the heart of the countryside. St Margaret's parish church stood to his left with Hall's Farm to his right. The sergeant gazed admiringly at the church for a moment. It looked idyllic in its picture postcard setting among the tree-lined fields. Built in the 12th century from local flint, the architecture was in the classic Romanesque style of the Normans, with narrow, arched windows, a square tower and weathervane, which swayed gently in the early morning breeze. It was an uplifting sight for a tired policeman. The farm opposite was more utilitarian in appearance, but beautiful in its own rustic way. Mayo eased himself out of the car and turned towards the barns and scattered machinery of the farm. It had belonged to an old family from St Margaret's village since the early 1900s, but was now owned by Jack McConnell. The sergeant opened the wooden gate at the entrance and scrunched his way up a gravel drive towards Napoleon and Parsons, who were standing next to a long, large barn and a tractor. They were watching four or five police officers loading boxes on to a trailer. Napoleon looked annoyed, his default expression, while Parsons appeared amused, her expressive eyes and features creased as if she was about to break into laughter.

Napoleon and Parsons had found dozens of boxes containing old VHS videos stored in the barn the previous evening after visiting Llewellyn. They had broken in and taken a couple of the boxes back to the office. Connecting an old VCR video recorder languishing in one of police station's storage rooms, they had played a few of the tapes back. Most were poor quality pornographic sketches, some with amateurish, harmless story lines and scenes, but others were more disturbing, prompting the early morning search.

"What's the matter?" Mayo said. Napoleon was more than a little annoyed. Parsons' amused expression turned into a broad smile. "Hi Joe," she said. "One of the police officers dropped a box in the mud. The inspector's not happy."

"It's evidence," Napoleon said grumpily. "And what are you doing here, sergeant? You should be tracking down Jim Buckler after his no-show in the graveyard last night. He might know something about these videos. I would wager some are home-made movies. The Bucklers probably did the filming."

Mayo leaned down and wiped a lump of mud off the top of one of his shoes with his handkerchief. Overnight rain had displaced some of the stones and pebbles, pockmarking the path with muddy patches.

"Shouldn't we pull Jack McConnell in?" Mayo said, straightening up and watching one of the police officers load the last of the boxes on to the trailer. "Isn't that the priority rather than Jim Buckler? McConnell's bribing the council, and now we've found a collection of video nasties in his own barn. There's bound to be some illegal, explicit stuff among this lot," he said, gesturing to the trailer. It was packed with 30 boxes, containing about 50 video tapes each. "I'd almost forgotten about VHS and video tapes," the sergeant added. "But it was big in its day."

Napoleon nodded. "McConnell closed down his VHS business about 10 years ago, probably when he stored this lot here. The little boy, Sean Cropper, also went missing about 10 years ago. He was used in porn videos. Is there one of him among these old VHS tapes? Is this linked to the deaths of Delgado and Rankin?"

Napoleon was off on a tangent again, Mayo thought, and glanced at Parsons. She was looking puzzled. "If there is a video of this little boy being abused, then that is very serious," Parsons said. "But how would it be linked to the deaths of Delgado and Rankin?"

She remembered Hunter's warning about Napoleon and his theories, which were usually based on some visceral instinct that could prove inspired but were more often, in the chief superintendent's opinion, irrelevant distractions. "Keep him out of the byways," Hunter had said.

"I don't know," Napoleon said, raising his hands in a gesture of frustration. He looked at Parsons, then at Mayo. "Yes. I know," he said, reading something in the sergeant's expression. "We need to pull in McConnell rather than making idle speculations. But I want to speak to Jim Buckler before we question McConnell. Buckler said he knew something bad about McConnell. And we need to talk to Charlie Dean, too. I've changed my mind on the bribery. With a little persuading, I'm sure he'll give us enough information for a prosecution against McConnell on the bribes. We must build a watertight case against McConnell on everything."

Mayo nodded: "Understood, sir. Anyway, the reason I'm here and not hunting down Jim Buckler is because my contact at Heathrow called. They've apprehended Ray Delgado and Sally Jones. They arrived at Heathrow early this morning on a flight from Paris. The Met also called. Sally Jones' red hatchback has been found in London. It was reported stolen on the Monday after Chief Inspector Rankin was killed."

"Why didn't we know about the stolen car sooner?" Napoleon said, closely watching one of the constables shut the back of the trailer.

"We should have been informed," agreed Mayo. "Some misunderstanding in traffic. There are a lot of cars stolen and a lot of red hatchbacks. But the Met quickly connected it to Rankin's hit-and-run. I had a very helpful forensic guy on the phone, who said there were traces of Rankin's DNA on the car. It was definitely the one that knocked him down.

Our forensic team are going to talk to the Met about similar DNA checks for Delgado."

"Good. Now go and find Jim Buckler," Napoleon said. "If he's not at home, search the local pubs. It sounds like he's on one of his boozy benders and the pubs will be opening about now. Go to The Wheel of Fortune, where you saw him yesterday. If he's not there, try The Nag's Head and then The Plough on Wellesley Road. You could even try The Rising Sun by Wellesley's football ground. When you find him, bring him back to the station and we'll get some answers."

———————————◆———————————

Sally Jones and Ray Delgado could have been brother and sister. Both were small and dark with Latin looks. But that was where the similarity ended. She was helpful and polite, while he was morose and rude. They had been taken straight to Wellesley police station from Heathrow and were sitting silently in separate interview rooms after being questioned by Napoleon and Parsons.

On the night of Peter Delgado's death, they had driven around the roads by Redfield University for about an hour, talking about Ray's difficult relationship with his brother, their families and their studies. They couldn't remember the exact route they had taken, but at no point had they driven near Wellesley at the estimated time Peter was hit by a car. "We drove around in circles near the university," Jones said.

They also insisted they had nothing to do with Rankin's death as neither of them were in the country. Delgado was in Spain, which the police were already aware of, and Jones was visiting her parents in Paris, where she had been for the past two weekends until this one had been cut short. Jones said her car had been stolen sometime over the previous weekend, but she only realised it was missing on her return home on the Monday morning.

"What do you think?" Napoleon asked Parsons, once they were back in his office. He remained standing, restlessly flicking through a pile of newspapers neatly stacked on a bookcase next to his desk, while Parsons sat in a chair by the office window, alternately watching the inspector and the traffic on the high street outside.

"I think they're both innocent," Parsons said. "She seems like a lovely young woman. Unless I've been totally fooled, she's telling the truth about Wednesday night. As for the young man, he's an arse. But he was in the car with her. If we believe she's innocent, so's he. He didn't tell us until now about his drive with Ms Jones because he was worried it would upset his girlfriend, which seems genuine. He's an arse, but not a murderer. As for the death of Inspector Rankin, they were both out of the country when he was killed. We know Delgado was in Spain and we can easily check whether she was in Paris. I'm 99 per cent sure that will be confirmed when we check her flights and talk to her parents."

"Yes," Napoleon said with a frown. He looked more world weary than ever. He stopped flicking through the newspapers and picked up a bottle of red wine that stood next to them. "Let's go back to the interview rooms and clear up the details on the stolen car. We'll interview them together this time to see how they react to each other," he said, taking a long look at the bottle before putting it back on the bookcase.

"Right, Ms Jones, can you tell us where your car was stolen from?" the inspector asked.

"I'm afraid, I'm not entirely sure. I left it outside Jack McConnell's house on the Wednesday evening last week after my drive with Ray."

Parsons' jaw dropped a fraction, while Napoleon's eyebrows rose a notch. "Why?" they said in unison.

"Uncle Jack is a friend of the family. Sorry, I often call him Uncle Jack, even though we're not related. It's from when I was little. Our families have been friends for years. He has a car repair shop on the Wellesley Road, opposite The Plough pub. He always services my car and he asked me to drop it off outside his house, so his mechanic could pick it up the next day.

"Uncle Jack said his mechanic is great with his hands, but doesn't have much up top and wouldn't find my house. It was a bit of a last-minute arrangement because the brakes had suddenly started squeaking. They were getting really bad on that Wednesday night when Ray and I went for a drive. I was worried they might fail at any moment. We might have driven around for longer if it hadn't been for my squeaky brakes.

"I dropped Ray back at the university library and then I drove back to Wellesley, parked my car outside Uncle Jack's house, put the keys through his letterbox and walked home. I live a short walk from Crookham Lane, down St Margaret's Road, and then a right turn on to the Wellesley Road. Number 93."

"Next door to Ted Cropper," Napoleon said. "Another coincidence."

"Yes. That's right. A coincidence to what?"

"Nothing," Napoleon said. But it was strange how there always seemed to be a link to McConnell or Ted in their enquiries.

"Go on," he added.

"Well, the mechanic picked up the car and fixed the brakes, but it took longer than the garage expected, and they didn't return the car until Friday morning. I'd already left to get my flight to Paris to see my parents by the time they'd finished. The mechanic texted me to say he'd parked the car down the road as he couldn't get a space outside my house. I don't have a driveway. He said he'd put the keys through my letterbox. He'd obviously found my house easily enough, despite Uncle Jack's worries."

"You shouldn't use McConnell. He's a crook," Delgado said suddenly. He had sat quietly, slouching in his chair, looking bored and defiant until now.

"You don't know that Ray," Jones said.

"I don't like him. Peter was convinced he'd bribed some of the councillors to get the backing for his plan to knock down that school."

"Do you have any evidence to support that?" Napoleon asked.

"No. It's just what Peter said. And McConnell tried it on with Chloe."

"That's not true. Chloe said he was nice to her. He didn't try anything on." Jones gave Delgado a dismissive look. "Uncle Jack likes the ladies and I have sympathy for his wife. Auntie Jo's lovely and I don't think Jack's always been faithful, but he wouldn't have tried it on with Chloe."

She gave Delgado another dismissive stare. "But, as I was saying, the mechanic said he parked my car on the road near my house. I still have the text."

"You only have the mechanic's word for that," Delgado said. His light-hearted mood in Paris had vanished. Coming back to Wellesley had brought back all the old worries about Chloe, the pregnancy and his course at university, and the strains were showing in his abrupt manner.

"Ray. Please. Why would the mechanic lie?" She turned to the police officers. "You can check with the mechanic. I'm not exactly sure how far down the road he parked the car from my house, but I'm sure that was where it was taken from, sometime between Friday morning and Monday morning. I don't know when because I wasn't here. I was in Paris."

"One final thing, Ms Jones," Napoleon said. "There was a copy of Hamlet in the car's glove compartment. I presume it's yours, or did the thief leave it in the vehicle? We may have an erudite villain on our hands." The inspector smiled wryly.

"It belonged to Ted Cropper," Jones said. "I wouldn't have thought Ted was a fan of Shakespeare, but he said he could relate to Hamlet. I'm not sure why someone like Ted would relate to a story about a mad Danish prince, but I was thankful for the loan. I needed a copy for one of my courses. I like a paper book rather than having to read things on a kindle or electronically. I find I can digest the information more easily when I have something tangible in my hand."

Napoleon nodded with approval. "Yes. I agree. It is good to hear someone so young still appreciates paper and print."

Jones smiled briefly, then a sad expression took hold. "Poor Ted, though. He was very upset about my car being stolen. I think he felt guilty. I'd asked him to keep an eye on my house while I was away. He has a key to the front door. I told him about my car being repaired and that a mechanic would drop it off outside the house and put the keys through my letter box. I asked him to check on the car as well as the house. I told him about 10 times that it wasn't his fault that the car was taken. He kept apologising, saying he hadn't noticed the car had gone because it had been parked down the road, a fair way from the house. He was more bothered about it being stolen than I was. It was just a little runaround. Not worth much. It was a nuisance that it was taken, but not the end of the world."

Back in his office, Napoleon picked up one of the newspapers on the bookcase, then sat down as he leafed through the pages. Parsons returned to her seat by the window.

"You're an avid reader of the local paper," Parsons said, noticing the pile of papers were mostly made up of the Wellesley Chronicle.

"Yes. I am." The inspector stopped turning the pages, stood up and reached for the bottle of red wine.

"And that looks like a quality bottle of wine,"
the constable said.

"Yes. It is. It was a present from Jack McConnell. He gave it to me yesterday after our lunch at his house."
Napoleon eyed the bottle pensively. "Could McConnell have left the golf club earlier than he said on the Wednesday night and killed Delgado in the red hatchback? It had been left outside his house and he had the keys."

Parsons shook her head. "He has a solid alibi from the banker who drove him home around midnight that evening. That was after the estimated time of Peter Delgado's death."

The constable pushed her hand through her hair, composing her thoughts. "But I suppose the estimated time of death could be wrong, and it's possible Delgado had evidence that McConnell was offering bribes to councillors over the school development. If he'd threatened to expose McConnell, then that would be a motive for murder. We can easily check with McConnell's mechanic to see if the car had been damaged from a collision when he collected it on the Thursday morning. But even if it was in a collision, we know McConnell didn't run over Inspector Rankin.

"He has a cast-iron alibi for the time of Rankin's death on the Friday morning. He was in his office. About 10 people said he was at his desk all morning on that Friday. And it wouldn't surprise me if forensic fail to find any traces of Delgado's DNA on the red hatchback. These hit-and-runs could still be two unconnected, random accidents."

"You know my thoughts on that, constable," Napoleon said. "These were deliberate acts. Delgado's body was moved to a place just on the edge of the first green on Wellesley's golf course, where it was carefully positioned so Jack McConnell would see it as he walked on to the green. That was deliberate."

"Assuming the person responsible knew Jack McConnell would be the first to arrive on the green?" Parsons pointed out.

"That someone could be Jack McConnell himself," Napoleon said.

"But why would McConnell move the body to a place where he would find it the next day?"

Napoleon sighed. "Good question and McConnell didn't run Rankin down. He's alibied up to his eyeballs, as you say. But whoever the driver was, they deliberately ploughed into the inspector. They were aiming to kill. No brake marks on the road suggest that."

"Not necessarily," Parsons said. "The driver may not have seen the inspector. That would explain why they didn't brake."

"It was broad daylight. The driver would have seen Rankin," Napoleon said belligerently.

"I'm sorry sir, but I think that's debatable," the constable replied, noticing a big man walking down the high street in the direction of the river from her seat by the window. It was Jack McConnell. He had a large golfing umbrella to protect himself from the rain, which had started to pour heavily, and he was walking quickly. "We really do need to question McConnell," Parsons said, the sight of him jogging her thoughts.

"He will know we've impounded his videos. The farm manager would have told him, so we should act quickly. If any of the videos have illegal pornography on them, then we can charge him straight away. One or two of those we played last night were very close to the legal line. One of the girls looked a lot younger than 18. Even if a lot of the videos are damaged or degraded after being stored in that barn for years, there will be plenty that work and I'm certain we'll find some that are illegal."

"Yes. We need to bring McConnell in for questioning, but not until we have sorted through the videos and found strong evidence against him. The team should have finished playing them back by now," Napoleon said. "Sean Cropper was used for pornographic videos. His father admitted it just before he killed himself. If Sean's on any found in the barn, then we really do have McConnell. We can leave McConnell to sweat for the time being."

The inspector was still holding the bottle of red wine. He gave it a suspicious, critical glance. "And I need to give this bottle back to McConnell. To think I once liked the man."

"But you don't like him anymore because of the pornographic videos and his lax attitude to the law?" Parsons said, anticipating the inspector's thoughts.

"Something like that," Napoleon said. "Since my lunch with McConnell yesterday, we've discovered he's bribing the head of planning at the council and found pornographic videos in one of his barns. He had a big business in videos for years. I don't know why I didn't connect it to Sean Cropper before. That poor boy, used in a porn video. Was Jack directly involved in his murder?"

"24 hours can be a long time in police work," Parsons said. She didn't add that she felt the inspector was jumping ahead again. One step at a time, she thought, remembering Hunter's advice about Napoleon and his wayward theories.

"Yes. I enjoyed my lunch with McConnell, enjoyed his company, but now he makes my skin crawl. My wife always disliked him. I should have taken more notice of her. Women are better judges of character."

"Not always," Parsons said, thinking of Mayo. "Some men are very perceptive."

"Maybe some," the inspector said. "But too often men are blinded by bravado, someone who can tell a good story, someone who's good company over a pint in the pub."

"Like Jack McConnell," Parsons said, once more anticipating Napoleon's thoughts.

The inspector smiled. It was a crooked, sardonic smile. "Yes. Like Jack McConnell. Men like him are fantasists, risk-takers. They think they're invincible and can get away with anything – and that is going to be his downfall. Women are more cautious, more sensible, more intelligent."

"You're quite a feminist, sir."

"No. Just a realist."

Napoleon put down the bottle of red wine and picked up his gold pen, which he put in his mouth, pretending to smoke it. Parsons laughed. Napoleon laughed too. "It's my impression of

McConnell. All smug with his wine and cigars. By the way, did forensic ever get back to you about that Beethoven tape you found on St Margaret's Road near where Delgado was hit? The collection of tapes I saw in McConnell's cellar suggests it may well belong to him," the inspector said.

"I'll text forensic to see what they've come up with. We may find McConnell's prints on it, but I'm not sure what that will prove. It must have been dropped there a few days after Delgado was hit, probably just before I found it. The scenes of crime team insist they didn't miss it in their original search."

"No. They wouldn't have missed it." Napoleon gave his gold pen a twirl around his fingers and took a couple of paces towards the office window, near where Parsons was sitting, and looked out on to the high street.

"We must talk to Jim Buckler," he said. "I'm sure he has something on McConnell, something even McConnell's slippery lawyer and weasel words won't be able to deflect or wriggle out of."

For the first time in a long while, Napoleon's expression looked lighter, even happy. Parsons wasn't sure it suited him. She was too used to his usual sour countenance, which gave the impression he had eaten something nasty. She smiled at the inspector, randomly remembering his look of utter disdain when the young PC dropped the box of videos in the mud.

Napoleon grinned crookedly back, although he wasn't sure there was much to smile about just yet. The inspector turned to look out on to the high street again. The rain had eased. There was even a glimpse of the sun. "Police work is about loose ends. Jim Buckler knows something that will give us some answers, explain some of the loose ends. I'm sure of it," Napoleon said.

CHAPTER 46

◆

Mayo found Jim Buckler slumped at the bar of The Plough, the last pub on his list. Buckler was only the second person he had come across in his tour of Wellesley's pubs, the other was the thin man with the fedora, who was nursing a whisky in The Nag's Head. It was only mid-morning, too early for alcohol except for the truly committed. The Wheel of Fortune had been deserted, while a desolate and broken-down Rising Sun was shuttered, leaving The Plough as the sergeant's final stop in his trawl of Buckler's drinking haunts.

But, despite finding his quarry, Mayo felt more depressed than elated. The sight of Buckler, looking like death, only slightly reheated, was enough to destroy the spirits. He reminded the sergeant of a scarecrow – and a malevolent, down-at-heel one – more than a man. His ravaged, drinker's face looked skeletal with pale, almost translucent skin pulled taut over prominent cheekbones, while the thinness of his scrawny frame was accentuated by threadbare clothes that were too big for him. He also gave off a ripe whiff. There were healthier specimens in Redfield mortuary.

"I've just opened," the barman said. "I refused to give him a drink because he was already drunk. He just nodded and put his head down and fell asleep. He can't stay there all day. He'll scare off the punters." The barman tutted, looking resigned. "But I suppose he's no trouble, unlike his brother. I wouldn't mind too much, except for the smell."

Buckler lifted his head and opened one eye. "Ah Yank," he said. "You're a good bloke. A good bloke." He spoke slowly and deliberately as drunks do. "I want to tell you summing."

"Yes, Jim," Mayo said. "I know. Why don't you come with me?"

"Where we going?" Buckler said.

"To sober you up, and then you can tell me everything."

"All right, Yank, show me the way." Buckler stood up, wobbling precariously. His left leg suddenly gave way as if it were asleep, prompting the sergeant to thrust a hand around his waist to hold him steady, while the barman grabbed one of his arms, slinging it over his shoulder to prop him up. The unlikely trio then walked unsteadily to the car park. "Are you family or a friend?" the barman said.

"Police."

"Ahh." The barman smiled. Everything clicked into place. "You don't look like a pal or a relation. Flash suit, clean shoes, expensive aftershave. Not really Jim's style."

"No. Guess not," Mayo said, raising his right eyebrow and guiding Buckler into the passenger seat of his car. "How did you get here, Jim?" he asked, looking around the empty car park.

"From over there," Buckler said, pointing to the car workshop across the road that belonged to McConnell. "I slept there, where Ernie was last seen alive before the bastards killed him. I can tell you summing bad about McConnell and my other bastard brother. They killed Ernie. They did. Bastards."

"Yes, Jim. Tell me when we get to the police station," Mayo said, shutting the passenger door. He thanked the barman for his help and got into the car on the driver's side. Once inside, the smell was almost unbearable, a ghastly combination of stale beer, old sweat and cigarettes emitting from the now comatose Buckler, whose head had fallen against the passenger window. Wincing, the sergeant put a hand over his nose and pressed the electric button to open the driver's window. Drinking in the taste of the cool fresh air, he hastily started the car, reversed, then turned on to the Wellesley Road towards the police station, immediately putting his foot down. For the first time in a long while, he ignored the speed limit. He needed to get to the police station quickly before the smell knocked him out too.

Napoleon was in his office, reading an article on Henry Llewellyn and the school closure cut out from the Wellesley Chronicle. Mayo noticed the inspector was also fiddling with a gold cross and chain, which was wrapped around his middle finger. "You've got Jim Buckler?" the inspector said.

"Yes sir. He's in the interview room. He needs to sober up, but we've got him. He's been rambling on about the death of his younger brother. He seems to think his other brother and McConnell murdered him."

"Hmm, very interesting," Napoleon said, standing up and laying the newspaper cutting on his desk. He unwound the chain from his finger and handed it to Mayo. "Does this belong to you, sir?" the sergeant said, looking at it blankly.

"No. It belongs to my wife. But Mick Buckler was lying when he said he couldn't remember losing a silver cross in a card game with John McConnell. I'm convinced that silver cross, the one Mick lost at cards, belonged to Sean Cropper."

Mayo handed the gold cross back to the inspector, who slipped it into his pocket. "You could be right, sir," he said. It had seemed a blind alley when Napoleon had first mentioned his suspicions over the silver cross, but now the sergeant was prepared to consider it as potentially relevant.

"The pornographic videos, the silver cross. They're connected to Sean Cropper's disappearance," the inspector said. "And now we have Jim Buckler claiming his younger brother was murdered by his other brother and Jack McConnell."

Napoleon pondered Mayo for a moment. "I think I might have said this before, but is there a link to the deaths of Delgado and Chief Inspector Rankin?"

"I don't know, sir. We need to talk to Jim Buckler first," Mayo replied.

The inspector picked up the newspaper cutting from his desk. "Take a look at this article," he said, handing it to the sergeant.

"What am I looking for?"

"Look at the pictures."

"Okay," Mayo said, puzzled. "The main one is of Henry Llewellyn and the smaller one is of Charlie Dean. What of it?"

"Yes, but what about them?"

The sergeant shrugged and scratched his head. "You've got me, sir. What about them?"

"They look very similar. They could be brothers." Napoleon took the newspaper cutting back and contemplated it in his outstretched hand.

"And that means what?" Mayo said. The conversation was now going in an odd direction, the drunken Buckler had made more sense at The Plough.

"Was Delgado mistaken for someone else in the dark? Did the driver kill the wrong man?" Napoleon said impatiently, as if this was the obvious conclusion from the likeness of Dean and Llewellyn.

"But sir. That still doesn't help us with Chief Inspector Rankin. He was run over in broad daylight. Both deaths could be unrelated, random accidents. The more we look into them, the more likely that seems."

"You know my view. They weren't accidents. They are connected. One person killed both men, and Jack McConnell is involved somehow," Napoleon said.

"That's what you want to believe. But that doesn't make it so," Mayo said.

Napoleon considered the cutting of Llewellyn and Dean in his hand one final time and put it back on his desk. "Sober Buckler up with as many cups of coffee as necessary. I'm going out," he said, collecting his raincoat from the hat stand in the corner of the office. "Go on then, sergeant. Boil the kettle and make Buckler a pot of coffee. And I want a report from the constables going through the videos when I'm back. They should have finished watching all of them by now. I won't be long. I'm going to the Wellesley Chronicle. I need to look through some of their files."

"Sure, sir," Mayo said, opening the office door for the inspector. Why Napoleon used the newspaper archives of the Wellesley Chronicle was beyond him when everything was on file at the police station. He presumed Napoleon liked the short walk and change of scenery. The newspaper offices were only three doors down from the station on the high street. He also suspected it was because the Wellesley Chronicle's archives still consisted of old newspaper cuttings, which the inspector preferred to the station's electronic files. He really was a Luddite.

Entering the offices of the Wellesley Chronicle was like walking back into the 1980s. They were cramped and cluttered and a smell of sickly, cheap polish pervaded the atmosphere. A picture of the high street in 1885, when the newspaper was founded, hung over the reception desk and the strip lighting flickered on and off in frenetic bursts as if some angry old ghost had got stuck in the elements. In the library, most of the space was taken up by dark green metal filing cabinets, filled with old newspaper cuttings. Scattered around them were a variety of chairs, some orphaned without desks, but most covered with piles of books. There were even a couple of typewriters stored in a cobwebbed corner.

The inspector found the article he wanted quickly. He knew his way around the library, having used it for years, and folded himself into a book-free chair at an old oak desk. The library's cuttings went as far back as the early 1970s. It was probably the only newspaper print library left in the country, kept by an old editor who refused to change and refused to retire. Shrugging off sentimental thoughts of times gone by, he smoothed down the curving edges of the newspaper cutting and began to read. It was more rewarding to find a real print article in a real cardboard file than through a computer search. Yet, reading the old newspapers made him wistful. It was like a nostalgic twinge to the heart. He could still touch the yellowing, deteriorating pages, but they recorded something that was gone forever.

The newspaper report on the inquest into the death of Ernie Buckler provoked unusually intense feelings, plumbing emotional depths the inspector found more disturbing than he cared to admit, even to himself. It was dated more than 10 years ago, but he could remember it as if it was yesterday. The youngest Buckler brother died a week after Sean Cropper went missing – and that was something he would never forget.

Buckler had wrapped his car and himself around a tree on the Wellesley Road on his way home from the car repair shop where he worked, the same garage where his older brother had spent the previous night in a drunken stupor.

"Have you got what you want, inspector?" a voice echoed from across the room. The inspector raised his thumb in assent. It was the old editor. "I'll be in my office if you need me," he said. "Thank you," the inspector replied. The old editor smiled, gave Napoleon a half salute and turned back to his office. The inspector watched him close the library door. The old man would probably die at his desk in his ancient swivel chair that he also refused to change. The inspector looked at his watch and read to the end of the article. Verdict: Accidental death, said the last paragraph.

Back at the police station, Napoleon found Mayo at his desk and motioned him to follow him into his office. "Get Parsons for the interview with Buckler," he said to the sergeant, putting the newspaper cutting on his younger brother's inquest in his desk drawer. "I want her in the interview. She's perceptive and keeps us focused. And get two of the constables on the video detail to pull Jack McConnell and Mick Buckler into the station for questioning. There's no point holding off any more. It's time to bring them in."

The inspector had been shown some of the most disturbing videos after his return from the Chronicle offices. Of the more than 1,000 videos stored in the barn, officers had found some of the most distressing in one of the smallest and last boxes they had opened. It featured children as young as 10 in explicit sexual acts with adults.

Mayo nodded and went in search of Parsons. Interviews with McConnell and Mick Buckler were now a priority. The videos were far more damning than first realised. It seemed likely that Jim and Mick Buckler and possibly McConnell had been involved in filming some of them. It also seemed likely that Sean Cropper had been one of their victims. The silver cross won by John McConnell in a card game with Mick Buckler quite possibly belonged to the young boy as Napoleon had suspected.

It would explain Buckler's angry eruption at the mention of the cross in his interview as the inspector suggested. It also meant that Jim Buckler's evidence was even more critical. Sobered up, he might provide answers, not just about his younger brother's death, but possibly Sean Cropper's disappearance as well.

In the interview room, Napoleon found it hard to contain feelings of disgust as he faced the gaunt and spectre-thin Buckler. But he needed to keep himself in check, despite the rising anger he felt on behalf of the children McConnell and the Bucklers had exploited. Parsons, seated next to him, read Buckler his rights, while Mayo, standing behind, looked on impassively. Parsons and Mayo had taken the developments in their stride, and the inspector was determined to keep his cool, too.

"So, Jim," Napoleon said, when Parsons had finished. "We've found more than 1,000 pornographic videos in a barn at Hall's Farm on the outskirts of Wellesley. You, your brother Mick and Jack McConnell handled, distributed and even made some of those videos before storing them there. That is correct, isn't it Jim?"

There was a long silence before Buckler replied. He gazed into the bottom of the coffee cup he was limply holding, then at Napoleon, then at Parsons, and lastly at Mayo. The sergeant remained impassive, except for a tiny flicker of his right eyebrow, which seemed to reassure Buckler.

"Yes," he said quietly.

"Is that a yes, Jim? Can you speak up for the recording?" Napoleon said firmly.

"Yes," Buckler said more loudly.

"Were you involved in the disappearance and murder of Sean Cropper?" Napoleon clenched his gold fountain pen as he asked the key question, his stomach tight as a drum.

Buckler's head jerked upwards as if he had been poked by a sharp stick or an electric cattle prod. "It wasn't my fault. Mick did it, and Jack McConnell covered it up, and then they killed Ernie," he said, his eyes moving from Napoleon to Parsons and back to Mayo.

"What did Mick do?" the inspector said slowly.

"He killed Sean Cropper. He didn't mean to. We were making a video. It wasn't supposed to be violent, just light porn for people who like that kind of thing, but Mick got carried away and choked the little boy."

"Your brother killed Sean Cropper?" Napoleon said. "That is a very serious allegation." The inspector remained calm on the surface, but the sensational news was playing havoc with his insides. An anxious mix of anger and excitement was tightening and churning his stomach.

The inspector had thought about the Cropper tragedy every day of his life since the boy had gone missing. At times, raw and bitter feelings had overwhelmed him. Yet now, Buckler had cleared up the puzzle in a confession that released him from the emotional punishment for failing to find the child. But was he entirely absolved? The guilt nagged again. He should have wrapped up the case a long time ago.

"Yes. I swear. He did it in the barn where the videos were stored. McConnell was furious when he found out, and then Ernie found out and threatened to tell the police. That's when Mick fixed Ernie's car."

"Slow down, Jim. Speak slowly," Napoleon said. "When did Mick choke the boy and what do you mean he fixed Ernie's car?"

"It was the day of the big cup game in the FA Vase," Buckler said.

"I remember," Napoleon said. That football match - the day Sean Cropper went missing - was burnt on his memory.

"Frank, his dad, had got drunk in The Rising Sun opposite the ground in the morning, and let me and Mick take Sean for a ride while he continued drinking," Buckler said.

"Did Jack McConnell know what you were doing?" the inspector asked.

"No. He wasn't involved. It was Mick's idea. It was sort of spur of the moment," Buckler said.

"We took the boy to the barn, and we set up the video. Mick was high on something. I can't remember what, probably coke. He was really into coke back then, still is. It was only supposed to be a harmless video, but Mick got carried away."

"Harmless," Mayo repeated from behind Napoleon.

"I know. It was stupid, terrible. I tried to stop Mick, but he just lost it. He was high on coke. I couldn't control him. We told McConnell what happened afterwards, and he was absolutely furious. But he was very calm and told us to take the body to the funeral parlour he owned in Redfield. He told us to incinerate it in the machine they use for cremations. The problem was that Ernie got wind of what we'd done.

"He knew something was up and wanted to know what was going on and Mick stupidly told him. That was a mistake, telling Ernie. Ernie wasn't going to take part in a cover up. I could have told Mick that. Mick soon realised he should have kept quiet. It was then that he told McConnell, warned him Ernie was going to the police and we were all done for. But McConnell remained calm and just said he would take Ernie for a drink, tell him it was a tragedy and there was no point going to the police. He told Mick not to worry, that he would deal with it. He said he would explain to Ernie that it was best for everyone and for business, if we covered it up. The little boy was dead and no-one could bring him back. McConnell always thought of business. He's a cold bastard, like Mick. But Mick had just killed a little boy. Ernie was never going to accept that, as if it was just an inconvenience."

Napoleon frowned. He could imagine McConnell making his calculations. He was a hard, practical man, a sunny and good-natured surface hiding the coldness of someone who was prepared to cover up the murder of a child for the sake of his business and reputation.

"What happened then?" Napoleon asked.

"That was the worst of it. I didn't realise what McConnell was really up to. He knew Ernie was a big risk to everything. He knew he could lose everything if it got out. I mean he was totally implicated. He was going to jail if Ernie went to the police. So, he took Ernie to The Plough and bought him a few drinks, telling him it was best for all of us not to involve the police.

"But McConnell knew Ernie wasn't going to keep it a secret. Me and Mick were his puppets. We weren't going to tell anyone. But Ernie. McConnell couldn't be sure he would keep quiet. McConnell was very calm, relaxed even, about what was happening. I couldn't understand it at the time, how he kept his cool with so much at stake. But he knew what he was doing. He knew that all he had to do was buy Ernie a few pints. Ernie loved a pint. Then, the car accident he was planning would be put down to drink. McConnell had told Mick to fix Ernie's car while he was in The Plough. I can see now that Mick was happy to play his part. He hated Ernie for being mum's favourite, her baby boy. He was so consumed with jealousy. And it was so easy to set Ernie up. Ernie leaving his car at McConnell's garage where he worked. All Mick had to do was drill a hole in the exhaust manifold of Ernie's car, while McConnell distracted him with drinks over the road in the pub."

"Yes," Napoleon said. "High levels of alcohol and carbon monoxide were found in Ernie's body, according to the newspaper report on the inquest into his death, but it was an old car. Carbon monoxide can leak from the engine. The coroner ruled the crash was an accident."

Buckler gave Napoleon a hollow look. "It wasn't drink, inspector. It was the gas that caused the accident."

He glanced at Mayo. "I told Yank that Ernie was last seen alive at McConnell's garage. He went back there after his drink with McConnell and drove home, but he never got there because he blacked out from carbon monoxide poisoning. The fumes from the exhaust got into the car after Mick drilled the hole in the manifold. It was an old car, as you said, but the carbon monoxide only got in after Mick tampered with the exhaust."

"Why are you telling us this now?" Parsons said. "Sean Cropper and your younger brother died 10 years ago. It's a long time to wait for a confession," she said.

Buckler turned to Parsons and gave her a grim stare, pained and haunted, almost primeval in its desperation. "Because it's got to stop. Because our mum died this year, and it doesn't matter now if this all gets out. It can't hurt her, humiliate her. It would have broken her heart if she knew Mick was a child killer and killed his brother. Now she's gone, and I can finally tell the truth. I was going to tell you this, confess. You just made it easier, asking me directly about the porn videos."

"But still, why now?" Parsons said.

"Yes. Why now?" Napoleon repeated. "Your mother died months ago. I remember reading it in the Chronicle."

"Because Mick killed the policeman."

Napoleon sat upright. "Sorry, Jim. You're saying Mick ran over Chief Inspector Rankin?"

"Yes."

"But how could he have done that?" Parsons said. "He was in Redfield with you on that Friday morning when the chief inspector was hit. You were working on a painting and decorating job in Redfield."

Mayo smiled fleetingly. Parsons was right. The pair of them had made a point of establishing where the Bucklers were on that Friday morning. Several witnesses had said the two men were in Redfield, nowhere near Wellesley, when Rankin was killed.

"That's when he told me, the day the policeman was killed, while we were on that painting job," Buckler said.

"He was lying," Parsons replied. "Surely, you must have known it was a lie. You were both in Redfield on that Friday morning."

"I dunno. I didn't see him until the afternoon. Anyway, the days come and go. I can't remember where I am a lot of the time. It's the booze, addled my brain. But Mick killed Sean Cropper and he killed my little brother. I know that. And if Mick didn't kill the policeman, then it makes no difference. He would have killed him, given half the chance. And he might kill a policeman next time. Mick's got to be stopped, even if it means I have to go jail. My mum has gone, and the truth has to come out. There's no reason to hide it anymore."

Napoleon looked from Parsons to Buckler. "You incinerated the body of Sean Cropper and after Ernie died you stored the videos in the barn? That's when McConnell decided to close the video business? Is that right, Jim?"

"Yeah. The videos were starting to go out of fashion, what with DVDs and the internet. Nobody wanted them anymore. McConnell was going to burn down the barn, get rid of all the evidence. He made Mick burn the video we made of Cropper, but then he changed his mind about setting the barn on fire.

"McConnell said the videos might come in useful later. We could transfer them to DVDs, still make money out of them, and no-one was going to find them. The guy who oversees the farm, where the barn is, was under strict orders to keep it locked up and told to keep his nose out. I think it also amused McConnell to have all that porn stored in a barn opposite the church."

"But Jim," Parsons said. "You have all this anger about Mick killing your little brother, yet you only tell us now? That's a big thing to keep secret. Ten years and you've kept this to yourself."

Buckler looked at Parsons for a long while. "I never really knew for sure that Mick had killed Ernie. I always suspected, but I wasn't sure. I guess I kidded myself he didn't. Mick only properly admitted killing Ernie when he lost his temper with me after we had a fight with McConnell's son outside The Nag last week.

"He was always aggressive and defensive when I asked him about Ernie and how he died. It seemed strange to me. But last week Mick just came out and said he killed Ernie. He told me everything. About McConnell taking Ernie to The Plough while he fixed the car. About how they had planned it without me knowing. He was laughing, manically, as he told me. He was high on coke, but even so. How could he just spew out all that evil stuff as if it was some kind of joke? I would have killed him then and there, but I was too gutted. It was like being punched in the stomach. I felt like all the air had gone out of my body. I could barely speak or even move. It was like the world had suddenly changed, become dark and evil. And my brother was responsible."

Buckler stopped. "You got any more coffee? I need another cup of coffee. I need a cigarette."

"Let's finish this," Napoleon said. "Then you can have a cup of coffee and a cigarette. Why did you have a fight with McConnell's son? Was that deliberate? Did McConnell tell you to attack his son?"

Buckler nodded. "Yeah. That's right. Jack told us to give his son a warning about selling drugs and videos. John had started selling drugs and porn videos with them. He must have got the videos from the barn. It had been broken into a while back. Jack didn't think anything had been taken at first, but later he realised a couple of boxes had gone, and it must have been John who had been responsible. Jack wasn't worried about John selling drugs, but he was worried about the videos. If John got caught selling them or if they got into police hands, it could have got back to Jack. He was thinking about setting fire to the barn again, but in the end, he decided to get us to give John a warning instead.

"That was when me and Mick had the row. We'd just had the fight with John. I'd got hit in the eye and my nose was bleeding and I was thinking, why are we, two old men, fighting a young boy, warning him not to sell porn videos? What had it come to? I said to Mick, why do we do this? But Mick just snarled at me. He says because Jack makes it worth our while. He then says don't go soft like Ernie did. I asked him what he meant. What had it got to do with Ernie? It was then that he told me about how he'd fixed Ernie's car."

"But why would Mick wait all this time to tell you?" Parsons asked.

"I dunno. Because he's back on coke and out of his brain most of the time. He's lost touch with reality. He's always been a mean, evil bastard, but he's got worse. He doesn't care about anybody and doesn't think he can get caught. But he told me. Right then and there outside The Nag's Head after we'd had the fight with John McConnell. He finally told me, finally told me he had murdered his own brother."

"And then he told you he had killed the policeman, two days later, on the Friday afternoon, while you were on the painting job in Redfield? That doesn't add up, Jim. Your brother was seen in Redfield on that morning by a number of witnesses," Napoleon said.

"I dunno, inspector. I didn't get to the painting job until late that day. I was in Redfield bookies most of the morning, and Mick was cross that I'd turned up late and had a go. I had a go back, called him a murderer, and told him not to talk to me. That's when he said he'd killed the policeman.

He was laughing manically again. But maybe he was just winding me up. I dunno. I walked out there and then, and didn't go back. I couldn't stomach talking to him anymore, couldn't stomach seeing his evil face. It was then that I realised I had to tell the police, tell you, about what Mick did to Ernie and Sean Cropper. He's got to be locked up and McConnell, too. Jack might not have killed the little boy, but he covered it up and he had Ernie murdered."

CHAPTER 47

◆

"McConnell and Mick Buckler are unlikely to comment or say anything to help us," Napoleon said. "But we'll give them time for reflection in the cells tonight. Then, tomorrow we'll draw up the various charges. I'm also going to bring in Charlie Dean for questioning. We'll throw everything we've got at McConnell and get him on bribery as well as murder and accessory to murder."

"Do you want one of us to come with you, sir, to pick up Dean?" Parsons said, glancing at Mayo, who was leaning against an old filing cabinet by the office window.

"I could do with some fresh air," the sergeant said, looking out on to the high street. "McConnell and Buckler might not have said anything, except a string of no comments, but it was intense in the interview rooms. And McConnell's lawyer. What a piece of work."

"I'll go on my own," Napoleon said. "You two can take a break, go to the pub or home for a bit. It's going to be a busy few days. I'll get Dean and we'll get a statement from him to add to our statement from Jim Buckler. Hunter wants to hold a press conference at headquarters in Kingham on Monday morning. We need to be ready for that. In the meantime, until the press conference, we're keeping McConnell and the Bucklers in custody here. It means we've got tomorrow, Sunday, to chip away at them. I doubt McConnell will give us anything, but Mick Buckler might crack, if he senses the game's up."

The doorbell rang and Molly woke up with a start. Her paperback copy of Hamlet, which had been resting on her tummy, slipped to the side of the sofa and she sleepily rubbed her eyes. She had dozed off while reading. She put the copy of Hamlet, which had fallen into a small gap between the cushions, on the coffee table and went to the door. It was Chief Inspector Napoleon. "Is your husband home?" he asked.

"No. He's at the pub, The Nag's Head. But he'll be home soon. He only went for a quick pint. Can I help?"

"I need to speak to your husband."

"You can come in and wait for him, if you like. He won't be long."

"Thank you," Napoleon said.

Molly led the inspector to the living room and offered him a seat on the sofa, while she sat on the chair opposite.

"What's this about?" Molly asked.

"Let's wait for your husband," Napoleon said.

"Okay. That sounds ominous," Molly replied with a faint grimace. "Do you want a cup of tea or coffee, while you wait?"

"Tea please," Napoleon said.

The inspector had picked up the copy of Hamlet on the coffee table and was flicking through the pages when Molly returned. "Very high-brow," he said.

"I suppose Shakespeare is high-brow, or perhaps middle-brow," she said with a smile. "I'm reading it because I had an interview with Henry Llewellyn for the radio station. He's playing Hamlet at Stratford. I was reading it on my kindle, but then I found my old paperback copy from schooldays, which was interesting as it had my teenage notes in it. I seem to have a different perspective now. I'm more sympathetic towards Hamlet. I think I've become kinder with age."

"If only we all became kinder with age," Napoleon said. "And it's good to see people still read paperbacks, real things." The inspector scratched his chin and pondered the book's cover, which showed the Danish prince clutching the skull of Yorick, the exhumed court jester. "It seems everyone is reading Hamlet these days. I wonder if Llewellyn and his production are responsible for its sudden wave of popularity."

"Hmm," Molly said. "But hasn't Hamlet always been popular? It's one of Shakespeare's best-known plays."

Napoleon grinned and turned to look at Molly. "I'd only met one person who had read Hamlet or any plays by Shakespeare for that matter before last week – and that was my wife. And I mean read in the proper sense, not someone with the plays on their bookcase, who've only read the title, a few select lines and the dust jacket. Now, I know four people who have read Hamlet and Shakespeare. No, five. I should include Henry Llewellyn."

Molly laughed. "Me, your wife and Llewellyn. Who are the others? Anyone interesting?"

"Not really. A young woman, I happened to interview this week. Oh, and Ted Cropper. Do you know Ted Cropper?"

"Yes. I do. He does plumbing and various jobs for us. He plumbed in our washing machine and fixed the bath when it leaked."

Napoleon took a sip of his tea and contemplated the book's cover again. "You wouldn't expect someone like Ted to read Hamlet, but apparently, he could relate to the play. It had some kind of meaning for him. My wife says I would enjoy Shakespeare, if I persevered. He was a genius, she tells me."

"He was. And I would agree with your wife. If you persevere, you get the rewards. I think Shakespeare is wonderful. Shakespeare is for everyone. He wrote so much and touched on everything - humour, revenge, jealousy, tragedy.

"In fact, I can see why Ted Cropper would relate to Hamlet after the terrible things he's suffered, losing his grandson. Abducted and probably murdered. And then the loss of his son who committed suicide. I can see how Ted would be moved by a story about a tragic Danish prince, driven mad with despair and by his obsession for revenge. Ted probably understands Hamlet better than most of us."

"Shakespeare's not for everyone," the inspector said, shaking his head. "The language is incomprehensible. And how would Ted relate to Hamlet? It's too, I don't know, too elaborate and grand, too unintelligible. It's not your everyday story of country folk, is it?"

"Hmm, but Hamlet is about revenge," Molly said. "Ted must have wanted revenge after his grandson was taken. Revenge is sweet. It can taste better than any meal. In his anger and grief, he would have wanted revenge like Hamlet did, it's the human reaction to injustice, and maybe like Hamlet he was unsure how to get it or what to do about his need for it. That's what I mean when I say I can see how Ted might understand and relate to the play."

Napoleon nodded, something deep inside him registering for the first time. It was obvious, why hadn't he thought of it before? It could explain everything. He nodded again. "Very true, Ms Dean. Very true. Revenge is sweet," he said dreamily, as if in a trance.

He was about to say more when Molly's mobile rang. "Hi Charlie," she said. "Inspector Napoleon is here and wants to talk to you. I'm not sure what about, but he's here waiting."

She paused, listening. "He won't say," she said. "How long will you be?"

She paused again.

"Okay," she said eventually. "I'll tell him. Hold on a second."

"Sorry, inspector. Charlie's at his office. He went there after the pub. He had to pick up some papers. He was just calling to say he'd be back a bit later. He'll be about 45 minutes."

"No problem," Napoleon said. "Just tell him to report to the police station when he's finished collecting his papers. Tell him to ask for me at reception."

Molly relayed the message and disconnected.

"What is this about, inspector? What has Charlie done?" she asked, frowning and looking worried.

"You need to talk to your husband," Napoleon said, finishing his tea and standing up. As he did so, he noticed a pile of Wellesley Chronicles stacked on the bookcase behind the sofa. He picked up a couple and began scanning the front covers.

"I've been meaning to file or throw those away," Molly said. "They're recent copies of the Chronicle with stories I planned to follow up for the radio station."

"Not that recent," Napoleon said. "This edition is about six months old. It has the story on John McConnell winning a bravery award for saving Peter Delgado from drowning."

"Okay, not that recent, then," Molly smiled crookedly. "My filing system's clearly not that organised, unlike the Chronicle's. The editor there is very hot on filing and keeping his library up to date."

"I know. It's a great library. I use it all the time. You worked at the Chronicle, didn't you? I recall you telling me that at the police station this week," the inspector said, flicking through the rest of the newspapers until he got to the bottom of the pile.

"Yes, I did. It was my first job in journalism. It's a very good local newspaper and the editor's top class."

"Yes, he is," Napoleon said. "Can I keep this edition?" he added, lifting up the copy with the story on John McConnell's heroics.

"Of course, please take it. I would have probably thrown it away anyway."

"McConnell pulled Peter Delgado out of the river and probably saved his life, only for him to die six months later," Napoleon said. "I remember you mentioning that, too. I meant to look into it further. McConnell's father found Delgado's body on the golf course, a coincidence of sorts, and I don't like coincidences. I don't believe in them."

Molly laughed. "You mean every coincidence can be explained, or as a policeman you would like to explain them."

"Something like that," the inspector said, tucking the newspaper under his arm while Molly showed him to the front door.

"Should I be worried about Charlie?" she asked as she opened the door.

"You should speak to your husband, Ms Dean." He would have liked to have reassured her that everything would be fine, but that would have been dishonest. He gave her a polite smile on the doorstep and thanked her for the tea and newspaper. "Do make sure your husband reports to the police station," he added, as he raised his hand in a parting goodbye.

CHAPTER 48

◆

Napoleon laid the Wellesley Chronicle with the story on John McConnell receiving a bravery award for saving Peter Delgado across his desk. The newspaper had become a tabloid about 10 years previously, changing from a broadsheet format around the same time as Sean Cropper's disappearance. The inspector had disapproved of the switch at first. He liked the broadsheet design, which could present up to 10 stories on its front cover, compared with the new compact version that had room for just three – a lead news item, a short story under a picture and a single column article running down the right-hand side of the page.

The single column slot on the front page was filled with the story on John McConnell's river heroics. It explained how he had plunged into the water at one of the most dangerous stretches near the weir, where powerful currents and an undertow had dragged Delgado below the surface. McConnell, a strong swimmer, had managed to pull Delgado back on to the bank without a thought for his own safety, the report said. The inspector furrowed his brow, his thoughts coalescing as he reached the end of the article. The coincidence that McConnell had saved Delgado six months before his father had found the young man dead on the golf course was a strange one. The pattern was too neat and tidy. There had to be a reason for it.

Means, motive and opportunity – the holy trinity of detection – surfaced in a separate thought. Those three tenets of policing had to be established, along with evidence and proof, to provide the basis for a successful conviction. John McConnell did not have the means, motive, or opportunity to kill Delgado six months after saving the young man's life, and neither did his father.

The inspector scratched his chin and frowned again, letting the random thoughts flow in the hope that something might emerge from the depths to make sense of Delgado and Rankin's deaths.

If the intended victim was John McConnell rather than Peter Delgado, then that changed everything. In that scenario, one person had the means, motive and opportunity that would explain why the two men were killed. In the case of Rankin's death, McConnell was standing in the middle of the road until his last-minute burst for the pavement and could have been the target rather than the policeman. But McConnell was nowhere near St Margaret's Road when Delgado was hit, and mistaken identity, an idea Napoleon had toyed with, was out of the question. Delgado and McConnell were too different in appearance.

The inspector folded the Wellesley Chronicle with the report on McConnell's heroics and pushed it to the corner of the desk. Reaching inside his top drawer, where he mostly kept cuttings and old notebooks, he fished out the newspaper profile of Henry Llewellyn, displaying pictures of the actor and Charlie Dean, the head planner at the council. The two men looked uncannily similar with their dark features and lean, athletic physiques. They were also of average height, their profiles and features matching the 5ft 9in Delgado, with his olive skin and Spanish complexion. John McConnell, on the other hand, was of an altogether different design. Fair and heavily built, he was unmistakably Anglo-Saxon or northern European, standing 6ft 4in in his sockless feet. Even on a dark night, no one could have confused the blond giant for Peter Delgado.

Napoleon put the cutting of Llewellyn and Dean back in the drawer and pulled out the copy of Hamlet that had been found in Sally Jones' stolen red hatchback. It was sealed in a transparent, plastic evidence bag, which the inspector considered for a moment before placing it on the desk in front of him. He stretched for his notebook in the pocket of his jacket, which was hanging over the back of his chair, and opened it to a fresh, clean page. On the top line, he wrote neatly – Hamlet: motive revenge. He then took Mary's cross out of his other jacket pocket and wrote in the line below - Silver cross belonging to Sean Cropper: motive revenge.

Next, he opened the bottom drawer of the desk, which contained an eclectic assortment of objects and picked out the red matchbox model of the Austin Maxi hatchback from his childhood. It was nothing like the Honda Civic hatchback that belonged to Sally Jones, but it would do in the methodical note-making process that he hoped might spark some inspiration.

He placed the model car next to the cross and the copy of Hamlet and wrote in the third line at the top of the notebook - red hatchback: means (ability to commit crime) and opportunity (resources to carry out crime). He wrote slowly and deliberately, letting his mind wander. It was a part of a routine he had used in the past, with varying degrees of success, to jolt or bring out some buried thought.

Finally, he reached into the same drawer for the piece of paper with the circle and words "Round Tuit" written inside and the cassette tape of Beethoven's symphonies, which Parsons had found on St Margaret's Road. The inspector put both objects, each contained in transparent evidence bags like the copy of Hamlet, on the desk along with the other items. He pondered them for a few seconds, and then on the fourth line of his notebook, wrote Round Tuit: evidence (Wellesley Primary School pupil). On the fifth line, he wrote Beethoven tape: evidence (classical music fan).

He sat back and flipped his gold fountain pen around his fingers, mulling his notes. He had made the notes simple and clear in the hope they would trigger something in his mind's recess. But still, despite the methodical and eccentric process, nothing new or fresh sprang out. Only one person had the means, motive and opportunity for killing Peter Delgado and Chief Inspector Rankin – and only then if the intention was to kill John McConnell. But that theory, like a stone aeroplane, would not fly, however much he tried to make it work.

He blew out his cheeks in frustration. He was trying too hard to bend the facts to fit an orderly pattern that likely did not exist. The deaths of Delgado and Rankin were probably random accidents, as Mayo had said. But why would someone carry Delgado's body to the first tee of the golf course. If it had been an accident, a law-abiding person would have stopped and reported the collision to the police. If it was a drunk driver, they might have sped off in a panic as quickly as they could. But no sane person, drunk or otherwise, would have moved a heavy body all the way to the first tee of the golf course at the risk of being seen, unless they had a reason or motive.

The inspector shook his head and stood up, stretching as he did so. After a few moments, he sat down again, stretched some more and reached for the copy of the Wellesley Chronicle with John McConnell's bravery award on the front cover, carefully moving the items he had taken out of his pockets and drawers to the back of the desk to make space for the newspaper. Sighing, he slowly turned the pages until he reached the centre spread, where there were more details of McConnell's rescue.

A picture of the river by the weir ran across the top of the two centre pages. Below was a photograph of McConnell and Delgado at the awards ceremony. They were smartly dressed in suits and ties, both grinning broadly, their arms around each other's waists. Beaming happily at the camera, they could not have looked more different, one dark and small, the other fair and large - mistaken identity impossible. He idly read the caption below, feeling despondent. He should be rejoicing in the knowledge that Jack McConnell and Mick Buckler were locked up and facing conviction. But instead, he felt frustrated that the one small thing that would explain Delgado and Rankin's deaths was evading him. They weren't random separate accidents, someone with a motive had been responsible for killing them both.

He drummed his fingers on the desk and picked up his pen, flipping it around his hand, again casting his eye over the caption of McConnell and Delgado. There was something not quite right. He squinted, picking up the paper, putting it close to his face. "My God," he said under his breath. He went over the words one more time to make sure he had not misread them. But there, in black and white, was the answer.

He sat back in his chair, a broad smile transforming his face, a feeling of pure joy flooding over him. At last, he could see why Delgado and Rankin had been killed. The full, glorious picture had neatly fallen into place.

He sat forward and read the caption one last time, shaking his head in disbelief at the reason for mistaken identity that had caused such a disastrous chain of events - a careless newspaper error in the Wellesley Chronicle.

Standing up, he stretched once more and paced across the office to the window. The evening was setting in with the light fading, the streetlamps bathing the high street in a yellowish, romantic glow. The inspector's thoughts were darkening too. There was nothing romantic or glorious in his next course of action. The exhilaration of discovery had quickly dimmed. The tragedy that had begun with the murder of Sean Cropper and ended with the death of Chief Inspector Rankin was precisely that. He had discovered the truth, but it was a wretched reality. There was nothing joyful or positive to be drawn from the deaths of Sean Cropper, Ernie Buckler, Peter Delgado and Patrick Rankin. They were all part of a miserable, heart-rending tragedy, and it was not over yet. There was one last, distressing scene to play out.

CHAPTER 49

◆

Napoleon fought his way through a crowd of people at the golf club bar, thinking of Mayo and Parsons in a pleasant distraction from the intensity of the murder investigation. He had watched them from his office window returning to the police station after their break at The Wheel of Fortune and was now puzzling over what he had seen. Mayo was laughing and Parsons smiling in that crooked way of hers. It was dark, not long after the inspector's Wellesley Chronicle breakthrough, but he could see them clearly from his first-floor vantage point, helped by the streetlights and a bright gibbous moon.

They looked more like a happy couple enjoying a night out than a plainclothes policeman and woman working on a murder investigation. He had noticed how close they had become in the past week. They worked well together and were often in the police station's kitchen area, laughing over a coffee or exchanging gossip. He was about to turn away from the window, his thoughts idling, when Mayo put his arms around Parsons' shoulders and kissed her on the side of the head. Parsons giggled and Mayo grinned back at her. For one moment, he thought they might stop and embrace, but instead they kept on walking.

Mayo's action could have been a platonic show of affection, although Napoleon had never had a hug from his sergeant. But did it matter if there was a romantic connection between them? It wasn't affecting their work. They had been models of professionalism when questioning Charlie Dean, who had arrived at the police station not long after their return from the pub. Dean had been amiable and helpful. Yes, he had been offered money by McConnell to back the leisure centre plan. No, he was not going to accept the bribe. And no, no money had exchanged hands, which meant the bribery case against McConnell was going nowhere. Still, it was more ammunition against McConnell that could be added to his charge sheet. Dean had left following his interview, and the inspector had come close to telling Mayo and Parsons about his eureka moment after reading the Wellesley Chronicle. But he had jumped too hastily to conclusions in the past. This time he would make sure he was right about the newspaper error, and its appalling consequences.

The Nag's Head had been his first port of call after dealing with Dean. Mayo and Parsons had gone home or back to the pub, probably the latter judging by the secretive glances between them, and he had gone in search of John McConnell, The Nag's Head the obvious starting point. McConnell's answers had backed up his theory. Now he needed to speak to Humphrey Christopher. If Humphrey gave the same answers as McConnell, then he was confident the case could be resolved.

Like McConnell, Humphrey's social habits would make him easy to find. The golf club was his home from home, a sedate bolt hole for mostly middle-aged men like the big man, although tonight the atmosphere was anything but serene with an unusually large crowd, even for a Saturday night. He gently pushed his way through a throng of golfers and finally made it to the bar, where a noticeboard above the row of spirit dispensers explained the activity. HUMPHREY 42 TODAY was written in big letters on a large piece of card pinned at the top of the board. So, Humphrey was definitely here, hopefully in a sober enough state for intelligent answers.

The inspector quickly decided against buying a drink. There was no point wasting time in the queue, there were at least three people ahead of him, and he could see Humphrey in the corner of the room. Squeezing back past the same group of golfers he had just disturbed, he made his way towards the fat man, who was holding court at a table of about 10 people. "Ah inspector," Humphrey roared as Napoleon approached the table. "What a fine man you are to honour my birthday." The inspector smiled thinly and declined an offer of a seat.

"I don't want to spoil your party, but could we talk privately? Somewhere discreet," Napoleon asked, feeling slightly awkward at breaking up the celebrations.

"I have no appetite for discretion inspector, but for you I will persevere against my instincts," Humphrey said grandly. He stood up, nearly taking the table with him, and pointed in the direction of the pool room. "This way," he said, moving swiftly for a man of his size. The inspector nodded and followed him.

"Should I shut the door?" Humphrey said as the inspector placed himself on a stool by one of the pool tables.

"Yes please," Napoleon said, relaxing a little. The room was quiet and empty. It was a relief to escape from the noise and crowd. "Nobody plays pool on a Saturday night anymore?" the inspector said, looking around the room.

"Not when it's my birthday," Humphrey replied, picking up a pool cue and rubbing its tip with his forefinger. "Do you want a game? I'm very good. I get a lot of practice. Everyone else is too busy playing golf." He grinned broadly, reminding the inspector of a very large Cheshire cat.

"No thanks. Just some answers," Napoleon said.

"Fine," Humphrey replied and slid into a bulky leather chair near the door to the bar, still fondling the pool cue. "Fire away, but make it quick. I've got a party to host. I suppose it's about the night the Delgado lad died? I was here. You know that."

"Yes," Napoleon said. "Tell me everything again. Who came in, who argued with who, who was drunk, everything."

Humphrey stared at the inspector blankly. He seemed at a loss. "I've already told you everything and now I can't remember what I said."

Napoleon sighed. "Okay. Let's skip that. Do you know John McConnell? Jack's son. Would you recognise him?"

Before Humphrey could answer, the door was flung open and his friend Bob, florid and sweating, stumbled into the room. "Your drink, Humphrey. I have saved your drink." His words came out in an exaggerated, intoxicated slur. He passed Humphrey an enormous, silver-plated tankard, which could easily have passed for a small bucket, and disappeared back through the door, slamming it shut on his way.

"Very drunk, inspector," Humphrey said, stating the obvious. "Strangely, for a big man, Bob can't handle his drink. But he has a heart of gold and answering questions from the police is thirsty work, so I am grateful for his consideration." He took a fish-like gulp from the tankard-bucket and eased further into the leather chair.

"Do you know John McConnell, Humphrey? Would you recognise him?" the inspector repeated, impatiently.

"Ah yes," Humphrey said, not noticing the irritable edge in Napoleon's voice. "No. I don't know John. Never met the boy and wouldn't recognise him, despite being friends for years with his father, who incidentally should be arriving at my party very soon."

The inspector's expression remained blank. There would be no party for McConnell tonight. He would stay in the police cells, but it was best to keep Humphrey in the dark.

"Why do you ask about Jack's son, whether I would recognise him?" Humphrey said, looking earnest.

"It just strikes me as interesting that you've never met John McConnell."

Humphrey took another gulp of beer and readjusted his bulk in the leather chair. "You pull me away from my friends and party to make this observation about my relations or non-relations with John McConnell. It strikes you as interesting that I have never met him. What is this all about, inspector?"

"Well, you only live two roads away from the McConnells, yet you've never met Jack's son. Both you and John have lived here in Wellesley your whole lives, but your paths have never crossed because you live in two different worlds."

"If the golf club is one world, then you're right, John McConnell has no part in it," the fat man said. "But what is the significance of this, and why have you pulled me in here to discuss it?"

Napoleon ignored Humphrey's question and asked his own: "The Nag's Head is another world. Do you drink there?"

"Never," Humphrey said indignantly. "It is a lavatorial hole for winos and no goods, where the music is always too loud and the leg room at the tables can only accommodate those people who wear skinny jeans and think a hearty meal is a plant-based salad."

Napoleon smiled. Not for the first time, he noticed Humphrey's tendency to act as if he was playing a part on a stage in front of a large crowd, even when talking privately to an audience of one.

The big man took another gulp of beer and ploughed on. "We live in an incommodious world inspector, as I may have pointed out in the past. The Nag's Head is an appalling example of the cramped conditions us larger than average folk have to put up with. Oh, how I despise this tightly fitting, overly snug little world we have created, created by the thin."

"So, no, you don't drink in The Nag's Head," the inspector said, sighing. It was hard work talking to Humphrey, particularly when he was oiled with drink.

"Even if I could squeeze through the pub's tiny front door, I have no intention of mixing with the dregs and low life that populate that pub."

The inspector watched the big man take yet another large gulp of beer and guessed, like Bob, he was now well on his way to oblivion.

Humphrey looked up, glassy eyed, at Napoleon. "Would you drink in The Nag's Head inspector, or would you choose the salubrious haven of the golf club bar? Golf may be a ridiculous game, but the clubhouse bar is one of the finest. The right sort of people are members of a golf club, no riff-raff here. I bet you would choose the golf club over The Nag's Head, that rat-hole of a hostelry."

"I guess I would," Napoleon said, nodding as he answered.

"The right choice, inspector. As Dr Johnson once said, or some such fellow of distinction, 'there is nothing which has yet been contrived by man, by which so much happiness is produced as by a good tavern'." Humphrey smiled to himself as he eyed the bottom of his nearly empty tankard-bucket.

"And in the words of another distinguished scholar, Humphrey Christopher: Good beer, fine wine and a decent malt are the ingredients of high civilisation and are best enjoyed in their natural setting, the English pub."

He raised his tankard and added loudly as if building up to a crescendo for a big audience: "The Nag's Head tarnishes the reputation of the great English pub. It is not a true pub. It is an imposter." He took one last gulp of beer from the now depleted tankard, then stared deeply into the jug, searching for any remnants of ale.

"You know inspector," he said, lifting his eyes, which he was now having trouble focusing, from the bottom of the tankard. "The problem with this town..." But the conversation was over. The inspector had gone.

Napoleon dialled Mayo's number in the partial darkness of his office. He hadn't bothered turning on the lights. It was oddly pleasant in the gloom and he could see clearly enough, thanks to the street lamp outside his window and the reflection of the moon that seemed bigger and brighter than ever.

"Joe, is that you? You sound strange," he said.

"Yeah, it's me sir. Who else would answer my mobile this late on a Saturday night?" the sergeant said.

"Good point. I want you in early tomorrow. 8am. I'll call Parsons too. I've made a breakthrough in the Delgado/Rankin case and we all need an early start."

"Err, sure sir. The early bird gets the worm. And you don't need to tell Parsons."

A woman's laugh suddenly burst through Napoleon's earpiece.

"That was Parsons, sir," Mayo said sheepishly. "We were having a nightcap at my place to discuss the case."

"Yeah right," Napoleon said. "Just make sure you're both in the office by 8am."

The inspector hung up and looked up at the clock on the wall. The hands had moved past midnight, the witching hour. It was Sunday, usually his favourite day, a day for the family, roast lunch and a relaxing, afternoon nap by the fire. But today would be anything but relaxing. It would more likely be highly stressful and upsetting, although he was confident it would at last close the book on the Wellesley murders.

CHAPTER 50

◆

"Why here, sir?" Mayo asked. The inspector had made himself comfortable in one of the seats in the middle of the main stand at Wellesley Football Club, about 20 rows back from the pitch, just in front of the covered section. The wind was whipping fiercely around them, and it looked like it might rain, not an ideal place to spend a Sunday morning.

"He wasn't at home, so he'll come here. I know his habits," Napoleon replied, looking unperturbed by the wind, despite it playing havoc with his hair, which he kept pushing back out of his face. "This is where he likes to read his Sunday newspapers, in his seat in the East Stand, where he watches his football team. And if he does break his weekly routine for the first time in 20 years, then Parsons can arrest him."

"So, we just wait?" Mayo said, thinking of Parsons, warm and snug in her heated car. Napoleon had decided to leave her waiting outside the suspect's house, just in case he decided to return home instead of visiting the football ground.

"He might have stopped off at the golf club before coming to the ground, but he won't be long," Napoleon said.

Mayo decided against sitting down and stamped his feet to generate some circulation and warmth, instead. "I can't believe he likes reading the papers out here in the cold, and I can't believe they don't lock this place up. We just walked in off the street."

"There's nothing to steal. That's why they don't lock it up," the inspector said. "The pitch looks good," he added. "It's rained heavily this week and they had a hard match yesterday, but the pitch still looks good. What do you think?"

"I really have no view, sir," Mayo said. "Baseball's my game. But tell me more about this newspaper mistake and why you're convinced we have our murderer." Napoleon had briefed him and Parsons about the error in the Wellesley Chronicle and why it was the catalyst for the killing of Peter Delgado and Chief Inspector Rankin. But he had left out a lot of the details on motive and reasons for the crime.

"All in good time, sergeant. Just trust me," the inspector said. Before Napoleon could add anything further, a man emerged from the tunnel by the pitch below them. He saw the policemen, dropped a collection of newspapers from under his arm, and darted back in the tunnel. Napoleon jumped up and followed, hurdling the rows of seats in front of him like an athlete until he reached the pitch. Mayo, without thinking, ran too, although he took the easier route down the aisle that led to the tunnel.

It was dark in the tunnel, but Mayo could just about see Napoleon up ahead. There was suddenly a clattering sound in the home team changing room at the far end of the tunnel. Napoleon swerved left, following the sound, and burst through the changing room door.

"I don't believe this," the inspector said as Mayo reached him in the changing room. He followed the inspector's gaze and noticed the cover over the air vent above the lockers had been prised off.

"He's made his escape through there," Napoleon said. "You'd better follow him."

"Me?" said Mayo.

"Yes you. You're smaller than me. I'm worried he might do something silly."

"And this isn't doing something silly?" Mayo asked as he used a chair as a step to climb into the shaft, which was just about big enough to squeeze into. It was dark and cold inside the vent, which twisted one way, then another before reaching an opening at the back of the stand about six or seven feet above ground level in front of a hot-dog van. Mayo shoved the grate at the opening, which had also been prised off its hinges and hastily replaced, out of the way and jumped on to the grassy space behind the van. He landed awkwardly and plunged forward, using his hands to avoid falling on his face. He went to stand up, but before he could do so he felt a thud on the back of his head. "Great," he thought randomly, then it went black.

He could hear whistling. What was it? Wind. He was cold and his head was throbbing. There was a smell of disinfectant, which reminded him of a football changing room, then it went black again.

The sergeant could just about focus. He could see Napoleon perched on a bench in front of him. Behind the inspector were several lockers and the broken vent. Its cover, he noticed, was leaning at a drunken angle against one of the lockers. It was the home team changing room. The sergeant remembered now. He was at Wellesley Football Club. A thin man with an extremely gaunt face was sitting in a chair beside him, saying something about not moving and remaining where he was. Mayo did as he was told and stayed still. He was lying on a small collapsible bed, which he presumed was used to examine injured players.

"I'm the club physio," the man said. "You'll be fine, but you should go for a check-up at the hospital." The thin man stood up and turned to Napoleon. "I'll be in the office if you need me. I'll be there until lunchtime. Just give me a shout when you're done here, inspector, and make sure you get the sergeant to hospital soon. He should be checked over." How about going now, Mayo thought, as he watched the thin man close the changing room door behind him. Napoleon nodded and sat down in the chair vacated by the physio. "How are you feeling?" he said.

"I'm fine," Mayo replied. "That man. That's the thin man," he said.

"Yeah," Napoleon said, looking blank. "Doug, the football team's physio, is quite thin."

Everything was swimming in his brain and Mayo felt dizzy, but the physio was definitely the thin man, with the raincoat and fedora, he had noticed in the pub on a number of occasions. He looked different in a tracksuit, but something in the sergeant's subconscious had randomly made the connection. "Funny old world," he thought.

It was only then that he noticed another man in the room, the one responsible for hitting him on the head, which he could feel had a large bump and a slight cut across the crown where his hair was starting to thin.

"Meet Ted Cropper," Napoleon said. Ted was sitting on another collapsible bed, a few feet away.

"Sorry," he said to the sergeant. "For hitting you, that is."

"No worries," Mayo replied. "What did you hit me with?"

"This," Ted said, producing a wooden walking stick. "I'm sorry. I didn't hit you hard."

"Hard enough," Mayo said.

"Sorry," Ted said again. "It's oak."

"Yeah, right," the sergeant said. He wasn't interested in its constituent parts.

Ted then produced a penknife. "I used this to get into the vent."

"I see," Mayo said, not sure whether Ted wanted praise for his ingenuity.

"Ted panicked. That's why he hit you," Napoleon said.

"Oh, that's fine then," Mayo replied. "How long have I been out?"

"Not long, about five or 10 minutes," the inspector said. "There's a door at the end of the tunnel at the back of the stand. It was open and I found Ted standing over you."

"You realised it was all over then, didn't you?" the inspector said, looking at Ted. The old man nodded. "We carried you here and Doug, the physio, turned up. He came over from his office to see what was going on when I turned the lights on in the tunnel, which was lucky as he's an expert on head injuries. He thinks you might need stitches, but there's no serious damage."

"Really? My head's pretty sore and I feel dizzy."

"You'll be fine," Napoleon said.

"Didn't the physio say I should go to hospital to be checked?" Mayo said.

"Yes, but that can wait," Napoleon replied. "You're young and fit. You'll be fine," he repeated. "We'll take Ted back to the station first. You can go to the hospital then, or interview Ted with me and Parsons."

"I'll do the interview," Mayo said. "I'm sure I'll be fine. I'm young and fit," he added sarcastically, mimicking Napoleon, who gave him a twisted smile.

Mayo rubbed his hands for warmth. It was cold in the police station interview room, and he was feeling groggy, probably because of the blow to his head. He should have gone to the hospital, but he was eager to stay for the interview as Napoleon still hadn't fully explained why he had suspected Cropper was the murderer.

The sergeant leaned forward, putting his elbows on the table in front of him for support, pondering the old man sitting opposite. He looked more like a victim than an assailant, miserable and hollowed out by life, a contrast to the young and vibrant Parsons, in the chair next to him. He gave her a quick smile. She smiled back and subconsciously gathered her hair into a ponytail, which she pulled round one of her ears and rested on her shoulder. She looked gorgeous. It had been fun in the pub the previous evening and at his flat later, where they had chatted for an hour or more before saying their goodbyes. As well as being a stunner, she was funny and great company. They also had their work in common, the perfect partner. But still, he was glad he hadn't made a pass. He wasn't sure she fancied him, and he wasn't going to risk everything with a clumsy kiss or some other embarrassing manoeuvre. He had kissed her on the side of her head on the way back from the pub, but that had been totally spontaneous because she was so funny and looked lovely under the streetlights, and she hadn't seemed to mind. In fact, she had smiled, and they had carried on laughing and talking.

Before he could ruminate further, the door opened, the squeak of its handle signalling Napoleon's entry. He had a newspaper wedged under one arm and a number of other items in plastic evidence bags in his hands. One looked like the cassette tape Parsons had found on St Margaret's Road, while another contained the piece of paper with the peculiar "Round Tuit" phrase scribbled inside a poorly drawn circle, discovered near Delgado's body on the golf course. The last item was the copy of Hamlet, retrieved from the glove compartment of Sally Jones' red hatchback. Mayo stood up and offered Napoleon his seat, wondering why he needed the props. He supposed they would help him with the questioning in the interview.

The inspector nodded at the sergeant and sat down, placing the newspaper and evidence bags on the table, arranging them in a neat row. He glanced at Parsons and turned to Cropper, asking if he wanted a solicitor. The old man, who had declined earlier, shook his head. Napoleon nodded again, switched on the recorder, and cautioned Cropper. The inspector took a further moment to settle himself, then asked Cropper in a detached, official manner to explain why he had killed Peter Delgado and Chief Inspector Rankin.

The old man hesitated for a long while. His ashen complexion seemed to fade to an even paler shade, as he despondently looked at the police officers, then at the floor. "What a mess," he finally said to the ground, seemingly too embarrassed to look at his interrogators in the eye.

"Just take your time, Ted," Napoleon said. "And start from the beginning."

Cropper took a long breath, and lifted his head, although he still could not meet the police officers' eyes. "I thought Peter Delgado was John McConnell. I didn't mean to kill that young man. And then the policeman was in the wrong place, right in the middle of the road. I didn't mean to kill him either."

"What a mess," he repeated and shook his head. "I don't know how it's come to this. I was going to come forward. I was going to hand myself in today after I read the newspapers at the football club. I knew I had no choice. I've been going over and over what I should do in the past week. Part of me still wanted revenge, but after accidentally killing the police officer, I started losing my appetite for that, for life. What's the point?"

Napoleon narrowed his eyes and opened the newspaper he had brought with him to the interview. It was the Wellesley Chronicle containing the report on John McConnell's award for bravery after his rescue of Peter Delgado from the river.

"This picture. The caption wrongly says Peter Delgado is John McConnell. Is that why you mixed up the two men?" the inspector asked.

"You knew then?" Cropper said.

"I only saw this report in the Wellesley Chronicle for the first time yesterday," the inspector replied. "It was only then that I realised you had killed Delgado and Chief Inspector Rankin and why. I was surprised you didn't know what John McConnell looked like, but then you and John's paths would never have crossed. He spends most of his spare time in The Nag's Head, you at the golf club, and I guessed he was never at the house when you went to the McConnells' to repair their washing machine or do work for them."

Cropper nodded. "Sons often don't look like their fathers, and it never occurred to me to double check what John looked like." Cropper looked very old and tired as he spoke, even more so than when the inspector had last seen him in his garden a few days before. The lines on his face seemed deeper and his deathly pale complexion had gone grey around the edges. His pallor reminded Napoleon of Jim Buckler, another broken man.

"I had been at the golf club that night when I killed the Delgado boy. It was a culmination of everything. My electrical repair business was going under. I was only doing occasional jobs. I just didn't have the energy for work. I was at a very low ebb. And then, that night when I killed the young man, Humphrey was going on about how wonderful Jack McConnell was. Then he started talking nonsense about that porn ring, the one that Jack was rumoured to have run. Humphrey can be so offensive. He was deliberately provoking me. He knew what happened to my grandson, taken and murdered by paedophiles, and he knew I suspected Jack McConnell was involved, and yet he started going on about how porn was great, and it was every man's right to watch it. How could he be so cruel and insensitive?"

The police officers shared glances. Everything was now fitting into place. "Why did you think Jack was involved in a porn ring?" Napoleon asked. "Was it because of the silver cross? You stole it from the McConnell household a few years ago because you believed it was Sean's. That's right, isn't it?"

"Yes. So, you knew about that too, inspector? You knew I had taken the cross. You're a clever man. I knew you were on to me that day in my back garden when you asked about Sean's cross. But how did you know? How did you guess I took it from Jack McConnell's house?"

"I didn't know for sure. It was just a theory."

"Well, you were right. I saw the cross hanging on a stand in Joanne McConnell's kitchen one day. I asked her about it. It looked just like Sean's. She told me her husband had given it to her. Then, when I looked at it closely, I knew it was Sean's. There was a small indentation at the bottom of the stem. That's where he used to rub it for luck with a coin. I'd bought it for him when he was a baby, and he always wore it as a little boy. So how come Jack McConnell had it. He must have been involved in his disappearance. And remember, back then, it must have been five years ago when I took the cross from the McConnells' house, the porn ring was big gossip.

"I was convinced Jack was involved in Sean's disappearance, so I asked him about the cross and the porn ring, and he just shrugged his shoulders and said he didn't know what I was talking about. But I could see he was uncomfortable. I knew then for certain he was involved in Sean's disappearance, so I broke into his house and took the cross. It wasn't difficult. Joanne always left the patio door at the back of the house open, and she was often out or drunk and Jack was never home, either. That cross was Sean's and Jack must have been involved in his disappearance and murder, yet everyone went on about how he was this wonderful businessman and upstanding pillar of the community. It made me sick. I trashed the house when I took the cross, except for the kitchen because that was Joanne's room. It gave me great pleasure."

He looked up and for the first time met Napoleon's eyes. "I wanted justice. But I didn't know how to get it. I couldn't prove Jack was responsible for Sean's disappearance. Then, on that Wednesday night at the golf club, Humphrey kept going on about how wonderful Jack was. I couldn't bear it and left.

"I got into my car in the golf club car park. I felt so angry, so I took a drive around the villages to try and calm down. Then, I decided to go home and get drunk. My wife passed away this year, so I had nothing else in my life. Nothing. Thanks to Jack McConnell. But then, all of a sudden, on my way back to my house, I saw John McConnell, or who I thought was John McConnell, walking up St Margaret's Road, near the golf course turning. It's difficult to describe my feelings. But I knew, it was my chance for revenge, so I just drove, right at him, my foot hard on the pedal. I wanted to kill him, like his father had killed my grandson. And, after I'd hit him, I felt an exhilaration, a joy even, and this idea came to me, how I could make my revenge even sweeter. I was just by Crookham Lane, where there's that passageway to the first green of the golf course.

"I knew Jack would be the first person to tee off the next day at the golf club. He always boasted how he was the first person to play on Thursday mornings. How he teed off at first light before anyone else was on the course. So, I lugged the boy to the green of the first tee through the passageway. He wasn't heavy and I've lugged washing machines around for years. I propped him up against a bush, where he could only be seen once you walked on to the green, which meant Jack would be the one to find his dead son. It made me feel somehow whole again. At last, I had had my revenge, retribution – and it tasted sweeter, finer than any meal."

"And you dropped this?" Napoleon said, pointing to the plastic bag with the piece of paper and words "Round Tuit" written inside a hastily drawn circle.

"Yes. You are very clever, inspector. Who else but you would have remembered that teacher, and his funny little notes. I can't even remember what that note was supposed to remind me to do. But, yes, it was mine. I deliberately wrote that mobile telephone number you wanted in my garden that day in a loopy style, totally opposite to my small, neat writing. I nearly confessed to you then, but at that point I still thought I might still try and kill John McConnell, or even Jack. I had nothing to lose. I'd already lost everything."

He turned his eyes away from the inspector's and wiped his nose on the sleeve of his shirt.

"Sean meant everything to me. You know that. My son Frank was an alcoholic and his suicide here in the police station was awful, but he had ruined his life with his drinking. Sean had his life ahead of him. His disappearance destroyed a part of me, most of me. He was such a bright, beautiful boy. I loved him to bits.

Me and Kitty, my wife, we virtually brought him up. Frank was never around, and neither was his mother, so it was left to me and Kitty, his grandparents, to raise him. He was my joy and Jack took him away. With Kitty, my lovely wife, now gone too, there really is nothing left."

"But how could you be sure that it was Jack?" Parsons asked. Her emotions were conflicted. She could understand Ted's grief and desire for revenge, yet he had murdered two innocent men.

"I knew because of the silver cross. It was Sean's. There was no doubt."

"But John McConnell gave Joanne the cross, not Jack," Napoleon said.

"No. It was Jack, not his son, who gave Joanne the cross. She told me," Ted said firmly.

"It was John who gave Joanne the cross. She had got confused and told you it was Jack by mistake," the inspector said.

"So, John McConnell killed Sean?" Ted replied, looking bewildered.

"No, Ted. John wasn't responsible," Napoleon said. He glanced at Parsons, then at Mayo and shook his head in a signal not to reveal the arrests of Jack McConnell and the Bucklers. Ted had been right about Jack, although for the wrong reason.

"I know Jack did it. I know," Ted said, trying to convince himself. "I've wanted revenge all these years."

He glanced at the copy of Hamlet in front of Napoleon. "I wanted revenge," he repeated. "Like Hamlet." He stopped for a moment, eyeing the book. "Why have you got a copy of Hamlet?"

"It was found in the red hatchback," Napoleon said. "The car you used to run over Patrick Rankin. It's yours. You lent it to Sally Jones, your neighbour. She'd left it in the glove compartment of her car."

"Oh. I didn't know it was in her car, but yes, it does look like my copy. I bought it after reading about that local actor and his production of Hamlet in Stratford. It was a play about revenge. It seemed worth reading."

He smiled forlornly. "It's not my normal reading material, but I read up on the plot. The story of a man who wanted revenge but was torn over how to get it. It struck a chord. I had the same dilemma and reading the play was therapeutic. I had the same suicidal feelings as Hamlet, the same torment. It helped me understand myself. Maybe, it even stopped me from taking my own life."

He sniffed and wiped his nose on his sleeve again.

"I dreamed of killing Jack, getting revenge, but I never really thought I would do anything. I'm not a violent man, but then that night, I saw John McConnell in the road in front of me and it was my chance, but it was the wrong man. It wasn't John McConnell."

He put his head in his hands, and then looked up. His expression was haunted, painful memories flooding back. "The next day was awful, when I realised my mistake. It was at the golf club I found out."

"You told Humphrey that the young man was hit by a car, when you found out. Didn't you?" Napoleon said. "Only you could have known he was hit by a car when the police hadn't revealed that information."

"Yes, I probably did. It's all a blur. I was in a state of shock. But there was no going back, and I still wanted revenge. I wanted Jack to feel the pain I'd felt all these years, to know what it was like to lose a child. And I wasn't going to make the same mistake a second time, so I did a search on the internet for John McConnell and found a picture of him. Once I knew what he looked like, I found out he drank in The Nag's Head. That he spent most of his time there.

"I didn't really have a plan. My van needed repairs after the collision with the Delgado boy, so I couldn't use that again to run him over. I had to think of something else. Then, by chance, Sally, my next-door neighbour, asked me to keep an eye on her house because she was going away for the weekend. She told me her car was being repaired, and a mechanic would leave it outside her house on the Friday morning after she'd gone. She was travelling very early to Paris. She told me the mechanic would put the car keys through her front door and asked me to make sure he'd done so. I have a spare set of keys to her house. I often keep an eye on her place when she's away.

"After that, everything seemed to fall into place. I took her car early that morning and waited outside The Nag's Head in the road opposite the pub. I guessed McConnell would go there at some point. And sure enough, he did. He went in at opening time and came out about an hour later. I saw him cross the Wellesley Road on his way into town and I drove straight at him, like I had with the Delgado boy, but he suddenly sprinted, and there behind him in the middle of the road was the policeman. I couldn't stop. I just couldn't stop. I was going too fast. There was no point braking."

Ted put his head in his hands again, and this time he started to weep. "I drove for miles," he said, his head jerking up and down as he sobbed. Mayo leaned over and handed him a tissue. "I was in a right state. I really didn't know what to do, so I kept on driving to London and dumped the car," he added, wiping his nose, and drying his eyes with the tissue. "I got a train home, let myself into Sally's house and put the car keys back on her door mat where I'd found them, so it looked like the car had been hot-wired and stolen by some joy rider."

"I guessed as much," Napoleon said.

"One final thing," the inspector added. "This tape cassette of Beethoven." He showed the old man the tape in the evidence bag. "Why did you drop it in St Margaret's Road after you'd killed Peter Delgado? Did you think it might implicate Jack McConnell? You stole it from Jack's collection, didn't you?"

"You knew that, too," Ted said, shaking his head, and wiping his nose again. "It was that day, when you and the sergeant were interviewing Joanne and her washing machine flooded her kitchen. I went into Jack's cellar to check whether it was flooded down there too, and I saw his tape collection. I thought why not try and put the blame on him for the young man's death? So, I took the tape and dropped it near where I ran him over."

"But it was never going to implicate Jack," Napoleon said. "We had already searched the area thoroughly."

"Yes. You're right. It was a stupid idea."

Ted looked at his calloused hands and sighed, and then glanced at the impassive faces of the police officers as he dried the last of his tears. "My late wife always said things would turn out right in the end, but they didn't. I still think Jack McConnell was responsible for Sean's death. I should have killed him a long time ago. Instead, I waited all these years, the hatred growing like a cancer, then I messed it all up. Everything is a mess. A total mess. It's like Hamlet, a revenge tragedy. But, I don't care anymore. That's the real tragedy."

Napoleon returned the bagged items to the evidence room and found Mayo and Parsons in the kitchen area making coffee. They were laughing as usual. He smiled at them. Why shouldn't they laugh? Life goes on, despite murder and tragedy and sociopaths like Jack McConnell.

"Do you want a coffee, sir?" Mayo said, reaching for a bottle of milk in the fridge.

"Yes. That would be good," the inspector said. "Are you going to get your head checked, by the way?"

"I'm going to the hospital after I've had a cup of coffee."

"You should. Doug, the physio at the football ground, did say you might need stitches."

"Joe!" Parsons said. "I didn't know you were told you might need stitches. You should have gone to the hospital earlier. I'll take you."

"I did say sergeant, that you should go to the hospital," Napoleon said in a mocking, ironic tone.

"That's not quite what I recall, sir," Mayo replied sarcastically.

Parsons shook her head and the three of them smiled at each other.

There was a brief, contemplative silence as Mayo poured coffee from a pot into three cups.

"It's interesting how Ted Cropper knew Jack McConnell was involved in his grandson's death," the sergeant finally said, putting milk in one of the cups and passing it to Parsons. "Do you want milk, sir?" he added.

"Just a splash," Napoleon replied.

"If only Ted Cropper had waited one more week before taking his revenge," Mayo said, tipping a tiny drop of milk into the inspector's cup and handing it to him. "Then, Jim Buckler would have made his confession and Jack McConnell would have been arrested. Ted Cropper wouldn't have needed to kill anyone. He would have had his justice, without having to exact revenge himself."

"That may be true," Napoleon said. "Ted stewed in bitterness for years, and did nothing. Then, by chance, he had the opportunity to kill the person he thought was John McConnell on St Margaret's Road, then killed Rankin by mistake too. But if he hadn't killed Rankin, Jim Buckler might never have confessed. It was Mick Buckler's claim that he'd killed the chief inspector that prompted Jim's confession about Sean's death and his younger brother's murder. He didn't realise Mick was lying."

"The slings and arrows of outrageous fortune," Parsons said, quoting Hamlet.

"Yes. The slings and arrows of outrageous fortune," Napoleon repeated. The three of them sipped their coffee silently. There was nothing more to add. Shakespeare's famous phrase seemed to say it all. The inspector thanked Mayo for the drink, which was smooth and not too bitter, the sergeant knew how to make a good cup of coffee and went back to his office. He sat down at his desk and let his brain idle, contemplating whether to phone Hunter. The chief super would be delighted that they were now ready to charge someone with the double murder of Delgado and Rankin as well as the murders of Sean Cropper and Ernie Buckler.

He smiled to himself and swivelled his chair towards the window. The sun had come out despite the rain, creating a blurry outline of a rainbow just behind the church opposite the police station. Wellesley looked idyllic in the sun's autumnal glow, the perfect embodiment of an English country town. It made him feel pleasantly contented. He was already feeling good, but it was a strange, unfamiliar emotion, not happiness or even satisfaction at a difficult job completed. It was more like feeling whole again. In fact, he was only now starting to understand the psychological impact of his failure to find the killers of Sean Cropper. It was as if a chunk had been removed from his emotional self or self-esteem, which had at last been replaced. Finding the killers of Sean Cropper had corrected some psychological imbalance, repairing, and making him feel complete again, and no longer a failure.

He stretched, breaking out of his reverie, then turned his chair back to face the desk, eyeing the telephone. Finally, after a few moments, he picked up the receiver and punched in Hunter's number. He would tell him the good news, then go home for lunch. Mary was making a Sunday roast for the children. He would just about make it in time, and after lunch, he would have a quick nap by the fire.

ABOUT THE AUTHOR

David Oakley is a British journalist and writer. He lives in Berkshire, is married, and has three grown-up children.

Death on The Golf Course is both his first novel and the first in the Napoleon Mysteries series.

For more information on David Oakley and his books, visit the Napoleon Mysteries website at napoleonmysteries.com and if you enjoyed the book please follow and share on social media.

You can also email david@napoleonmysteries.com

Printed in Great Britain
by Amazon

82332603R00176